Clive Graham Lord worked at Sotheby's in New Bond Street, London for 22 years, the last 15 of them as chief operating officer. Many of the incidents, apart from the murders of course, are based on real-life experiences and have been woven into the book with a little added literary license.

This is Clive's first novel since moving from Sotheby's in 2020; he lives in London and Surrey with his partner.

This book is dedicated to Jenneke Kelly, my cousin, who sadly lost her life from pancreatic cancer in July 2022 at the age of 52. She was an avid reader and had recently qualified as a funeral celebrant. The character, named after her, is loosely based on her and she was delighted to be memorialised in this book.

'Your inclusion of me as a funeral celebrant in your forthcoming murder mystery novel is splendid. Thank you for thinking of placing me in this role, I'm truly honoured and the prospect of longevity through fiction is highly appealing.' – Jenneke, Tuesday, 17 May 2022.

Clive Graham Lord

MURDER MAKE$ THE WORLD GO ROUND

AUSTIN MACAULEY PUBLISHERS™

LONDON * CAMBRIDGE * NEW YORK * SHARJAH

A CIP catalogue record for this title is available from the British Library.

ISBN 9781035816828 (Paperback)
ISBN 9781035816835 (Hardback)
ISBN 9781035816859 (ePub e-book)
ISBN 9781035816842 (Audiobook)

www.austinmacauley.com

First Published 2023
Austin Macauley Publishers Ltd®
1 Canada Square
Canary Wharf
London
E14 5AA

I would like to acknowledge and thank the following people for their help and support in bringing this book to fruition.

Jennifer Conner
Rafal Golaj
Clare Harris
Brian Masters
Olga Matthias
Rena Neville

Table of Contents

Prologue

Anita sat at her desk in her new office overlooking the River Thames. As the newly appointed head of the UK's Anti-Terrorism Unit, she was due to attend her first COBRA meeting on Zoom. The first item on her agenda was to ensure that all future meetings were held face to face. Zoom was a terrorist's gift, as it could be hacked by almost anyone. She was going to sort this government out, and there would be no arguing with her.

As she had five minutes before the call started, she reflected on the last twelve months, which had been full of ups and downs. Her brief time running the Art Squad, that investigates crimes in the art world, had exposed her to all sorts of characters, and the extensive travel around the globe was insightful, educational, and interesting. She had learnt a huge amount during this time, mostly about herself. She thought about her wife, Juliet, and her intern Camau, who was now a close personal friend.

Her original views about the art world as a hot bed of international crime, proved to be way off the mark, but she had done her bit uncovering some pure wickedness. She had seen how the super-rich, live in a glamorous, parallel universe, almost detached from the rest of humanity, and how for some of them, their motives and behaviour were driven by greed and money.

Her screen came alive with a grid of sixteen people attending the COBRA meeting, sitting in their respective offices, kitchens, or bedrooms.

'Firstly, Home Secretary…'

Part One

The Barman

Thursday, 9th December.

It was eight forty-two in the evening when the auctioneer banged his gavel down on the final lot of the day.

'Thank God for that. We can now go for a drink,' Riccardo whispered under his breath to his colleague Ursula.

Along with another seventy-auction staff, they had spent the last three working days in Mount's largest auction room, standing on the phone bank. The auction room was huge, cavernous and could seat four hundred and fifty people. It was twenty metres wide, thirty-nine metres long and twelve metres tall. There was room for several television crews and their camera equipment, an area for journalists, who were seated in a separate section that was roped off, and space for clients and bidders who wished to stand at the back of the room. As well as clients in the auction room, there were usually dozens of auction house staff, standing around or wandering about, doing absolutely nothing productive at all.

The auctioneer was centre stage facing the audience and the phone bank took up the entire left-hand side of the room. It was a long continuous desk just above waist height, with a front panel flush to the floor, and a privacy screen hiding sixty telephones. The screen was there to prevent prying eyes, especially journalists, from seeing which phone numbers had been dialled and potentially identifying who an anonymous bidder might be.

Supposedly, the staff stood behind the phone bank to place bids on behalf of absentee clients, and to attract the attention of the auctioneer, who would acknowledge their bids. However, the primary purpose for standing on the phone bank was to be seen, both in the auction room by the audience, and more importantly on the live television and internet channels that were broadcast globally in real time. Being seen at an important auction was vitally important for all serious auction staff, as it reinforced their status, value, and credibility. The auction house management would frequently send round an all-staff e-mail, requesting that only staff with phone bids should stand on the phone bank. Like most of the management's emails, they were simply deleted, unread.

What did management know about the importance of being seen?

Riccardo Hofstadt was twenty-eight years old, six feet tall, good-looking, tanned with a swimmer's build, and cropped dark blond hair. He worked for Mount's Auction House in the Zurich office and only ever wore Giorgio Armani clothes, never Emporio Armani, and looked like a male model whether wearing sportswear, casual gear, or more formal clothes.

He had been recruited to work at Mount's four years ago, because of his multi-lingual skills, his good looks, but most importantly because of the fact that his father was a Swiss banker. Based in Zurich, both Riccardo and his parents were well connected with the secretive wealthy residents in the city. His Italian mother was a sculptor who produced awful works, but nobody dare tell her as she had a classic Italian explosive personality. The family home was in Zug, one of the tax havens in Switzerland, and Riccardo's parents had bought him a penthouse in the centre of Zurich. He lived there with his boyfriend, Stephan, who was also Swiss, twenty-eight, and worked in the rapidly expanding Crypto industry, doing something that Riccardo was simply not interested in, or even pretended to understand. Like most gay men, both Stephan and Riccardo played around, which to them was as innocuous as having a cup of coffee.

Ursula Baumann was sixty-two years old and had worked for Mount's for almost forty years. She lived just outside of Zurich, was the head of the office and knew everybody that was worth knowing. She was petite, almost bird-like, and sported a formidable head of hair that was set rock hard with hairspray, her helmet hair. She always wore two-piece suits and for some unknown reason modelled her looks on Nancy Reagan. Her German husband was older than her, a retired physics professor, who stayed at home, researching, reading, and commenting on physics papers with the on-line scientific community. Ursula worked, travelled, and had no intention of retiring as she loved her work.

Riccardo and Ursula packed up their things and left the auction house to go to Knight's Bar, which was located in the five-star Bridge Hotel, just across the road from the auction house in Knightsbridge, London. The hotel had been purpose built in the nineteen thirties, with eleven floors housing two hundred and twenty-five rooms and three suites. The bar and hotel had recently been refurbished by a well-known interior designer, Glenda Bloom. The bar was stunning with large comfortable, plush velvet armchairs in jewel colours. They surrounded unique and solid Perspex illuminated tables, each one embedded with a lump of charred wood. The walls were filled with huge contemporary works of art, representing knights, in honour of the historic origins of Knightsbridge, supposedly knights and a bridge, but no one is exactly sure. The art works were hung against shimmering, metallic polished plaster walls in a soft gold. To complete the look, the room was illuminated by a sophisticated lighting system that created a wonderful intimate atmosphere.

The bar was in effect a company bar, as it was primarily populated by Mount's auction staff. Ursula and Riccardo entered the bar via the main front entrance, and joined two other colleagues; Gregory Petrov, who was the head of the Budapest office, and Taric Abbas, who was of Iraqi heritage and based in the Paris office. Gregory called over the waiter and ordered four vodkas and slimline tonics, the preferred drink for everyone, as it was low calorie and would not sit on the hips.

Taric immediately started the conversation.

'Who the hell paid four thousand pounds for that last lot, an ashtray?'

'God knows. They must be mad. Just because it once belonged to Zena Sparks, they must think it is special. You can buy them online for a couple of quid,' answered Riccardo.

'Well darlings, it keeps us all in business,' added Ursula.

'Cheers to that,' agreed Gregory and they all clinked glasses and took a drink.

All four of them, along with other colleagues who had travelled to London for the auction, had been there since the previous Thursday afternoon, in order to sell the sale. This was the period before the auction took place when all the lots were put on public view.

Selling the sale entailed auction staff meeting with clients who came to the view and persuading them to place a bid. They were also engaged in calling and e-mailing clients who they thought might be interested in bidding on a lot. Then of course they attended the evening client reception, which in this case had been held on the previous Monday evening. On top of these activities there were also breakfasts, lunches, dinners, drinks, and extra-curricular activities, all of course on expenses.

The auction that had just finished was the single owner collection of Zena Sparks, a famous British popstar who had died a few months earlier. It had been the largest auction ever in terms of value and took place over three days. As with most large single owner collections it had been sold in a number of auction sessions, according to the value and type of property. The most important and valuable session was held on Tuesday evening, which covered major world class and rare paintings. Several world records were set including almost two hundred million dollars for a Francis Bacon triptych. During the following days there were sessions covering lower value paintings, furniture, decorative arts, jewellery, and the final session that had just ended this evening which covered miscellaneous, including ashtrays.

The Monday evening reception had been held between six and eight thirty and was the hottest ticket in town. It was attended by a whole host of people, all invited for free, including international popstars, art professionals and rich clients all of whom were invited in the expectation that they would place bids. There is no such thing as a free lunch, or a free reception. The larger the number of bids placed on each lot increased the competition and hence the final selling price.

The reception took place in Mount's gallery complex, which consisted of fourteen galleries, all interlinked so clients could wander through from one to the other. Each gallery had items on display from Zena's estate and her music was played throughout the evening, as the champagne flowed and the canapes, all styled with a musical theme, were handed out to over one thousand and eight hundred guests.

'Shall we have another drink?' suggested Riccardo.

Everybody nodded in agreement.

'I have got a seven thirty flight back home in the morning, so one more drink then I am off,' Riccardo announced as he beckoned the barman over.

'Same again please,' ordered Riccardo as he slipped a folded up post it note onto the tray that the barman was carrying to take the empty glasses away.

In due course, the barman returned with the drinks, placed them on the table and nodded to Riccardo. The note simply read, twenty twelve, ten thirty. This was Riccardo's room number in the hotel and the time for Cezary Bukowski, the barman, to meet him there. Cezary was twenty-three, a Polish student, studying marketing in London and worked at Knight's Bar to help fund his studies. Cezary was stocky, well-built and went to the gym three times a week. He had shaved hair and an olive-coloured complexion with dark, deep eyes. Riccardo and Cezary had been seeing each other for about eighteen months, every time Riccardo came to London. Riccardo knew that Cezary's shift always finished at ten thirty.

'It is ten twenty-five and bedtime for me. Good night and see you around.'

Riccardo left and went to take the lift to his room from the main reception. Once there, he switched on the lights, closed the curtains as the window overlooked the auction house, and laid down on the king-sized double bed waiting. Soon there was a knock at the door and Cezary was standing there as Riccardo opened it. He pulled Cezary into the room and pinned him against the wall as they kissed passionately for several minutes. Their hands roamed around each other's body and then moved to undoing the buttons on their shirts. Topless, Cezary led Riccardo to the bed, and they fell onto it in unison. Intertwined, side by side they fumbled to undo each other's trousers and remove their shoes, until they were just in their Armani socks and underwear. Riccardo had given Cezary some of his socks and underwear to wear when they met. It turned them both on.

'Wow, that was good. Now get out of here, I have an early morning start,'

'Cheers, till next time,' Cezary replied as he dressed, kissed Riccardo, smiled broadly then left the room, closing the door behind him.

Riccardo climbed into bed and set the alarm for five thirty in the morning. He thought to himself, that really was a quickie, as it was still only eleven. He turned the lights off from the central switches by the side of his bed and fell asleep.

The Platinum Card

Friday, 10th December.

The alarm went off at five thirty and Riccardo jumped out of bed and straight into the en-suite bathroom. Like most men, his morning routine was simple and quick, but in Riccardo's case a little bit longer because he applied moisturiser and aftershave. All were done in fifteen minutes, then he dressed in Giorgio Armani underwear, socks, a crisp white shirt, a black suit accompanied by a black crocodile skin belt, and black loafer shoes, always easy to get on and off at airport security.

He packed up all his things into his Armani carry on and with his briefcase he left the room and took the lift down to reception. He left his key card on the desk, knowing that the bill would be charged to his credit card and emailed to him later that day.

Riccardo had ordered a taxi to take him to Terminal Six, the recently opened exclusive terminal for GB Airlines at Heathrow Airport. Mount's Travel, Entertainment and Expenses Policy stated that staff should use public transport to travel to and from airports when on business. There was no way Riccardo was going to walk over to Knightsbridge tube station and take the Piccadilly line to the airport. Did management not realise that he had been working until eleven the previous evening and had only had six and a half hours sleep? No one in their right mind dressed in Armani would take the tube at this ungodly hour. A black bus was in order, as after all, London taxis were public transport because they could be used by anyone. Plus of course, Ursula, as head of office, would sign off his expenses, so there was nothing to worry about.

Ursula and Riccardo had travelled to London together, and because she was an office head, she was entitled to fly business class, unlike Riccardo. He travelled in business class with her as they had to 'work together on the flight,' a frequently used reason so that a junior colleague could sit upfront with a senior one. Ursula had changed her return flight to one later that day as she had a hastily arranged breakfast meeting in the hotel in London.

At this time of the morning the journey to the airport was exactly twenty-two minutes. As all frequent business travellers will confirm, maximum speed and efficient use of time are paramount to get to, in and out of an airport as quickly as possible, hopefully without encountering any of the masses.

Like all the major airlines, GB Airlines had a loyalty scheme, with various levels for different types of clients, depending upon how much they spent. Some GB Airlines' marketing person came up with the colours of the rainbow, in order to be seen to be inclusive, and to represent the different client levels, starting with red, orange, and yellow. Subsequent budget cut backs meant that the rest of the rainbow colours never materialised, with the exception of white, which is of course the blend of all the colours of the rainbow and became the White Platinum level. Riccardo had a Platinum card.

When Riccardo arrived at the airport, he paid the taxi driver and went straight to the Platinum check in area, which of course was the closest to the entrance. There were no queues at all as he passed through the electronic gate with his on-line boarding pass, went straight through to the Platinum security area, again no queues and then into the Platinum Club lounge. The lounge was hush silent, like an old-fashioned library, with deep pile carpets, leather armchairs arranged in small groups and lots of contemporary art on the walls.

Once inside the lounge he took a seat, ordered two croissants, some fresh fruit, and an espresso from the waiter who appeared out of nowhere. Thirty minutes later he was seated in one A, in business class on the seven thirty GB Airlines flight to Zurich.

In reality, the airline never really cared about any of the clients, apart from those in the Platinum Club. Riccardo was greeted in his seat by a member of the cabin crew staff, who was holding an iPad and introduced herself as Violetta. She asked him how he was, and if he would like anything.

'I am good thank you, and yes I would like a bottle of Evian, a pillow and a small glass of champagne.'

'Of course, sir.'

GB Airlines cabin crew had all been trained to adopt a WTF (what the fuck) face when they had to deal with any customers who were not in the Platinum Club. This entailed a stare that could freeze hell over.

When a traveller in seat twenty-seven C, asked for a bottle of water, the response was.

'That will be seven pounds fifty.'

'What the f...' exclaimed the traveller followed by the WTF face from the crew member.

When a traveller in seat fourteen B, asked for a pillow, the response was.

'That will be twenty-five pounds, and we will collect the pillow at the end of the flight.'

'What the f...' exclaimed the traveller followed by the WTF face from the crew member.

When a traveller in seat seventeen D, asked for a glass of champagne, the response was.

'We do not serve alcohol anymore in this cabin, Covid.'

'What the f...' exclaimed the traveller followed by the WTF face from the crew member.

Riccardo's requests were delivered to him, and he settled into his leather seat, with no one next to him, playing games on his mobile phone as the plane taxied and took off.

Riccardo did not actually qualify to be in the Platinum Club, because he did not travel or spend enough with GB Airlines. His father had use of the Bank's private jet, which the whole family used. Riccardo had been given the Platinum Card by the member of Mount's management team who managed the corporate account with GB Airlines. The corporate deal included three gratis Platinum cards to be handed out to whoever the manager thought deserved them.

Woody Smith was Mount's Human Resources manager and managed Mount's corporate deal with GB Airlines as well. He was forty two, married to Jayne, was bi-sexual and liked to have discrete fun on the side. Riccardo met Woody early one evening in a gay bar in London's Soho, just after they both started working for Mount's. After a brief chat to introduce themselves to each other, Woody had to leave to take the tube back to Fulham for dinner with his wife. They did however meet the following morning in Riccardo's hotel room, and this became a regular liaison, whenever Riccardo was in London. In return for his favours, Riccardo was given a Platinum card by Woody.

Ursula came down to breakfast in the hotel and joined her colleague, Sadi Leclere, who was a jewellery expert from the Geneva office. The breakfast room was sumptuous, like the bar, with tables dotted around dressed in crisp white linen tablecloths. On each table was a single red rose in a small white vase. A waitress came and took Ursula's order.

Sadi was fifty eight and had been in Mount's for almost as long as Ursula and they were exceptionally good friends. Sadi was one of the foremost jewellery experts in the world and travelled around the globe constantly on business. She was in London to do a jewellery valuation for a Saudi client, that she was meeting later that day at the Ritz Hotel.

Ursula had severe type two diabetes. She had to monitor herself constantly, to watch what she ate and to check her blood sugar levels regularly. She would self-administer insulin, usually about four times a day, from an insulin pen that she always carried around with her. Whenever she stayed in a hotel, she would always give her second room key to a colleague, just in case anything happened to her, and they needed to gain access to her room.

She always carried three insulin pens in a bespoke handbag that was designed at the Louis Vuitton workshop in Paris. The bag was about the size of a standard iPad and about ten centimetres deep. It had a handle on top and the two large sides of the bag opened when unclipped to allow three pens to be held horizontally and individually on one side, and her regular handbag contents on the other. The bag was made of bright red ostrich skin, her favourite colour, and was lined inside with a protective layer to prevent any x-ray damage to her insulin when passing through airport security checks. Along with the pens she always carried her prescription paperwork in a compartment located behind the pens that opened with a hidden catch. She would present the paperwork, if requested, to the security staff on duty, who would inspect the bag and allow her to pass.

Ursula was having a light breakfast of an egg white omelette with mushrooms and chatting with Sadi when she received a text.

'Royal, five.'

She glanced at the text on her mobile phone and turned it over, face down. She opened her handbag, took out a small vanity mirror and checked her make-up before touching up her bright red lipstick.

'That is my breakfast meeting. Got to go. See you darling,' as they air kissed.

Ursula left the restaurant and took the lift to the Royal Suite situated on the eleventh floor of the hotel. She walked out of the lift looking confident and sexy in her red two piece Chanel suit, Louboutin red stiletto shoes and of course her trade mark helmet hair. She had arrived in exactly five minutes as the message stated.

She knocked on the door and entered.

The GB Airlines flight landed in Zurich at ten twenty local time. Riccardo was the first passenger off the plane, then through passport control and in a taxi by ten thirty. He was at his desk by ten forty five.

Ursula left the suite fifty minutes after entering.

Zena and Raindrop Sparks

Zena Sparks died at her seventieth birthday party. She had been an iconic popstar from the late nineteen sixties, until her death. She had broken every mould and convention, whether it be related to music, fashion, or her personal life. Her music was complex, intriguing, and the words to her songs dealt with issues and topics that were always relevant to her fans.

Zena was five feet eight inches tall, slim with bleach blond hair and blue eyes. She looked more Scandinavian than English. She used to wear her hair short and kept it in a tousled, casual style. She would occasionally wear makeup, but as she associated it with her stage performances, for most of the time she was makeup free and looked much younger than her actual age.

In terms of fashion, she had changed her image frequently, way before Madonna did the same thing. For example, she would dress like a man, then a barbie doll, then a punk, but lately she had taken to wandering around in a sort of Druid style long flowing outfit in her favourite colour, aquamarine.

In the nineteen seventies she had covered the popular song, "The Age of Aquarius" which was a major international hit for her. A couple of years ago she had re-released this song but updated it as a dance anthem for today's audience. It was also a major global success as it spoke to today's generation. Aquarius is associated with democracy, freedom, humanitarianism, idealism, modernisation, and humanity.

Her personal life had been just as colourful as she grew up in the swinging sixties and had regularly engaged in sex orgies with both men and women. She became pregnant in nineteen seventy one and had absolutely no idea who the father was. Her daughter, Raindrop, was born the following year and almost immediately Zena was back on the road earning money from her concerts. When she was travelling, she would leave her daughter in the commune in which she was living, located just outside Guildford in Surrey, England. Raindrop was cared for, and in effect brought up by a number of women, who combined looking after their own children along with Raindrop. Zena was considered the star of her generation, and people made huge allowances for her, hence they brought up her daughter for her. Although Raindrop did not have a sister, she was close to Rose, who was born a few months after her, and they grew up together.

Raindrop was the absolute opposite of her mother. She was a quiet, introverted, studious child who loved reading in order to escape, from what she perceived to be, the chaotic lifestyle of her mother. As close as sisters and having names like Raindrop and Rose, meant that both girls were teased mercilessly at school. "Raindrops on roses and whiskers on kittens," followed them wherever they went. When they changed schools, they both decided to change their names. Raindrop started to call herself Jane, which was about as plain a name as she could think of. Rose took a book of girls' names, opened it, and randomly selected a name using a pin. She then became Jenneke, which is of Greek origin and means wise woman.

Raindrop, or Jane, never wanted anything to do with her mother's world. She grew up to have similar looks to her mother, was about the same size, had blue eyes and long flowing blonde hair. Perhaps her father had been Scandinavian, but she had long given up the notion of ever finding out who he was. Although she never showed it, this was a source of real trauma for her. It was as if an air of melancholy hung over her all the time.

She kept herself to herself when growing up, remained close to Jenneke, and eventually studied to be a physiotherapist. Her mother supported her until she was twenty one, then cut her loose to find her own way in the world. Zena had made her money on her own and believed that her daughter should do the same, without any further handouts or support from her.

When Jane qualified, she had various jobs in hospitals and private practices, until in her early thirties she went to work in a beautiful health resort in Switzerland. This was an exclusive and expensive private clinic in a large nineteenth century villa, offering cosmetic surgery, where the guests could have their procedures done, spend the rest of their holiday recuperating around the nearby lake and mountains then return home looking fabulous. She worked helping clients, before and after surgery, restoring their strength as well as dealing with any physical issues the clients may have, apart from wrinkles and misshaped bodies.

It was in Switzerland, during her mid-thirties that she met her husband, Dave. He was English and worked for the largest insurance company in Switzerland. The clinic and his company often had dealings if there were any claims from clients who were not happy with their cosmetic procedures. Dave was a typical English gentleman, the sort of man who looks like they are from the nineteen fifties, even though he was only thirty-eight. He wore blue pinstripe suits with a shirt and tie, now a rare sight, was slightly rotund, balding, and about five feet seven inches tall. He was sensible, dependable, and honest. Jane quickly fell in love with him and after a few dates in and around the ski resorts in Switzerland, he asked her to marry him.

They married in an old small church in Lausanne, on the banks of Lake Geneva and honeymooned in Sicily. Her mother attended the wedding and was remarkably demure and kept in the background, even though she was the mother of the bride. Mother and daughter had a relatively formal relationship, which was distant but respectful. They talked perhaps once a week but had lifestyles that were polar opposites.

Jane and Dave continued to work in their respective jobs, and they lived in the small mountain village of Gruyères, the home of the famous cheese, in the canton of Fribourg. The village is typically Swiss with the main street lined with perfectly formed chalets, a few essential shops, and some famous gastronomic restaurants, all serving fondues. There was also access to some great skiing in the Pre-Alps.

They bought an apartment with a large mortgage, in the centre of Gruyères, on the upper floor of a chalet. It had stunning views towards the mountains, three double bedrooms, two lounges and a huge wrap around balcony, that was protected by the overhanging roof, so that when it snowed it would slip off directly onto the ground.

They both longed for a child and as Jane was thirty-six when she married, time was ticking. It was not until four years later, after two miscarriages that her daughter, Amy, was finally born. Jane gave up work as she wanted to be a full-time mother to her daughter, the kind she never had.

As an insurance expert, Dave was cautious and did not do anything without thoughtful consideration. There was however, one exception. He loved to ski and would abandon his cautiousness when on the slopes. It was his form of escapism from constantly analysing everything and being bound by probabilities. On the ski slopes he was as free as a bird. Dave was an accomplished skier and would ski as often as possible, even in the summer when he would drive to the highest mountains and glaciers to seek out somewhere to ski. As a cautious family man and father, he had taken out a life insurance policy for ten million Swiss francs, just over eight and a half million pounds, to provide for his wife and daughter should anything happen to him.

Six years after Amy was born, the weather in early March in Switzerland had been unseasonably warm. Many lower level ski resorts had already closed earlier than normal due to the lack of snow, which was a devastating blow for both the resorts and the skiers.

Dave frequently went away for a night or two, to ski with his friends, leaving Jane and Amy at home in Gruyères. Jane was happy with this as it meant she could spend time alone with her daughter. Dave travelled to Zermatt, the highest ski resort in Switzerland as he wanted to ski Piste Fifty-Nine, an advanced black run situated in the valley of Cervinia in the Italian part of the resort. He had skied this many times and knew it inside out. When he arrived, by ski-lift, at the start of the Piste on a glorious sunny Saturday morning with his ski buddy Klaus, they noticed that officials were putting out notices stating that the run had just been closed due to the weather conditions.

'That is for the faint hearted,' Dave said to Klaus as they fastened on their skis and set off.

Neither of them wore a crash helmet because they felt that helmets took away the feeling of exhilaration of taking risks and overcoming their fears. The run was exciting and the views as always out of this world.

They stopped after about ten minutes just to check things over and were happy with the conditions they could see. Dave leapt off the area he was standing on and continued skiing down the section of the piste that was almost a vertical drop. His speed was increasing when suddenly his skis hit a jagged rock that had been exposed by the melting snow. He flew head first down the slope and almost immediately his head smashed against another rock that was jutting out. His skull cracked open and there was blood and flesh all over the snow. His body continued to fall down the piste for about another five hundred metres until it was finally halted by a group of pine trees.

Klaus arrived at the body of his friend a couple of minutes later. He was mortified by what had happened and also terrified of skiing further. He was not sure what to do. He could not go back up and could not do anything to help Dave as it was obvious that he was dead. There was no-one around as everybody else had heeded the closure notices. There was no option but to ski down the rest of the slope for several kilometres to reach help. Klaus had been in the Swiss army as a younger man and had been trained to handle all sorts of obstacles and situations. Today however, his body was shaking uncontrollably which made skiing down the slope even more challenging.

He tried to control his speed and be as careful as possible. After about twenty five minutes he finally reached the lower part of the run which joined other open runs. He approached a member of staff who was working on the ski lifts and explained what had happened.

All the lifts were halted, the runs were closed immediately, and sirens sounded to get people off the slopes. Klaus was driven by a colleague of the lift worker to the helipad, and by the time he had arrived the helicopter's blades were spinning round. Klaus joined the Italian mountain rescue team already on board and spoke to them in Italian.

'He is at the top, near a group of trees. He will be easy to spot because there is so much blood.'

The helicopter lifted up in the air and followed the contour of the mountain as it climbed up towards the start of the black run.

'There he is,' shouted out a member of the team to the pilot.

It was obvious that the helicopter could not land on the almost vertical slope near the trees, so it would have to hover as a crew member was lowered down on the winch with a stretcher attached. The crew member stepped gingerly onto the ground near the body and pulled the stretcher closer. He had to remove the one ski that was still locked onto Dave's foot and pulled the body onto the stretcher. He struggled as there was so much blood on Dave's body which meant that getting a good grip was tricky. Eventually he fastened the body to the stretcher and indicated to his colleagues to winch them up.

The helicopter climbed upwards and then swung around to the left to return to the helipad. It arrived there five minutes later. An ambulance was waiting, and Dave's body was transferred in it for the short journey to the local hospital.

Klaus called Jane on his mobile phone. She screamed and howled like a wild animal when she heard of Dave's death.

The funeral was held a couple of weeks later, after the inquest, at the local crematorium next to the church in which Jane and Dave had been married in. The small and private funeral was officiated by Jenneke, who was now a non-religious celebrant and had flown in from England to support her friend. Zena did not attend as she was on a promotional tour in the USA for her latest album, which really upset Jane. Jenneke stayed with Jane for a couple of weeks helping her to recover from her devastating loss, but eventually she had to return home to England to look after her own family.

A couple of months after Dave's accident, Jane was thinking about what to do with the rest of her life. She would have the insurance money, be able to pay off the mortgage and live comfortably. She even thought about going back to work part time.

After several weeks of phone calls, many meetings and lots of delays, Jane finally received the letter from the insurance company she had been waiting for.

They apologised but said that they were unable to pay out the policy.

They explained that the Italian authorities had been at fault by failing to close the lift access to the start of Piste Fifty Nine. The insurance company had referred this matter to the local police. They further explained that Dave had ignored the closure notices that were being handed out when he arrived, and although not against the law, he did not wear a crash helmet, which would have been the sensible thing to do to minimise the risk of injury. The final nail in the coffin, so to speak, was the testimony from Klaus, that they had stopped after ten minutes, surveyed the area, and made the conscious decision to carry on. The accident was therefore the result of Dave's negligence and consequently the insurance company would not be paying out.

Jane was in shock.

How was she going to survive?

How was she going to pay the large mortgage?

How was she going to be able to look after her daughter?

She could not afford the mortgage, so decided to sell the flat in Switzerland and return to the UK.

The sale of the flat went through quickly as demand for property in Gruyères was strong. She ended up with just over three hundred thousand pounds after paying off the mortgage. Her mother helped her with the necessary funds to buy a lovely three bedroomed, semi-detached country cottage, called Pipe Passage, in Dorking, Surrey, England for eight hundred thousand pounds. She moved in five months after Dave's demise.

Zena agreed to provide an allowance for Amy and to pay for her private schooling, but she insisted that Jane got a job to support herself.

Jane took a part time job in the physiotherapy department at the local Dorking NHS hospital. She worked three days a week and earned just under twenty thousand pounds a year. Whilst Jane had a house and a job, she was angry, frustrated, and unhappy at the situation she found herself in. She had become accustomed to having an extremely comfortable and pleasant life with Dave, a secure future, but now all that was shattered.

Zena had made an enormous amount of money in her career but had no accurate figure about how much she was really worth. She knew the broad value of her house and art, but not an absolute number. She was financially astute and from the start of her career had always controlled the financial side of her business. She employed managers and accountants, but she always retained control and importantly she always signed everything herself. She had never granted anyone else the power to sign on her behalf. Even as a young teenager she was well aware of many women in show business who had lost out either to a partner, husband, or business associate. So many successful women had lost almost everything they earned, for example Doris Day. Right from the beginning of her career she made sure that it would never happen to her. Many of her contemporaries in the music industry had failed to do that and had lost enormous amounts of the wealth that they had generated and earned.

Just after the success of the release of the upbeat "The Age of Aquarius" Zena cannily sold the rights to all her songs. All future copyright income now belonged to the largest media company in America. In return she received just over thirty five million dollars. She had calculated that it was worth her while to have the cash upfront in her bank account now, as she believed passionately that the income stream would dwindle away over time. She had deliberately released that hit to boost her income, increase her value, and attract a good price for her body of work. There were many of her contemporaries from the sixties, seventies, eighties and even nineties that were unknown to people under thirty. In time, her fifteen minutes of fame, which had been more like fifty years, would wane like the setting sun and she would be forgotten.

Zena had bought a beautiful nineteenth century mansion with eighteen bedrooms, in the Surrey Hills, England, in the mid-nineteen seventies. It was a bit run down when she purchased it, but she had restored it sensitively, and then proceeded over the years to fill it with all sorts of works of art. She had exquisite taste and bought the best art and furniture from all the top auction houses and dealers, mixing everything up in an eclectic style. She was also conscious of the struggle that creative artists often go through to be successful, so she would buy art from anybody in order to support them and stored these works in a warehouse in West Byfleet near her home. There were thousands of pieces, some of them good, others that should never see the light of day again. The huge collection of over three thousand works of art was looked after and curated by a local art dealer, Heather Beech, who managed the collection alongside her own art business.

As Zena was growing older, she began to contemplate the future, her legacy and naturally to look back at her life. She was becoming increasingly spiritual and concerned that she had accumulated so much wealth in her lifetime, but that many millions of people around the world lived in dire poverty. She had been pondering what she might do with all her money but had not yet made any decisions. She talked openly about this topic and especially so when she was on the chat show circuit. She was a frequent guest on shows in the UK and the USA. Over the last couple of years chatting to Graham Norton, Seth Myers, and James Cordon, she dropped lots of hints that she was going to do something philanthropic.

It was now almost four years since Dave had died and it was Zena's seventieth birthday on June twenty first. She had decided to hold a birthday party at her home to celebrate.

The house was situated in the most glorious position almost at the top of a valley and looked across the rolling hills to the other side. There was a large driveway off the main road that led down to the entrance to the house. It was laid with polar white pebbles that made a lovely crunching sound when any one walked on it, or even better drove on it. The mansion was built in the eighteen fifties and was constructed of Portland stone in the Palladian style, with all the charm, grace, and simplicity that this style entails. At the rear of the house was a terrace which spanned its entire width and led to a large staircase of forty steep steps that followed the contour of the valley down some twelve metres to a further terrace and a beautiful English rose garden.

Zena had planned the party for months and had invited all her friends as well as colleagues from the music industry. She had engaged a professional events company, Clare Harris Special Events, the best in the industry, which managed the whole evening, overseeing all the floral arrangements, the pre-dinner drinks, the canapes, and the birthday dinner that would be held outside on the lower terrace, weather permitting, in candle light. The theme of the evening was The Age of Aquarius.

White flowers had been stood in water for twenty four hours, into which turquoise food dye had been added, so that they absorbed the hint of aquamarine in their petals. Aquamarine tinted roses, carnations, jasmine, and lilies in several huge bouquets festooned the terrace, filling it with their fragrance. There were huge storm lanterns, each holding a large church candle, which adorned the terrace as well as on each end of the forty steps leading down to the lower terrace.

On the lower terrace, a long table had been laid for dinner for the sixty guests, thirty on one side, thirty on the other, Zena at the head and her daughter at the other end. The table was covered with crisp, white linen tablecloths and all the cutlery was solid silver which glistened in the fading sunlight. There were six huge silver candelabra each holding thirty candles, and in between each one were solid silver centre pieces about eighteen inches tall, holding white grapes that cascaded like waterfalls. The grapes had all been dipped in egg white, then in silver and aquamarine coloured sugar so that they sparkled like jewels. The sets of four glasses for each guest, were Irish cut glass and similarly glistened. The crockery was plain white Wedgewood, so as not to appear too ostentatious. Around and above the table a large wooden frame had been constructed from which hundreds of individual flower heads hung upside down on invisible thread, interspersed with aquamarine crystals. The effect was mesmerising.

On the balcony at the back of the house, overlooking the terrace from the first floor drawing room, a twenty one piece orchestra played light classical music as the guests arrived from eight pm onwards. Amongst her guests were several leading lights from the art world, who were either dealers or who worked in the main auction houses that she frequented, and she classed as friends.

The guests arrived and mingled on the terrace as they were served champagne, cocktails, or elderflower cordial for those who did not want to drink alcohol. The mid-summer evening weather was perfect. It had been a lovely clear bright sunny June day that had turned into a balmy English evening. There really is nowhere better in the world than England on a perfect summer's day. The catering staff, who of course had all been selected for their good looks, served the drinks and canapes to the guests.

At nine thirty precisely, the orchestra conductor standing on the balcony, asked all the assembled guests on the terrace to form a semicircle around the terrace facing the large staircase, but leaving a gap underneath the balcony where the large French doors to the ground floor library were closed. The guests did as they were requested with an air of anticipation, as this was going to be the moment when Zena arrived. The conductor asked for silence and in a moment, you could hear a pin drop. The orchestra started to play the first introductory bars of "The Age of Aquarius" and the French doors were opened by a couple of staff.

Zena emerged in all her splendour. She was wearing a floor length Dior dress in aquamarine silk, encrusted with over five thousand hand sewn aquamarine crystals. Her impossibly high stiletto shoes, which were barely visible, were the same colour and also crystal encrusted. She wore a large necklace, drop earrings, bracelets on both arms and rings of the finest aquamarine. To cap it all she wore a huge Marie Antoinette, or Bridgeton style, tall white wig that must have been four feet tall. She entered and raised her arms revealing an attached cape of the finest gossamer silk also encrusted with crystals. The microphone attached to her dress was hardly visible. The music continued, she moved centre stage and sang her heart out to her adoring guests.

At this point Zena moved round to her right to get closer to her guests and moved around the semi-circle of friends as she continued singing.

When she reached the other end of the semicircle, she started to touch her guests and shake their hands as they stretched them out to her. She turned around to see all her guests for her final notes when suddenly she fell backwards and tumbled down the forty stairs. Her body gained speed as it fell towards the bottom terrace, landing just beside the dining table.

Her neck was broken instantly.

The guests screamed in horror as most of them descended the staircase to help her. They held her twisted body as her wig fell off onto the ground.

'Get an ambulance,' screamed several of the guests, in harmony.

The music had stopped, and people stood around in a haze of disbelief.

'What had happened?'

'How had she fallen?'

'Did she slip?'

'Were her shoes too tall?'

'God this was awful, the worst party ever.'

A Porn Scandal

Tuesday, 14th December.

It was lunchtime and the Home Secretary, Amol Patel, was incandescent with rage. One of his young assistants, James, was standing in front of his desk showing him a video on an iPad.

'Get me the Mayor of London now,' he bellowed to another young assistant, Amelia, sitting in an adjacent office. She called City Hall and then popped her head around the open door.

'Sir, the Mayor of London is in a meeting and will call you back at the end of the day.'

The Home Secretary picked up his landline and pressed one, two one. The department, on the Home Secretary's insistence, continued to use old fashioned landlines because internet based phone services, including mobile phones, were not dependable in the event of a power cut. God knows how the country would operate in such a crisis once all the landlines were phased out in three years' time and all phone calls were operated via the internet. The country would be back to eighteen thirty eight before the first telegram was sent.

The person at the end of one, two one answered.

'Home Secretary.'

'I want you to send two squad cars to City Hall and bring the Mayor of London to my office in the next thirty minutes. This order is covered by Section Two.'

'Yes, Home Secretary.'

Section Two was the recent legislation that enabled the Home Secretary to issue any command in the name of national security. The order was not to be questioned or challenged but would be reviewed in due course by a House of Commons committee, that of course sat in private.

Amol was part of the new government that had only been in power for a few months. The election had been fraught with uncertainty but in the end the winning party had a huge majority. Amol had been the Member of Parliament for Bradford West for the last fifteen years. He originally came from Nairobi, Kenya, was of Indian heritage and had moved to the UK after studying law at Birmingham University. He was in his early forties and was extremely ambitious.

He was principled and could not tolerate laziness, sloppy thinking or people playing politics. He was married to an Indian woman from Yorkshire, they had two children, a boy, and a girl, who all lived in the family home on the outskirts of Bradford. Amol looked as though he could be a Bollywood star. He had thick jet black hair that was swept back and verged on being too long for a politician. He always wore a black suit, black shirt, and no tie. His unconventional dress and style endeared him to his constituents, and he had increased his majority in the last election.

The four police officers arrived at City Hall and two of them entered the building, showed their credentials at the entrance desk, and asked where the Mayor was. Escorted by a security guard they duly took the lift to the third floor, knocked, and entered a large meeting room where about twenty people were sitting around a large rectangular table.

'Madam Mayor. Please come with us. Section two.'

The Mayor stood, asked the deputy Mayor to take over the meeting, collected her things and left with the officers.

'What is this about?'

'Just following orders, ma'am,' one of the officers replied.

The Mayor got into the rear of one of the police cars, quietly seething at being treated so indignantly, as she made the journey to Whitehall.

Ivana Marku was sixty-three and the first female Mayor of London, elected about six months ago. She was five feet ten inches tall, with shoulder length dark blonde hair, that was kept that colour on a monthly basis. From her days as a management consultant, she still wore business suits, generally navy or black, with either trousers or a skirt and always a white blouse and black stiletto shoes. She meant business.

Her parents had come to the UK just after the Second World War, settled in Chiswick, London and worked in the National Health Service. Her mother, who was Slovenian, worked as a nurse and her father, who was Albanian, worked as an auxiliary in operating theatres.

Ivana was a bright child, did well at school and attended Manchester university where she studied Business and Law. She too worked in the National Health Service for a few years and quickly became a manager. She then set up her own management consultancy business advising the NHS on efficiency improvements in procurement and service delivery. The business was extremely successful and soon expanded to provide consulting services to nearly all of the NHS trusts in England and Wales.

As she reached her forties she became increasingly interested in politics and was elected as a ward councillor for Hounslow local authority. She was left of centre and passionate about overcoming what she saw as the injustices and barriers that hold people back. Two years ago, she started her campaign to become the Mayor of London, standing as an Independent, and to her surprise, as much as everyone else's, she was elected.

When the police cars arrived at Whitehall, they drove through an entrance into an underground car park. The cars stopped and two of the officers escorted the Mayor via the lift to the Home Secretary's office complex.

'What the hell is all this about?' she roared as she entered the Home Secretary's office.

'James, come in and show the Mayor the video,' shouted the Home Secretary to his assistant sitting outside his office.

'Yes, sir.'

James came into the office and positioned the iPad so that the Mayor could see it clearly. On the screen was a porn movie showing two naked women having sex, one of them wearing a police hat.

'What has this got to do with me?' asked the Mayor.

'See the tattoos on the buttocks on the woman wearing the hat. One, a red rose for England and the other, a yellow chrysanthemum for China. They belong to Anita Wu.'

The Mayor's face went bright red, and she sat down in an adjacent chair. The Home Secretary, sitting at his desk, leant forward on his elbows, and looked into the Mayor's eyes.

'This is the woman that you convinced me should be our next Head of the UK's Anti-Terrorism unit. Now, we have a major security breach and potential blackmail situation on our hands with this video. God knows how long it has been live on Pornweb and who knows where else, and are there more videos? There is no way she can be appointed now.'

'Are you sure it is her?'

'As part of dealing with the increased security threats that we face in this country, we have introduced a new body scanning process for all individuals in sensitive roles. Fingerprints, retinal and face recognition have not proved to be secure enough. Our enemies have no qualms about using body parts cut off from kidnap victims to gain entry to our premises and systems. Hence, we have been trialling this new secret, state of the art security system, which scans the naked body and then is used digitally wherever we think it can be useful. All candidates for selected roles are now required to be scanned. We have recently been assessing its effectiveness against material on the internet, and thank God we did, as this video was spotted,' replied the Home Secretary.

'Has parliament approved this?'

'Mayor, there are some things that are done behind closed doors, for the sake of national security and are subject to the Official Secrets Act. We cannot have any loose cannons, members of parliament or worse still sensationalist journalists getting on their high horse about this. Whether you like it or not, we are at war with our enemies and so have to use every possible means to defeat them.'

The Mayor looked uncomfortable with this whole situation. It was the first time that she had really come into contact with the world of serious government, and what she perceived to be some of the underhand methods and techniques that were used.

'James, get me Mr Rose, the Head of Human Resources in my office.'

'Yes, sir.'

The Head of Human Resources arrived a few minutes later and entered the Home Secretary's office.

'James, show Mr Rose the video.'

'Yes, sir.'

After watching the video, the Home Secretary explained the whole situation again to Mr Rose.

'I want you to work with the Human Resources team at the Metropolitan Police and get this woman fired in the next twenty four hours for gross misconduct. No payoff, no pension, no nothing.'

'But we will have to conduct an investigation and make formal recommendations before we can do that, Home Secretary. At best, that will take us several weeks.'

The Home Secretary was about to explode with anger and frustration.

'Sod that. I have just done the investigation and made the recommendation. You either implement it or I will fire you for gross misconduct and move your entire department out of these plush offices in Whitehall to an industrial estate on the outskirts of Warrington. Do you understand?'

'Yes, Home Secretary.'

'Amelia, call those police officers back and get them to bring in Anita Wu.'

'Yes, sir.'

'You can all leave my office now whilst I call the Prime Minister. We will regroup here at four o'clock to sort this out, once and for all,' The Home Secretary announced.

'Mayor,' the Home Secretary beckoned her to stay.

'What were you doing when my office called earlier, and we were told that you would call back at the end of the day?'

'I was in a meeting with my team to discuss how we can implement the use of appropriate gender pronouns across the Mayor's office so as not to discriminate against any members of staff.'

The Home Secretary took a deep breath.

'My primary task this week is to work out how to save one and a half billion pounds from the Home Office's budget, of which the Mayor of London's office is a part. The Chancellor of the Exchequer, rightly, is insisting that as a government we must bring down government expenditure, which under the last administration was out of control. As we have a substantial majority in parliament there are going to be some changes to the remit of regional Mayors, including you. To start with, your budget will be reduced by one hundred million pounds, so I suggest that you and your team focus on that.'

The Mayor was taken aback, and her face looked like a thundercloud.

'Let me have your savings proposals by the end of the week.'

'Amelia, set up a meeting on Friday afternoon for the Mayor and me.'

The Mayor left the Home Secretary's office and slammed the door as she left.

Anita Wu had been kept waiting in an office in Whitehall since she had been brought in by the police officers. She was a senior police officer and about to be appointed to one of the top jobs in policing, the press announcement was expected any day now. She was forty seven, five feet six and extremely physically fit. She had short cropped black hair, flawless skin, and an attractive face.

She had been a police officer for twenty five years since joining the police force in her native Hong Kong. Of mixed parentage, her mother was English and her father Chinese, she had always longed to move to the UK and be an officer in the Metropolitan Police force. She moved to London about twenty years ago with her girlfriend, an actress, who she met whilst she was on tour in Asia. After a whirlwind romance and the end of a Shakespeare tour, Anita moved to London and shared her home with Juliet Brioche, who was by now a well-known actress on stage and screen. Although Anita had always been open about her sexual orientation, she and Juliet were extremely private and were never seen in public.

At four o'clock, The Home Secretary, the Mayor of London, Mr Rose from Human Resources and James were joined in the Home Secretary's office by Anita Wu. The video was played, and Anita broke down in tears.

'Oh my God, I am so sorry.'

'How did this happen?'

'I was away at that Interpol conference last year in Helsinki and met that woman in the video. She told me she worked for Interpol in Copenhagen and like me had moved to Europe although she had been born in and grew up in Shanghai. After the conference ended, we had dinner and a few drinks, and one thing led to another. I tried to contact her afterwards but could not find her anywhere and Interpol had no record of her.'

'Oh my God. You were clearly set up by the Chinese. This is worse than I thought.'

'May I go to the ladies?'

'Yes fine.'

Anita left the room and Ivana followed to accompany her.

'Home Secretary. I have a proposal.'

'What, Mr Rose?'

'Rather than firing Anita for gross misconduct, the Human Resources manager at the Metropolitan Police, suggested that it would benefit everyone if she were kept in the fold, better in the tent, than outside.'

The Home Secretary looked non plussed.

'Let me explain.'

'There is a small department within the Metropolitan Police force that investigates crimes in the art world. The current head of the department has been wanting to retire for some time, he is nearly seventy. The problem is that no one wants to do the job. The department has no staff and an annual budget of twenty thousand pounds. We could put Anita in that department on a much reduced salary and she could keep her pension. There is a risk that if we let her go completely, she might go to the press or worse to one of our enemies as she knows so much about how we tackle terrorism in this country. She has been fully briefed for the last few months in preparation for her new appointment.'

'That makes good sense Mr Rose.'

'So, you say there are no staff in the department Mr Rose?'

'Yes.'

'That is a problem as we need to keep an eye on her. The Chinese clearly thought they could extort her with that video, and she has already proved that she is a risk. They probably released it so they could use her as soon as the announcement of her role was made, which would have been tomorrow. Once the announcement was in the public domain and the video was in circulation the trap would be set. James, I want you to get on the phone with our counterparts in the USA and ask them to get Pornweb to remove this video from all its sites.'

'Yes, sir.'

Anita and Ivana returned to the Home Secretary's office and sat down next to Mr Rose.

The Home Secretary addressed Anita.

'Anita, you understand that this situation is gross misconduct, and you would leave the force in disgrace with no payoff and no pension. It is unlikely that you will ever work again because you will require references, and these will not be forthcoming. I do, however, have an alternative. You can stay in the force as head of the Art Squad, dealing with crimes in that world, on a reduced salary and you will not lose your pension benefits you have accrued to date. The department has a budget of twenty thousand pounds and no staff, but I am willing to appoint a junior member to work with you. My nephew has just left university and has been asking me to arrange an internship for him. There is no such thing as nepotism in Her Majesty's government or police force, but in matters of national security, needs must.'

Anita realised she was cornered. She had no choice other than to accept the position on offer.

'I accept your offer, Home Secretary.'

'Good. Mr Rose will sort everything out.'

'Yes, sir.'

'You can all leave my office now, and Mayor remember I am waiting for your savings proposals.'

The Home Secretary picked up his mobile phone and dialled his nephew.

'Hi Camau, it is Uncle Amol here. I have finally got you a great internship. We have just appointed a new head of the Art Squad and there is a position for you to work alongside her.'

'That is great Uncle. When do I start?'

'You can start next Monday. I will have my office send over the details. Camau, I would like to ask you one important thing.'

'Of course.'

'Whilst Anita is part of the Metropolitan Police force and reports to the Assistant Commissioner, I would like you to be my eyes and ears in case you see or hear anything that you think is suspicious.'

'So, you want me to be a spy, Uncle?'

'Not really. I just want you to let me know if you come across anything that you think I should be aware of, that is all.'

'Okay.'

'And Camau, this is totally off grid and just between you and me. Never talk to me about this on the phone, only face to face. Understand?'

'Yes, I understand Uncle, but how can the Art Squad be doing anything that you would want to know about?'

'Hopefully, they are not, but just in case let me know of anything.'

'Sure. Got to go, see you later.'

'Bye Camau.'

The Art Squad

The Art Squad was based in two offices on the lower ground floor of an eighteenth century town house, located on Thyme Street in Knightsbridge, which was owned by one of the auction houses based in London. Over the years the budgets for the Art Squad had been gradually reduced. There used to be a team of ten officers but over time this was reduced to today's one. The auction houses, dealers, and the art market in general enthusiastically supported the Art Squad which they saw as a defence against crime, but the Metropolitan Police did not see it as a priority.

When there was a proposal, a couple of years ago, to close the department completely to save money, and to release office space in New Scotland Yard, which was at a premium, a deal was done with one of the auction houses. Office space on a long term lease for a peppercorn rent of ten pounds per annum was provided to the Art Squad. The lower ground floor offices had been used to store files, so handing them over to the Art Squad was no great loss.

The current head of the department was Stephen Smith, who had been a regular police sergeant in London for thirty years. When he retired from that role, now fifteen years ago, he agreed to run the Art Squad for five years to enhance his pension. He had been asking to leave and retire for several years, but no one would come forward to take over the department.

Stephen was six feet tall with collar length grey hair, seventy years old and still as fit as a fiddle. Stephen's wife had died unexpectedly when he was fifty-six, leaving him devastated. He now lived with one of his ex-clients, who Stephen helped after she had some paintings stolen from her house in the Cotswolds. Once the case was closed, he and Lady Penelope Greyshot became an item and a couple of years later he sold his house in Battersea in South London and moved into her stunning Queen Anne mansion, stuffed with art and antiques, in the town of Burford in the English Cotswolds.

Lady Penelope was a force to be reckoned with. She was now seventy five and had been born in India towards the end of the British raj. She had a privileged upbringing, being brought up by a nanny, attending a private school for girls in Surrey and finally a finishing school in Paris. She would have been a debutante, presented at Court to the young Queen Elizabeth the Second, if that entire system had not been abolished in March, nineteen fifty eight.

She was fearsome, the most politically incorrect person in the country and behaved in an aristocratic manner, even though her title came from her fourth husband who was now deceased. He had been a major player in the printing industry and was knighted for services to printing, as well as for chairing the successful fund raising campaign to restore St Paul's cathedral, in London during the nineteen nineties.

Stephen rarely went into the office any more, preferring to work from home, long before it became standard practice. When he received the call from human resources saying that an immediate replacement had been found, he was as happy as Larry.

When Anita left the Home Secretary's office she was taken to another office in the building where she handed over her security pass, her mobile phone and divulged her passwords so that her email account could be deleted. All the files that she had been working on were shared so she simply lost access to them. A press officer came into the room with a draft press release announcing her new appointment as head of the important Art Squad.

"The Home Secretary and the Mayor of London are pleased to announce the appointment of Anita Wu to the important position of head of the Art Squad. Anita was due to be appointed as head of the UK's Anti-Terrorism Unit, but due to personal reasons has decided to accept this other important, critical, strategic role. She will be stepping down immediately from her current role and will be taking a few days holiday before taking up her new position on 20th December. As the art market has grown over the last few years and has become more and more international, there is an increasing level of sophisticated crime that warrants the attention of an exceptional officer. Both the Home Secretary and the Mayor of London wish Anita all the best in her new role."

As always press releases can be spun to get across whatever message is needed.

One of the female police officers who had escorted Anita to the Home Secretary's office, took her back to her old office a short ride away to retrieve her personal items. There were emotional scenes once her colleagues discovered that she was leaving so abruptly as none of them could understand why, and Anita could not explain. Finally, she was handed a key for the Art Squad offices in Knightsbridge.

Anita had started the day as one of the most important police officers in the country, about to be appointed to a major role, but ended it, disgraced, her financial security significantly reduced and in a new job that she had taken because she had no other choice. On top of that, she had no interest in art or the art market.

She left her office, with her belongings in a cardboard box and a couple of carrier bags, and the police officer dropped her off at Piccadilly Circus. She took the number fourteen bus to Putney Heath, where she lived with her girlfriend. She was not looking forward to going home and having to explain to her partner what had happened.

The Team Meets

Monday, 20th December.

It was a damp, grey morning as Anita waited at the bus stop at seven fifteen for the number fourteen bus to take her to her new office in Knightsbridge. This was the first time in a long time that she had not worn her police uniform to work. Today she was dressed in a grey trouser suit with a black polo neck jumper, knee length black boots, a large navy blue overcoat, a black woollen skull cap, black woollen gloves and carrying a large black golf umbrella. It felt strange to be wearing what she considered to be casual, weekend clothes.

She had not had a good few days. When she arrived home on the previous Tuesday evening, she had waited for her girlfriend to come home so she could explain to her in person what had happened. Her girlfriend was in a new, successful play in the West End and did not get home until just after eleven thirty in the evening. Anita had some camomile tea ready and when her girlfriend sat down at the kitchen table, she explained everything and the consequences for her career.

'You can sleep in the back bedroom tonight,' her girlfriend responded icily.

For the rest of the week, Juliet was at work doing the play and Anita stayed at home, contemplating what had happened to her. She felt so ashamed and upset. How had she been so stupid? She spent the next three days in a sort of haze, dressed in her pyjamas watching day time television. She never even went to the gym. She thought a lot about her life and how she had to overcome this catastrophe. She thought about her Chinese heritage, then on Friday afternoon it came to her. Her difficulties today were nothing in comparison to those that her grandparents and great grandparents had suffered in China during the Communist and Cultural Revolutions. She quickly decided that she should stop being so self-indulgent and she should embrace the opportunity she was being given. It was not what she planned, but the measure of a successful person is to overcome setbacks and get on with it. In addition, watching day time television was enough to make anybody want to go back to work.

Anita and Juliet had a large five bedroomed house that was one of four in a block that was built in the nineteen twenties in the art deco style. The houses were located in a private drive, off a road with multi-million pound detached houses, and the soft red brick was complemented by mullioned windows and dark timber woodwork, giving the illusion of age. They had bought the house as an investment and not done anything to it since buying it seven years ago. The kitchen and bathrooms were dated, probably from the nineteen eighties, when taste and interior design generally went out of the window. Juliet was always concerned, as an actress, about having enough money and a steady income and Anita was careful with money, the result of her Chinese upbringing.

At the weekend, Juliet and Anita had gone about their usual weekend routine. Grocery shopping, cleaning the house, walking their dog, and eating late after Juliet came back from her play. They went for pre-arranged drinks to a gay bar on Clapham High Street on Sunday afternoon with a couple of girlfriends. They both asked them if everything was okay, and they simply replied that they were a bit tired from working long hours.

The conversations between Anita and her girlfriend were polite, efficient, and devoid of any real emotion. Anita continued to sleep in the back bedroom.

Mr Rose, from Human Resources, had proposed that the new Art Squad team would meet today with the outgoing head. Stephen had agreed to come into the office to do a handover and Camau Kumar, the Home Secretary's nephew, would also be there.

The bus crawled in the heavy morning traffic through Putney High Street, Fulham Broadway and finally arriving in Knightsbridge forty five minutes later. It was just after eight, which was the usual time that Anita started work. She arrived at the address she had been given and walked down the metal steps to the office front door which she opened with her key and entered. She immediately noted that there was no alarm which now made sense to her as she had not been given any entry codes. How odd for a police department, she thought.

The office comprised of two interconnected offices, a small kitchenette, and a lavatory. It was dark and miserable with papers all over the desk in the larger of the two offices. The second office had box upon box of files, which she soon realised after investigating had nothing to do with the department but related to the auction house that owned the building. These would have to go she noted.

There was no computer terminal on the desk, just a landline. How strange she thought. How was she ever going to work with this set up?

She made herself a coffee using the items she found in the kitchen. Well at least that was something she approved of. She detested buying coffee from coffee shops and walking round holding a paper cup with a plastic lid that simply added to the environmental mess that the world was already in. Plus of course the cost was ridiculous, and she could not understand why people wasted so much money on buying drinks that they could so easily make themselves.

Anita looked around the office, picking up the odd piece of paper here and there. Everything was so disorganised, and she noted that there was hardly any stationery items around. She almost had a fetish for stationery and decided that getting the necessary items would be a good first step, and a good job for her intern. On the subject of her intern, where was he? It was now eight forty five and, in her world, people started work in the office at eight.

At nine twenty, Camau arrived carrying a Starbucks coffee.

'Hey, how is it going?' he asked Anita as he entered and closed the door behind him.

'My name is Camau.'

'Good morning Camau, I am Anita. Were you delayed this morning?'

'No, everything is good.'

'So why are you late?'

'What do you mean? I was getting a coffee and you would not believe there was such a long queue in Starbucks. Anyway, my mobile phone is always switched on so you can always call or message me anytime.'

'Okay.'

'We will talk about this later.'

'I understand that Stephen Smith will be coming in to do the handover.'

'I dunno,' Camau answered as he shrugged his shoulders.

Anita was getting the measure of Camau. She had never really come into contact, let alone worked with a Gen Z before. She had read that they were a distinct species, but she was shocked at Camau's casual and laissez faire attitude. She was used to discipline and a command-and-control structure where things got done when she ordered. Camau would be in for a bit of a shock.

Camau, like his uncle was of Indian heritage, born in Kenya and lived between London and Nairobi. His mother, the Home Secretary's older sister, worked as a magazine editor in Nairobi and his father was the Managing Director of Jomo Kenyatta International airport in Nairobi. Camau was a brilliant mathematician and statistician and had recently graduated from Cambridge University with a first class honours degree. Since graduating, a few months ago, he had been travelling around South America having a post graduate gap trip as he did not have one before starting university.

He was six feet tall, clean shaven with long black hair that he swept back and kept in a ponytail. He always wore denim jeans, designer trainers and a white Nehru collar shirt. He carried a black leather courier bag over his shoulder in which he kept his iPad and mobile phone.

'Whilst we are waiting for Stephen to arrive, I would like you to pop out and get these stationery items for the office.'

'Nah, I do not feel like going shopping, I have just arrived.'

Anita stared at him in a way that he recognised from his mother. No other words were necessary.

'Okay then. Have you got a card?'

Anita opened her handbag, took out her purse and handed him her debit card.

'Do not spend more than fifty pounds.'

Camau left and went to the local Ryman's stationery store, returning about thirty minutes later. Anita checked everything that Camau had bought and arranged the items neatly on a shelf that she had just cleared. Anita sat at the desk and Camau sat on one of the two chairs in front of it checking his phone.

At ten thirty, Stephen arrived.

'Good morning, everyone. I am Stephen. Wow, you two are early birds.'

'Good morning, I am Anita, and this is Camau. We are taking over from you, and I understand you will help us in the handover.'

'Yes, that is correct. That is why I came into town today. I never take the train before nine in the morning, too busy. Now, first things first. Where are we going to go for lunch?'

Anita could hardly contain her dismay. This department was a complete shambles. It was no wonder it was treated with so little respect by New Scotland Yard.

'Do you like Italian?' Stephen asked as he picked up the phone and called Zio's, just around the corner.

'Morning Luigi, Stephen here. Three people for lunch today at one, my usual table please.'

'Of course, see you later.'

'Stephen, please take a seat.'

'I will just make a coffee first. Would you all like one? I only drink Sumatra Mandheling,' as he wandered off to the kitchen, returning five minutes later.

'Got to let it brew properly. Penelope and I are going on a cruise on Wednesday to celebrate my retirement, flying to Montego Bay in Jamaica, then Grand Cayman, Cancun, Cozumel, and Cuba. Should be fantastic. We are flying in an Airbus three fifty from Gatwick.'

'Stephen, please take a seat then we can start on the handover.'

'Of course.'

At that point, the phone rang, and Stephen reached over the desk and picked up the receiver.

'Good morning, Stephen.'

'Good morning, Rodney, how are you?'

'I am good thanks. Shame about Rovers at the weekend. Phillips should have got that goal in.'

'Yes, I know. Did you hear that I am retiring and then off on a cruise on Wednesday with Penelope?'

'Where are you going?'

'We are off to the Caribbean.'

'Well, that will be lovely at this time of the year.'

'Anyway, I just wanted to let you know that I have finished those repairs on Penelope's dinner plates. You can collect them anytime.'

'Great, I will pop in after lunch. See you later.'

Stephen placed the receiver back in its cradle.

'Just got to pop to the loo, the consequence of getting older.'

Stephen left the room.

Even Camau was getting frustrated, and Anita disconnected the phone at the wall socket.

When Stephen returned Anita asked him to take a seat next to Camau.

'Stephen. As you know I am taking over this department and am likely to be here for a number of years for several reasons which we do not need to go into. To be honest I know nothing about the art world, and I am not really interested in the arts. I would like you to tell us about it and the cases on which you are currently working. I understand that you will be away over Christmas, but if necessary, I may need to call you when you are back if Camau or I have any questions. Is that okay with you?'

'Yes, that is fine.'

Stephen settled into his seat next to Camau and picked up his cup of coffee.

'The global art market is relatively small but more than makes up for that by the scale and intensity of feelings. Whilst there is a degree of rationality in the marketplace the level of emotion in this market is unparalleled anywhere else. It always seems to attract personalities who thrive on being prima donnas.'

'When trying to understand the art market the first thing that people often ask is. What is art? People have attempted since the dawn of time to define what art is. In my view art is simply anything that a human being has created that is cherished by another. Of course, scholars and academics like to speak of Fine Art to distinguish between certain works and others, but the distinction is a matter of opinion. There is a whole industry devoted to explaining and maintaining the mystique around art.'

'Whilst there is an almost infinite number of objects that have been created by humans, the ones that people covet and are traded in the art world are paintings, prints, photographs, sculptures, works of art, books and manuscripts, furniture, jewellery, precious stones, cars and motorbikes, clocks, watches, coins and medals, ceramics and glass, toys, modern collectibles, wines and spirits, sports, music, film and television memorabilia, scientific instruments, space ephemera, stamps, silver and vertu, rugs and carpets, musical instruments, fashion and latterly handbags and sneakers.'

Anita was listening intently.

'I never realised there were so many different fields in the art world.'

'Yes, and it grows every year. Now even old computers and game consoles are considered collectors' items.'

'The market though is highly polarised. Imagine if you will a pyramid. If you could stretch the apex of the pyramid and pull it upwards and then let the base melt and spread outwards, you get a sense of the shape of the art market. There is an enormous number of low value items with a few extremely expensive ones, and the rest in the middle. That is why there is so much competition at the top of the market. There is a huge amount of cash washing around in the world looking to find a home, hence the almost obscene prices paid for certain items. The good thing about the art market though is that the best things are preserved over the generations. An active market ensures this, irrespective of whether one might think that some prices are extortionate.'

'Some parts of the art market are truly global, but many are local. There are lots of sub markets which serve national or even regional tastes and do not travel well. Swiss paintings of cows and mountains rarely leave their home valleys. These markets are the base of the pyramid that I mentioned. There are only four truly global markets. These are the Impressionist and Modern Art, Contemporary Art, Old Master Paintings, and Jewellery and Watches markets. These four markets account for the bulk of the international art trade, whether sold at auction, at art fairs or through dealers. It is almost impossible to get a handle on the true size of the art market because the lower value segment is so fragmented across so many players, in so many countries. Therefore, the only measure that is accurate is the summation of these markets in London, Paris, Geneva, New York, and Hong Kong, which together account for about ninety per cent of the total global art market.'

'This is fascinating Stephen. I never realised the art market was so complex or international.'

'Next, I should move onto the key players, or actors.' That sent a shudder down Anita's spine, just hearing the word actor, but she remained calm and said nothing.

'There are several groups of people in the art world, including living artists. The majority of living artists have a tough time and are generally excluded from the high value transactions. They are fighting back with the use of technology, but more of that later.'

'The clients maybe buyers, or sellers, or both. Some may have inherited their collection; others may have acquired it over time. Art is the ultimate form of showing off. Once an individual has houses, cars and maybe a yacht, the only other thing they can acquire is art, and it becomes an intense competition to see who can show off the most. Some of these people have limited taste and need a lot of help to make sure they buy the right things and build up a good collection. The mistake, many people make, is to invest in art in the hope of a financial return. The fundamental issue with art is that people fall in love with their purchases, and then just as with people, rationality goes out of the window. It happens, repeatedly.'

Stephen continued.

'The people who inherit are the ones I feel sorry for.'

'Why the hell would you do that?'

'Inheritance can be a burden. I am not talking about inheriting a couple of hundred thousand pounds from your parents to pay off your mortgage, buy a new car or having a holiday of a lifetime. No, I am talking about inheriting large collections of works of art which always come with additional burdens. They may also have inherited historic houses, which cost a fortune to run and maintain, and which can be difficult to sell as they are often owned by trusts with legal restrictions. Inherited land may also come with tenants or other restrictions and covenants. For these people managing a collection of works of art is a full time job and a real burden. Art has to be maintained and does not generate an income, unlike many other assets. If they wish to sell something there can also be complex legal, heritage and tax issues to be dealt with. In many ways these people are trapped.'

'I never thought of it that way, Stephen.'

'Galleries showcase living artists in their spaces. They take a percentage of the selling price and can make or break the career of an artist. As I mentioned many of the tech savvy artists are selling to clients directly on Instagram or other platforms, bypassing the galleries and some of them are doing very well indeed.'

'Agents and advisors assist clients by helping them to build and edit their collections by buying or disposing of works of art, all of course for a fee.'

'There are many dealers around the world in every major town and city that operate in the secondary market. There are however a few, large international dealers that shadow the auction houses, and will often have premises in the same cities. There is a sort of love hate relationship between the auction houses and these dealers as on one hand they poach business from each other and on the other hand need each other to feed their respective business. It is a symbiotic relationship.'

'I like this complexity,' added Camau, as Anita noticed that he was finally waking up and engaging.

'Time for lunch now, everyone.'

'It is only around the corner.'

'Stephen, can we continue talking during lunch?'

'Yes, of course, but after lunch I have to pop into see Roddy, the restorer, to collect Penelope's plates, then it will be time for me to catch my train back home. I always buy a super saver so must be on the train by three o'clock.'

Anita sighed inside but realised that she could not do anything about Stephen's timekeeping. Best to get out of him what she could and then move on.

She reckoned it was unlikely that he would come to the office tomorrow and then he was off to the Caribbean on Wednesday. Soon it would be Christmas and before you know it, January in the New Year.

All three left the office and went to Zio's, the Italian restaurant three doors away. The restaurant was one of the few remaining old Italian restaurants left in London. It looked like it was untouched from the nineteen fifties, because it was untouched. The walls looked as though they had absorbed years of the smell of pasta and the dark patterned carpet looked as though it was hiding a multitude of stains and spills. There were old pictures of Italian holiday seaside and mountain resorts on the walls, that were all faded.

Stephen was welcomed with open arms by the Head Waiter and was escorted along with Anita and Camau to the best table in the room, positioned nicely in the window.

'Great table.'

'Yes, I have been coming here for many years. When I am in London, I come here every day.'

Anita was astounded. How was it possible in today's world to operate like this, with no technology, a chaotic office, lunch in a restaurant when in London, working at home the rest of the time?

She wondered how effective Stephen really was and what he focused on.

'Lady and gentlemen, the special today is farfalle con tartufo bianco, butterfly pasta with fresh truffle.'

Stephen looked around the table. 'Is that good for everyone?'

Everyone nodded in agreement.

'Then, three Luigi.'

'Perfetto.'

'And to drink?'

'Tap water is fine for me.'

'And me.'

'I will have a large glass of Valpolicella.'

'Of course, Stephen,' Luigi acknowledged and went to the bar, returning with the drinks momentarily.

'So, Stephen can you continue and explain a little about the auction houses?' requested Anita in an attempt to get everyone focused again.

'Of course. The auction houses are the other players in the art world. Whilst there are auction houses all over the world in most towns and cities, the vast majority operate at the lowest end of the marketplace, just like those that you see on television programmes such as Hunt the Lot, or Bang the Gavel, where the audience gets excited when the bidding reaches one hundred pounds. There are only three major global auction houses, and they are all based here in London.'

'I thought that the Chinese had auction houses?'

'Yes, they do Camau, but they do not operate internationally, only in mainland China, so we do not count them.'

'Okay.'

'The oldest house is Mount's, which was founded in sixteen seventy. They started in St James' when that area of London was being developed but soon moved in order to expand to what was then no man's land, Knightsbridge, now of course one of the most exclusive parts of London. Their brand colour is still claret burgundy, selected by Mr Mount in the seventeenth century. He simply chose that colour as he was drinking claret when asked what colour to paint the outside of his premises. You will have seen Mount's in the news last week following the success of the auction of Zena Sparks, the largest estate sale ever. That was an incredible sale of some amazing works of art. Kudos to Mount's for putting in on and achieving a great result.'

'Stephen, why did Mount's manage that sale?'

'They would have won it against the competition by having the best deal and offering the most marketing promises. I will explain how all that works another day.'

Stephen continued.

'The second oldest auction house is Balfour's, founded in sixteen ninety-four. They are based just next to Knightsbridge, actually on the border, in Belgravia. Their brand colour is Bottle Green which was selected during the Georgian period, and they have kept it ever since. Balfour's is now owned by two Italian sisters who own the company that makes those famous chocolate covered almonds, Gocce D'Amore or Love Drops.'

'The third auction house, Seton's, the newcomer, was founded in seventeen eighteen. They were originally based in Mayfair but when it was taken over about twenty five years ago by a group of Turkish billionaires, they moved to Vauxhall. God knows what they were thinking of, moving south of the river.'

'Why is that a problem?' asked Camau.

'There is a saying in London that no one lives north of the park or south of the river.'

'You mean Wembley Park?'

'God no. Hyde Park.'

'Wealth in London, like in all cities, is concentrated in certain areas. The wealthy always have, and still do, select the best places to live and make it their own. The price of property in these areas is exorbitant and creates a real barrier to keep people out. Postcodes with the highest property prices in London are all located north of the river and south of the park. Whether you like it or not it is the reality. People live in their own small area and crossing the river for some people is still a barrier.'

'About five years ago Seton's also changed their brand colour to black from a lovely navy blue, in the belief that black would be classy, as used by many fashion brands. The problem with using black in an auction house is that death is a key part of the business, therefore it is appropriate to be subtle, stylish, and timeless, not look like a funeral house.'

'What do you mean death?' asked Anita.

'The auction houses thrive on the three Ds. Death, Divorce, and Debt. People with assets sometimes build up substantial debts and then struggle to pay them off. If someone owns art and antiques, it can be difficult to get a loan from a bank using art as collateral because banks do not know the value of art, although some do offer art backed loans. All three of the main auction houses have filled that gap by agreeing to lend money using art and antiques as collateral. They of course take possession of the collateral and if the loan is not paid off the items are sold to repay the debts. It is a lucrative side business.'

'Divorce is never a pleasant business for either the people or professionals that are involved, including the auction houses. Petitioners often state they want an amicable divorce, but the more money that is involved the more acrimonious the divorce. Assets usually have to be sold to realise the funds necessary to settle the divorce between the parties.'

'Death is the cleanest and easiest D to manage as it is clear cut. Estates are sold to raise funds to settle inheritance commitments as well as death duties and taxes that may be due. All the three Ds keep the art market going round and round.'

'Tre farfalle con tartufo bianco,' Luigi announced as he placed the pasta dishes on the table.

'Buon appetito.'

'Why are there only three global auction houses?' asked Anita.

'The global art market consolidated years ago, long before anyone thought about Monopolies and Mergers legislation. These three houses bought up the competition or forced others out of business. They expanded to all the key centres of wealth where they all now have offices whilst at the same time consolidating their auction rooms to just five centres, London, New York, Paris, Geneva, and Hong Kong. Auction houses are incredibly costly to run, so despite the headline jaw dropping prices they achieve, they have to manage their operations and costs extremely carefully in order to generate a profit. I will explain more about the economics another time.'

'This pasta is wonderful, don't you think?' Stephen stated, not actually expecting anyone to disagree with him.

'Yes, it is really good.'

'So, within walking distance, apart from having to cross the river, we have the three main auction houses in and around Knightsbridge.'

'Yes Anita, that is correct. It is all here.'

'Ah, ah Luigi, may I have another glass of wine?'

'May I ask a question?'

'Of course, Camau.'

'As we are the Art Squad focused on identifying and solving crimes in the art world, what sort of crimes are there?'

'You would be amazed my boy.'

Luigi cleared the plates away and asked if anyone would like a pudding or coffee. All three agreed just to have an espresso each.

'And I will have a grappa, please Luigi. Anyone else?'

The two others at the table shook their heads.

'Where do I start with the crimes?'

'Okay. First there is good, old fashioned theft. This is the area that I focus on. I manage to recover about ten percent of reported thefts. The rest just disappears even though there is a register of stolen goods against which all potential sales have to be checked.'

'Sometimes criminals swap items particularly jewellery and watches. By this I mean people who go into a shop and request to try something on when it is on display. They then come back another day, perhaps seeing different staff, and replace the item they tried on with a fake that they have brought with them. People usually operate in twos or threes so they can create a diversion. It is easy to swap a diamond ring for one with glass or switch a valuable watch with a fake.'

'We have also recently seen an increase in smash and grabs where thieves will drive a car at full speed into a shop front and steal whatever they can.'

'Whenever goods are being transported it is relatively easy for thieves to track, follow and hi-jack the vehicle and steal the items on board.'

The coffees and grappa arrived and were placed on the table.

'Wherever you have money and staff there is always a risk. Thankfully, cash is rare in business today but there are instances where staff steal cash or create false receipts to defraud their employer. There was a case in one of the dealers where a member of the accounts team creamed off all the pence on invoices to his own account. When a client might be paying tens or even hundreds of thousands of pounds for an object, they simply do not notice that an invoice has been rounded down. It took the auditors in this instance several years to work out why the books did not balance by a few thousand pounds each year. The person in question slipped up by purchasing a Porsche nine eleven and bragging about it to his colleagues. He was then watched for a couple of months and his game was up. He is now doing time in Wormwood Scrubs.'

'As values have mushroomed over the years, the prevalence of fakes has also increased at an exponential rate. Fakes are cheap and easy to make and if they fool the right people can generate enormous amounts of money. You can order a copy of any painting you want on line and have it delivered almost as fast as Amazon Prime. Many people have been duped over the years and rigorous scientific analysis is now being used to detect fakes.'

'The art market is subject to laws developed mainly for other purposes. Although there has been much talk globally about introducing art market specific regulations, the authorities do not want to commit the time and resources as the return is not perceived to be high enough. Therefore, the market is considered to be ripe for money laundering and could be a cover for all sorts of illicit activities.'

'Oh my God,' said Anita. 'I had no idea that this genteel world could be involved in such topics.'

Privately, she was excited at discovering these issues as it ignited her interest. Perhaps this job would not be so bad after all. She would have to work things up a bit, get more resources and could perhaps be exonerated from her indiscretion.

'The tax authorities check on sales in their respective countries to make sure that capital gains taxes are accurately calculated and paid. Often clients cannot remember, or do not know, what was paid for an item, so it is challenging to work out the amount of tax due.'

'Cyber-crimes are endemic everywhere, including the art market. Crooks will attempt to steal identities or re-direct bank transfers by hacking emails and amending bank account details.'

'And finally, last but not least is the wild west of digital art known as non-fungible tokens (NFTs), and crypto currencies that are taking the art world by storm. Although more and more regulations are being implemented in many countries the Law is not yet up to speed in this area and disputes are developing over ownership, inheritance, source of funds and tax implications.'

Stephen took a drink of his grappa.

'Wow. So would I be correct in summarising all of these into the following seven categories of crime:

- Theft, in all its forms
- Fakes
- Money laundering
- Fraudulent claims
- Tax evasion
- Cybercrimes including NFTs.'

Summarised Anita.

'Yes, that is correct.'

Anita was even more excited, now that she could see that the art world was a hot bed of crimes and could potentially be responsible for some of the most heinous ones that were happening today. Perhaps her move from the Anti-Terrorism Unit was not so bad after all. She would be able to operate without scrutiny as this world and her new department were so far under the radar as to be virtually unnoticeable. It was only the auction houses and trade bodies that lobbied the government and the Metropolitan Police to keep the Art Squad going.

'Stephen, that was absolutely fascinating. I hope you have a wonderful cruise over Christmas, and I look forward to staying in touch with you in the New Year.'

'No problem. I would like to invite you both to come and stay with us in January when we are back. Come and stay for the weekend in the Cotswolds.

We can show you around and I am sure we will have lots of photographs from our cruise to show you.'

'That would be wonderful,' Anita said as she looked at Camau and the look of horror on his face.

'Luigi, il conto, per favore.'

'Si, Stephen.'

The bill arrived and Stephen passed it to Anita.

'You are the senior officer here, so your shout.' Anita opened the folded bill and gasped in horror.

Item	Number	Cost per Unit	Total Cost
Cover charge	3	£5.00	£15.00
Large glass of Valpolicella	2	£9.50	£19.00
Farfalle con tartufo bianco	3	£45.00	£135.00
Espresso	3	£4.50	£13.50
Grappa	1	£8.50	£8.50
Sub Total			£191.00
Service @ 15%			£28.65
Total ex VAT			£219.65
VAT @ 20%			£43.93
Total			£263.58

She calculated that with the stationery bill this morning she had spent nearly one point six per cent of her annual budget and it was not even two thirty on her first day. This was the last time this was going to happen, period. She paid the bill, and they all left the restaurant. Stephen said his good byes and walked off to visit Rodney, then to get the tube to Paddington station and take the train home.

'You and me, back to the office now.'

Once seated back in the office, Anita got out one of her new pens and a pad that Camau had bought this morning.

'What are you doing?'

'I am making a plan.'

'On paper?'

'Yes.'

Camau rolled his eyes and got his iPad out of his bag.

'There are two weeks until the return to work in the New Year. In that time, I want you to do the following:

- Contact the auction house and get those boxes removed from that office. I believe this building belongs to Balfour's.
- Clean and tidy the whole place and tomorrow, I will bring some paint from home so you can decorate the place.
- Contact the IT department and get two computers and Wi-Fi installed in here. The office may need cabling.
- Contact security and have the locks changed, an alarm fitted and a security audit to assess if there are any other areas that need securing, for example the windows.
- Contact facilities and have some appropriate flooring, office desks, chairs, filing cabinets and equipment brought over. I want this office looking like it means business.
- You can use the office back there which will also be a meeting room when needed, so make sure we have a meeting table.
- I also want a fridge and microwave putting in the kitchen. There will be no more lunches in fancy restaurants and by the way Starbucks, Costa Coffee and any other take away coffees are banned in this office with immediate effect.'

'Yes, boss.'

Anita was surprised at Camau's enthusiasm. All he needed really was to be given plenty to do and to deliver something that he could be proud of. Perhaps Gen Zs were not so different after all.

'So, let us get all this done ready for January the forth next year when we will start in earnest. I am certain there is plenty to do. Once we get more insight from Stephen, I want you to do a detailed analysis of the art market so that we can really understand what is going on, and to work out where we should focus our attention to root out the criminals operating in this world.'

'Brilliant.'

The New Year

Tuesday, 4th January.

It had snowed overnight, leaving half an inch of snow across London and consequently public transport was in chaos. Buses had been taken off the roads and tube lines that run overground had been severely disrupted. Being a no nonsense sort of person, Anita had ordered a taxi the day before, so she arrived at her office on time at two minutes to eight.

Christmas had been tricky for Anita and Juliet as the consequences of the video strained their relationship. They went through the motions on Christmas Eve and Christmas Day, then decided to go for a walk on Putney Heath on Boxing day with their chocolate brown two year old Springapoo, Mabel. At lunch time they found themselves at The Printers Arms pub where they ordered a bottle of wine and some dry roasted peanuts. The pub was a typical gastropub that was huge and had been done up in the nineties in a style that was now looking dated. They made small talk and fussed over their dog, when Juliet suggested that they needed to talk.

'Anita, we cannot go on like this, it is unbearable. I think I might have overreacted about what has happened. I am genuinely sorry about the impact on your career which I know means so much to you. However, our relationship is strong and can withstand the knocks that life throws at us.'

'Go on.'

'I have a confession to make, which has been praying on my mind for months. When I was in Edinburgh last year for the festival, I had a one night stand with a stage hand. We had finished the final performance and there was an after show party when we all got drunk in the main dressing room. This young girl, aged about twenty, made a pass at me and I reciprocated. We went to one of the small dressing rooms where there was a day bed and locked the door. I had great sex.'

Anita remained silent.

'The following morning, I felt so guilty and have been longing to tell you ever since. I have never done anything like this since we have been together, and I am so sorry. I cannot even remember the girl's name and I am sure I will never see her again.'

Anita breathed in deeply and exhaled pointedly.

'So, you have been giving me a hard time over the last few days when you have done exactly the same thing but were not caught out like I was.'

'Yes, I know, and I am ashamed and really sorry.'

'Look, we have a long history, nearly twenty years, and we would be fools to throw all that away for a couple of incidents that really do not matter in the scheme of things. Yes, I have had to change my role in the Met, but to be honest I think it might prove more interesting than I first imagined. Anyway, you are the most important thing in my life. Will you marry me?'

Juliet was taken aback as this was not what she was expecting after coming clean about her indiscretion.

'Yes, of course I will marry you. I love you.'

'And I love you too.'

'Shall we get a bottle of champagne to celebrate and order some lunch?' Anita asked as she took Juliet's hand.

'Yes, perfect.'

As Anita walked down the steps to the office, she could see that the lights were on. She knocked on the door as her key did not open the lock anymore. Camau opened the door and welcomed Anita. The office had been totally transformed.

Along with the new security lock that required an electronic pass, the office was now a contemporary office space. It had been decorated in a soft grey paint with a white ceiling and white woodwork. The floor had been laid with dark oak, almost black flooring and each office had modern electric standing desks that could be raised or lowered for standing or sitting. A seated area had been created in the larger office with a couple of sofas in lapis lazuli blue fabric. An oval meeting table had been added to the second office and the kitchen had been kitted out with a coffee machine, microwave, and a new fridge.

'How did you manage to do all of this?'

Camau smiled.

'I called my mother and told her where I was working and how awful the office was. She subsequently called her younger brother, the Home Secretary, and told him to sort it out. He ordered the facilities team at the Home Office to refurbish this place over Christmas. They only finished yesterday.'

'I am extremely impressed, Camau. This is great.'

'Plus, I got your budget increased to fifty thousand pounds a year.'

'Oh my God, fantastic.'

'Would you like a coffee?'

'Yes, I most certainly would. Thank you.'

Anita's opinion of Camau had completely changed. He was smart, resourceful and had made this office, by whatever means, a really nice place to be in.

Over coffee, Anita spoke to Camau.

'As you know, Stephen has invited us to stay for the weekend at his home in Burford. We can take the train to Charlbury from Paddington at sixteen fifty eight, which arrives just over an hour later. Stephen will then pick us up and drive us to his home. We will come back to London on Sunday afternoon. Can you sort the tickets?'

'Sure.'

'Then for the rest of the week I would like you to pull together all the figures that you can about the art market. I want to really understand what is going on so we can start to look at all those crimes that Stephen mentioned and then prioritise where we should focus our attention.'

'Great. I am on it.'

'Meanwhile, I am going to visit all the auction houses and main dealers to introduce myself.'

Weekend in the Country

Friday, 7th January.

Anita and Camau left the office in good time to get to Paddington Station to take the train to Charlbury. Anita insisted they take the tube, so they took the Piccadilly line from Knightsbridge to Earl's Court, then the District line to Paddington. As they were travelling on the tube, they discussed what each of them had been doing for the last few days.

Camau had being doing an analysis of the art market and had collated as many statistics and reports as he could muster. He had filed them all electronically in the cloud, so they were accessible to both of them from anywhere and on any device.

'Camau, what are your conclusions about the art market?'

'Well as Stephen said the marketplace is highly polarised. I have never seen a market or set of statistics that did not follow Pareto's Law.'

'Remind me what that is?'

'The eighty, twenty rule. For example, eighty per cent of profits come from twenty per cent of a range of products. It is almost a law of nature because it applies to all sorts of things. What is strange in the art world is that the ratio is ninety seven to three. That is ninety seven percent of profits or sales come from three per cent of the items sold. Stephen was right when he said the market was like a stretched pyramid with a wide base.'

'Interesting.'

'Also, the market is almost a perfect duopoly, except it is a triopoly. All the auction houses copy each other in everything that they do. They all operate in the same markets, in the same countries, and their operations are a mirror of each other. It is impossible to distinguish between any of them. Of course, they try to say that one is better than the other for whatever reason, but the reality is that they are all the same.'

'It is impossible to get accurate financial information for each house. The auction businesses are all counted as part of other private companies, so their figures are combined with other businesses. For example, Balfour's sales, revenues, costs, and profits are included with the UK company that distributes and sells all the Gocce D'Amore chocolates. It is the same in every country in which they trade. It is clearly a deliberate strategy to avoid having their data in the public domain, and more importantly available to each other.'

They arrived at Paddington and located the platform for the train to Worcester. Soon they were seated in the second class carriage and the train departed, unusually Swiss like, on time.

'Camau, where does the art come from, and who buys it?'

'The majority of the lots that are sold come from a few countries. The USA, the UK, France, Germany, Switzerland, and Hong Kong. There is a second tier of countries that includes Italy, Spain, Belgium, Netherlands, Austria, and Canada. Then occasionally there are works that come from other places such as South America, South Africa, and Australia. Contemporary works of art are currently being generated everywhere, especially Africa, India, and Asia. These new markets are red hot.'

'The buyers tend to come from all over the world. They are global, sophisticated citizens at ease in Europe, America, India, Africa, or Asia. They have nearly all made their money recently through commerce, and either because they earn so much or because they have sold their businesses, they are cash rich.'

'I understand the market is extremely international then?'

'Yes, very international. Money flows all around the world from one jurisdiction to another.'

Erm, thought Anita.

'And how were your visits to the dealers and auction houses?'

'All the dealers were absolutely charming and could not have been nicer to me. They were extremely interested in what we could do for them. They complained about all the regulations that apply to them for money laundering and the identification of clients, which I understand can be a burden for small businesses. They were all positive about the market place and I could see that they genuinely cared about the art and the clients. I have to say I was taken aback as the impression I had was that this market place and the players were all dodgy. However, I am not so easily taken in. I have seen so much in my career, and it is wise to be cynical in a healthy way.'

'I see.'

'The auction houses were the same. I managed to get appointments with all three houses to see some managers. I did not meet any of the owners as I get the impression that they do not really work in the business, they just own them. I met two or three managers in each auction house and again they were all charming, intelligent, passionate, and articulate. They know their business inside out and I was impressed. I did ask about their numbers, but just as you said, there is no transparency. They were firm however that market share was not a relevant measure because the focus was on making money.

But as I said, I have known many criminals in my long career and the more charming they are the more devious they are. I am not going to be taken in by these people. Everyone suspects that the art market is riddled with crime as Stephen pointed out the other day. If they think that charming me will stop me, they have something coming to them. I will find out what is going on and bring the criminals to justice.'

'Okay,' acknowledged Camau, not really agreeing with her as he could not see from the data what or where the issues were.

Stephen was waiting for Anita and Camau at Charlbury station as the train arrived on time. They got into his old BMW five series which had obviously seen better days, and he drove them the ten miles to his home. The house that he shared with Lady Penelope was absolutely stunning. It was a quintessentially English country house built in seventeen ten during the reign of Queen Anne. Constructed of soft brick with a staircase leading to the central door and rows of sash windows set flush in the brickwork, it was picture perfect.

The garden surrounding all sides of the house was stocked with a whole range of plants that still had a scattering of snow from earlier in the week. The inside of the house was impeccably decorated in that relaxed English style that looks as though it has always been there. Everything was harmonious and complimentary. There was nothing that should not have been there.

As the car drew up on the side driveway the front door opened, and Lady Penelope stood waiting for her guests to enter. She was five feet three inches tall, with blond shoulder length hair that was tied in pigtails, like a school girl. She was wearing a shocking pink knee length dress, bright purple tights, a scruffy blue faded anorak, and a pair of wellington boots.

'Hello. I have just been feeding my chickens and sheep. Anita, how lovely to see you. Stephen has told me so much about you. And you must be Camau. Well, you are a good looking young man.'

Camau blushed.

Lady Penelope invited them in and then removed her jacket and wellington boots, throwing them into an understairs cupboard and putting on a pair of sheepskin slippers.

'These used to be Freddy, my favourite sheep who died a couple of years ago. Let me show you to your rooms. Anna, my daily has made them up for you.'

The bedrooms were equally splendid, each with four poster beds with drapery in a fine floral print that matched the floor length curtains on either side of both windows. The rooms were larger than some apartments in London and had sofas, chairs, desks and tables and there was still plenty of room. Both rooms had en-suite bathrooms with fittings that looked as though they were from the nineteen thirties.

'I will let you unpack then come down for cocktails. No need to dress up, we are totally relaxed here.'

Anita and Camau unpacked, freshened up and then went downstairs to the drawing room. It was an extremely comfortable and relaxing room with three large well-worn sofas, with lots of mismatched cushions and throws, positioned around a roaring fire. The large stone mantelpiece had lots of candles on top of it alongside the family Christmas cards. It was a wonder they did not catch fire. All the other Christmas cards that had been taken down that day were stacked in a pile next to the fire, ready to be burnt when needed. There were piles of magazines and catalogues everywhere. On several occasional tables were collections of silver and gold boxes, which are highly sought after and unbelievably valuable. The walls were covered in all sorts of paintings in different sizes. They looked like the walls of the summer exhibition at the Royal Academy of Art in London.

'Do come in and sit down.'

'Gin and tonics all round? Stephen, be a dear and prepare the drinks will you.'

'Yes, Pen.'

Stephen brought the drinks in from the kitchen on a large silver tray. On it was a bottle of gin, several bottles of tonic, a plate with slices of lime, an ice bucket filled to the brim and four huge cut glass goblets, the size of fish bowls, each filled to the brim with fizzing, refreshing gin and tonic.

'I hope you like lime slices in your drinks. I cannot abide lemon in a gin and tonic, so down market.'

'Fine.'

'Cheers, bottoms up and welcome to Burford House.'

'This is a beautiful house, Lady Penelope.'

'Darling, call me Penny and thank you. Yes, it is a lovely house. I inherited it from my last husband. I have had four husbands, two divorced and two died, but now I have Stephen and I am not going to marry him as my track record is pretty hopeless. I hope you like fish. We are having coquille St Jacques followed by fish pie.'

'Sounds lovely Penny.'

'Do you enjoy cooking?'

'God no. I have never cooked in my life, ironed any clothes, or cleaned a house. I had nanny who was with me until she died when I was thirty-three, then I have always had staff, who were paid for by my husbands. The problem today is that staff are so dammed expensive. Thank God for Marks and Spencers and prepared food. I just read the instructions, pop the food in the oven or microwave and there you have it. Everything else is done by my Latvian daily Anna, who really is a bi-weekly as she only comes in on Mondays and Thursdays.'

Stephen stood and moved towards the drinks tray.

'Shall we have another drink?' Everyone agreed.

Penny turned to Camau.

'Where do you come from?'

'I was born in Nairobi.'

'Oh, I love Africa. When my parents left India after independence they settled in Nairobi for a while, in Muthaiga.'

'That is a lovely area. Full of colonial houses that look just like Surrey,' commented Camau. 'My parents live next door to the Muthaiga club.'

'Oh, how wonderful.'

'How come you are in the UK?'

'I was at Cambridge and graduated in the summer and I have just been travelling for a few months. My uncle is the Home Secretary and I asked him for an internship, and he suggested working in the Art Squad. I am excited about getting to grips with all the art crimes.'

'That will not be easy,' added Stephen. 'There are so many crimes and not enough time. All I do is concentrate on thefts from country houses, as I like visiting them. The rest of the crimes I just ignore.'

Anita was horrified. There were serious crimes that were going undetected, and it grated with her that these were not being pursued. Things were going to change.

They finished their second drink then moved to the farmhouse kitchen, all sitting around the large table that was laid out casually. The food was put in the oven and Penny asked Stephen to open some wine.

'We will have red. I do not believe in that rubbish of white wine with fish. One should drink what one likes.'

'May I ask why you are joining the Art Squad? Stephen told me you were lined up for a serious job in the Metropolitan Police but turned it down. Why would you do that?'

'I thought about it long and hard, but I have come to the conclusion that there are more important things in life. I am getting married soon and I want a life that is a little less stress-free.'

'So, who is the lucky guy?' asked Stephen.

'Actually, I am getting married to my girlfriend, Juliet Brioche, the actress.'

'Oh, that one that was in the television thriller recently. So, you are a lesbian then? I was a lesbian for an afternoon once at school with Paula Harrison-Smythe. She is now a judge at the Supreme Court.'

After they had enjoyed the starter and main course, Penny handed everyone a banana.

'Good for vitamins and minerals.'

'Brandies, everyone?' asked Penny as she stood up to get the bottle out of a cupboard.

'Not for me.'

'Nor me. Do you have any camomile?'

'Yes, of course,' said Penny as she located a tin with dried camomile flower heads.

'These were fertilised by Freddy,' as she added some to a teapot and added some boiling hot water from her Quooker tap that provided instant hot water. She placed two mugs on the table as the tea brewed.

'Thank you,' Anita and Camau politely replied realising they were about to drink sheep fertilised herbal tea.

'We have got a busy day planned for you tomorrow. Stephen will make breakfast in the morning, then we will walk down to see my good friends, Jake, and Laura, who run a wonderful smokery. You will be able to see how they smoke local trout and salmon as well as smoking my wonderful chickens. After that we will go to the local vineyard and brewery. They make the most wonderful beer, wine and champagne, well English sparkling wine. In the evening I have booked a table for us to have dinner at a pig restaurant.'

'Sounds lovely. Stephen, when will we be able to continue our conversation about the art world?'

Penny answered.

'Oh, we can talk about that as we are walking.'

This was not what Anita had planned. She wanted to hear about the art market from Stephen, not from Penny who was dominating everything. She decided that she had to hatch a plan. Camau would be tasked with entertaining Penny whilst she would get Stephen on his own and pick his brains.

'What is a pig restaurant?'

'Literally a pig restaurant. All the meals are pork based, starters, mains, and puddings. They use all parts of the pig.'

'Fascinating.'

Saturday, 8th January.

Everyone slept like a log as it was so quiet in the country. In London, the noise never stops with general traffic, boy racers revving up their ridiculous sports cars, the never ending sound of aircraft taking off and landing, and worst of all emergency vehicles using their sirens. Silence is golden, although it was shattered by the sound of several cockerels crowing at dawn and the incessant chiming of the local church clock in the distance, every fifteen minutes that started at six am.

Stephen cooked a full English breakfast. The sort of breakfast that you know you should not eat because it is unhealthy but is actually one of the best meals you can have. Rich home produced eggs, locally sourced bacon, sausages and black pudding, tomatoes and mushrooms from the local farmer's market and sourdough toast from a newly opened bakery in the town centre. Accompanied by freshly squeezed orange juice and recently ground coffee it was a breakfast that both Anita and Camau could easily get used to.

As they finished breakfast Anita asked Penny if she and Camau could go for a walk in the garden to take a couple of photographs as it was a lovely crisp, but cold sunny morning.

'Of course, we shall be ready to leave for our walk to the smokery at ten.'

'Great.'

Anita and Camau grabbed their coats and went outside into the garden.

'Camau, you have to get Penny on her own and keep her busy as I want some quality time with Stephen. This was after all the prime reason we came here. I need to understand more about how the auction houses work.'

'Sure, of course. I will link arms with her and flatter her whilst we walk ahead, and you can walk slowly behind us with Stephen.'

'Good plan.'

Soon they were both joined by Penny and Stephen and the plan was put into action as Camau took Penny by the arm and walked on. Anita and Stephen chatted and naturally fell behind the other two.

'Stephen, as we discussed the other day, can you explain to me how the auction houses work? I visited all three of them last week and popped into a few of the larger galleries and dealers. The auction houses have such an air of mystique about them it is not easy to see how they operate.'

'Well, where shall I begin? Firstly, all auction houses operate in the same way, so if you understand one you understand them all. It would also be useful to understand who owns each one. Mount's is owned by Kerem Akbarov. He is from an Azerbaijani family who made their money in the early twentieth century when Azerbaijan was the world's leading oil producer. Kerem's great grandfather sold his oil company in nineteen ten to a major US oil producer. The family has lived a luxurious lifestyle throughout the twentieth century, having homes all over the world as well as being based in Baku, the capital of Azerbaijan.'

'In nineteen seventy five, Mount's was in serious difficulty. The family that owned the business had not invested in their old building in Knightsbridge and the local authority condemned it. The cost to relocate to a new building was out of their reach so they had no choice but to sell the business to cover existing debts.'

'Kerem's father decided to buy Mount's in order to give him privileged access to the rich and famous. Owning Mount's became his calling card and gave him access to the highest levels of society. He was no longer considered just the grandson of an oil baron, but the owner of the most venerable and oldest auction house. It was, and is, like being royalty. The Art world is truly glamorous and one in which the world's richest people prefer to socialise and spend their time. Other comparable worlds of fashion, television, cinema, theatre, and music, pale into insignificance, with their vacuous focus on celebrity and momentary fame. Art is the real deal and outlives everything and everybody else.'

'He bought the freehold of a department store in Knightsbridge that had recently closed down and relocated the auction house there, where it has been ever since. A department store was the ideal premises for an auction house. It had lots of wide open spaces on the ground floor in which galleries could be created, lift and escalator access between the floors to several private entertaining suites, offices and meeting rooms, excellent basement storage as well as outstanding goods inwards and outwards facilities. Plus being located in the West of London it had easy access to Heathrow Airport and all the relevant services for importing and exporting goods, such as transport and customs clearing handling services.'

'Kerem was born in nineteen seventy five and always wanted to be a doctor. Although his family was wealthy and Kerem knew he would inherit a large amount of money from his father, he studied and eventually became a doctor in his early twenties. He decided to specialise in cosmetic surgery, eventually opening his own practice in Harley Street in London, which was extremely successful. He further decided to focus on Botox treatments, which were becoming extremely popular.'

'Kerem's cousin, Tural, worked at the Institut de Medicine in Geneva, Switzerland, and during a casual conversation when they were both in New York for a medical conference, Tural mentioned that he was working on developing a more effective form of Botox, one that lasted longer. Kerem was excited at the prospect because it would give him a competitive advantage. He agreed to fund Tural's work privately on the condition that only he would be permitted to use the new improved Botox. It took Tural another six months to refine the formula and the results were spectacular. Instead of having to have injections every four to six months, the new formula would last for eighteen months. The new formula did not require a new license or approval as it was simply a variation of the standard Botox that was in use globally. Kerem began to use the new formula in his clinic. His patients were so happy with the results that they readily paid a premium for this youth elixir.'

'At the age of forty, Kerem inherited Mount's when his father died in twenty fifteen. He decided to take an active part in the business and takes a keen interest in what is going on. He kept his plastic surgery practice going but staffed with employees.'

'Kerem is extremely handsome, five feet ten inches tall, perfectly proportioned and invariably has a suntan with jet black medium length hair that is swept back off his face. He has a swarthy Middle Eastern look about him, is clean shaven and his eyes are captivating. He prides himself on wearing designer clothes, which suit him perfectly.'

'Shortly after inheriting Mount's, Kerem married an English girl, Rosemary, who was two years younger than him and was working in one of the departments in Mount's. Rosemary is tall, statuesque, with long blond hair and azure blue eyes. She is charismatic, charming, and entertaining. It is rumoured that although she was once sexually voracious, she is now not too keen on sex. Apparently, she has sex with Kerem, once a week on a Sunday morning, but only before breakfast, never after. It is well known that Kerem on the other hand loves sex, and often does it several times a day, including self-service. He is happy to do it with both men and women.'

'How do you know all this?'

'Penny knows everything, about everybody.'

'Mount's has a loyalty card for their most important clients. These cards are like gold dust and the criteria for who gets one is not public knowledge. Generally, they are for the wealthy who either have a lot of assets or spend a lot of money with Mount's. The card has a range of benefits including private and privileged access to Mount's events, such as behind the scenes tours of museums and artists' studios, exclusive offers from luxury companies, for example, yacht and private jet hire, plus a number of free meals per year in Mount's in-house Michelin one star restaurant. It is rumoured that one of the really special benefits is free Botox injections for selected clients and that this has been a critical competitive advantage that has enabled Mount's to win business. Vanity and money go hand in hand.'

'Balfour's is owned by two Italian sisters, Michela, and Adrianna Fraganese, who own the largest fashion and confectionery empire in Italy. You probably will not have heard of them as they keep out of the media and their holding company is not well known. However, they own most of the major Italian fashion brands. Plus of course, as I mentioned, they own Gocce D'Amore, Love Drops, the world famous almond chocolates.'

'They inherited the auction business from their mother who was given it by her rich husband in order to keep her occupied, so she would stay out of the fashion and confectionery businesses. The sisters are passive in the business and employ a team of managers to run it for them. They visit the offices when they are in London, but they spend most of their time on the fashion circuit.'

'Seton's is owned by a group of Turkish billionaires who bought it in nineteen ninety seven, after offering the family that previously owned it so much money, they would have to have been mad to refuse it. The new owners wanted to expand the Seton brand into all sorts of new fields, but it has not worked out. What they failed to understand was that old established brands rarely translate into new markets. One would be better off creating a new brand.'

'All three auction houses operate in exactly the same way and in the same markets competing for business. It really is a zero sum game. What one does, the others follow almost immediately. It is impossible to create any differentiation between them, despite them trying.'

'The houses all have offices in all the major cities around the globe and in smaller locations they will have representatives, whose sole purpose is to find things to sell. The main challenge for the auction houses is to secure art to sell. Selling rare art and antiques is relatively easy as there are lots of people who want to buy.'

'So how do they win business?'

'Well, they have people in offices all around the globe, plus they have teams of art experts who travel everywhere to value art and convince the owners to sell it. On top of that they all have teams of client relationship and business developers who befriend clients and their families in the hope of winning business. The closer one can get to a client, the more chance there is of winning the business.'

'The art world consists of a relatively small number of people globally. There appears to be a lot more of them, simply because the same people pop up around the world time and time again at the main Art Fairs, and during the auction seasons. In London and Europe, there are three auction seasons, February, June, and October. In the states the season is January, May, and November. In Hong Kong it is March, July, and December. This ensures that people can fly around to all the events comfortably on an annual cycle, with time off, of course, for the main holidays. The auction houses also employ a sun and snow strategy, ensuring that their key people happen to be on holiday at the same time and in the same locations as their clients. Even better if you can be invited onto a client's yacht, where the client is a sitting duck for a few days.'

'If you are wealthy and own art and antiques, you are never more than a few feet away from a member of staff from one of the auction houses.'

'Auction house staff will do almost anything for their clients, buy them gifts, attend their parties and dinners, make contributions to their charities, or give their children internships.'

'When there is a beauty parade of the auction houses, during which the sales and marketing people present their proposals to the owners of estates for holding a successful auction, they will throw everything and the kitchen sink into the mix to win the contract. Marketing promises, which often make no sense at all, are banded around to appeal to the vanity of the owners.'

'It is rumoured that at the proposal presentations for the Zena Sparks auction, Mount's won it by offering to invite the granddaughter's cat to the evening reception. Apparently during the meeting with Jane and her advisors, the cat ran into the room followed by the ten year old granddaughter, Amy, chasing after her. It was Ursula Baumann, I believe, who suggested on the spur of the moment that it would be a great idea if the granddaughter and her cat attended the reception to be held before the auction. The little girl screamed and screamed in excitement until her mother gave in and awarded the contract to Mount's.'

'The cat did attend the reception and wandered around the galleries along with the guests. It was totally bizarre but not the craziest thing of which I have heard. For one collection, the owners wanted to have some sheep at the reception to wander around their collection of Lalanne sheep inspired furniture. The expert in charge of the event asked her intern to get a mixture of sheep for the event, expecting different breeds. What she got was a mixture of ewes and rams who naturally had sex in front of the guests all evening and were impossible to catch. The intern lost her job.'

'The auction houses entertain their clients or potential clients on a regular basis. Mount's, like all the auction houses, has a special department that just manages invitations and guests lists. It is run by Lady Bute, who is fearsome and makes the Dame Maggie Smith character in Downton Abbey, look like a pussy cat.'

'Lady Bute is a stickler for protocol and although most countries have abolished titles and varying forms of address, they are alive and kicking in the UK. She has a department of gals, who are tested upon arrival to see if they will last the day. When a new joiner, Pashmina, arrived one morning in the department she was seated on a broken desk in the corner of the office with a wobbly chair. Lady Bute asked her to write a note to invite the Duke of Padchester, the richest man in England, to luncheon.'

'When she read the note that Pashmina had written, Lady Bute was shaking with anger.

The note read:

Dear Bumper,

I would like to invite you to luncheon at Mount's next Tuesday at 12.30 for 13.00.

Lots of love

Pash xx

Lady Bute asked her why she had written the note as she did. The reply floored her.

Pashmina replied that David, or Bumper as he is known, was her cousin, and they had grown up together on their respective families' estates that are next door to each other in Yorkshire. Lady Bute continued to ask Pashmina how she would address the divorced wife of a Marquess. The reply was, her name, for example Belinda, Marchioness of wherever. And a Privy Counsellor? Pashmina replied, The Rt. Hon. name of the person.'

'Apparently, Lady Bute told one of her team, Fenelia, to pick up her things, move to the broken desk and let Pashmina have her desk which was next to Lady Bute's. Pashmina had a successful career at Mount's, finding a husband after two years and now manages their estate in the country, whilst her husband works in the City as she is bringing up their five children.'

'If you are smart you can have breakfast, lunch, and dinner by attending all these events. The minor royals, Prince and Princess Holstein have this down to a fine art. They have hardly two beans to rub together. They have sold all their pictures and replaced them with copies in their grace and favour apartment. They will go to the opening of an envelope and as the guests of honour are out somewhere almost every day.'

'One of the people you must meet is Deirdre, Penelope's sister. She works at Mount's and has been there forever. Deidre does deaths. She is a department of one, apart from the poor interns assigned to her. She reviews all the major international newspapers every day for death notices. She fervently believes that only interesting and rich people are listed in the right newspapers. She circles any that she considers important with a red pen and has the intern cut them out and stick them with glue onto a card which is then filed. She refuses to use a computer and threw the technology guys out of her office when they tried to install one. Only a few select senior people are allowed into her office.'

'So, is that where Penny gets all her gossip?'

'I could not possibly say.'

All four had been walking for about fifty minutes and were now arriving at the Smokery. It was a ramshackle collection of wooden buildings, many in a dilapidated state on the banks of the River Windrush.

'You two, hurry up. What are you talking about?'

'Darling, I was just explaining to Anita how the auction houses work.'

'Never mind that. Camau and I were just discussing his upbringing in Nairobi. I have had my fill of the Caribbean. I want to go on a safari next.'

'Yes dear.'

'Now let me introduce you to Jake and Laura. They produce the best smoked produce in the world.'

Everyone greeted each other and followed Jake into the so called shop. It was in fact just another hut where the items they sold, smoked trout, salmon and chicken were stored already vacuum packed in large chest fridges. There was absolutely no merchandising or attempt at marketing.

Laura handed out cups to everyone.

'I have made some hot chocolate for us as it is such a chilly day.'

'Oh, wonderful, thank you.'

'After this we can go down to the trout ponds and see how we nurture the fish from hatchlings to full grown.'

They drank their hot chocolate, laced with a dash of brandy, and topped with mini marshmallows and powdered cinnamon. Then all six of them walked the short distance down to the various ponds which were laid out on the banks of the river, each separated by a removable wooden barrier but fed by fresh water directed by various sluice gates from the river.

Jake pointed to the ponds.

'We grow the fish in batches and when we remove the mature batch for smoking, we open each barrier in turn and allow each batch to move into the adjacent pond. The whole cycle from egg to maturity takes just over three years,'

'And where are the salmon?' asked Anita.

'Ah, we fish for these on certain rivers in this area which we do not disclose. If the location of the salmon became well known, poaching would become more of a problem than it already is.'

'There is crime everywhere.'

Laura agreed with Anita.

'Poaching is one of the oldest crimes and shows no signs of falling by the wayside.'

'Jake, shall we go into the smoke house?'

'Yes of course Penny. Follow me.'

They returned to a building next to the shop and entered a dark world with the only light coming from a hole in the ceiling. There were racks and racks of filleted trout and salmon hanging across wooden poles that were themselves hanging over wood chips that were producing a glorious woody smoke.

'Not too long in here,' Laura insisted.

'We put these in here to smoke yesterday afternoon and they will be ready tomorrow.'

'It smells amazing in here.'

They all left the smoke house and returned to the shop.

'Now what would you like to buy?' Penny asked both Anita and Camau.

Anita wised up immediately. This was not just a friendly visit, but a shopping trip, with the vineyard and brewery to follow. She thought that Penny was really an old trout herself.

Anita and Camau both bought some smoked trout, salmon, and chicken breast after being informed by Penny that the chicken, Jemima, was one that she had killed and brought to the smokery earlier in the week. The bill for the lot was forty five pounds.

'I will drive you to the vineyard as it is a fair way.'

'That is so kind of you.'

'Come along, Stephen. No dawdling.'

'Yes, Pen.'

They all squeezed into an ancient land rover and held on for dear life as Luke drove like the clappers down the country lanes, until they reached the winery. It is one of the few vineyards in England, was located in acres of vines and included a large organic farm shop, a fairly tacky wedding reception facility, a large gift and wine shop as well as the production facilities that were open to the public.

They got out of the vehicle and were ushered to join a group for a tour of the winery. The leader of the tour group repeated everything in four languages, Chinese, Italian, Polish, and English. Impressive though the tour leader's language skills were, this was not what Anita had expected.

As the tour progressed through all the stages of how wine was made, Anita pulled Stephen back to the rear of the group in order to continue their discussion.

'Stephen. Who runs the auction houses?'

'Well, that is a leading question.'

'As we are in a vineyard and brewery it would be useful to think of the people that work in the auction house in three ways, beer, wine, and champagne. First, there are the beer people and departments. They are the ones that do all the hard graft. Auctions are physical and require people to move things around and display them properly. Each house sells thousands of lots a year and every lot needs to be handled several times. I have heard that a lot is likely to be handled up to twelve times on average.'

'At the top of the tree you have the champagne people and departments. These are the ones that run the business. They are primarily the expert departments plus the client and business development teams. They operate on their own with hardly any reference to anybody else.'

'In the middle you have the wine people and departments. These are the people and departments that help the champagne people to achieve what they want. They include for example, the shipping, graphic design, finance and client accounts departments.'

'What about management?'

'Management really just administer what goes on and generally makes sure that everything is legal and above board. They think they are in control, but they are deluded. It is the champagne people that decide everything. For example, the human resources department can hire who they want for the beer departments, and for some of the wine departments, but the champagne people recruit who they want and on what terms for their departments. Bright, young things are hired into the champagne departments and if they do not hack it, they will be offered up to the wine departments, which are therefore staffed by champagne rejects. A lot of recruits are trust fund kids, the sons, and daughters of wealthy clients, who are offered jobs in the hope of the auction house securing some future business.'

'Come along you two. Wine tasting now,' ordered Penny who was still linking arms with Camau.

'I have arranged a private room for us, instead of sitting with this group. I thought you might prefer that.'

'That is wonderful Penny, how thoughtful.'

They entered into a side room and sat at a table laid out with six bottles of wine, two red, two white, one rosé and one sparkling. Each person had six glasses in front of them and a score sheet to rate each one. In addition, there was another sheet of paper, an order form.

'These are all the wines that they produce here. They are all impressive,' beamed Penny.

'Stephen, do the honours will you?'

Stephen did as he was instructed and opened each bottle in turn and poured a small amount in each glass for everyone. It was not yet lunchtime and Anita and Camau were not used to this level of drinking, at any time of the day.

The group proceeded to taste the wines one by one, discussing each one in turn as they progressed through all six wines. Anita and Camau only took a sip of each one and soon reached the conclusion that all six wines were awful. They were bitter, sour, and unpleasant to drink.

Penny and Stephen were having a fine old time and drank each of the six glasses then topped them up from the remaining amounts in each bottle.

'Has Stephen explained everything to you that you wanted?'

'Yes, thank you. Along with the data analyses that Camau produced and my visits to the dealers and auction houses we now have a good understanding of the art market.'

'I want to focus our efforts on money laundering and how proceeds from the art market are funding serious international crime.'

'Well, that would be a complete waste of time,' Penny scoffed with a slight slur in her voice.

She continued.

'The only area in the art world worth looking at are single owner collections. Each year a small number of large, valuable collections come to the market and the house that secures these will maximise their profits. It is this marginal business that makes all the difference.'

Penny tapped her glass indicating to Stephen to replenish it. She took a couple of drinks from her glass and carried on, slurring even more.

'All the houses send me their catalogues for their single owner collections in the hope that, before I fall off my perch, I will give them my business. You can see all the catalogues in the drawing room, piles, and piles of them. What I have noticed in the last few years is more and more, valuable collections coming for sale. It does not make sense to me. I would not be surprised if some of these clients were being bumped off.'

Anita was stunned. She thought she had understood the market and that she had identified the areas to investigate where she would be able to uncover serious major international crimes. Penny in a slightly drunken state without any data analyses seemed to have identified a potential area of the market to investigate.

'After lunch when we get back to the house, I will give you some catalogues that you can take back to London with you. I suggest that you look into the circumstances surrounding those collections. There is something fishy going on, I just know it.'

'Okay, thank you. We will do that.'

'We will buy one bottle of each wine,' announced Anita to the server as Camau looked at her in total surprise.

They all had a good lunch in the winery, followed by a quick tour around the brewery and more tasting and shopping. After eating and sampling the wine and beers, everybody became relaxed and sleepy. Penny ordered a taxi to take them back to the house, which pleased everyone and avoided the need to walk back in the fading light on a cold January afternoon.

Once back at the house, everyone went to their room for a nap.

Working Out Where to Look

Monday, 10th January.

Anita and Camau arrived at the office bright and early. They had left the weekend with Stephen and Penny each carrying a full suitcase of catalogues. Penny had spent the remainder of the weekend expanding on her hunch that there was an increase in single owner collection sales. Over dinner in the pig restaurant, which was surprisingly good, she ran through all the collections that she could recall, and after breakfast the following morning located all the relevant catalogues to give to Anita and Camau to take with them.

When they emptied their suitcases, they counted them and realised that they had three hundred and fifteen catalogues, that either came from Mount's, Balfour's or Seton's and covered the last ten years.

'Where on earth shall we start Camau?'

'I propose we sort them into three groups for each auction house and then sort them by year so we will have thirty piles.'

'Then what?'

'I think we should sort them by value.'

'But how can we do that when each lot is listed with a photograph and low and high estimate. It will take us days to add up all these manually.'

'One of the things I found when I was doing the analysis is that auction sales are a matter of public record. Each result is listed on their respective websites.'

'Very good, Camau.'

'But the problem is that the data is not easy to download, and each auction house's format is slightly different, therefore it will be difficult to pull all this together.'

'Ah, wait a moment.'

'I have a friend, a fellow student, who is brilliant at scraping data off websites and putting it into a format or database, that can be interrogated easily.'

'Great. How can we get in touch with this guy?'

'He is now down in Cape Town as he went to see his family for Christmas and New Year. Let me message him and see what he can do.'

Camau Whatsapped his friend and in a matter of moments they were in conversation.

'Sorted.'

'He wants two grand to scrape all the sales data for the last ten years from all three websites and to create a database that can be filtered and analysed as we choose.'

'Done.'

'I think we should ask him to ensure we have the following data,' proposed Camau

- Auction House
- Saleroom location
- Sale Date
- Sale Name
- Sale Number
- Lot Number
- Lot Description
- Lot Category
- Low Estimate
- High Estimate
- Hammer Price
- Buyer's Premium
- Total Price
- Currency
- Converted into $
- Sold or unsold.

'Sounds good.'

The Database

Tuesday, 11th January.

As Camau was standing on the tube going into the office he received a message from his friend in Cape Town, saying that the database was ready and available in the cloud with an encrypted password. Camau thanked him and messaged Anita to send the money to him, which she did as she was sitting on the bus.

They were both excited as they arrived at the office, made coffees and Camau accessed the database. It contained over four million, three hundred and forty thousand records, one for each lot that had been offered for sale globally over the last ten years in all three auction houses. His friend had also added some state of the art artificial intelligence, that could for example, distinguish between a violin which would be classed as a musical instrument and a painting of a violin, which would be classed as a painting.

Camau quickly realised that because they had all the sales data for the last ten years, he would be able to work out the market share of the auction houses.

'Surely the auction houses have been able to do this themselves.'

'I expect so, but it is time consuming to arrange all the data in the same format. My friend used the technology that he created that takes flat text, that is printed text, along with other data and converts it all into data that can be fed into a database. He is setting up his own company and will no doubt make a fortune. The auction houses probably have to do all this part manual, part automated, enter everything into a database and convert into a common currency, probably American dollars.'

'What does the data show?'

'If you look at this graph, it shows the net sales globally for each of the last ten years by auction house.'

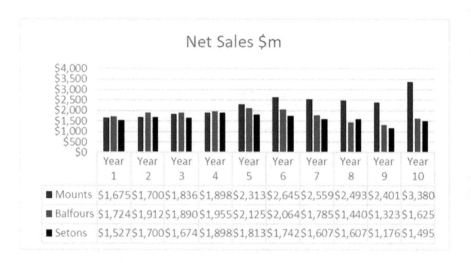

Net Sales $m

	Year 1	Year 2	Year 3	Year 4	Year 5	Year 6	Year 7	Year 8	Year 9	Year 10
■ Mounts	$1,675	$1,700	$1,836	$1,898	$2,313	$2,645	$2,559	$2,493	$2,401	$3,380
■ Balfours	$1,724	$1,912	$1,890	$1,955	$2,125	$2,064	$1,785	$1,440	$1,323	$1,625
■ Setons	$1,527	$1,700	$1,674	$1,898	$1,813	$1,742	$1,607	$1,607	$1,176	$1,495

'Wow. Mount's sales have been growing over the last five or six years, clearly at the expense of the other auction houses.'

'And if you look at market share, the situation is even more pronounced as the total art market tends to go up and down.'

Market Share

	Year 1	Year 2	Year 3	Year 4	Year 5	Year 6	Year 7	Year 8	Year 9	Year 10
■ Mounts	34%	32%	34%	33%	37%	41%	43%	45%	49%	52%
■ Balfours	35%	36%	35%	34%	34%	32%	30%	26%	27%	25%
■ Setons	31%	32%	31%	33%	29%	27%	27%	29%	24%	23%

'In a triopoly it does not make sense that one player will have over half the market when they all operate on an even playing field. Penny was right, there is something suspicious going on.'

'I have estimated the net profit at five percent, which cannot be far off given the heavy costs that the auction houses bear. When you look at these figures you can see that Mount's is now making significantly more profit than the other houses.'

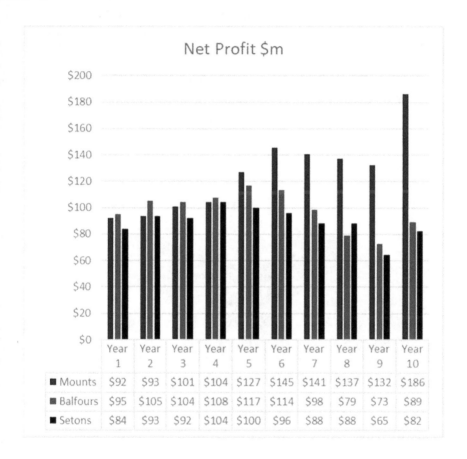

Net Profit $m

	Year 1	Year 2	Year 3	Year 4	Year 5	Year 6	Year 7	Year 8	Year 9	Year 10
■ Mounts	$92	$93	$101	$104	$127	$145	$141	$137	$132	$186
■ Balfours	$95	$105	$104	$108	$117	$114	$98	$79	$73	$89
■ Setons	$84	$93	$92	$104	$100	$96	$88	$88	$65	$82

'Camau, this is absolutely fascinating. Can you work out the cumulative sales difference between Mount's and the other auction houses over the last ten years?'

'Sure, easy.'

'The total market size for the last ten years for Mount's, Balfour's and Seton's has just been shy of fifty seven billion dollars. Mount's sales difference over the last ten years has been just under four billion dollars or just under seven per cent.'

'That doesn't seem so much.'

'But if you look at the last five years the total market was just over twenty nine billion dollars, but Mount's cumulative difference was three point seven billion dollars or well over twelve percent,' Camau explained. 'Plus, the percentage difference has been growing from eight per cent five years ago, ten per cent four years ago, twelve per cent three years ago, sixteen per cent two years ago and nineteen per cent last year.'

'Now that is starting to look interesting.'

'And even more interesting, Anita, is that the fact that the thirteen largest collections over the last five years amounted to over four point four billion dollars.'

'Therefore, if we investigate these collections, we might be able to see if there really is anything going on, or if it is just the luck of the draw.'

'Right, let us find these thirteen catalogues then shall we go for lunch?'

'Great.'

The Louvre

Thursday, 13th January.

It had been over twenty one years since the French auction market had opened, allowing the international auction houses to hold sales in Paris. The celebration of this important development had been delayed twice because of the pandemic, but it was now finally taking place.

The glitterati of the art world had descended upon Paris for the major event to be held at the Louvre, hosted by the new French President, Madame Duval. The auction house staff from all three houses were out in force and included all the heads of the main global art departments, heads of offices, client and business development staff, Chairmen and Chairwomen as well as unusually the owners of each house. All in all, there were about one hundred and twenty auction staff in attendance.

The team from Mount's included Kerem and his wife Rosemary, the global heads of the Impressionist and Modern, Contemporary, Old Master and Jewellery and Watch departments, the Chairs of the American, European, African, Indian, Israeli, Middle Eastern and Asian businesses, the office heads from the UK, Switzerland, Germany, and France along with several key client and business development staff. Among them were Ursula Baumann, Riccardo Hofstadt, Taric Abbas, Gregory Petrov and Sadi Leclere. All in all, there were over forty staff from Mount's.

Mount's staff stayed in a beautiful Parisian hotel, the Hotel Deauville, just off the Champs Elysée, and were transported the short distance to the museum by coach, for the evening reception that started at eight. The men were in black tie, and the women were all dressed in full length evening gowns, and all adorned with the most amazing jewels, some real, most not.

Kerem was staying in his apartment in the seventh arrondissement and arrived at the museum by chauffeur limousine after all his staff. His wife, Rosemary, was dressed in an off the shoulder white floor length Armani Privé ball gown. Rosemary had a birthmark on her left shoulder, which vaguely resembled a butterfly and about the same size. Her tattooist had incorporated it into a stunning butterfly tattoo that was emphasised by her dress. Her blond hair was swept up in an elegant beehive and she wore a dazzling diamond parure of European Royal heritage. She was the most stunning person in the room and every single man and woman stared at her discretely as she and her husband moved around chatting to the guests.

The reception was held under the large glass pyramid at the Louvre and with the clear night sky, the stars twinkled and shone on all the guests. There were over three thousand attendees at the reception as they drank the best champagne, ate intricate and stunning canapes and following a welcome speech by Madam President, they listened to the exquisite voice of Barbara Volte, the world's leading opera soprano as she sang a selection of arias. Following this there was a series of tableau, that recreated classical paintings and sculptures, which then transformed into outlandish, ethereal creatures that moved throughout the audience, enchanting everyone.

Ursula was wearing a floor length Versace dark green evening dress to complement her real emerald necklace and drop earrings. She grabbed Riccardo by his right elbow and steered him towards Kerem.

'Kerem, may I introduce Riccardo Hofstadt?'

'Good evening, Riccardo. I have heard so much about you. May I introduce you to my wife?'

'Enchanté,' Riccardo greeted her as he bowed his head and kissed her white satin gloved hand.

'What a beautiful evening Mr Akbarov,' Riccardo said politely as he shook Kerem's hand.

'Rosemary, come with me to the powder room,' Ursula requested in a firm manner not expecting any refusal.

'Of course.'

Ursula and Rosemary left, leaving Kerem and Riccardo standing together.

'I like to get to know the people that work for me, to understand how things are at the coal face as it were, although in this world we are about as far removed as we could be from a coal mine. When are you leaving Paris Riccardo?'

'I am going to the Business Development meeting in the morning then I have a few other things to do tomorrow before taking the train back to Zurich.'

'How fascinating. I have never been on a train before, it must be so exciting. Come to my office at five o'clock tomorrow to continue our conversation.'

'Certainly,' agreed Riccardo, as Rosemary and Ursula returned.

'Rosemary, come with me and let me introduce you to the American Ambassador,' Kerem insisted as he put his arm around her waist and guided her away.

'Lovely to meet you,' Rosemary said politely to Riccardo as she was whisked away.

Riccardo leant in towards Ursula.

'What the hell was all that about?'

'Nothing, that is just what he does.'

The Dinner

Thursday, 13th January.

At ten o'clock, Kerem and his wife left the reception in their limousine and went to La Tour D'Or, the most prestigious restaurant in Paris, founded in seventeen eighty two. It has the largest wine cellar in the world, which was preserved during the German occupation of Paris in the Second World War, when the then owner bricked it up. The cellar was never breached, and it now has a collection of wines from the eighteenth century onwards that is unrivalled anywhere.

The limousine entered through a street level garage door, and when it closed, the whole car was lifted in the car lift to the fifth floor. Their car door was opened, and the occupants were greeted by the owner and escorted to the private dining room. The room was decorated in high French Empire style, with classical designs and geometric patterns, and soft draped fabrics in azure blue, rich green, red ochre, and acid yellow. The room was adorned with laurel wreaths, urns, lions, hieroglyphics, palms, winged griffins, cobras, and sphinxes, plus an abundance of marble and tortoiseshell.

There were five other people in the room. Adrianna and Michela Fraganese, Altan Ozdemir, Hasad Soydan and Neval Ersoy. This was a meeting of all the owners of the three auction houses. Adrianna and Michela from Balfour's and Altan, Hasad and Neval from Seton's.

'How lovely to see you all,' Kerem announced as he entered the room, kissing all the guests twice on the cheek. Rosemary followed doing the same and then they all sat down.

As they ate an exquisite meal, accompanied by pre-French Revolution wines, they discussed the evening reception and how their respective families were doing.

Coffee was served, the staff dismissed, and the doors closed.

'I thought this would be a great opportunity for us to meet to discuss our business in general. Obviously, we do not want to do anything that is illegal, but I do think it is healthy to have an open conversation,' Kerem suggested to the diners.

'I think I speak on behalf of everybody here, when I say that this is a great idea,' Neval agreed.

Everybody round the table nodded in agreement.

'Adrianna and Michela, can I suggest you start and tell us your thoughts about your business?'

'Va bene.'

'Over the last couple of years, we have noticed some seismic shifts in our fashion and confectionery businesses. The world is changing, and we need to change with it. We are going full steam ahead to be organic, sustainable and to create a closed circular economy in the fashion business. By the end of this year all our clothes will be made of re-cycled fibres and will be coloured using natural plant dyes. We are also introducing a buyback programme in which the company will buy back your old clothes for twenty per cent of what the buyer paid and we will recycle the material.'

'Fascinating,' Rosemary said as she looked at the recycled dresses that they were wearing.

Michela continued.

'In the confectionery business, our one product, Gocce D'Amore has seen global sales starting to falter. We did some research and found that people now want more than just a beautiful almond encased in milk chocolate. We are therefore going to diversify by offering them in plain, white and milk chocolate, and we will be offering organic, vegan, semi-sweet, bitter-sweet, sugar free, stevia, and fair trade versions. We are going from one line to twenty-one but can still use our same production line in Apulia, without any capital investment.'

'We are going to stop using fertilisers on our almond trees, that our grandfather planted, and are going back to nature. We have installed an underground watering system, on our two hundred hectare orchard, using clay pipes that siphons water from our underground reservoir. Do you know it takes four and a half litres of water to grow one almond? We are aiming to reduce that by eighty per cent. We are also planting wild herbs and flowers in the orchard and have reached an agreement with our neighbour who will graze his goats in our orchard, and we get free manure in return.'

'We have added dozens of bee hives into the orchard and are changing our packaging to honeycomb shape, which is the most efficient use of materials to create a container. All our boxes will be recyclable, dyed in natural colours and we will differentiate each product by a letter after Gocce D'Amore, for example V for vegan, SF for sugar free.'

'That is amazing,' Kerem added as all the guests smiled in agreement.

'And what about Balfour's?'

'Balfour's fits perfectly with our strategic direction because it is the ultimate recycling business, and we love it. We let our management team run the business and offer any guidance when they ask us. One thing they have raised with us, is how are you winning so much business? You seem to have had a good run lately. How are you doing it, Kerem?' Adrianna asked.

'I just employ the best people, take care of them and make sure we offer fantastic client service.'

Michela was about to ask something further when Kerem turned to Altan.

'And how are things going at Seton's?'

'Well, I agree with Michela and Adrianna. We have really noticed that Mount's is winning all the big collections. The Zena Spark's collection was spectacular, it raised over one point two billion dollars.'

'As I said, people and service. How are you doing south of the river?' Kerem asked changing the subject.

'With hindsight that was a serious strategic mistake. We have a beautiful, modern, state of the art building that is efficient and easy to use, but clients will not go there. As the cost of property has soared in the right postcodes the business simply cannot afford to move back. Therefore, we are going to concentrate on the on-line business. We are having some great success with handbags and sneakers.'

'We are going to concentrate on selling art. We are not going to sell second hand handbags or sport shoes. Surely that is what e-bay is for?' Kerem suggested.

'You would be surprised who is engaging with us in these new fields. We really are reaching a new type of client who will become loyal to us and move into art over time. It is a long game but one that we are confident of succeeding in.'

Kerem wrapped up the evening.

'It is interesting that we are all owners of the three global auction houses, and each have a different game plan. I wish you all the best and thank you for coming this evening. This restaurant is spectacular. We must do this again,'

Everyone agreed and then stood to leave. They shook hands and kissed as they all left just before midnight.

Kerem turned to his wife as the car left the lift and continued onto the main street.

'They are all fools those people. Recycling, handbags, and sneakers. It is no wonder Mount's is winning business.'

'Yes, darling,' Rosemary agreed as she laid her head on his shoulder.

'I love you,' she whispered into his ear.

'And I love you.'

'Can I take the car tomorrow as I have an appointment at Balgavi when you are seeing Riccardo? They have some new jewels they want to show me.'

'Of course, darling.'

Spot

When Kerem inherited Mount's, over seven years ago, he discovered that the existing computer systems were, to put it bluntly, out of the Ark. He engaged a software company owned by Rosemary's brother, Charles, to completely overhaul and redesign the systems and to bring them up to the state of the art and beyond.

Charles had a small team based in the UK, in Swindon, but most of the software developers were contractors based in Prague, Czech. They created a brand new company wide system that had a number of sub-systems, that were all interconnected to each other, and to the central system called SPOT.

Departments and business functions no longer owned their systems. Instead access to the central and sub systems was granted on a needs basis. This approach annoyed many middle managers who felt that they owned their systems, even though they did not pay a penny for them. When the new systems were implemented, after just nine months of development, the software team managed to transfer over from the old system, the huge database of historical transactions and client information that dated from the early eighties. There was considerable resistance when the new system was introduced, but most staff fell in line. Those that did not, either left or were replaced. It is a pretty standard outcome for ten percent of staff to fall by the wayside when a major new system is implemented.

The new sub-systems:

- supported the auctions themselves where the details of each lot for sale were entered, the bids recorded, catalogues produced in print and on-line, and the successful bidder added.
- produced insightful reports about the business.
- recorded all the data and information about individual clients, their families and support networks, for example lawyers, advisors, or their

staff. The system relied on manual input from the business and client development teams. Of course, they complied with all relevant world-wide data protection legislation.

- held all the relevant information about employees.
- produced all the invoices, monthly and annual accounts including the calculation and payment of various taxes.
- recorded information about the prices realised for lots that were sold in all the auction houses. At the press of a button the system could produce a guide price for virtually any work of art. However, a human eye was always needed to assess the condition, provenance, subject matter, and size of any object. Two Blue Period Picassos can vary widely in price depending upon these factors.

The central system, SPOT, was the real jewel in the crown. This brand new system had been built using Artificial Intelligence and its sole purpose was to identify opportunities, hence SPOT. As it was connected to all the sub-systems it could work through and identify connections, links, and opportunities. In addition, SPOT was also connected to many external information sources such as wealth reports, real estate transactions, company formations and liquidations, that it could match with the client information it had on file.

For example, if a painting by Gustav Klimt was sold at any of the auction houses, SPOT would search itself and find other Klimts that were owned by Mount's clients. It would generate a report for the relevant business development person so that they could have a conversation with their client about the recent price, what their painting was worth now, and whether they might want to sell it in one of Mount's auctions. The early signs of this new system proved to be extremely promising. The new systems were transformational. Efficiency and productivity shot up by at least thirty per cent, as transactions that had previously taken hours to process, whizzed through the system in a matter of minutes. Charles subsequently became the Head of the IT department.

The Business Development Meeting

Friday, 14th January.

Mount's senior management had decided, in their wisdom, that it would be a good opportunity to have a Business Development meeting on the Friday morning after the reception, because so many key people were in Paris.

The attendees begged to differ.

The purpose of the meeting was to review a list of orphan clients, ones that were not assigned to any business development person in particular, and to agree action plans in the hope of winning some business. The list had been produced by SPOT, as it used all its intelligence to identify these potential high value clients who were not being looked after properly by the business development teams.

These were the sort of meetings that the attendees hated, sitting around in groups pretending to work collaboratively. The only reason they attended, begrudgingly, was the fear of missing out on something. The meeting was scheduled to start at nine thirty in the morning in a large conference room attached to the hotel where everyone was staying. The room was a brutalist monstrosity that had been built onto the back of the hotel in the nineteen seventies. The badly lit room had no style at all, and behind the old net curtains there were steel window frames that slid up and down, like the ones in airport hotels that look onto the runway.

The management had engaged a consultant to run the meeting. This was a classic tactic that they used frequently. If the meeting turned out to be a failure they could blame the consultant, and if it were successful, they could take the credit for having brought in a consultant. Either way the management would be credited with making the right decision.

The attendees started arriving just after nine thirty and immediately went straight to the refreshment area to get a cup of coffee, tea, herbal tea, water, or juice. They greeted and kissed each other and chatted about the previous evening.

Every time someone new arrived, they all kissed each other, and the conversations continued.

The consultant was getting frustrated, as the meeting was due to start at nine thirty and it was now nine fifty. He moved around the groups of people asking them to take their seats. Each person had been assigned to one of five tables, each with eight seats, totalling forty. He was ignored as the attendees continued with their conversations and started to take a second cup or glass of refreshment.

A loud klaxon sounded.

'Please take your seats,' the consultant requested in a loud voice.

'How rude. There is no need to shout,' Barbara from the New York office commented to the group of colleagues she was standing with.

Armed with their cups or glasses, the attendees made their way to their tables, moving around from one table to the other in order to locate their named place card.

'I am not sitting on this table,' announced Reza from the New York office as he promptly switched his card, moved to another table, and sat down with his friend, Idris, from the Cape Town office.

Finally, at ten past ten, everyone was seated as the consultant stood at the front of the room.

'Good morning, ladies and gentlemen.'

A hand shot up immediately.

'I am a Princess, not a Lady,' insisted Princess Margarethe from the Netherlands.

'And I am a Duke, not a gentleman,' proclaimed the Duke of Alburgh from Germany.

'Well, I am a Countess,' added Countess Sophia from Madrid.

'And I am the only Lady here,' added Lady Cecelia.

'Good morning, everyone,' The consultant interjected above everyone.

'I would like to start with an ice breaker. Could each person introduce themselves, stating your name, where you come from, what your role is, and add one interesting fact about you that no one else knows in this room?'

There was an audible sigh.

The consultant, Darren, was a lot smarter than the people in the room would believe. He had worked with many other companies in the art world and knew exactly how they behaved, although he thought that this group from Mount's was particularly difficult. He would have them all wrapped around his little finger in no time at all.

'So, let us start with table one.'

Suddenly the door opened.

'Apologies for being late. I had a breakfast meeting that overran, and the traffic around here is beyond,' Ursula announced as she swept into the room and found her allocated seat.

'Table one please.'

'I am Geoff Chung from Hong Kong, the Chairman of the Asian business. I have just been accepted to appear on Master Chef Asia.'

'I will have a number forty two,' requested Eric who was sitting on the same table.

'Ha, ha.'

'I am Silvia Thomas, the Chairman of Switzerland based in Geneva. I am having a torrid time with the menopause. It is so hot in here.'

'Brava,' shouted out a colleague and the whole room burst into spontaneous applause as Silvia wiped away a tear.

'I am Octavia Drakolopolopolos, the head of the Athens office. I have been asked by the Greek Ministry of Culture to arrange an exhibition of Greek Contemporary Art, that will tour the ten largest tourist islands during the summer months, so that is my summer holiday sorted.'

'Well done,' everyone shouted.

'Can I come with you?' several people requested.

'I am Eric Felps, the Head of the Old Master's department based in London. I am training to run the London marathon.'

'In how many days?' Yaris from Paris asked.

'I am Cristoff Russo from the Rome office. I have just proposed to my boyfriend, and he has accepted.'

The room burst into applause.

'My name is Jacinda Carlstein from the Impressionist and Modern department in the London office. My family produces lager.'

Ursula practically exploded as she turned to her colleague, Lady Cecelia, sitting next to her, the Head of the Impressionist and Modern Department.

'I have been trying to get to the Carlstein family for years. They are impossible to get close to. That young girl must be the daughter of Herr Franz Carlstein, in which case she is the sole heir to his billions.'

'Yes, I know,' replied Lady Cecelia. 'He went to school with my ex-husband, and I refused to sign the divorce papers until he introduced me.'

'You scheming bitch,' scowled Ursula.

'She works in my office now,' Cecelia smiled gleefully.

'I am Olaf Lindgren from the Business Development in the office in the Stockholm in the Sweden. I just found out yesterday that we are having triplets. My bitch is doing good.'

'Is that the right way to speak about your wife, Olaf?' questioned Darren.

'No, no. It my Swedish Elkhound that is having triplet, not my wife bitch.'

The whole room burst into laughter.

'I am Hakam Noor, I am Egyptian, an expert in Middle Eastern Contemporary art and am based in the Dubai office. I am descended from the Pharaohs.'

'Like everyone in Egypt,' shouted most of the room.

'Thankyou table one and now to table two.'

'I am Reza Amiri, Co-Chair of the Americas, based in New York, Jackson Hole and now Carmel, California. I just bought Betty White's house.'

'Who is she?' asked Darren.

'OMG, The Golden Girls.'

'I am Xandy Schlom, and I am the Head of Israel. I am building a house down on the coast at Jaffa, the oldest port in Israel.'

'Is the house orange?' Gresham shouted.

'I am Xin Cheng, the boss of the Beijing office. I do private tours of the inner sanctum of the Forbidden City, for a suitable fee, of course.'

'Typical communist,' announced Countess Sophia.

'I am Idris Khoza, the Chairman of Africa, based in Cape Town. I just got divorced and am looking for a new woman or two.'

'That was a sexist remark. Hey, I am Lala Greggs from Los Angeles, Lalaland, specialising in female Contemporary artists. I am the founder of Women in Power, dedicated to overthrowing the Patriarchy.'

'God help us,' several people lamented.

'I am Countess Sophia Gonzalez, head of business development in Espagne, based in Madrid. This evening I am taking my PJ down to Marbella for the weekend, if anybody would like to join me?'

'What is PJ?' asked Darren.

'Private Jet,' everyone shouted out in unison.

'I am Fabiana Ferrari, and I am ze 'ead of the business in Roma. I have just done a deal with Italian Pogue and will appear on their front cover next month, posing at the new Caravaggio exhibition.'

'Brava, brava,' exclaimed all the other members of her table.

'Good morning, everyone. I am Gresham Horde, Chairman of the UK. My new alter ego is Laura Lard, and I shall be performing at the Savoury Club in London tomorrow evening, if anyone would like tickets.'

'Bravo, bravo or brava, brava,' shouted all the other members of his table.

'Thankyou table two. Now table three please?' Darren gestured to move the proceedings along.

'Hi, I am Florence Green. I just started last week in the New York office as an intern. I am working on this project with Darren, who is my uncle.'

'I am Javinda Singh from the Mumbai office. It is so nice to be here in Paris where I can eat a steak.'

'Ooh, please I am a vegetarian,' grumbled Florence.

'Ciao tutti. Sono Riccardo Hofstadt from the Zurich office where I work with the amazing Ursula. Just like sailors have a woman in every port, I have a man in every five star hotel.'

There was a round of applause as everyone knew about Riccardo's reputation.

'Hi y'all, I am Kalvin March from the Contemporary team in the Big Apple. I have just booked a ticket on the first tourist space flight in three years' time.'

'Is that one way?' Lady Cecelia asked sarcastically.

'Hello, I am Sullivan Clarke from the London jewellery department. I am going to climb Mount Everest next month.'

'Wow, that is impressive,' enthused Darren.

'I am Her Royal Highness Princess Margarethe Van Herdt, the head of the Amsterdam office, and on Sunday I am being ordained as a lay member of the Protestant Church of the Netherlands.'

There was a round of applause as several people in the room crossed themselves.

'I am Yaris Fontaine, from the Impressionist department in Paris. I am an avid collector of sneakers.'

'You should go and work for Seton's,' Riccardo suggested.

'I am Gregory Petrov from the Hungarian office in Budapest. I am an astrologer; a Virgo, and I did my chart this morning. The Moon is rising, Saturn is falling, and Mercury is retrograde. There is going to be a big change today.'

'Great, now table four?' Darren urged the next table to speak as time was running short.

'I am Taric Abbas from Paris business development. I just received confirmation that I am taking part in the Paris to Dakar rally next year.'

'It would be a lot quicker to fly,' Kalvin from New York stated.

'I am Naresh Chaudry from the Contemporary department in London. I play the Viola and am in a string quartet with my brothers and sister.'

'Can you give us a tune on your fiddle?' Fabiana from Italy requested.

'I am Quarren Der Zut, the head of the Brussels office. I am a ceramicist and I have my own exhibition coming up soon.'

'Exhibition of what?' asked Idris.

'What do you think?' Quarren replied.

'Good day everyone, I am Nancee Wilson all the way from the Sydney office, down under. I have just discovered an amazing collection of Aboriginal paintings that will be coming up for auction in the summer.'

There was a round of applause and cheers.

'I am Lady Cecelia Abbots, the head of the Impressionist and Modern department in London. I am writing a book about the English Impressionist artists; Impressionism is not always about France and the French.'

There was a loud cheer from the Brits in the room.

'Darlings, I am Sadi Leclere. I am Scottish, but live in Geneva, and I am pleased to announce that Mount's will be launching a new diamond business in London this year.'

'Any special offers going?' several people shouted.

'Guten Tag, I am Ursula Baumann from the Zurich office. I think I have been at Mount's longer than any of you here. I am the grossmutter or grandmother of you all.'

'Gross nutter, more like it,' Lala Greggs murmured under her breath.

'I am Meera Samil, the Chairwoman of India based in the Mumbai office. I have just set up a charity to save the Mountain Snow Leopard.'

There was a loud cheer from around the room.

'Thank you, and now finally to table five.'

'I am Jake Turner from New York where I am the Head of the Contemporary Department. I am competing in the America's Cup in two years' time in Barcelona.'

'Why is the America's Cup in Spain?' Barbara asked Jake.

'I am Aldo Di Nobili, the head of the office in Milan. I have just been selected for the Italian Winter Olympics downhill slalom team.'

Again, there was another round of applause, cheers, and whistles.

'I am Kapryce Foster from the Contemporary department in Hong Kong. I am about to publish a book of my black and white photographs, in colour.'

'What?' everyone thought.

'I am Barbara Middleton, the Co-Chair of America. I have just taken up bee keeping as the world is in real danger if bees disappear.'

Lots of people in the room gave her the thumbs up, not realising what thumbs up actually meant in the Roman times.

'I am Elene Dacron, the Chairwoman of France. I have just received an award from the North American Lilium Society for my new hybrid lily, Clintonia Eleaneum, a beautiful miniature blue lily.'

'Clitoris what?' asked Silvia from Geneva.

'I am August Meyer, the Duke of Alburgh, the Chairman of Germany. I am a Chess Grand Master and will be challenging the world champion robot in Leipzig next month.'

'Is it called SPOT?' asked Gresham.

'I am Agata Jergman from the business development department in Vienna. I bake a beautiful Sachertorte and have brought some for our coffee break.'

'Oh, fantastisch,' exclaimed August.

'I am Paulo Gracca, the office head in Lisbon. I will be officiating at the mass at Lisbon Cathedral next month when the Pope visits Portugal.'

'In nomine patris, et filii, et spiritus sancti, amen,' the Catholics in the room said with reverence.

Almost immediately after Paolo had introduced himself, most people picked up their mobile phones. Some listened to their messages, as others were typing furiously on their keyboards. Two people stood up and announced that they had to take these calls, which were urgent.

Cecelia Abbots, Lady Abbots went into the lobby and made a call.

'Oh hello, Cecelia here. I got your message. I can bring Atos in for his wash and shampoo at ten thirty instead of ten o'clock next Monday, that is fine.'

'Thank you, Cecelia. See you next week.'

'My little angel Atos, he is a pedigree Maltese and the love of my life, after my husband ran off with his secretary,' she informed Eric who had also left the room with her. 'My sister looks after him when I am travelling.'

'Good morning, this is Eric Felps. Tuesday at three in the afternoon is perfect to see the hygienist and then the dentist.'

'Thank you, Mr Felps, see you then, bye,' as the dental receptionist ended the call.

'I suppose we had better get back,' Eric proposed to Cecelia.

'Yes, I suppose so,' she agreed reluctantly.

The klaxon sounded.

'Can I have your attention?' Darren shouted firmly.

'Senior management has initiated a review of all those clients in the system that are not allocated to a business development person. We have done some analyses and have identified eight hundred clients that could potentially generate some good business for us. Florence will hand out envelopes for each one of you, which contain a list of twenty clients that we think, based on the new Artificial Intelligence algorithm, will be clients that you may know or should know. We would like you to review these clients and to code them according to the categories also included in your envelope. If you do not know the clients then you have the opportunity to trade them with your colleagues sitting on your table, but at the end of the day you must have twenty clients that you have coded and who will then be assigned to you.'

'Christ, this looks like hard work,' Sullivan complained under his breath to his colleagues on table three.

Darren continued.

'Plus, there are going to be some major changes to the company's Travel, Entertaining and Expenses Policy. From Monday morning, any travel bookings must include the name of a client, and any expense claims must also have client names attached, along with the specific action that was planned and carried out.'

The room exploded in a riot of protest. It was impossible to hear all the comments and complaints as everyone in the room was enraged.

'How dare management question what I am doing?'

'Who do they think they are?'

'They never have to do the tedious work of entertaining clients.'

'I am going to go to the opposition.'

'Well thank God I have my PJ.'

The Klaxon sounded again.

Darren continued.

'Now that I have your attention, I want to point out that this policy change has come straight from Kerem Akbarov, and he has insisted that it is implemented. If there is anyone in the room who does not intend to comply with these policy changes, you can leave now. Woody Smith from Human Resources is sitting outside and will hand you your termination papers for failing to comply with company policy which, as you know, is gross misconduct. The termination of your contract will be immediate with no severance pay. Is that clear to everyone?'

You could hear a pin drop.

Darren had finally got their attention and they were now putty in his hands. Of course, they were all going to comply. Not one single person wanted to give up their luxurious lifestyle, funded by the company.

Sadi Leclere covered her mouth and spoke softly to Ursula sitting next to her.

'Here we go again. This has all been tried before. All that happens is that people make up clients and put them in the system to justify what they do. I still have a client, called Mr Ogadodo from Kenya who lives in Geneva, from the last time that they did this. I still meet with him for dinner all over the world and use his name to claim expenses for my non-business dinner guests and nobody has yet spotted that he is made up.'

'Yes exactly, then there will be even more dormant clients in the system, and they will need another project and consultant to sort it out,' agreed Ursula wearily.

The envelopes were handed out to each table and each addressee opened theirs. Inside each was the list of codes that were to be used.

1	Dead	10	Tax problems
2	Dying	11	Government investigation
3	Ill but not dying	12	Impending birth of a child
4	Getting married	13	Impending marriage of a child
5	Divorced	14	Impending divorce of a child
6	Divorcing	15	Any other life event
7	Relationship in trouble	16	Inheriting
8	In debt	17	Selling business
9	Financial Issues	18	Anything else-list

'When we have all the codes we will enter appropriate comments into the system, for example, not receiving visits, could describe a client who is not well. We have until three this afternoon to do this work then you can leave. We have a buffet lunch which will be served at one. When you have completed your list, please hand the sealed envelope back to Florence,' Darren explained.

Everybody got on with the job, worked through lunch, and had all finished by three. All forty envelopes were handed in to Florence with the completed coding and all the attendees gradually drifted away.

Riccardo and Kerem

Friday, 14th January.

Riccardo took a taxi from the hotel to Kerem's office. The journey took far longer than it should have, because the traffic in Paris, as usual, was completely gridlocked. However, he arrived just before five o'clock. The office was located in the heart of the luxury district on Rue du Cirque. This was not Mount's office, but Kerem's own private family office located in the penthouse suite of an old Palais that had been converted into offices.

Riccardo went to the ground floor reception desk and announced himself. He was escorted by the receptionist, Miriam, to a secluded lift, the doors of which seemed to open as soon as they stood in front of them. Miriam used a key to activate the button for the penthouse suite and left the lift just before the doors closed. The lift moved silently and in a matter of seconds the door opened into an entrance area where another receptionist was sitting.

'Welcome Mr Hofstadt. My name is Adela, please follow me.'

Riccardo walked behind Adela down a long corridor until finally they arrived at a door. She used an electronic pass to open it and they entered a staggering apartment with floor to ceiling glass walls with views across the city of Paris. The apartment was ultra-modern and furnished with a mix of contemporary works of art, combined with stunning Old Master paintings and renaissance furniture.

'Please take a seat, Mr Akbarov will be with you shortly.'

Adela left leaving Riccardo sitting quietly to admire the works of art around him. He particularly admired a stunning Botticelli and a David Hockney landscape.

Kerem entered the room from a side door. 'Apologies Riccardo, I was on the phone with the President. Come into my office.'

Riccardo followed Kerem into the office which was similarly furnished but without the glass walls.

'Please take a seat,' Kerem gestured to Riccardo to sit on the sofa as Kerem sat beside him.

'How was the Business Development meeting?'

'It was feisty. People are up in arms about the new travel rules.'

'Yes, that is only to be expected. It is important that people are focused on the job at hand, which is to win business against the competition. There has been too much unfocused activity recently.'

Riccardo was surprised that Kerem knew so much about the details of the business.

'Anyway, lets focus on why I wanted to meet you privately.'

'I am sure that you know that my family come from Azerbaijan. I have decided to create a new museum in the capital city, Baku, focused on Azerbaijani art and design throughout the ages, right up to the modern day. I have the backing of the President, who I was just speaking to, and many other influential people.'

'However, you may or may not know that being gay in Azerbaijan is frowned upon, even though it is legal. I therefore have to be careful about who I involve in my new project. You are clearly an up and coming member of Mount's team, but I know from Woody Smith that you are gay.'

Riccardo was seething inside. How dare Smith compromise him. Riccardo decided in that moment that he was going to deal with Smith the next time he was in London.

'I would like to involve you in the museum project but being gay is an issue. There is however a solution, and we could come to an arrangement that would suit us both.'

Riccardo was unsure where this conversation was going.

'Whilst I am not gay myself, I do like people to help me achieve orgasm, and I would like to propose that every now and again you could help me. I can help you by bringing you onto the Museum project and I am prepared to waive the new travel rules for you.'

Riccardo's mind was working ten to the dozen.

Was he being threatened?

Was he being blackmailed?

What if he refused?

Is there an advantage in this for me?

'Okay, so you want me to jerk you off occasionally and I get a major role on this new project and travel freedom?'

'Yes.'

'And if I say no?'

'Well, there are always ways and mean to terminate someone's employment, but I am sure that we do not need to go there.'

Riccardo realised that if he wanted to keep his job, he would have to accommodate Kerem. Well at least Kerem was the boss and Riccardo was sure, that in due course, he could manipulate this situation to his advantage, so best to play ball.

'So do we have a deal?'

'Yes, we have a deal,'

'Good. I will be in touch.'

'Yes, boss.'

'You do know that I am not gay.'

'Of course. There are lots of men just like you who just want someone to jerk them off. It is good exercise, like a trip to the gym. Think nothing more of it.'

'I appreciate your candour, Riccardo. A real man's man.'

Riccardo smiled.

'I had better get going to the hotel to pick up my luggage and get to Gare du Lyon.'

'Ah, yes you are taking the train to Zurich. I must try it.'

'It is actually much more relaxing than flying these days.'

'I am sure it is. My driver will take you to the hotel and then onto the station.'

'Thank you.'

As they walked to the door, Riccardo thought to himself that perhaps it was a good thing looking after Kerem, if he could get certain privileges. Perhaps he would thank Woody Smith after all.

Kerem shook Riccardo's hand.

'That was a great meeting and I look forward to working with you on the Baku Project.'

'Likewise.'

Riccardo got into the lift with Adela, the doors closed, and it descended to the basement level.

'So, you are working on the Baku project?'

'Yes, it sounds extremely exciting.'

'It is. Kerem is spending over half a billion dollars creating the museum,'

The lift doors opened and Kerem's car glided silently in front of them. The chauffeur, Brad, got out of the car and opened the rear passenger door. Mrs Akbarov emerged after her trip to the jewellers and greeted Riccardo.

'Hello Riccardo. Good meeting?'

'Great,'

'Brad will take you to your hotel. See you again,' Rosemary said as she entered the lift with Adela and the doors closed.

Riccardo was impressed with the service around him, and the fact that Mrs Akbarov knew that the chauffeur was taking him onto his hotel. Perhaps the arrangement with Kerem was perfectly above board. He got into the rear of the black Rolls Royce with dark tinted windows, sank into the sumptuous black leather seat and smiled to himself as the car left the basement and emerged into the Parisian traffic.

'Hi, my name is Riccardo.'

'Yes, I know.'

'How come you have an American accent?'

'I am American and after college I joined the US Navy, then became a Navy SEAL.'

'That is impressive. I have never met a US Navy SEAL before. What brings you to Paris?'

'I work for Mount's as the bodyguard for the Akbarovs, overall company security advisor and chauffeur. I love it.'

'Ah, okay, well nice to meet you and thank you for taking me to my hotel and the station.'

'Not at all, my pleasure.'

They arrived at the hotel and Riccardo went in to get his luggage from the concierge and returned to the waiting car. Brad took the luggage placing it on the rear seat and put his arm around Riccardo as he helped him into the car. Riccardo thought that Brad was perhaps being a bit too familiar, but he loved the thought of a fit, muscular US Navy SEAL in a chauffeur's uniform, touching his body and protecting him with his powerful hands.

Brad was extremely good looking, five feet ten inches tall, with a chiselled clean shaven face. Like many military men he had a high and tight haircut, mostly shaved with a slightly longer section on the top of his head, which corresponded to the size of his palm, which was used as a guide when wet shaving the rest of his head.

The Rolls Royce arrived at the VIP entrance to the Gare Du Lyon and glided effortlessly to a halt. Brad got out of the car and opened the rear door for Riccardo who had his luggage in one hand. Brad grasped Riccardo's other hand and aided him to step out of the car. Once out of the car Brad shook Riccardo's hand and winked at him.

'I am certain our paths will cross again. Have a good journey and see you soon.'

'Sure, see you around and thank you, merci, grazie,' Riccardo said as he shook Brad's hand and stared into Brad's piercing blue eyes. Riccardo felt a wave of energy flow through his body unlike anything he had ever experienced before. It was powerful, overwhelming and took his breath away.

As Riccardo walked away, he glanced back at Brad who was just standing there looking at him. Riccardo felt as though fireworks were exploding inside his body and he felt transformed. He was tingling all over and thought to himself that if that were the effect that Brad could have on Riccardo after a few minutes and a handshake, his mind boggled at the thought of a night with the gorgeous US Navy SEAL.

Thirteen Collections

Monday, 17th January.

Since Anita and Camau had identified the thirteen collections that they wanted to investigate, they had spent the last few days developing a plan about how to go about this work. The challenge was that the deaths of these thirteen people had occurred all over the world. Whilst they could do much desk research using the internet it would be essential to visit all these locations. Anita was concerned about how much this would cost in air fares and hotels for both her and Camau to travel. The deaths and the value of the collections in millions of dollars that they wanted to investigate were:

Client	Location	Mount's	Balfour's	Seton's	Total
Aoki Fujiki	Dubai	$517			$517
Darian Amani	Jackson Hole		$85		$85
Ehuang Zhang	Beijing		$135		$135
Eleanor Dupre	New York	$342			$342
Gavin Johnston	Cape Town	$478			$478
James Settle	Everglades			$18	$18
Johannes Blomfeld	New York		$68		$68
Melvin Easton	Iceland	$290			$290
Myra Sharma	San Diego		$145		$145
Patrick Van Roots	Puducherry			$38	$38
Sophia Lazarini	Australia	$352			$352
Yves Gaston	Hong Kong	$735			$735
Zena Sparks	UK	$1,213			$1,213
Totals		$3,927	$433	$56	$4,416

Camau looked at the locations and developed the following plan. He and Anita could buy round the world tickets, which are reasonably priced, and generally allow up to fifteen destinations, but not enough to visit all the locations. Plus, they would be able to travel in first class if they booked with the right agency. They would travel west, firstly to Iceland, then to the US to visit New York, The Everglades, Jackson Hole, and San Diego, followed by Australia, Beijing, Hong Kong, India, and Dubai.

He proposed asking Stephen and Penny if, when they went on safari to Kenya, they would fly down to Cape Town first and also to visit Surrey, either before their departure or after their return. He was sure that Stephen and particularly Penny, would be flattered to be asked to be involved. Stephen had not yet formally retired so he was still a serving police officer and would be able to speak to local police to access police records where necessary.

Anita was impressed with Camau's thinking and so agreed that they pursue this plan. Anita had called Stephen on the previous Friday evening, a good time to drop a suggestion, and had agreed to call back today to get his and Penny's reaction. She need not have worried as Penny was thrilled at the prospect of combining a safari trip with some investigative work.

Everything was agreed so that over the next few weeks Anita, Camau, Stephen, and Penny would visit all thirteen locations and collate as much relevant information as they could to assist them in their investigations.

Camau arranged and booked the tickets and made hotel reservations in each location. They would depart the following Monday, 23rd January. Penny and Stephen agreed to go to Cape Town before their safari holiday and everybody would be back in London by the beginning of April and would hopefully be able to reach some conclusions.

For the rest of the week Anita and Camau did desk research and created briefing packs for each of the thirteen collections. These included background information, family members, the value of the estates and who had inherited or benefited from the sale of each collection.

Using her authority as part of the Metropolitan Police, Anita arranged for either her, or Stephen, to meet with the respective police departments in each location.

New Image

Friday, 21st January.

When Camau came into the office, Anita did a double take. He had shaved all his hair off and was wearing a white, formal business shirt, navy blue suit, and black brogues.

'Wow, that is a change.'

'Yes, I thought it was time that I grew up and started to look more professional, especially as we will be travelling around the world and speaking to all sorts of people.'

'Well, you look fantastic, Camau.'

'Thank you.'

'I have loaded all the briefing packs up to the cloud, so we can access them wherever we are, and no need to take any papers with us.'

'Great. I am having lunch today with Stephen and Penny to brief them on their cases. Do you want to join us?'

'Do you mind if I miss that, as my parents are in town, and they want to meet before I go travelling with you?'

'Of course, no problem.'

Confronting Woody

Friday, 21st January.

Riccardo had flown into London on the first flight from Zurich in Business Class. As he had exemption from providing any reasons why he was travelling, the company travel agency simply booked his flight without asking any questions. He was going to meet a client who had asked him to source some art for his and his wife's new five bedroom house in South Kensington. However, the main purpose of his trip was to speak to Woody Smith face to face, following his encounter with Kerem in Paris.

Riccardo took the Heathrow Express to Paddington, in first class, then jumped into a taxi for the final part of the journey. He arrived at Mount's around ten thirty, went through the front door, the reception area and into the Large Gallery. He disappeared behind a secret door that led into the back office. Whilst the public face of Mount's was glamorous, like a swan moving gracefully, the back office was a totally different picture all together. It was like the back of a theatre. A bit ramshackle, doors, offices, and equipment everywhere. He took one of the lifts and went straight up to Woody's office in the Human Resources department where about ten staff were sitting in an open plan office. Riccardo had requested a meeting at eleven, but as Woody's office door was open, he went straight in, closing the door behind him and sat down on what was known as the crying sofa. This was the sofa on which staff would unburden their troubles and invariably burst into tears. A box of tissues was placed on a side table next to it.

'Good morning, Riccardo. How are you?'

'I am good thanks, but I want to have a serious conversation.'

'About what?'

'Kerem.'

'Ah, I see. Listen Riccardo, you have a bright future ahead of you here at Mount's, irrespective of any arrangement that you and I have. If you want to be in the upper echelons of the company, there are certain things that you will have to do. Kerem is the boss, and he calls the shots. Whilst you may think that I betrayed your confidence, nothing could be further from the truth. I am helping you to get on in the world. If I had told you about this beforehand you would probably have resisted. I like you a great deal Riccardo, so do not be angry with me. This is just how the world works.'

'So, what else will I have to do?'

'Kerem is fair and protects those people around him who he appreciates. You have nothing to worry about, everything will be fine. You are already exempt from the new travel rules. There will be more benefits in due course, if you prove your worth, and money will not be a problem. Your salary will increase, and your bonuses will be significant. You really do have the world at your feet.'

'Okay, I get it, but I want you to promise me that you will be completely honest and upfront with me in the future. I do not want any further surprises or to be compromised again.'

'Agreed.'

They shook hands.

'Any chance of a meet up whilst you are here?'

'Sorry no, my boyfriend Stephan is flying in tonight for a weekend in London.'

'Next time, then?'

'Sure.'

A Chance Meeting

Friday, 21st January.

Stephan, Riccardo's boyfriend, was spending the weekend in London, prior to attending a crypto currency conference the following week. It seemed a good opportunity to spend some time visiting London, especially as Riccardo would stay in London until Monday afternoon as he had conveniently arranged a meeting on Monday morning. It was a classic tactic when travelling somewhere nice, to arrange meetings either side of a weekend, meaning it was imperative to stay over.

As usual, Riccardo was staying in the Bridge Hotel and Stephan joined him around eight in the evening. They changed into casual clothes and then went out to Soho to hit the bars. They loved going out in Soho as it was so much more fun than the bars in Zurich. Soho still has lots of characters and you can see virtually every style of dress and image, even on one night out. They went to Comptons, the Admiral Duncan, the Duke of Wellington and finished up at Comptons. They talked to several guys in the friendly atmosphere and then took a taxi around midnight back to the hotel. After getting to their room, they undressed, got into bed, and fell asleep almost immediately.

Saturday, 22nd January.

Stephan was six feet tall, well built like Riccardo and had naturally blond hair in the same style as Robert Redford. As he woke around eight fifteen, he cuddled up to Riccardo who was lying with his back to him. He kissed Riccardo's neck and stroked his body They hugged each other and held each other tight. No matter whatever they did with other people nothing beat being together. They loved each other so deeply and had a strong and powerful connection, it was truly special, magical, and out of this world.

'I love you,' Stephan whispered to Riccardo.

'And I love you too, more than ever.'

'I am starving. I propose we get showered, dressed, and go down for breakfast.'

'Great.'

Camau was up early sorting out the things he needed to pack for the round the world trip. Both he and Anita had agreed that they would take only hand luggage to avoid delays when flying. He, like Anita, therefore had to be ruthless what he packed. With careful thought and planning, and laundry services in hotels it was entirely achievable.

When Camau got to his iPad and mobile phone, which were probably the most essential items, he realised that he had left both his chargers in the office the previous day. It was a bit frustrating, but not the end of the world. He would simply pop into the office, collect the items and he decided to treat himself and go for a nice breakfast, like the one Stephen cooked, in Bridge's hotel. Once the items were collected, he arrived at the hotel's restaurant at eight forty.

Unusually, the restaurant was extremely busy. The Finnish national football team were playing later at Wembley and the team along with a large contingency of supporters, were staying in the hotel. Camau managed to get the last available table which was set for four. Almost at the same time Riccardo and Stephan came into the restaurant and the only table the restaurant manager could offer was to share the table with Camau.

'That is fine,' agreed Stephan.

The manager approached Camau and asked if he would mind sharing his table.

'Sure, no problem.'

'Hi, my name is Camau,' as he introduced himself to Riccardo and Stephan.

'I am Riccardo, and this is my other half, Stephan. It is super busy in here this morning.'

'Yes, apparently some football match.'

'God, how boring.'

The waitress gave them each a menu and asked if they would like coffee or tea. All ordered black coffee as they perused the breakfast menu.

'Are you staying in the hotel?' Riccardo asked Camau.

'No, I work just across the road and had to pop into the office to pick something up as I am going on a long world-wide business trip on Monday,' Camau replied.

'That sounds interesting. What do you do?'

'I work at the Art Squad, part of the Metropolitan Police Force. We are investigating a number of deaths that maybe suspicious. We have analysed that there has been an increase in the number of single owner sales over the last five years at the auction houses. As nearly all the people concerned died abroad, we are going to visit each location to see if there is anything untoward,' Camau explained.

'That sounds even more interesting,' Stephan commented 'And part of your world,' he added addressing Riccardo.

'So where do you work?' Camau asked Riccardo.

'I work for Mount's in the Zurich office.'

'What a small world. Well, we are not visiting Switzerland so nothing to investigate there.'

'Good to hear.'

The waitress returned to take their orders. They all ordered full English breakfasts, with brown toast and fresh orange juice.

'I have never heard of the Art Squad. What does it do?' Riccardo asked Camau.

'It investigates crimes in the art world but has recently only been focused on thefts from English country houses. We now have a new boss, Anita Wu, who is a high powered police officer and is intent on rooting out all the criminal activity that she suspects is happening in the art world.'

'Crimes such as?'

'Money laundering, fraud, funding terrorism, drug and people trafficking,' replied Camau.

'I have never come across any of that.'

'Well, I am sure that our investigations will get to the heart of the matter and uncover whatever is going on.'

'How did you get this job, it sounds fascinating?' Stephan asked Camau.

'My uncle is the Home Secretary and after I graduated from Cambridge, I was looking for an internship somewhere, and my uncle proposed the Art Squad.'

'Who is the Home Secretary?'

'Amol Patel.'

'Never heard of him. Neither of us has any idea who any politicians are in the UK.'

'Probably the best way to be.'

Breakfast arrived which they all ate practically in silence as it was so good. They ordered more fresh coffee and chatted about the day ahead.

About twenty minutes later Riccardo asked the waitress for the bill and indicated that he would pay all together.

'No, no, let me get mine.'

Riccardo raised his hand as if to say talk to the hand.

'It is all on expenses and as you work in the art world, this was a legitimate working breakfast.'

'Well thank you very much, that was most kind of you,' Camau said thankfully as he picked up his things, shook Riccardo's and Stephan's hands and left the restaurant.

'Are you sure Mount's will pay for this?' Stephan enquired.

'Oh yes, nothing to worry about. I will update Kerem about this meeting and all will be sorted.'

'So, you call Mr Akbarov Kerem now?'

'Yes, I met him the other day in Paris, and he is really friendly. I think he will be good for my career and for both of us.'

'Shall we get out of here and do some shopping?'

'Yeah.'

Part Two

Tectonic Plates

Monday, 24th January.

Anita and Camau landed in Reykjavik after taking the GB Airlines flight from Heathrow. They had both travelled in first class, which was a new experience for Anita who had only ever flown economy before. The cabin was spacious with only about seven passengers, and she was amazed at how luxurious the service was, and how she was treated. For Camau, it was nothing new as his father frequently got his son an upgrade when flying between London and Nairobi. What was the point of running an airport if there were no benefits?

After clearing passport control and customs, they took a taxi to the GEO Town Hotel in central Reykjavik. They were staying in this hotel because it was the sister hotel of the one they would be visiting tomorrow. The hotel was Scandinavian style, ultra-modern with minimalism as the overriding design style, but the service was welcoming, and the hotel was warm.

Today, they intended to meet with the local Chief of Police to understand the circumstances surrounding the death of Melvin Easton.

Melvin Easton was seventy eight years old when he died. He owned the largest group of department stores in his native Canada. He had inherited one shop in Toronto from his father in nineteen sixty nine and had built a retail empire by buying up stores around the country, and developing the Easton brand, which stood for luxury at affordable prices. He had one son, Gary Easton, whose mother had died in childbirth. Melvin never remarried but devoted himself for the rest of his life to his business. Right up to his death, he still went into the office every day in downtown Toronto and maintained a firm guiding hand on the business.

Unfortunately, his son, who was now forty eight, did not share in his father's passion, but used his inheritance from his mother to feed his gambling addiction. He would travel all over the world to gamble in Monte Carlo, Las Vegas, and Macau.

Melvin was proud of his Canadian heritage and had amassed a large collection of early Canadian artefacts. These included many items from the Viking era, who were the first Europeans to arrive on the American Continent, long before Christopher Columbus. Viking relics are few and far between, and new discoveries are greeted with great acclaim. A stone Viking chess set discovered in the Shetland Islands in Scotland a few years ago was considered to be one of the greatest finds. As the Vikings generally worked in wood and animal products, it was only stone items that survived.

The rarest location for discovering such items was Iceland. The last major find, of several stone items, including religious artefacts, was found buried in a cave almost one hundred years ago. When the GEO Experience hotel was built a couple of years ago, about an hour outside of Reykjavik, in a geo thermal location, several more items had been discovered as the foundations for the hotel were excavated. Although these items belong to the state, they were now displayed in a museum style room that was attached to the hotel, and which added another dimension to the hotels' facilities.

The GEO Experience hotel was powered by geothermal energy that produced hot water just below boiling point. The water was used for heating and to drive a generator that produced all the electricity for the hotel. It was the ultimate green carbon neutral hotel. The green ethos was carried throughout the whole building. All the materials used in its construction were reclaimed, and all the organic food that was consumed came from within walking distance. Like its sister hotel, it was decorated in Scandinavian minimalist style and was pleasing to the eye.

Melvin wanted to visit the hotel to see the collection, even though he knew he could not purchase anything. He had been putting off making the trip but finally set a date and arrived in the summer when the weather was at its best.

The curator from the Reykjavik Viking Museum had agreed to meet with Melvin as part of an organised trip of art scholars who were touring Scandinavia and would finalise their trip in the GEO Experience hotel.

Melvin arrived in the hotel on a Tuesday evening, had dinner and an early night as the group would be arriving early in the morning. The three days for the art group were broken up into a number of outdoor activities to experience all that Iceland had to offer, along with private lecture sessions about the rare Viking objects. The outdoor activities including walking inside a glacier, horse riding in the nearby hills and, if it were not summer, late night views of the northern lights, which from this location were spectacular, and a once in a lifetime opportunity.

The first activity on the Wednesday morning was a snorkel dive in the pristine sea water between the two tectonic plates that were only a couple of metres apart in this area. The curator had arranged for Melvin to join the trip and at nine thirty, after breakfast, he along with ten other people were sitting on a mini bus and driving the fifty five minutes to the departure location. It was a fine sunny day and about fifteen degrees centigrade as the bus travelled along a tarmac road, then continued along a shingle track, until they arrived at their destination.

The bus stopped in a make shift car park where there were another four groups, already getting prepared, who had driven directly from Reykjavik. Each person had to wear a waterproof rubber diving suit with built in boots and gloves, with a tight cuff around the neck. They were not becoming at all but were essential as the sea water was just above freezing. People also wore a skin tight rubber hood that left their eyes, nose and mouth exposed so they could wear a snorkel, leaving almost no bare skin exposed.

Each person waddled across the car park to the water's edge and climbed down some natural stone steps into the water, until it was waist deep. They fixed on their snorkels, then launched themselves into the water, bobbing around and being carried by the powerful current to the area between the plates. It was impossible to see the bottom of the crevice, even though the water was crystal clear. All the swimmers glided along, powered by the current, as they touched both sides of the channel they were in. Uniquely, they were touching Europe and North America at the same time, and this was the only place in the world where this was possible.

It was imperative to only stay in the water for a maximum of thirty minutes, because despite the heavy rubber suits, the cold water was pernicious. Each person, as part of their respective group, swam the channel which was only the length of an Olympic swimming pool, touched the plates, marvelled at the stunning sights around them, then climbed out of the water using more natural steps at the end of the channel. They then waddled back to the parked buses and removed their suits.

Naturally, everybody was buzzing with excitement, having just experienced something that was truly unique. They all removed their rubber suits, chatted and were grateful for the hot drinks on offer of coffee, hot chocolate, or tea.

There were well over forty five people standing around, including drivers and tour guides. Everyone was mingling together, until just before midday, people were asked to get back on their bus ready for the return journey.

It was at this point that the curator of the group which Melvin had joined, noticed that he was not around. He double checked the headcount on his bus, then realising that he was one short, he ran to each of the other buses asking frantically if Melvin had got on the wrong bus. He was nowhere to be found.

Two of the tour leaders from the other buses agreed to get into their diving gear again and to check the channel. Within five minutes they had dressed and entered the water. They swam along the channel until one of them noticed a snorkel sticking out from behind a rock. At the left hand side there was a narrow side channel where the pressure of the water was even greater than the main channel. In this channel they found Melvin's body lodged at the narrowest point. They managed to free him, and swim pulling him along with them to the steps. Melvin's body was lifeless and stone cold.

It was pointless to call the emergency services as they were in a remote location, and it would take nearly two hours for the nearest ambulance to arrive. Several people helped to carry Melvin's body to one of the buses, in which he was placed, and one of the tour leaders agreed to drive the bus back to the hotel. All the other people crammed into the remaining four buses, dropping some people back at the GEO Experience hotel, then continuing on to Reykjavik.

Anita and Camau had an appointment at two o'clock with the Chief of Police, Kristian Sturluson. They arrived at the modern looking police headquarters and were ushered straight in to meet with Kristian, in an office on the ground floor with a large window looking towards the hills covered in snow.

Kristian was forty five, five feet ten inches tall, with collar length blond hair, blue eyes, and a chiselled jaw. He was dressed in jeans, desert style outdoor boots, a denim shirt, and a classic Icelandic woollen jumper with a traditional motif around the neck.

Kristian shook both their hands.

'Good afternoon, please come in and welcome to Iceland.'

'Good afternoon, and thank you for agreeing to see us,' Anita said as she sat down with Camau, opposite Kristian.

'It is not often that we get high flying fellow officers visiting. It is generally pretty quiet here. Most of the crimes are domestic, caused by too much drink, the darkness, and the cold.'

'I am sure. We just want to talk to you about Melvin Easton. We are investigating the deaths of several people who have died over the last few years and had their valuable estates sold at auction. His sale raised five hundred and ninety one million dollars.'

'Well, that poor guy just spent too much time in the water and died of hypothermia, it is not rocket science. If you live around here, you know from childhood, that if you fall into the water then you had better get out pretty quickly, otherwise it is curtains.'

'I have no doubt that is the case. Did you question the people that were with him that day?' Anita asked.

'Of course. It was just a tragic accident. There were too many people around and people got confused, nothing more to it than that. We have now limited those tours to a maximum of twenty people to avoid anything like that happening in the future.'

'We are going to visit the hotel tomorrow and have a look around. Is that okay with you?'

'Of course, be my guest. There is nothing more to add, but I am sure you will have a good time. The hotel is beautiful, with great food, and the outdoor hot spa pool at night with the northern lights is awesome.'

'Thank you, but we will stick with policing, all the same.'

'Well, it was nice meeting you both. Let me show you out.'

Kristian escorted them out of his office and to reception.

'Good afternoon, and have fun both of you,' Kristian said as he shook both their hands and left them.

'This is extraordinary, Camau. They should have used the interviews from everybody on that trip and created a detailed timeline so they could work out exactly what happened. Plus, they should have looked at the tour operators' policies and procedures for managing these high risk expeditions.'

'Yes, boss.'

'It really is sloppy work.'

Tuesday, 25th January.

The following morning Anita and Camau had breakfast, checked out of the hotel, and used the hotel's courtesy bus for the one hour drive to the GEO Experience Hotel. They travelled with a party of two American couples, in their sixties, from Florida who had included Iceland on their whirlwind tour of Europe as it was a good stopping over point on their return journey, and they wanted to see the Northern Lights. It was still dark as the sun did not rise until ten twenty three.

The bus arrived at the hotel just after ten in the morning and everyone alighted, then went to the reception desk to check in. Twenty minutes later, Anita and Camau were back in reception, after unpacking, and agreed to have a coffee and plan their day. They sat in the hotel bar and ordered their drinks. As the sun rose, the beguiling landscape was unmasked.

'It is stunning here. I have never been anywhere like this before. It is as though we are on the moon with sky and sunshine.'

'Yes, it is Camau, but we are here to work. I propose we speak to the hotel manager and arrange a visit to the Silfra fissure in the Þingvellir National Park.'

Their coffees arrived and they sat drinking them in silence staring out of the huge windows at the mesmerising scenery.

'This blows my mind. Nature here is out of this world.'

Anita just nodded. It was as though they were drugged by the views and surroundings.

After finishing their coffee, they went to speak to the hotel manager, Klara Baldvindottir, who happened to be at the reception desk. She was a local Icelandic woman, aged thirty eight, who had trained in the hotel industry in the Middle East, then returned to her native Iceland three years ago to manage this hotel.

'Good morning. I am Anita Wu from the Metropolitan Police in London, and this is my colleague Camau. May we have a word in private?'

'Of course. Please follow me,' as Klara gestured for them to follow her into her office.

'Please take a seat. What can I do for you?'

'We are investigating a number of deaths all over the world which resulted in large sales at auction houses. We are trying to discover if there are any questionable circumstances as we have some suspicions that not everything is above board. We have come here because we want to understand how Melvin Easton died, and where.'

'That was terrible. He was elderly and obviously fell behind the rest of the party, was caught up in the narrow section with the currents, got stuck and died of hypothermia. The Reykjavik police reports were clear that it was a tragic accident.'

'Yes, we spoke to Kristian at the police headquarters yesterday.'

'How was he? He is my cousin, but I do not get to see him so often as I am on duty here nearly all the time.'

'He was in good form. We would like to visit the Silfra fissure to see for ourselves.'

'Okay. As the weather this time of the year is unseasonably warm, we have a group going this afternoon and I believe there are a couple of spare places. We only have four hours to do the tour as it is dark most of the time in late January. That will be twenty five thousand Kroner each.'

'We have to pay?'

'Yes, we are not running a charity here and it is expensive to put on these tours. Either take it or leave it.'

'Okay. Two places this afternoon. Just add the cost to our bills.'

'The bus will leave at twelve thirty, so you will have time for lunch which is on me. Just go to the restaurant when it opens at eleven thirty and your table will be ready.'

'Thank you.'

Anita and Camau left Klara's office and went for a walk outside.

'I am not convinced that everything is as they say. The investigating police officer is the cousin of the hotel manager, and they all assumed Melvin fell behind, got stuck, and died of hypothermia. It all seems to me as though they have jumped to conclusions without proper evidence.'

Camau attempted to placate Anita.

'We will see this afternoon how things are, and then we can take it from there.'

'Maybe.'

'Well at least we are going to have a nice lunch.'

Anita just looked at him.

Lunch turned out to be a mind blowing experience. They ate a salad of wild foraged herbs with a concentrated seaweed essence, succulent prawns sauteed in local butter and wild garlic, roasted cod cheeks with wild redcurrants and crispy cod skin, followed by the lightest wild strawberry mousse.

'I think we will be sinking after eating all this,' Camau joked.

At twelve thirty, Anita and Camau were on the bus along with the four American tourists who had travelled with them earlier in the morning, and another Italian couple who were on their honeymoon. They were escorted by a driver and diving instructor, and they followed the same route that Melvin had travelled two years ago. When they arrived in the car park, they put on their rubber dry suits and hoods, then went over to the steps.

Anita pulled back the diving instructor and explained who she was, and what she wanted to see.

'Sure, that happened way before my time. That little channel is dangerous, and we steer clear of it,' the instructor explained, 'but I will show it to you.'

'Thank you.'

The driver, who was also a diving instructor entered the freezing cold water first, followed by the Italian couple, the two American couples and finally Anita, Camau and the other instructor. The water was unbelievably cold and could be felt even through the thick rubber suits. Both Anita and Camau put on their snorkels and dipped their heads in the water. The shock of the icy sea water against the small areas of their exposed faces was heart stopping. It was perishingly cold.

As the party moved through the channel, the instructor who was with Anita and Camau, guided them over to the channel on the left. The water in the main channel was a force to be reckoned with, as the seawater was squeezed through the narrow six feet wide opening. It was obvious to both Anita and Camau that the pressure in the side channel was even stronger as it was only eighteen inches wide. The instructor placed a stem with a few leaves on it that he had picked up off a ground plant before they entered the water. He tapped Anita on her visor indicating to her to watch what he was doing. He let go of the stem and it sped through the side channel at a rate of knots. He then indicated to both Anita and Camau to follow him to the steps so they could get out of the channel.

Anita and Camau arrived at the steps, stood, and removed their snorkel masks. Their faces were numb with the cold. They walked up the rest of the steps and onto dry land. Neither of them had ever been so cold before.

'I can totally see how a seventy eight year old man would die quickly in that water if he were trapped. I am sure a person could only survive a few minutes.'

'In fact, it is about fifteen minutes at this water temperature. Once the core body temperature drops a person will lose consciousness.'

'How do you know that Camau?'

'I once did a project on the mathematics and statistics of the impact of temperature on the human body in space, where the temperature is minus two hundred and seventy point four two Celsius. It was a quick project as death is instantaneous.'

'Fascinating.'

Everyone enjoyed the hot coffee, chocolate, or tea as they gradually warmed up and got back into the bus which was cosy as the heater had been kept on whilst they were in the water. Just like all the people who swim this channel, they were all buzzing with excitement and the thrill of what they had just experienced.

'Camau, I want you to contact Kristian and have him send us the details of everyone who was on the snorkelling trip at the same time as Melvin, along with their interview notes. I should have asked him yesterday.'

'Sure, will do once we get back to civilisation and mobile phone reception.'

'Gee, this was awesome,' one of the Americans announced to the group.

'Si, stupendo,' replied the husband of the Italian couple.

'I hope you will join us tonight for a hot tub and the Northern Lights,' asked one of the American women.

'They are best around midnight.'

The other American and Italian couples both confirmed they would be there. Anita was unsure as this was a work trip, not a holiday.

'Come along Anita. We might never get a chance to see them again. Life is full of ups and downs, and you never know what is going to happen next, so best to seize the moment when you can.'

'Okay.'

When the bus arrived back at the hotel, they all got out and walked into reception. They were greeted by the Manager.

'Did you all have a good time?'

Everybody confirmed that they did and how awesome, amazing, and stupendous the dive had been. The Manager led Anita by the elbow away from the group.

'Did you discover anything?'

'That the water is beyond cold, and I can see easily how someone could die of hypothermia. I do think it was negligent that the guides did not notice that one of their party was missing. I am surprised that there were no prosecutions for that.'

'Well as I said, my cousin Kristian investigated Melvin's death and recommended to the coroner that it was a tragic accident.'

'Well, I am keeping an open mind. I have asked for the names and interview notes of all the people that were there that day. I will have a good look at them when I am flying to New York tomorrow.'

'Okay. Are you staying to watch the Northern Lights tonight?'

'Yes, we are.'

'Great. I suggest that you have an early dinner, have a rest, and come down to the hot tub around eleven thirty.'

'Yes, we will do that.'

Anita moved back towards the group, said good afternoon to the Americans and Italians then walked Camau to the lift. She explained the plans for the evening and suggested they should meet for dinner at seven thirty.

Klara went back to her office, closed the door, sat at her desk, and picked up her mobile phone, searching for and then dialling a number.

'Kristian, how are you?'

'I am good thanks, and you?'

'I am a bit concerned about that English policewoman who is sniffing around. I do not want any bad publicity for the hotel.'

'Nothing to worry about, Klara. The coroner and police commissioner are all satisfied that what happened was a tragic accident and it is a closed case.'

'She tells me she has asked for all the interview transcripts.'

'Yes, that is correct, but believe me there is nothing from any of the tourists, art specialists, drivers, or guides. They were all out for a fantastic afternoon and there was an accident. Everyone knows that too long in the water around here is a death sentence.'

'So, I have nothing to worry about?'

'No, and I hope you are coming down to my birthday party next Saturday? No water involved at all.'

'Yes of course. I will see you then, bless.'

'Bless, bless.'

Anita and Camau ate dinner, took coffee in the lounge, and then played a few rounds of snooker. Anita was a good player and Camau a quick learner. Soon they were battling each other to win each frame when Anita realised it was almost eleven twenty.

'We had better get changed and get off to the hot pool.'

'Sure, see you there.'

Soon Anita and Camau had joined the American and Italian couples who were already in the large hot tub. The steam was rising from the highly mineralised water when suddenly all the lights were switched off around them. It was totally dark, but then the black sky started to dance with the most vivid colours of green, pink, red, yellow, blue, and violet as the solar winds interacted with particles in the earth's atmosphere.

'Oh my God, this is awesome,' the Americans said almost in unison.

'E bellissimo,' the Italians shouted.

'Do you miss your girlfriend in moments like this?'

'Yes, I do very much. She is on tour in Australia with her latest play which has finished in the West End, and we will meet up there in early March. We are going to get married in Sydney. Can I ask if you would be a witness, Camau?'

'Yeah of course, that would be awesome.'

They both laughed at Camau picking up Americanisms.

'Sorry, yes I would love to accept.'

'These lights are special. These are the moments that you should cherish in life. You never know when they will come along or when they will stop.'

'Now steady on Anita, do not get carried away.'

They both laughed.

Piranha Bar

Wednesday, 26th January.

Anita and Camau checked out of the GEO Experience hotel, and took the hotel's courtesy bus to the airport, where they took an IceAir flight to JFK, New York. The weather in New York was dreadful, as a heavy snow storm had covered the city in twelve inches of snow and the temperature had plummeted to minus ten degrees. They were lucky that their flight had landed, as many flights were cancelled, but IceAir was used to inclement weather and nearly always managed to operate.

With the time difference in New York, it was lunch time when they arrived in their hotel. They each had a room in the Cambridge Hotel, on the Upper East side of New York, which was in the middle of the art district, and where the wealthy had their homes.

This hotel is one of the most prestigious hotels in New York and has been frequented by well-known people over the years and has an unrivalled reputation for service. Many of the staff have spent their entire working lives at the hotel and are treated as family members by the hotel guests.

A lot of the guests are regulars, or indeed live there permanently in one of the twenty four apartments located on the top six floors of the fifty storey building. Each apartment has stunning views across the city or Central Park, and most are furnished with priceless antiques.

The hotel has a dedicated spa for dogs, who are taken out for a walk in their doggy wellington boots and designer dog coats either by their owners, or the hotel staff, twice a day.

The regular hotel rooms were equally sumptuous with beautiful furniture, the finest linens, bathrooms with underfloor heating and spa whirlpool baths. The one thing that the hotel did that really made a difference to people, was to embroider the snow white, thousand thread pillow cases with the initials of the guest staying in the room. A.W. for Anita and C.K. for Camau. It really was one

138

of the most personal touches that a hotel could do and made both Anita and Camau feel special and welcome.

'Camau, let us have some lunch, then we have a meeting this afternoon at two o'clock at the precinct on Fifty Third street, to meet with Senior Detective Bill Huckley. He was involved in both the cases we are looking at.'

'Great. We can eat in the bar here. It is beautiful and decorated with hand painted murals by Andy Warhol.'

'Perfect.'

At one thirty they were both in a yellow cab, driving down Madison Avenue towards Fifty Third street. Fortunately, they had both purchased jumpers in Reykjavik and brought with them the latest hi-tech lightweight warm coats, that protected them from the bitter cold and the biting wind that was blowing through New York from the northern lakes.

When they arrived at the precinct, they were asked to wait in a dismal reception area. The building felt like a prison. It was grey, drab, in poor condition with strong metal grilles over each window, and the seating was hard metal benches fastened securely to the floor.

'God, this is grim.'

'Yes, I agree. It makes our places in London look five star.'

After waiting for twenty minutes, Detective Bill Huckley finally arrived, greeted them, and welcomed them to New York.

'I think it is best if we go out for a coffee to talk, as it is crazy back there.'

'Sure, that would be great. How do you work in a place like this?'

'You sort of get used to it. Some of the people we have coming in here are sometimes mad, sometimes dangerous, and sometimes mad and dangerous. I have only three more years to go, then I can retire to the Hamptons.'

'That sounds like a good plan.'

All three went along to a diner just one block away. It was a relief to get back to a nicer environment, although the diner had red plastic chairs, and tables covered with plastic tablecloths.

The server showed them to a table, and they all ordered black coffees.

'So, let me get this straight. You have come all the way from England to enquire about two deaths that happened here in New York city?'

'Yes, that is correct.'

'I do not understand why you would do that. We have so many deaths every year so why are you interested in these two?'

'Camau, show Bill your charts of auctions sales and profitability.'

As Camau was opening the charts on his iPad, Anita explained that they were investigating thirteen deaths that had occurred all over the world and had resulted in sales at the big auction houses.

'Okay, I get it. These deaths are part of a bigger picture.'

'Exactly. These deaths have all occurred in different countries and jurisdictions so no one would be suspicious. One of my colleagues, Penelope, spotted the increase in large single owner sales and suggested we look at them,'

Camau raised his eyebrows.

Camau showed Bill the various charts on his iPad and the list of thirteen deaths that they were investigating.

'So, you are interested in Johannes Blomfeld and Eleanor Dupre?'

'Yes exactly.'

'Johannes Blomfeld was an international television journalist. He was born in South Africa and after initially working as a newspaper journalist in Johannesburg, he moved to London in the mid nineteen eighties and joined the BBC. His rise in the corporation was meteoric and he became the lead political editor. He interviewed everyone of note from all political persuasions and in numerous countries.'

'He moved to New York with the BBC in two thousand and two, where he remained the lead international political journalist until he died at the age of sixty two. He was also a prolific author and wrote many books on geopolitical issues which won him lots of acclaim, awards, and riches.'

'As a black South African he was passionate about correcting what he called the 'text book history of the African continent,' which bore little or no reflection to its rich and varied reality. African history is much more complex and sophisticated than the commonly held view. There was the rise and fall of many kingdoms and empires, the flows of international trade during the Middle Ages with Asia, India and Europe, and the ensuing political connections, the battles between the religions, the impact of colonialism, slavery, and the extraction of minerals, in particular diamonds and gold, that were all distorted in the received narrative.'

'Bill's overriding obsession was the arts of Africa, which demonstrated the sophisticated nature of African societies throughout the ages. He used his earnings to build a superb collection of African Art, which rivalled that of any museum.'

'He worked with leading African Art experts and academics from across the globe, and in particular with Janette Litz, who is acknowledged as the world's leading expert. Janette works for Mount's and is based in the London office. She would source objects for Johannes, which she could either arrange to sell to him privately or she would guide him through the auctions to ensure that he bid at the right level to secure the objects he wanted.'

'Johannes' collection consisted of over two thousand and three hundred objects spanning all regions of the continent and through all the ages. I understand that he had one object in particular that was especially coveted, a bronze sculpture of a head from Benin, dating from the twelve century.'

Camau interrupted Bill.

'Was he married?'

'No, he never married and there were never any rumours about any personal relationships. He was married to his work and to his devotion to Africa. Johannes died four years ago.'

Camau checked on his iPad.

'Yes, and his collection of art was sold at Balfour's three years ago. It sold for fifty two million dollars and his collection was dispersed around the world,'

'I know nothing about that.'

'So how did he die?' asked Anita.

'Johannes had arranged, supported by Janette Litz, to hold an exhibition of his collection at the Museum of the World in New York. The exhibition of some three hundred objects supported by a book he released and a television documentary series on Netflix, had been a major international success. He attended the closing night of the exhibition, along with all the rich and powerful in New York. Normally they would have attended the opening night, but Johannes wanted the exhibition to be a success in its own right before the power players, fashionistas, glitterati, and Park Avenue princesses would claim it for themselves.'

'This unusual strategy worked like a treat as they all wanted to be seen in person, and in the media, and to bask in the exhibition's success. The closing night occurred at the same time as a strike by New York taxi drivers, which brought the city to a standstill, as everyone had driven into the city. It was completely grid locked and it would take hours to get from one part of the city to the other.'

'Johannes was staying in his New York apartment near Astor Place, and when the exhibition finished around eleven, he only had the option to take the subway from the station at Eighty Sixth street in the Upper East Side. He was standing on the platform, which was busy, waiting for the train, when suddenly someone pushed him onto the track just as the train was pulling into the station. It was not a pretty sight and the train cut his body up into several pieces.'

Anita was keen to find out.

'Was he murdered?'

'He was pushed onto the track by a woman who we suspect was high on the synthetic opioid Fentanyl. It is a truly awful drug that destroys people's lives. There are almost seventy thousand deaths a year from Fentanyl overdose in the USA alone. She managed to evade capture that evening as there were no police or security around, and the public would not go near her. I suspect she is probably dead by now.'

'A tragic accident then?'

'Yes. I am sorry to say,'

'Nothing further to discuss then about Johannes. Can we move onto Eleanor Dupre?'

'Yeah of course. More coffee?' Bill asked both Anita and Camau.

Camau declined anything further, but Anita wanted some water.

The server came over and Anita asked for some water in her English accent.

'Oh my God, you sound like the Queen of England,' the server said in her broad American accent as she returned momentarily with one of the best things about America, iced water in a pitcher.

'Thank you,' Anita said politely, slightly emphasising her cut glass accent.

'Awesome, I just love you Brits, I just love you Brits,' as she filled the glasses and walked away.

'Eleanor Dupre's case is a little more interesting, although she was a hundred years old when she died.'

'Wow, we had no idea she was that old?'

'Well as you know she was the Queen of cosmetics, who as a young woman, inherited from her father a company that produced face creams. She expanded the business which grew into the international Dupre brand that it is today. It is probably the world's leading beauty brand, trading everywhere and selling all manner of perfumes, potions, and lotions. She maintained that she was in her early eighties and like all ladies of a certain age in New York had undergone significant amounts of plastic surgery, being scraped, and pulled into an unnatural look.'

'To maintain the mystique that she was in her eighties she held a birthday party in her Park Avenue apartment to celebrate being eighty five. Her daughter had already passed away several years ago so her granddaughter, Suzanne Dupre who ran the company on her behalf, organised the party. Her son was not interested in the business and had left the states to live in virtual poverty in Goa, India. He had previously been married to Barbara Middleton, the Co-Chair of Mount's in America, who had in effect become a surrogate mother for Eleanor's granddaughter.'

'Eleanor's apartment was the largest on Park Avenue with ten bedrooms, all en-suite, several reception rooms, a library, a games room, a music room, a cinema, a meditation room, an art gallery, an office complex, two ballrooms, a gym, pool, spa and sauna complex, a beauty parlour, a panic room, a jewellery vault, a flower room, a present wrapping room, and an entire wing for the staff that contained all the functions necessary to run a large household including several kitchens and a wine cellar.'

'The party was held in the smaller of the two ballrooms and along with her granddaughter and Barbara, who were her only family, she had invited the powerful elite of New York. These included the Mayor, politicians, judges, the police chief, museum directors, fashion and cultural icons, media moguls and the board members of her company. Although she was eighty five going on a hundred, she ruled the company with an iron fist, making all the major decisions. With so many powerful people at the party it was not an enjoyable experience, more like a jungle where predators lay in wait for their prey.'

'Eleanor was stick thin, still tall, with a full head of snow white hair coiffured immaculately, dressed in a black dress exquisitely tailored for her by Givenchy and set off by her trade mark triple row pearl necklace.'

'She had flown in the world's top chef from Paris to prepare canapes for her party and the only drink that was served was Krug Clos d'Ambonnay champagne, the emblem of wealth. The ballroom made the Gallerie des Glace, the hall of mirrors, at Versailles look dowdy. The room sparkled with crystal chandeliers as the room had gold panels embedded into the walls that were encrusted with semi-precious stones, in the style of the Pala D'Oro in St Mark's Basilica in Venice. There really was nowhere else in the world like this. The guests were invited, and indeed expected, to arrive promptly at six in the evening and would leave at eight thirty precisely.'

'That sounds like a swell party.'

'It sure does, Camau.'

Bill continued.

'There were around one hundred guests and Eleanor held court sitting on a raised dais at the head of the room. Her throne was covered in gold, also encrusted with precious stones and she was seated on a blood red velvet cushion. She greeted each of her guests as they paid homage to her. Everything was going swimmingly and according to plan when Eleanor suddenly collapsed on her throne and fell to the side. The New York senator, who was also a doctor, rushed to her side, raised her from her slumped position and checked her pulse and eyes. It was no good, she was dead. Her real age had caught up with her.'

'Nothing suspicious then?'

'Not when you are a hundred. Come on, she had had a good life and lived life to the full to the very last moment.'

'Her granddaughter pushed for a police investigation and the Police Chief agreed, but it was determined at the autopsy that she had died of heart failure, therefore nothing to report.'

'Okay Bill, so thank you for your time and it seems that there is nothing fishy here. It is just convenient that her granddaughter inherited her whole estate including two hundred and forty two million dollars from her estate sale at Mount's in twenty sixteen.'

'Yes, I would agree. Just part of life's rich tapestry here in New York. Where are you going next on your travels?'

'We are going down to Florida to the Everglades, but we do not have a meeting until next Monday as we expected to be in New York a bit longer, but it seems that there is nothing further to investigate here.'

'Well why not enjoy a couple of days sightseeing in New York? It is a great city with lots to do.'

'Perhaps we will and thank you for your time,' Anita said as she shook Bill's hand and she and Camau left the diner.

'Anita. shall we go back to the hotel and plan what to do for the next couple of days?'

'Yes, I suppose so, but it does not seem right sightseeing when we are here on business.'

'Look we have achieved what we came to do and our flight, which we cannot change, is on Saturday morning, so why not spend a bit of time taking in the city. Sometimes you need to lighten up, you are too tough on yourself.'

Anita laughed. 'Yes, I agree, sometimes I am too hard on myself. You are a good antidote to my puritanical self.'

Camau hailed a cab and they returned to the hotel.

'I propose we meet downstairs in the bar at six thirty for a drink and to discuss our sightseeing plans, then we can go for dinner and see what happens then.'

'See what happens then?' Anita looked puzzled.

'This is the city that never sleeps, so who knows where we might end up,' Camau replied with a smile on his face.

They both came down to the hotel bar a few minutes after the agreed time. They were both dressed in blue jeans and the hand knitted jumpers they had bought in Iceland and managed to squeeze into their hand luggage, plus they were both carrying their hi-tech coats. They entered the same bar, with the Andy Warhol murals, where they had taken lunch earlier. The lights had been dimmed and a pianist was playing a grand piano. The murals were a cartoon like panoply of life in New York that seemed to be alive.

'I suggest we should have their signature Manhattan cocktail?'

'Perfect, Camau.'

Camau ordered two Manhattan cocktails which contained the finest ingredients; a fifty year old Scottish whisky (instead of bourbon), sweet vermouth from Turin, French dry vermouth, the newly created mandarin flavoured angostura's bitters from Venezuela, German kirschwassweror or cherry eau de vie, and the purest ice that was specially imported from a glacier in the arctic. As the mixologist placed the drinks in front of Anita and Camau on the bar where they were sitting, he spritzed concentrated mandarin oil over each glass. The aroma was heavenly, and the taste of the cocktail was literally the most beautiful thing that either of them had ever tasted.

'OMG, I do not know what to say.'

'Exactly, words are inadequate, just enjoy the experience.'

They both drank their cocktails, then ordered another one each.

They chatted about their time in New York and how despite their expectations that foul play played a part in the deaths of Johannes and Eleanor, the facts as they were, did not seem to support any such notion.

145

'Perhaps Penelope was mistaken, and given that she is an old trout, she played a blinder by getting us to travel halfway around the world and for her and Stephen to get the safari on the house.'

'The department is paying for their safari?'

'Yes, it was the only way I could get Stephen to agree, or rather Penelope to agree.'

'Okay. Drink up and let us go for dinner.'

'I have booked a table at Peking Café, the smartest Chinese restaurant in New York city.'

'Brilliant Camau, needless to say I love Chinese food.'

They arrived twenty minutes later at the restaurant which was virtually pitch black inside. Once their eyes adjusted, they could see that each table was spot lit, and the serving staff were fully dressed in black with luminous white gloves. All you could see was their faces, their gloves and the plates of food that seemed to magically appear on the table, all on black crockery so that the focus was completely and totally on the food. By removing all other distractions, the mind was focused on the look, smell, and taste of the food which all came in small portions. They ordered and ate:

- Hot and spicy crispy eel
- Frogs legs with cayenne pepper
- Pork trotters with chilli oil
- Twice cooked cumin lamb
- Smoked blackened duck
- Purple rice
- Chrysanthemum ice cream served with toasted coconut shards.
- Narcissus tea.

Anita and Camau ate in virtual silence as their senses were overwhelmed with the exquisite food.

'Do you know that I have a chrysanthemum tattoo?'

'No, I did not. Where?'

'That would be telling,' Anita said coyly as she was a little bit drunk from the two powerful cocktails.

'And a rose on the other one.'

'The mind boggles,' Camau said shaking his head.

After they had settled their bill, Camau proposed that they took a cab and went on to a bar for another drink which Anita readily agreed to. Once inside the cab, Camau asked the driver to take them 235 West 32nd Street.

'Where are we going?'

'Chill, you will see when we get there.'

A few minutes later they arrived at the Piranha Bar, the oldest and most famous drag bar in New York.

'So, you thought that because I am gay that I would automatically like drag?'

'No, that never occurred to me. I just thought we could have a drink in a bar with a good reputation and a bit of entertainment. We are just having some fun and a laugh, not making any statements. You are so touchy sometimes, relax.'

'Okay.'

They made their way into the dark bar which was busy with all sorts of people clearly enjoying the stage show. Anita ordered two beers and they found a bar table with high stools and sat down. The bar was stylish with dark crimson walls that showcased many black and white photographs of previous artists. The staff, all men, were handsome, bare chested, tanned, and wearing skimpy sports shorts, sports socks, and sneakers.

The artist on the stage was a drag king, a woman dressed as Freddie Mercury and belting out Queen songs, almost better than the original.

'Well, that is a first to see a drag king.'

'You see Anita, everything is not always as you expect.'

'I agree.'

Camau beckoned a server over and ordered two more beers. As the beers arrived the stage changed from a rock band set to a dressing room where several drag queens were getting themselves ready. They were all generally about half dressed and continued during the routine to complete their looks and to emerge as their full drag personas.

During this they bitched and joked at themselves, the audience, and the world at large. It was savage, on point, hilarious, hugely entertaining and Anita and Camau could hardly speak for laughing. There were crude jokes about the realities of sex, vicious comments about well-known people and political observations that were cut throat.

As the set finished, Anita lent over to Camau.

'That was fantastic, thank you for arranging this.'

'No worries, boss.'

'The show is over now; shall we get back to the hotel?'

'Great idea.'

Sightseeing

Thursday, 27th January.

Anita and Camau had two more days to sightsee around New York. Camau had put a programme together that covered the best things to do in a couple of days. He presented his thoughts to Anita at breakfast.

Today, Thursday:

- am – American Museum of Natural History
- pm – Metropolitan Museum of Art
- evening – Helicopter tour

Tomorrow, Friday:

- am – Museum of Modern Art
- pm – Whitney
- evening – New York catacombs by candlelight.

'That looks great Camau, thank you.'

'Yes, there is a lot to see, so I want us to focus on some really special things. In the Natural History Museum, we should see the Okavango Blue Diamond, the Blue Whale, the Mammoth, the Dinosaurs, and the Willamette Meteorite. In the Metropolitan Museum of Art there are Monets, Van Goghs and Bruegels, along with thousands of other works of art. The helicopter tour by night is the best way to see New York and we will be passing the Statue of Liberty, Times Square, the Rockefeller Centre, the Empire State Building, and the Chrysler Building, as well as passing by the George Washington Bridge and NYC neighbourhoods.'

'On Friday we will visit the Museum of Modern Art and see Cézanne, Matisse, Rousseau, Picasso, Dali, and Warhol. In the Whitney we can view

Rothko, Calder, Hartley, Bellows, Hopper, and more Warhol. Then in the evening we will tour the catacombs of Saint Patrick's cathedral by candlelight and see where bishops rest alongside prominent New York Catholics, such as the Delmonico Family and the first resident Bishop of New York, Bishop John Connolly. This labyrinth of vaults belongs largely to bankers, lawyers, captains of industry, merchants, political candidates, and even to a Civil War-era general Thomas Eckert.'

'This sounds amazing. I am looking forward to today. Thank you again Camau.'

Key Lime Pie

Saturday, 29th January.

Anita and Camau had thoroughly enjoyed the last couple of days in New York and seen some outstanding, world class works of art. Anita was beginning to see the inherent value of art and how important it was to the whole human race. Having never really thought about art before, she felt that she was blossoming internally and opening up to new ideas, thoughts, and different perspectives.

She was generally left brained in everything that she did, and she realised that the brain has two halves, each of which should be stimulated and used properly in order to optimise human existence.

This trip was turning into much more than a technical investigation into some deaths, but a life enhancing experience. She had Camau to thank for this. He really was an extraordinary young man who was far wiser than his age and dare she say it, a beautiful soul. Never before had she thought about anyone having a soul. She had been so focused on the practicalities of life and the demands of her police career, that she now understood that she had been missing out on so much.

The flight from New York La Guardia to Miami was around three hours and they arrived around three thirty in the afternoon at Miami International Airport. Camau had reserved a car as they would be driving to their meeting in the Everglades on Monday. They picked up the car and drove into downtown Miami to the hotel where they were staying. The weather was warm, pleasant, and sunny, so different from the ice and cold of the last few days.

As they were driving from the airport to the hotel, it was noticeable how neighbourhoods changed along the route. There were clearly areas that were not for tourists, which were truly frightening, and others that were solely for tourists.

Camau was driving the car with the windows up and doors locked.

'I think we should stick to the main road and get to the hotel.'

'I agree.'

They were staying in the Colonial Hotel on South Beach, one of the famed art deco hotels that had recently been refurbished and freshly painted outside in candy soft pink and sky blue.

Once ensconced in the hotel they decided to go for a walk along South Parade and get an early dinner. They quickly found the Atlantic Café Grill nearby, got a table outside by the edge of the beach, ordered some crisp white chardonnay to go with a dozen oysters, shrimp tempura and grilled lobster.

'Camau, I want us to drive over to the Everglades tomorrow so we can check out the area for ourselves, before we meet up with our contact on Monday.'

'Of course, great idea. It is about seventy miles from here, so it should take us about an hour and a half to get there.'

The server came to their table and removed the empty plates.

'Key lime mousse pie for anyone?'

'Most definitely, for both of us.'

Camau was taken aback at the new adventurous Anita, she did not even hesitate. He thought about the request from his uncle to gently spy on her, but as he was unable to speak to him face to face and had agreed not to use a phone, he would wait until he was back home. Anyway, there was nothing untoward to report to his uncle. He thought that she was hardworking, a bit frugal and frankly a bit too serious, but he could see that was changing during this trip.

The key lime mousse pie arrived which was light, fluffy, and imbued with the fragrance and aroma of key limes, which are more intense than regular Persian limes. The body of the pie was yellow as key lime juice is yellow not lime coloured, and when mixed with egg yolks and condensed milk produces the classic lemon colour. Interestingly key limes are not grown in Florida anymore but imported from Central and South America.

As they walked back to their hotel Anita suggested that they should both return to their hotel rooms and familiarise themselves with the briefing pack on James Settle, the individual who had died in the Everglades three years ago, ready for tomorrow's trip.

The Cartoonist

James Settle was Welsh, and a well-known cartoonist and artist, who used his artistic skills to make observations and commentary about daily political life, especially in the UK. He started drawing when he was a young child, absorbing things he had heard on the television news and then creating an image that captured the story perfectly.

His signature style was to take one or two characteristics of an individual, or their personal style, and to emphasise them to the extreme. He was ruthless in exaggerating people's flaws or negative characteristics, and although all his subjects dismissed his work as nonsense, they craved his attention as it kept them in the spotlight. He traded on his subjects' ego and vanity.

Throughout his long career, he was sixty three when he died, he had produced regular, daily cartoons for two broadsheet newspapers, a weekly political magazine, as well as producing sketches focused on the issues of the day. Over the years, he had built up a sizeable body of work that represented an important social and political commentary. In many ways he was a modern day Hogarth.

It was rumoured that Queen Elizabeth the Second was an avid collector of his sketches, in particular any to do with her prime ministers. No one had ever seen the collection, but it was believed that Her Majesty kept them displayed on the walls of a room off the audience chamber in which she met the Prime Minister of the day each week on a Tuesday evening. Apparently, she loved and appreciated the exaggerations that were evident in each sketch.

James was in Florida for two reasons. Firstly, he had curated an exhibition of his works at the Miami Art Basel Fair, which was held in December twenty nineteen. In addition to observations about well-known British public personalities, he had a sizeable body of work covering American politicians and personalities. These were the subject of his exhibition and had been a great success.

Secondly, accompanied by his wife, Flora, he gave his daughter away at her wedding which had taken place during the Art Fair in the Sanibel Beach Resort, just outside Fort Myers. His daughter Kathryn had been married before to a loser and an alcoholic. Kathryn subsequently divorced him and wanted to marry the new love of her life, Marcus who she met at work. They were both Financial Advisors for a major UK bank.

Kathryn was Roman Catholic, like her mother and father so was unable to remarry in the Church. She and Marcus decided to marry in Florida and so combined the trip to her father's exhibition with her wedding.

The bride wore a white dress of Welsh silk designed by Julien MacDougall. It had a high neck, a huge bow at the back and a long train that was almost three metres in length. She wore a veil of the finest lace, held in place with a diamond tiara, that she had borrowed from Tiffany's for the day. Intentionally she looked like the Virgin Mary, pure, pious, devoted, dedicated, and serene. The bridegroom, who was Scottish, wore a black watch tartan kilt with all the regalia.

The wedding took place in the grounds of the Sanibel Beach Resort, overlooking the Gulf of Mexico on a sunny, Sunday afternoon. The weather was perfect, the views were magical, and the gardens manicured down to the last blade of grass. The wedding party stood at the edge of a cliff, overlooking the ocean, under an arch of freshly picked hydrangeas and orchids. Her parents were the witnesses, and the officiant was a local woman who conducted a beautiful service that brought tears to the eyes of all of them.

Following the wedding, the family, which now included Marcus, posed for photographs by a local photographer and then along with the celebrant they drank a toast of champagne as they posed for more informal pictures.

A couple of hours later, they took a white stretch limousine to the best restaurant in town, Luigi's, about fifteen minutes away. When they arrived the happy couple, who looked stunning and incredibly beautiful, were applauded by all the guests who stood up as they entered the restaurant to go to a private dining room.

'Oh my God, she looks like a princess.'

'And he looks scrumptious.'

'Is it true that you are wearing nothing underneath your kilt?' one diner asked as the bridegroom walked by.

'Aye, that is right,' the bridegroom answered in a Scottish accent.

'Oh Jesus, I am going to faint,' the woman declared who had asked the question.

After the dinner, the four of them returned to the hotel, once again in the stretch limousine and had drinks in the bar. By midnight everyone was exhausted, and they all retired.

On the following day, the newly married couple left to go on a Caribbean Honeymoon cruise and James and his wife returned to their previous hotel in Miami for the remainder of the Art Fair. James had already booked a trip to the Everglades, which his wife declined as she said she would prefer to go shopping rather than sailing around some infested swamp. James frequently used animals and their characteristics in his drawings, and he preferred to draw them from having seen the animal in the wild. There is a world of difference between a lion sitting in a zoo waiting for its lunch from a zoo keeper, and a lion in the wild hunting for its dinner. James always wanted to capture those wild moments and the feelings that they elicited.

Whilst in Florida, James wanted to see the American Alligators in their natural habitat, as he often used them to represent people lurking beneath the surface, plotting their next moves, or pouncing on their prey. He had never seen them in the wild before, so this trip was a golden opportunity. James had booked a tour from the hotel for the Tuesday, after the wedding.

At one o'clock in the afternoon, the tour consisting of ten people, left the hotel in a mini bus for the ninety minute drive to the Everglades. James was still tired from the wedding celebrations so slept most of the journey.

When he woke up, he had been transported into a pre-historic world of swamps and lush vegetation. He left the minibus along with all the other passengers and they were soon seated on an air boat, which was really a flat plastic base, with a small lip around the edge, some seats attached and a large air fan at the rear to propel the craft along the water.

James was seated at the left hand side on the middle of three rows which each had four seats. The pilot was their guide and sped them away at a fair rate of knots right into the middle of the Everglades, He started to explain the geology, ecology, history, climate, the restorative work underway, and breeding and re-wilding programmes. It was all fascinating, yet all James wanted to do was to see some alligators so he could photograph them and sear their mannerisms and behaviour into his mind.

'Would it be possible to stop for a few minutes to take some photographs of the alligators?' James asked the pilot.

'Sure, buddy. We will stop over there by that clump of vegetation where there are always several alligators hanging out.'

'Thank you.'

The pilot steered the boat to the area in question, positioning the right hand side of the craft next to the vegetation's edge and switched off the engine. The pilot suggested everybody should be silent, which they duly were. All that could be heard was the call of birds and the buzzing of insects. As their eyes got used to the vegetation and the camouflage, they could see several young alligators with their noses just poking out of the surface of the water. One of the group pointed out a nest containing several eggs, and everyone tapped each other in turn to ensure that everyone got to have a look.

James was looking in the other direction towards the open water by the left hand side of the craft, as he had spotted a large alligator lurking in the water. When he was tapped on the shoulder he turned round, and at the same time the alligator leapt out of the water and snapped its jaws around James's waist. As the alligator fell back into the water, it dragged James with it, and proceeded to pull him under the water to drown him as it thrashed around and twisted its body. In a matter of seconds, James was dead, there was blood everywhere in the water and the other people in the boat were hysterical. The pilot switched the engine on immediately and got everyone out of the area as quickly as possible and back to the landing stage.

'This never happens,' the pilot informed the group. 'It must have been the mother protecting its nest.'

As soon as they arrived at the landing stage, a heavier craft was dispatched to retrieve James's body and bring it back to dry land. Before they had left the hotel for the trip, everyone had been asked to sign a waiver, absolving the boat company of any responsibility for any mishap, including loss of private property, injury, and death.

James's wife was naturally devastated, and his daughter and her new husband left the cruise to join her and to take what was left of his body back to the UK.

The Park Ranger

Monday, 31st January.

As planned, Anita and Camau had driven to the Everglades on the previous day to check out the area, returning to the hotel in the evening. Today, they drove to the Ernest F. Coe Visitor Centre, which is located on State Road 9336, fifty miles south of Miami, on Florida's east coast. They were meeting the head Park Ranger, Bud Little. He looked like a typical cowboy, which seemed a bit out of place in the tropical wetlands. He wore tight blue well-worn jeans, black alligator cowboy boots with spurs, an open necked red checked shirt and a Stetson. He was rugged and his leathery skin was deeply tanned from a life outdoors. Bud was of mixed heritage, half Seminole Indian and half Caucasian, was forty seven years old and a been a park ranger in the Everglades since the age of sixteen.

Anita and Camau arrived just before ten thirty in the morning. Bud greeted them and escorted them into his office which was a short distance away from the modern sophisticated visitors' centre. Bud's office was a bit like an old log cabin and inside it was scruffy and grubby. He dusted off a couple of wooden chairs and placed them in front of his desk. He sat behind it and managed to toss his Stetson so that it landed perfectly on a coat hook on the wall to his right, then placed both his feet on his desk crossing his boots at the ankle. He laid back in his reclining chair, chewing a piece of tobacco.

'Would ya all like some coffee?'

'Yes, that would be lovely.'

'Dyllis, three coffees,' Bud bellowed to an elderly lady sitting in the next room.

'I understand from your e-mail you want to discuss what happened to James Settle.' Well, it is simple, he was attacked and eaten by a "gator."

'Is it not unusual for that to happen?'

'Yes, it is pretty rare, but it does happen from time to time.'

'Was there any foul play at all that contributed to James's untimely demise?'

Dyllis arrived with three mugs of coffee.

'Morni' all.'

'Good morning to you and thank you very much,' Camau said as he smiled at Dyllis and took a cup of coffee.

'Good morning.'

Anita focused on Bud again.

'Was there any foul play?'

'It was just unfortunate that was all.'

'But why stop the airboat next to a nursery and a nest where the risk would be much higher than normal.'

'It was what the pilot was asked to do. He did not know there was a nest there.'

'Are you sure?'

'Look, we interviewed all the people on the boat, and you can have all the notes. James wanted to take photographs and requested the boat the stop.'

'But should the pilot not have known that it would be risky?'

'The pilot was skilled; these things just happen you know. There are one point five million "gators" in Florida, and two hundred thousand here in the Everglades. Tourists flock here by their thousands each year. You have to remember that it is their habitat, not ours, and fundamentally we put lunch in front of them on a plate. I am surprised there are not more incidents.'

Anita continued pressing Bud.

'But the marketing materials for the Everglades say that humans live in harmony with the alligators and there are no accidents.'

'Look lady, tourists are the lifeblood for people who live in this neck of the woods, without them we would starve. Of course, we are not going to say, come to the Everglades and get eaten by a "gator" are we?'

'How many deaths have there been involving alligators in the Everglades?'

'We have had about twenty odd since the year two thousand, so about one a year?'

Anita was mortified.

This whole industry promoted itself on harmony with nature when the truth was anything but.

'That is shocking Bud.'

'Hey, wait a minute. I think you should look in your own backyard first. Do you know how many deaths there are per year in the UK from dangerous dogs?'

'Er, no sorry I do not.'

'Plus, deaths from cattle and horses. It is probably about one hundred people a year in total, that is ten thousand per cent more than "gator" deaths.'

'Okay, understood.'

'And there were no prosecutions?'

'No, it was nobody's fault. Everybody who goes on those trips knows the potential risks and signs the waivers. Just the luck of the draw.'

Anita continued to be unconvinced.

'I am not so sure. Can we take a copy of the interview notes?'

'Sure, be my guest.'

'Thank you, Bud.'

'Dyllis, can you print out a copy of the "gator" death notes?' Bud shouted out to her.

'Can we have them e-mailed to us?'

'Not sure Dyllis can do e-mail,' Bud replied as he chortled to himself.

'Let me help her,' As Camau he stood and went to see Dyllis.

'Thank you Bud, for seeing us. I know we might seem overly suspicious but all the deaths we are investigating led to multi-million dollars of sales at auction, in total just under four and a half billion dollars.'

'Well bugger me, I had no idea. So, you think these people were murdered for their money?'

'Yes, but it is extremely difficult to prove anything. All the deaths, like James' look like genuine accidents, plus they all occurred in different countries and jurisdictions, so it is almost impossible to identify any patterns or modus operandi.'

'Well, no hard feelings and sorry if I was a bit gruff. It looks like you have got a tough job on. If you need anything at all just give me a call.'

'Thank you Bud, I will.'

Bud stood up and moved from behind his desk and as Anita stood, he embraced her and gave her a big kiss on the lips.

'Happy investigating,' Bud said as he turned to shake Camau's hand who had returned to the office after having sorted Dyllis and the e-mail.

The Layover

Tuesday, 1st February.

The next stop on Anita's and Camau's trip was Jackson Hole, which entailed a long journey and would take all day. Starting from Miami airport they had a two and a half hour flight to Houston, Texas, a layover of one and a half hours, then a further three and a half hour flight to Jackson Hole airport.

When they arrived in Houston George Bush Intercontinental Airport Terminal A, they disembarked the flight knowing that they would have to sit around at the departure gates for the next flight. Anita proposed that they went to the coffee shop and have a review of their trip so far.

'We have now visited four locations out of the eleven that we will be visiting, Stephen and Penny will be visiting the other two. On the surface all these deaths look like genuine accidents, but my instincts tell me that they all look too easy. There are little things that are peaking my interest.'

'Such as, Anita?'

'Let us take Melvin Easton first. He was with a group of over forty people, and no one noticed that he was missing, nor did he shout for help or splash around in the water when he felt he was being pushed into that narrow channel. The police guy, Kristian Sturluson, seemed too quick to assume it was just hypothermia that killed Melvin. Plus, the Manager of the hotel, his cousin, Klara Baldvindottir, seemed more interested in the reputation of her hotel than the truth.'

'Johannes Blomfeld, I have to say does look like an accident. An unfortunate death by a crazed, drugged up woman.'

'Eleanor Dupre is a tough one. It is rare for people to just keel over. Most people suffering heart failure are visibly distressed.'

'James Settle's death looks too easy. Why would you position an airboat next to an alligator nursery and a nest? That is about the most dangerous place you could stop and all those people working on the Everglades know that.'

'Perhaps we need to have a closer look at the autopsy reports, who were present in each situation, what possible motives there might be and who benefitted from these deaths. In James's case his wife inherited eighteen million dollars from his auction sale at Seton's in twenty, twenty one.'

'Yes, I agree. We cannot just accept the conclusions that we are being fed. I really do not know what is going on, but my Police Radar tells me to be wary.'

'You mean like gaydar?'

'Or poldar?'

'Very funny, go and get us some coffees.'

'Yes, boss.'

Just a Coffee

Wednesday, 2nd February.

Jackson Hole in Wyoming, a valley between the Gros Ventre and Teton mountain ranges is one of the most beautiful places on earth. It is surrounded by steep mountains on both sides and the Snake River runs through the whole of the valley. With twenty four thousand acres of protected land, it is one of the last few remaining wild places on earth. It can be extremely cold in the winter and the summers are mild.

Teton County, in which Jackson Hole is located, has the largest income from assets per capita in the USA, and the state of Wyoming has an extremely favourable tax regime with respect to real estate, income and inheritance taxes.

Mere millionaires do not have a chance to live in this area. It is the preserve of billionaires. Most of the properties in this area sell for millions of dollars.

Anita and Camau were visiting Jackson Hole to investigate the death of Darian Amani six years ago. Darian was a world famous film director who had produced some of the most well-known films over the last thirty five years. He had won several Oscars as well as other international awards around the globe. He was born in Iran and his family had moved to the USA when he was a child.

Darian had travelled to Jackson Hole to attend a Gala party for Chuck Hanson who had been one of the most influential art dealers in New York. Chuck was celebrating fifty years working in the art world and held his Gala party to celebrate. Chuck was married to Anabelle Hanson, the major shareholder of Sutton's, the largest food company conglomerate in the states. They lived in the most expensive house in Jackson Hole which was really a luxurious ranch with stunning views of the surrounding mountains and the Snake River.

Darian had been at college with Chuck, and they were lifelong friends. Anabelle had agreed to let Chuck hold his Gala party in her house, providing it was contained within the entrance hall. She did not want people wandering through her home gawking at her extensive and valuable art collection. The entrance hall was perfectly large enough to accommodate the fifty guests that were invited. The marble flooring could be cleaned easily, by her cleaners, plus there was access to kitchen facilities for the serving staff, and cloakrooms for the guests, if absolutely necessary, as she detested strangers using her lavatories. As always with these types of events there was a strict starting time and more importantly a strict ending time. Arrive five thirty, depart eight thirty sharp.

Darian arrived in Jackson Hole on the day of the party with his wife, Joy, and they stayed at the Amangani Resort. This luxury resort was nestled in the mountain side overlooking the Grand Teton mountains. Constructed of wood and stone, all the rooms were suites with high ceilings, balconies and large picture windows framing the views of the mountains and forests.

His wife had visited Jackson Hole several times as her old school friend lived there, but It was the first time that Darian had visited, and he wanted to explore the area including an early morning balloon ride and a river float on the Snake River. The balloon trip was booked for the following morning and the river excursion for that afternoon.

The trip on the river was a ten mile floating experience in a shallow canoe with just the two of them and a guide. As the craft floated along with the natural flow of the water, which was only about ten inches deep, the silence was magical, only pierced with the occasional sound of insects buzzing around. Bald and golden eagles circled high in the sky and on the banks of the river were otters, elks, and a few moose.

When the trip was over it was time to return to the hotel and get dressed for the Gala party. It was attended by people from the art world who had all been Chuck's colleagues over the years. The guests duly arrived on time, drank champagne, nibbled on canapes, listened to a speech by Chuck reminiscing about his lifetime in the art world, and left as scheduled, without any one stepping into Anabelle's private space. She spent the whole evening occasionally talking to guests but looking as though she had a bad smell under her nose, which she held aloft. When it was all over, she retreated to her snug to watch American Pop Idol.

The following morning, Darian and his wife got up before sunrise and when dressed they went downstairs to meet the driver who would take them to the balloon departure point. When they arrived in the middle of a field there were six other guests, all of whom Darian knew from the art world.

The balloon was virtually fully inflated as the pilot continued to burn the propane heater. The basket gondola was tethered to the ground with ropes that were attached to what looked like tent pegs. On the side of the gondola was a gate that allowed the guests, a maximum of eight, plus the pilot, to step into it. All the guests got on board and the pilot locked the gate shut with a bolt on the inside. He carried on pumping heat into the balloon and when the moment of lift off arrived, the assistant on the ground released the tethers and the balloon glided upwards, silently.

Occasionally, the pilot would give the burner another boost of gas and the balloon lifted higher. As it rose, the sunrise could be seen over the mountain tops. Their blackness contrasted with the orange glow building behind them, until the vibrant golden globe of the sun could be seen. Light rays shone everywhere, and the sky became a riot of different colours as the light cloud cover reflected the rising sun.

'Darling, this is amazing,' Darian's wife said to him as she pecked him on the cheek.

'Yes, it is pretty special.'

The pilot attracted all the passenger's attention.

'In a moment we will pass over the Bison herd which will be drinking water at this time of the day down by the river's edge. Cameras ready.'

The sun was now fully risen, and the balloon floated on for another five minutes until it reached the banks of the Snake River. The pilot added some more heat and the balloon rose by at least a hundred feet. Everyone in the gondola was taking pictures of the Bison herd, which was enormous. Darian was standing by the gate when he leant on its edge as it flew open, and he fell out of the gondola right on top of the herd. Bison are extremely dangerous, and he was gored, and stampeded to death.

Darian's estate was sold at Balfour's in twenty sixteen and realised seventy five million dollars.

Anita and Camau took a taxi into the centre of Jackson hole from the Amangani Resort, where they were staying. They were going to meet Lieutenant Jane Todd at eleven o'clock. They had read the briefing notes and asked the taxi driver to take them around the impressive and wealthy town before their meeting started. There were no signs of depression or run down shops or houses. Everything was perfect and even the snow piled on the sidewalks looked clean and orderly. The taxi stopped at East Pearl Avenue in front of the police station. Anita and Camau got out of the cab, paid, and thanked the driver and entered the station by the front door where Jane was waiting for them.

Jane welcomed them and shook both of their hands.

'Good morning and I hope you are having a good stay.'

'Yes, it is beautiful here but a bit cold.'

'Nah, this is nothing. Sometimes it is nearly minus fifty. Today it will be plus five, positively spring like. Come with me into the cafeteria.'

'Thank you.'

The cafeteria was like a full scale restaurant with several food stations, drink dispensing points and a large bank of vending machines offering what looked like really nice food and snacks.

'I am going to have a skinny, de caff, double shot, oat milk cappuccino.'

'And for you, Camau?'

'Just a coffee please.'

'Yes, but what sort of coffee?'

'Anita?'

'Black, hot, wet, strong coffee please.'

'You mean just a regular filter coffee?' Jane asked with a puzzled look on her face.

'Yes, I suppose so, two please.'

'Okay.'

Once they had their coffees they sat at a table in a quiet corner.

'I re-read your e-mail last night explaining a bit more in depth what you are looking at. I have always had my suspicions about the tragic death of Darian Amani. We looked at all the evidence and interviewed everyone on the balloon ride, but nothing could be proved. Somehow the bolt on the gate came undone or was never bolted in the first place. The pilot was adamant that he bolted it and he has many years of experience flying these balloon trips. There was no forensic evidence, no additional fingerprints and no one admitted to seeing anything. One theory was that he undid the bolt himself and jumped. That must be a possibility because suicide victims can hide their pain and look as right as rain.'

'Do you think the wife was involved as she benefited from the sale of his estate to the tune of around seventy five million dollars?'

'I do not think so. She was traumatised by what happened and not faking her distress, she was genuine.'

'May we take a copy of your notes and add them to the others so that we can see if there any patterns, threads, or connections we can identify?'

'Of course, I will e-mail them to you now.'

'Not a Dyllis situation then?'

'Ignore him, just a private joke and thank you,' Anita said as they all stood up, shook hands, and left the cafeteria.

'I will drive you back to your hotel.'

'That is kind of you.'

'It is clear to me that one of those guests opened the bolt and allowed Darian to fall or pushed him out of the gondola. I just cannot prove which one and I cannot arrest all of them. You have your work cut out, but I am sure your efforts will prove worthwhile,' Jane added as they walked to her police vehicle.

Once back in the hotel, Anita asked Camau to join her for lunch to discuss the meeting.

'It seems to be the same pattern again. A death made to look like an accident, but even Jane has doubts like I do.'

'Yes, I agree. What I have noticed is that all the deaths so far seem to have taken place with a crowd of people around. Melvin with a large group of divers, Johannes on a crowded subway platform, Eleanor at her party, James on an airboat with a group of tourists, and Darian with a group of people in a balloon gondola. Do you think the crowds are being used as a cover?'

'Good thinking. Let us keep that in mind.'

'California tomorrow. Hopefully, it will be warmer than here.'

'Yes.'

Monika

Friday, 4th February.

As Anita and Camau were landing at San Diego airport, the captain made the usual arrival announcement including that the time was just approaching three in the afternoon and that the weather was a lovely, balmy twenty degrees with a gentle breeze. They both purred. It had been another long journey, leaving at nine in the morning from Jackson Hole for the flight to Los Angeles which took two hours and forty minutes, then a layover of an hour and forty minutes, then the final flight to San Diego, which was just over an hour.

As the plane was taxiing to the terminal, Camau leant over to Anita, who was sitting on the opposite aisle seat.

'I have got a surprise for you, here in San Diego,' he said with a glint in his eye.

'What?'

'We are going to stay in the Hotel Del Coronado, established in eighteen eighty eight.'

'We cannot afford to stay there; it is one of the most beautiful hotels in the world.'

'Chill. My cousin is the assistant manager, and he has arranged a condo for us, at a super discounted price.'

'Are you sure?'

'Of course. He owes me, as my father always gets him in to business class when he is flying back to Nairobi from here.'

'Okay, well great.'

They arrived at the hotel after a twenty minute cab ride, and Camau's cousin, Jag, was waiting for them. He was wearing a classic black suit, a white shirt and black tie. He had shaved hair and was like a slightly smaller version of Camau. It was obvious that they were related as they looked so similar.

'Good afternoon and welcome to this wonderful hotel.'

167

Jag shook hands with Anita, then with Camau, and embraced him.

'Follow me and I will show you to your condo. I got the best one for you.'

'Thanks.'

'I like your name Jag, that is so cool,' Anita said as they walked along the corridor together.

'It means, man of the world.'

'Impressive.'

Jag took a key card from his pocket and opened the door.

Anita was shocked.

'Oh my God.'

'Let me show you around,' Jag insisted as he closed the door behind them.

'The whole condo is decorated in white and oyster, to create a sense of purity, cleanliness, and sophistication. The floor tiles throughout, are off white Turkish marble, streaked with pale gold, and you have electric day curtains and night time black out blinds. This is the luggage room where you can store your suitcases and this is the guest bathroom with power shower, Japanese loo and illuminated dressing table. This is the kitchen which has a welcome pack of food and drink items in the fridge. You can use the kitchen yourself, or you can ring for your on call chef who will cook whatever you like, twenty four hours a day.'

'You also have an on call maid and butler as well, twenty four hours a day. This is the laundry room, should you need it, or your maid will do whatever you require. This is the dining area with a Carrara marble dining table and eight chairs. There is of course a fully stocked drinks cabinet and if you want a mixologist to make you a drink, just press this buzzer any time. The lounge has three, five seater leather sofas in Italian, oyster coloured leather. You have televisions in every room with access to three hundred channels and full internet access. Netflix is included of course. The veranda has a hot tub, lounge furniture and a heater, should you need it. You have private access down to your own beach and the Pacific Ocean,' Jag explained, as he moved back into the lounge to show the bedrooms.'

'There are two bedrooms, one to the left and the other to the right, they are both the same. Each room has two King size beds with thousand thread Egyptian cotton linens. Each bathroom has a sauna, steam shower, power shower, Japanese loo, and the pièce de résistance is the large sunken bath which you can enter using these steps. If you wish you can call the aromatherapist to run your bath and add the perfect mixture of oils and fragrances to suit your mood. I hope this is to your liking, Anita?'

Anita was speechless and just nodded.

'Well, I will leave you both alone now. We should have a drink later when I finish at six thirty.'

'Perfect, see you then. Which bar?'

'Ah right, we have eight bars in the hotel. I think we should have sun downers on the Terrace Bar.'

'Perfect and thank you,' as Camau shook his cousin's hand.

'Anita, shall we call the aromatherapist and have a bath before going for a drink with Jag, we have plenty of time?'

'I am not sure.'

Camau gave her a look of exasperation.

'Yes, all right.'

Camau called the aromatherapist who arrived at the condo ten minutes later. She was thirty four, five feet six, with dark hair that framed her face, wearing a white lab coat, sensible black leather laced up shoes and carrying a tan leather gladstone bag. She looked like a cross between a Bond movie villain, a nurse, and a beauty therapist.

She introduced herself in a strong accent, that was probably Romanian.

'Good afternoon, my name is Monika. May I ask you to go into your bedrooms and undress down to your underclothes? I will run the water, then assess each of you to see what combination of oils and fragrances your body requires.'

Monika knocked and entered Anita's bedroom. She closed the door behind her and saw Anita sitting on the edge of the bed in her bra and knickers.

'Okay, please stand up over there and let me have a look at you?'

Monika circled Anita as if she were examining a life size sculpture from every angle. She poked and prodded Anita in various places, looked at her palms, the soles of her feet and eventually her eyes.

'Oh dear, you are under the weather. You look as though you have the world on your shoulders. You are holding yourself so tightly and I can see all the blockages in your body.'

'Blockages?'

'What do you mean?'

'In your aura.'

'Aura, what sort of nonsense is that? Oh, I get it, I am in California, I should have known better than to agree to this.'

'Whether you agree or not, your aura is a mess and needs sorting. I like your tattoos.'

Anita blushed.

'Now undress and put that robe on whilst I prepare your bespoke mixture and add it to your bath. When you get in the bath, you must stay in it for forty minutes. Do you understand?'

'Yes ma'am,' Anita replied as if she were addressing a superior police officer.

Monika added lavender, bergamot, ylang-ylang, and clary sage oil to Anita's bath. She then added a dozen yuzu fruits which floated on the surface. Finally, she popped into the kitchen and prepared some jasmine tea.

'Now as I said, forty minutes in there and drink the tea. You will feel like a new woman when you get out.'

Anita removed her robe and got into the bath. She was expecting nothing to happen and resented the fact that she had ever agreed to this in the first place. God knows how much this mumbo, jumbo was going to cost, she thought to herself.

Monika went into see Camau. She did the same inspection with him and declared that his aura was perfect, shining in every direction.

'I will just add some rose oil and red rose petals to your bath.'

'Enjoy.'

Forty minutes later, Monika knocked and went into Anita's bathroom. Anita had drunk the jasmine tea and was relaxed.

'May I suggest you get out of the bath slowly, as I hand you your robe, then please go and lie down on your bed for at least fifteen minutes?'

'Of course,' Anita agreed in a voice that was calm and stress free.

'Good.'

'Then you can shower and enjoy the rest of your day.'

'Thank you.'

As Anita and Camau were leaving for drinks with Jag, Camau asked her how the bath had been.

'Not what I expected. She basically told me my aura was a mess, whatever that is, but I do feel lighter and a bit strange.'

'I thought that is what she might say,' Camau said as he opened the door.

'What do you mean?'

'Well, even I can see your aura needs sorting.'

'Sorting? I have no idea what you mean.'

They bumped into Jag and went for sun downers on the Terrace Bar.

'I do not understand all this Californian trendy new age stuff,' Anita told Camau as they were on their second tequila sunset.

'We have plenty of time this weekend to sort this out before we have our meeting at the zoo on Monday.'

'Sort this out?'

'Just trust me.'

Saturday, 5th February.

It was another glorious day and both Anita and Camau were enjoying the gorgeous weather. They both slept well and felt refreshed and renewed as they came down to breakfast in the outside restaurant overlooking the beach. They both had fresh fruit, scrambled eggs and smoked salmon, a basket of pastries, freshly squeezed grapefruit juice and coffee.

'After we have finished breakfast, we can go back to our rooms and read up on the notes for Monday's meeting.'

Camau counter proposed.

'Come on, it is beautiful here. I think we should go down to the beach. We can read and discuss the notes there, enjoy the weather and get a bit of a tan.'

'Okay, I agree.'

'Then tomorrow I have arranged to meet Jag for lunch as he has Sunday free. Would you like to join us?'

'Of course.'

Once on the beach they read up on the case of Myra Sharma.

Myra Sharma was a world famous Indian jewellery designer and had died in San Diego a couple of years ago. She designed classic Indian jewellery, as well as modern contemporary pieces, and had built up a successful business with a string of jewellery boutiques around the globe to serve her clientele. Her parents had been killed, when she was a teenager, in a traffic accident on India's notorious roads. Her only other family was her sister, who was four years older than her.

Myra's sister, Paavni, emigrated to America in her twenties and was now a successful art gallery owner, with premises in New York, Chicago, San

Francisco, Miami and a soon to be opened new one in San Diego. She focused on representing Contemporary artists and was a well-respected gallerist.

Myra lived internationally with homes in Delhi, Sydney, London, New York, and Dubai. Although Myra was fifty six, when she died and her sister sixty, neither of them were currently married. Both had been divorced and were childless.

Myra looked much younger than her age, as she took great care of her body and used all the best cosmetic and beauty treatments available. She wore beautiful designer clothes, usually from her favourite designer, Donna Karen. Her preference was pure white cotton clothing, that emphasised the jewellery she was wearing at the time.

Her sister was a naturalist and advocate of organic products. She refused to dye her hair which was now almost snow white and kept long. She wore a mixture of traditional Indian and western clothes.

Myra had recently been on a singles holiday to Greece, and met a young man, Omar, from Oman. He was twenty five years old, six feet tall, handsome and would often wear a pure white classic Arab starched thobe with a white gutra and black egal.

Myra was infatuated with her new admirer, and he quickly latched on to her and her lifestyle. He enjoyed travelling in style and staying all over the world with Myra. He did not work and told Myra that he had a private income from his family, but he was not too keen on spending money at all.

After a whirlwind romance, Myra announced in a telephone call to her sister, that she and Omar were going to get married in two months' time. Paavni was about to open her new gallery in San Diego and really wanted her sister to be there for the opening evening. Myra agreed that she would attend and because Omar was visiting his family in Oman, he would arrive a couple of days after the opening.

Myra had been working on some new ranges of jewellery for her stores. She was impressed by how the Victorians in England had incorporated the language of flowers into jewellery. She subsequently created a modern range of flower inspired jewellery that won her many awards. She now turned her attention to how insects had been represented in jewellery which goes back at least to the time of the Pharaohs. Insects were associated with re-birth and transformation, for example a caterpillar becoming a butterfly or moth. Butterflies, beetles, bees, dragon flies and lady birds have all been used in jewellery designs throughout the ages.

Myra had recently become fascinated with spiders, following the social media frenzy after Lady Hale, President of the UK's Supreme Court wore a large spider brooch, when delivering a verdict on the UK government. Some people are frightened of spiders and associate them with death, Halloween, and horror movies. Others see them as fascinating, resourceful, strong, and adaptable.

Whilst in San Diego, Paavni suggested that she and Myra visit the zoo, which has the largest number of species in the world. They have an outstanding collection of insects, and Paavni thought that it would be a great opportunity for Myra to study them in real life, to help her to create more realistic designs.

Paavni's friend was one of the keepers in the Entomology department and had agreed to show Myra and Paavni a behind the scenes tour. Myra was delighted by such an opportunity.

Myra and Paavni visited the zoo after hours, one Wednesday evening. Ernesta Lavender had worked in the department all her life and was passionate about the role and importance of insects to the world. She was also well aware of the serious danger that many insects were in, as their numbers were declining rapidly around the globe. She was supportive of Myra producing a range of insect inspired jewellery because it would raise their profile.

Once inside the department there were hundreds of glass containers, like fish aquaria, stacked on top of each other lining the walls, that each held all sorts of spiders. In the centre of the room was a large stainless steel table, upon which Ernesta had placed a number of the glass containers.

'I have selected a range of different sorts of spiders that I thought you might be interested in,' she explained to Myra and Paavni as they arrived.

'You can take lots of photographs and if you want you can open the lid to get a better image. These are all harmless spiders so no need to worry if one of them gets out. This room is sealed, so there is nowhere for them to go.'

Ernesta then invited Paavni to go with her to the cafeteria to buy some iced peach tea, whilst Myra was studying and photographing the spiders.

'See you in a few minutes,' Paavni said as she left with Myra.

Once in the cafeteria, Ernesta bumped into a couple of colleagues and after introducing Myra, they all agreed to sit down at one of the tables on the outside patio and enjoy their iced peach tea in the evening sun.

Time flew by, and before they knew it, nearly an hour had passed since they had left Myra.

'We had better get back and see what my sister has been up to,' Myra said as she and Ernesta stood up to leave.

'Lovely to meet you and I hope your sister has enjoyed her time here with our spiders,' one of Ernesta's colleagues said.

'I hope so. Bye.'

When Paavni and Ernesta returned to the Entomology department they were horrified to find Myra lying on her back on the floor with a spider clinging to the underside of her forearm. She was hardly breathing, barely conscious and was having muscle spasms, with tears streaming down her face. She had been drooling and had vomited.

'Oh my God,' Ernesta screamed as she bent down over Myra and firstly brushed off the spider that was attached to Myra's arm. Paavni also bent down and cradled her sister in her arms. Ernesta picked up a telephone and called for help.

A medical team of two personnel arrived almost immediately. There were frequent incidents in a large zoo such as the one in San Diego and they had their own Fast Responder team on site.

'We need the antivenom for the Sydney Funnel Web Spider,' Ernesta explained to the medical team.

The team looked at each other.

'We do not have any. We threw the last batch away a few months ago and we have not yet received fresh supplies. There is nothing we can do as it is the only antivenom that works.'

Paavni screamed and one of the medical team helped her to her feet and tried to comfort her. Myra continued to convulse, then suddenly she stopped. The other medical team member checked Myra's pulse and declared that she was dead.

Myra's collection of art and jewellery was sold at Balfour's for one hundred and forty five million dollars.

The Chakras

Sunday, 6th February.

Jag, who lived in the grounds of the hotel ordered a cab to take him, Anita and Camau for lunch. As it was his day off, he wanted to get out of the hotel and enjoy an Indian lunch at the best vegetarian restaurant, located a couple of miles away, downtown. The restaurant was located in what looked like the Indian quarter and it was clearly off the tourist route. When the taxi arrived, they entered the main door of the restaurant, then climbed the staircase to the dining room. It was simple but elegant and the staff were charming and the food delicious.

They had the fixed lunch menu which consisted of:

- Aloo Cabbage
- Palak Paneer
- Chana Masala
- Tomato Dal
- Basmati Rice
- Whole Wheat Rotis
- Almond and Rice Kheer
- Khandvi
- Mango Mousse with Coconut Milk Cream.

They all thoroughly enjoyed the lunch and had a great conversation. Anita enjoyed seeing Camau with his cousin as it was clear they had a strong bond. As they were having coffee, an elderly gentleman approached the table in traditional orange robes. He was a swami, a Hindu monk.

'Namaste,' he said as he pressed his two hands together, held near his heart and gently bowed his head.

'Namaste,' both Camau and Jag responded as they also held their hands together and bowed their head.

'Namaste,' stuttered Anita as this greeting was alien to her.

Jag stood up.

'Please take my seat next to Anita,' Jag insisted to the monk.

'Camau, come with me and we will sort the bill,' Jag beckoned his cousin, who stood and followed him to the front of the restaurant where the teller was situated.

Anita was feeling a bit uneasy and unsure what to do.

'Hello, my name is Sarvajna,' the monk introduced himself to Anita.

'Hi, I am Anita.'

'Yes, I know.'

Anita realised that she had been set up by Camau.

Sarvajna took hold of both of Anita's hands and held them gently. She instantly felt a flow of energy as if she were experiencing a mild electric current.

'I have been told, and I can see, that your aura is disturbed.'

'I am sorry, but I do not know what this whole aura thing is about, and I think you are wasting your time.'

'Let me explain, just listen.'

'Okay.'

'I want you to imagine a house. A stand alone, or I think you call it detached in England. Think about the house and what it looks like on the outside and how you imagine it on the inside. Now within the framework of the house there are wires in every room, that are all connected via junctions and fuse boxes, and through which electricity flows to power all sorts of things inside the house.'

'Okay?'

'Yes, fine.'

'Normally you cannot see the wires and you can rarely, if ever, see electricity unless it causes a spark.'

'Okay?'

'Yes, fine.'

'Now imagine if you take the physical building of the house away and you are just left with the wires that would in effect look like a wire frame with the junctions and fuse boxes.'

'Yes, I get that.'

'Now I want you to pretend that you can see the electricity. All the electrons flowing around the wires in the house, faster than you can imagine, doing their work.'

'Okay?'

'Yes, fine.'

'Now I want you to imagine your body, just like the house, with a "wire frame" inside it, that carries electricity to all your organs and cells, therefore keeping you alive.'

'Okay?'

'Yes, I get that.'

'Now imagine that if you take your body away there will just be your wire frame remaining. The good thing about your wireframe is that there are only seven junctions or fuse boxes. Each one is a different colour, that happens to correspond to the colours of the rainbow, which are the colours that make up white light energy. The first one, red, is at the base of your spine, the second, orange, around your groin, the third, yellow, around your stomach, the fourth, green, around your heart, the fifth, blue, around your throat, the sixth, indigo, between your eyebrows on your forehead, and the seventh, violet, at the top of your head, your crown. It is a lot simpler than your average house. In a house these fuse boxes and junctions control the flow of electricity. If there is a problem somewhere in one of these, something will not work. Perhaps the fridge, the television or the bedroom light, and the flow of electricity, assuming you could see it would be disrupted.'

'Okay?'

'Yes, I get that.'

'So, in your body when your junctions or fuse boxes are faulty, it shows up in the flow of electricity running around your body, your aura.'

'Ah, now I get it. My aura is my personal electricity flow running around my body.'

'Exactly.'

'But sometimes that flow of electricity, or energy, can be disrupted for any number of reasons. If you are ill, at dis-ease, it will show in your aura. If you are holding some emotions or feelings in your body, without expressing them, they will block your flow and show in your aura. If you are dishonest, or lie, these will fester in your energy system and disrupt it. When your energy system does not flow at its optimum speed, your happiness is reduced, sometimes to the point of depression. Does this all makes sense, Anita?'

Anita burst into tears.

Sarvajna held her hands.

'Just let it all out,' he said gently, as he seemed to be passing his energy to her to clear her blockages, or fuse boxes.

Anita sobbed and sobbed for at least five minutes, her body convulsing, her breathing increasing in its depth. Eventually she felt a light above her head as if she were connected to some energy machine that was refuelling her.

'That is the universe, taking care of you. It is always there for you. All you need to do is ask and it shall be given.'

Sarvajna kissed her on her forehead.

'I have done a terrible thing. I embarrassed myself, my country, my colleagues, my partner, and I feel like I am living a lie here doing all of this work which looks like it is proving to be a waste of time. I am such a horrible person. I have no feelings and am frankly miserable all the time. I try to be nice to Camau and he has the patience of a saint, when I want to hold back and be sensible and serious.'

'My child. You are a daughter of the universe, which holds you dear and precious, and will do everything it can to make you happy. The past is the past. Whatever you have done, cannot be undone, so like the best souls in the world, learn from your mistakes and go on as an improved and holy being. You are special and remember that the purpose of being born into the human realm, is to refine your soul through earthly physical trials, so that when you return to the universe, your soul and your energy will vibrate at a higher level, and you will be at one with The One.'

'Let the energy of the universe flow through you and let go of all your baggage. And smile my child, you are beautiful. Your fuse boxes or chakras will work superbly.'

Anita composed herself and kissed Sarvajna's hands.

'Thank you.'

'No, thank the universe. I am just the electrician, come to fix your fuse boxes.'

Anita laughed as Camau and Jag returned. She hugged them both tightly in a group hug and whispered.

'Thank you both. I am sorry I doubted you.'

Sarvajna told Anita that Jag and Camau would be able to explain to her how to clear her own chakras herself. It was easy to do, would not cost anything and could be done anywhere. He stood up, folded his hands together and bowed.

'Namaste.'

'Namaste,' all three replied.

The Zoo

Monday, 7th February.

The meeting this morning was with the in-house team that manages the security at San Diego Zoo. The zoo is a complex environment with lots of dynamics, many of which can be unpredictable and interact with each other unexpectedly. There are thousands of species, looked after by a large team of staff and there are hundreds of thousands of human visitors annually.

Creatures escape and some of them are extremely dangerous and a threat to human life. There are incidents and accidents that need attending to, plus where there are lots of people, things always happen. The San Diego Zoo, like many others, has its own security team to deal with all these issues, and being on site means they were much better placed to respond to anything that might happen.

Anita and Camau were meeting with Capt. Angela Foscani, a former USA soldier, who had served tours in Iraq and Afghanistan, before joining the Zoo's security team as its head. Angela was forty nine and had been working at the zoo for six years, including the three prior to the tragic death of Myra Sharma.

Angela greeted Anita and Camau as they arrived at the front entrance to the zoo.

'Good morning and welcome to San Diego Zoo. Just follow me through the ticket hall and we can go to my office.'

'Good morning and thank you. I am Anita and this is Camau.'

They all shook hands.

They arrived in Jane's modern office on the ground floor which had photographs of her army days all over the walls. Behind her desk were two American Flags as tall as a person positioned in a V shape. On her desk were three mini USA flags in small holders.

'I am jealous of you having your world tour investigating all your deaths. I really miss all the international travel from when I was in the army.'

'Well, I am not sure it is as exciting as being in the army. There is just the two of us and honestly it is looking like we are on a wild goose chase. We are not really getting anywhere.'

'Yes, I am sure it is challenging. When you are in battle you generally only have one enemy but, in your case, it must be like playing three dimensional chess, in a different language and blindfolded.'

'Yes, I agree.'

'I know the types of people you are dealing with, rich, clever, and tricky. Take the characters in your spider case. A rich, international jewellery designer and her arty sister, both swanning around the world, and an insect obsessed scientist. My instincts tell me they were up to something, but I am unable to prove anything. The jewellery sister was about to be married to Oman.'

'Sorry you mean, Omar?' Anita asked.

'Well, yes, the Arab. They were going to be married, then suddenly the sister dies, the other sister inherits a fortune, and the insect doctor gets a sizeable donation for her department. Those critters.'

'You mean the spiders?'

'Yes, those critters get everywhere. The zoo does a headcount every year, which when you are counting elephants, tigers or even penguins it is always accurate. Two people can count the same critters and get answers that are often ten percent apart. The critters disappear, hide, re-appear and it is almost impossible to keep tabs on them.'

'But I thought from reading the report that the room was sealed?'

'Sealed or not, they hide in your clothes, climb down sink holes, love the air conditioning pipes. It is impossible to keep on top of them.'

'But what about the poisonous ones, like the one that killed Myra?'

'They are all the same. Nobody has died from one of those spiders since nineteen eighty one after the antivenom was discovered. We always have some stock in the fridge, but a couple of years ago in the height of summer we had a power cut and all the items in the fridges had to be thrown away, including the antivenom for the Sydney spider. We were waiting for a fresh supply from Australia, but as it takes seventy male Sydney spiders to be milked of their poison to produce the antivenom, there was a delay. We thought we had all the population of Sydney Funnel Web Spiders in one tank, but as I say they are slippery critters.'

'So do you think it is possible Myra was murdered?'

'Yes, there is a real possibility that she was, but impossible to prove. There is no evidence at all. Either the sister and the insect woman were clever, or there is nothing in it and it was just an unfortunate spider bite.'

'There were no prosecutions?'

'No, as the case would not pass the evidence threshold, the file was closed.'

'Angela, do you think Camau, and I could have a look around the insect department?'

'Of course, just follow me.'

They all went along to the Entomology department and saw what looked like millions of creatures.

'I can see how they would struggle to count all these,' Camau commented as they walked passed tank after tank, with every known species of spider and insect.

Anita and Camau started to itch all over, as the thought of the critters hitch hiking a ride in their clothes was getting to them.

'Enough?'

'Yes, I would like to go back to the hotel and have a shower.'

'Me too.'

'Angela, thank you for showing us round and explaining things to us. I can see your dilemma as it is hard to prove one's instincts.'

'Exactly,'

'Shall we go and look at the new Panda cubs that were born two months ago? They are scrumptious,' Angela suggested to change the subject.

'Perfect.'

The New Advisor

Tuesday, 8th February.

Kerem had arrived in London the previous evening, on his private jet from Mumbai, where he had been meeting with the person he had appointed to oversee his new museum in Baku. This week was the Spring season of sales in London, with the prestigious Impressionist and Modern, and Contemporary sales taking place at all three auction houses. Each house would have two evening sales and four day sales, therefore eighteen auctions during the whole week.

There was an unwritten convention that no auctions were held at the same time, therefore each house took it in turn to go first every three years. This meant that the clients had access to all the auctions and ensured a level playing field.

Kerem had arrived at Heathrow alone and passed through the exclusive VIP passport and security in a matter of seconds. Access to this service costs several thousand pounds every time it is used, but it meant that Kerem was in his chauffeur driven black Mercedes ten minutes after landing. He was in his apartment on Mount Street in Mayfair, twenty five minutes later. Kerem's family apartment in London was attached to the seven star Cornell Hotel, so it was fully serviced twenty four hours a day without the need for Kerem to maintain his own team of staff.

The apartment had three bedrooms and was decorated in a cosy English style that was timeless and elegant.

After an early morning swim in the hotel's pool, before it was opened to the regular hotel guests, Kerem had breakfast in his apartment, then after dressing took his chauffeur driven car the short distance to Mount's. Once at his auction house he went straight up to his office, which was solely for his use.

Kerem had arranged to meet Riccardo at eight o'clock to discuss the plans for his museum and how Riccardo could help. Riccardo was in town, along with all the other international auction staff for the auctions, all part of the annual migration from one set of auctions and art fairs to the next.

Riccardo was dressed immaculately in a dark navy blue Armani suit and a crisp white open neck shirt which emphasised his tan from the previous weekend's skiing on the outskirts of Zurich. Riccardo was staying in the Bridge Hotel and had arrived at the office early, finding a hot desk in the business development department on the second floor where all the visiting staff based themselves. This large office had over twenty hot desks in two rows as well as the regular desks for the permanent members of staff who worked there.

He was the first one in the department this morning, as early starts and business development are mutually exclusive. The excuse being that most of the staff worked long into the evening entertaining clients and there was no need to start early in the morning. As the Head of the Department believed this, all her juniors followed suit.

Riccardo took the lift to the sixth floor and knocked on Kerem's office door just before eight o'clock. The office was basic, with a mahogany three part pedestal desk, a dark green swivel leather chair, a dark brown chesterfield sofa, and an oval oak meeting table with six chairs around it. There was no art on the walls as they were all panelled in oak, matching the meeting table.

'Good morning Riccardo. How are you?'

'Good morning. I am great and you?'

'Yes, I am good and looking forward to the auctions this week. I will only be attending the two important Mount's evening sales.'

'Of course.'

'Take a seat at the table over there, then we can discuss the plans for my new museum.'

Riccardo took a seat at the meeting table and waited for Kerem to join him.

'Before we start Kerem, can I just mention something?'

'Of course.'

'The other day I had breakfast in the hotel across the road and because it was so busy, I was asked to share a table with another guest. It turned out that the guy works for the Art Squad.'

'Who the hell are they?'

'It is a department within the Metropolitan police, here in London, that investigates crimes involving art, and they are looking into the deaths of some people whose collections were sold at auction over the last five years.'

'Why would they do that?'

'Apparently they have been analysing the sales and profits of all three auction houses and seem to think that Mount's is doing way better than the other two.'

'God, those idiot police. Of course, Mount's is better. We employ the best people, and they provide the best service as I keep telling everyone. Balfour's are focused on being green and Seton's is focused on selling sneakers and handbags on line. It is no wonder we are doing better.'

'So, nothing to worry about?'

'Nothing. Now let us get down to business.'

'I just met last week in Mumbai with the advisor that I have appointed to help oversee the museum. She is a professor of Islamic arts and a collector herself. She is proposing that we follow a timeline from the earliest known human settlements in Azerbaijan to the present day and to display their art and design in a chronological sequence. I am funding the museum so that it can purchase everything that it needs to make this happen.'

Riccardo looked unfazed.

'Kerem, sorry but that is not going to be exciting. I understand that you want to build a world class museum that represents the vibrancy and creativity of Azerbaijan. Displaying everything in a timeline sequence is totally boring.'

Kerem was stunned.

'I suggest that you present everything in themes that look visually attractive, stimulates discussion and debate, and makes a powerful statement. For example, you could group objects according to colour, to material, to the tools used, by who created them, or themes of relationships, power, warfare, peace, magic, stories, or morals,' Riccardo finished, half expecting to be fired.

'That is fantastic. That is what I want, a totally unique museum which is unlike any other in the world. I agree with you that so many museums simply lay out their artefacts by timeline. I am done with that.'

'Riccardo, I want you to be an advisor for my museum.'

Kerem stood and went to his desk to pick up his mobile phone. He pressed speed dial and after a couple of rings the call was answered.

'This is Kerem Akbarov here. You are fired.'

'Who was that?'

'The ex-advisor of my museum. I want you to work up your ideas and then we can meet in Baku in a couple of weeks to go through them.'

'Sure, of course.'

'And Riccardo, come back here at five tonight for our little arrangement, before the auction starts at seven.'

'Yes, boss.'

Riccardo went back to his hot desk, still reeling from the conversation he had just had. His mind was exploding with ideas and how was he ever going to fit everything in. He called his boyfriend Stephan and explained what had just happened.

'That sounds great,' Stephan enthused. 'Well done, I am really proud of you, you will be fantastic.'

'Thanks, that means a lot.'

By three o'clock the business development area was buzzing with phones ringing, people talking and others tapping away on their keyboards. The intensity of an evening sale builds up throughout the day as the auction staff frantically try to secure bids from clients.

Just after quarter past three, Ursula entered the room after returning from her lunch and greeted Riccardo. Immaculate as ever from the front in a Chanel toffee pink two piece suit, she unfortunately looked a little different from behind and sideways on. Her coiffured helmet hair was as flat as a pancake against the back of her head. Clearly, she had been having a lunch date lying on her back. Riccardo wondered to himself, what was she up to? She often had meetings when she would slip away for an hour or two. Obviously, she was having an affair. But who with?

Just Life

Wednesday, 9th February.

The flight to Sydney had been another long journey. Anita and Camau had left San Diego the previous day at eight in the morning for the just over six hour flight to Honolulu. They had to wait an hour and a half for their connection, and Camau regretted that they had not included a night in Hawaii. He decided not to mention this to Anita as she would undoubtedly tell him that they were on a business, not pleasure trip.

Once again in first class they flew to Sydney, arriving in the evening after a ten and a half hour flight. Although several of their flights had been long, the luxury of flying first class meant that the time passed quickly. Sumptuous meals, endless films to watch, and plenty of space to walk around including sitting on high stools at the bar. To cap it all there was the ultimate pleasure of having a shower on board in one of the two huge bathrooms. This was one of the highlights of the whole trip. All that Anita could think of when she was having a shower, is what would she do if there was any turbulence and she would have to return to her seat immediately, naked and dripping wet through, in order to fasten her seat belt. She was pleased to note that in the bathroom there was a bench and a seat belt.

Although the airlines would never admit it, the quality of air at the front of the plane is far superior to that at the back. There is more oxygen up front and a lack of it at the back which induces sleep to keep everyone calm. When passengers disembark after a first class trip they are never exhausted or looking like they have just come out of a tumble dryer.

Once Anita had finished watching her second film she asked Camau how she could clear her own chakras as Sarvajna has suggested.

'Ah, it is easy. Lie down, or relax in a chair, preferably in a reclining position. Close your eyes, relax your body, and hold your thumbs and forefingers together.'

'Why?'

'It improves the flow of energy around your body. Now focus on your first chakra at the base of your spine. Imagine it is red, a spinning red crystal filling your body with red energy. Allow yourself to be completely transformed by the red energy for a minute. Next, move to the orange chakra around your groin. Now imagine it is an orange crystal and do the same, then you move onto your yellow chakra around your stomach, then green around your chest, blue around your throat, indigo on your forehead and finally violet at the top of your head. You can also imagine white light, and shimmering gold flecks flowing down into your body. You will be totally relaxed and may fall asleep.'

'Is that all there is to it?'

'Yes that is it. It is a simple, but powerful technique. Try it now. Recline your seat, pop on the sleep mask, and relax.'

Ten minutes later, Anita was fast asleep.

Anita and Camau left the plane looking as fresh as a daisy, and after getting through passport control and customs, they were met by Juliet who had finished the run of her play, was taking some time out to be with Anita, and of course to get married.

Anita and Juliet hugged and kissed each other, then Camau was introduced by Anita to Juliet.

'Welcome to Australia and lovely to meet you,' Juliet said as she embraced and kissed Camau twice on the cheek.

'I will just pay the parking ticket then we can go to the house and have drinks and dinner.'

Juliet had rented a beautiful white modernist house overlooking Sydney harbour, with views of the Opera House. It had three bedrooms, all en-suite, so there was plenty of space for Camau to stay.

'When we get to the house, I will fire up the barby, grab us some tinnies and we can have dinner and enjoy the evening.'

'Sounds perfect darling.'

'I will leave you two alone as I am sure you have lots to talk about. You do not want me being a gooseberry,' Camau stated as he sat in the rear of the convertible.

'Utter nonsense, Camau. I have lived with Juliet for twenty years; we have been speaking twice a day whilst we have been travelling and I insist on you joining us for dinner.'

'Yes, I agree totally.'

'Okay, I just do not want to be in the way.'

The journey to the house was around thirty minutes and when they arrived Juliet showed Camau to his room, which had its own private balcony overlooking the bay. Anita and Juliet disappeared to their room for some intimate private time. A few minutes later Juliet came down to the main patio, followed by Anita, switched on the gas barbeque then took three cans of cold lager from the fridge.

It was already dark, but the harbour lights twinkled and danced on the water's surface.

'It is beautiful here,' Anita said as she drank her beer.

'Yes, it is, and it is close to the location where we will be getting married on Monday.'

'May I ask why are you getting married on a Monday? It seems a strange day to me.'

'Because it is the fourteenth, Valentine's day.'

'Ah, okay I get it.'

'We have the meeting with the police department on Friday, then after the wedding we have a couple of days in Sydney before we fly onto Beijing for our next investigation, on Thursday. Juliet is going to teach some acting masterclasses at Sydney Drama School for a month, then will join us in Egypt for our honeymoon Nile cruise.'

'Sounds wonderful.' Camau had decided he would spend the time in Egypt exploring the country and perhaps go to Hurghada on the Red Sea.

'Tomorrow, Anita and I have an appointment at the wedding store to select our outfits, then in the evening we will be joined for dinner by Nisha, who will be our second witness, along with you.'

'Perfect. I will go and sort out my outfit as well. I have been researching on the internet and have decided what to wear to honour you. They are going to make it to my exact measurements in twenty four hours.'

'Impressive,' Juliet said as she gave an approving look to Anita.

'Yes, Camau is a wonderful man. He is delightful, resourceful, thoughtful, and caring. Throughout this trip he has made me a better person.'

'Now steady on Anita,' Camau said as he tried to stop Anita from being so effusive.

'It is true.'

After a wonderful barbeque, they continued their conversations.

'So how was your play?' Camau asked Juliet.

'It has been a huge success. It was a new play by the Irish playwright, Ron Brown, which was extremely funny. It dealt with international stereotypes of people, eventually debunking them all, and concluding that people are really the same all over the world. Nisha, who you will meet tomorrow played an Indian Maharajah's daughter and absolutely stole the show. She lives in England and will be going to drama school in London next September.'

'And how are your investigations going?'

'Truthfully, a bit frustrating.'

'We have investigated six deaths now, the first one in Iceland, two in New York, one in each of the Everglades, Jackson Hole and San Diego. All the deaths look like accidents, but they could also be murder. We have had deaths by hypothermia, pushed in front of a train, an old lady who was a hundred, a "gator" snatch, a fall out of a balloon and a nasty Australian spider in California. There are no consistent patterns that we can identify, all the causes of death are different and generally there are lots of people involved. Either we are dealing with some extremely sophisticated people, or it is just life.'

'Well, on that note, I am going to bed. Good night both.'

'And make sure you both get some sleep if you know what I mean.'

Anita and Juliet just looked at each other.

The Outfits

Thursday, 10th February.

Anita and Juliet had an appointment at the wedding store at ten in the morning. They had both discussed what they wanted to wear for their wedding and agreed upon wearing floor length white culottes with a white blouse and a long white, almost ankle length jacket. They would both wear the same outfits, as they did not want to dress like a straight couple, with one in a suit and one in a dress. They would both look elegant and equal.

They attended the appointment, selected their outfits, which required a little adjusting, and would be ready to collect on Sunday morning.

Camau went to downtown Sydney for his appointment to be measured for his outfit. He selected exactly what he wanted and was promised that it would be ready the following afternoon. He called his mother in Nairobi who transferred the money instantly to his account so he could settle the bill.

Soul Mates

Thursday, 10th February.

Dinner was arranged for seven thirty at one of the coolest restaurants in Sydney, The Harbour View. Juliet had booked the table weeks ago as there was always a long waiting list. Anita, Juliet and Camau were all dressed in blue jeans with white shirts and when they arrived by an Uber, they entered the Brazilian restaurant. The inside was like a tropical rain forest, with faux vegetation everywhere and the faint sound of jungle sounds piped throughout. They were escorted to the terrace bar by a tall, skinny woman with the shortest skirt and longest legs, to wait for Nisha to arrive.

Anita caught sight of Juliet looking the girl up and down.

They perused the drinks menu, and all agreed that they would each have a Death Flip, an Australian cocktail that combines blanco tequila, yellow chartreuse, jägermeister, simple syrup, and a whole egg, garnished with freshly grated nutmeg.

The bartender brought over the three cocktails and Juliet toasted, to murder or life. Camau thought that Juliet clearly had a wicked sense of humour.

'Here is Nisha,' Juliet waved as she put her drink down on the table.

Nisha was of Indian heritage, twenty two, five feet three and ravishingly beautiful. She had perfect skin, long black hair, dark eyes and was dressed in a bright yellow cotton catsuit and flat yellow pumps.

Camau stood up to greet Nisha and that was it. He looked at her and realised in that instant that she was his soul mate. The feeling was overwhelmingly powerful, and he just stared at her. Nisha felt the same and smiled at Camau.

'I have always known you, and once again we have found each other.'

Camau kissed her twice on the cheek and they both sat down.

'What is going on here?'

'We Indians believe in reincarnation and when you find the other half of your soul there is no need to say anything. You simply know. Nisha and I have always been together and always will be. That is right, is it not?'

'Yes, that is true.'

'Wow. Well would you like a drink, Nisha?'

'Yes, please. I will have a Sydney Sunrise Sunshine.'

This is a light, non-alcoholic cocktail made with fresh orange juice, lime juice, honey, and an egg. Juliet called the waiter over and ordered the drink for Nisha. When it arrived Juliet toasted, to us. They chatted about the success of the play, the investigations into the various deaths, the upcoming masterclasses that Juliet would be running with Nisha assisting, and of course the arrangements for Monday's ceremony. Camau and Nisha were glued to each other, and at the dinner table sat side by side, seemingly edging closer together with each course. They had a wonderful tasting menu of:

- Watermelon mousseline with cucumber essence
- Scallop ceviche with pickled lime and hazelnut
- Tuna tartare with chipotle chili
- John Dory with black fried crispy onions
- Slow roasted suckling pig with honey glaze
- Duck breast with warm plum and vodka sauce
- Ginger and mandarin panna cotta
- Rich dark chocolate tartlet with a light whisky cream foam.

Each course was paired with an appropriate Australian wine and to finish the meal they had a cold press coffee liqueur.

'Darling, this is a wonderful restaurant, and the food is out of this world. I feel so lucky to be here and in such wonderful company.'

'You really have changed. You were always so worried about spending money and holding yourself back. This trip has done you a world of good, even if you cannot find any murderers.'

'All down to Camau, but I think he is now occupied with something else,' Anita said as she winked at Juliet.

Juliet paid the bill, ordered two Ubers and they all went to wait in reception. Anita pulled Juliet back a little, so that Camau and Nisha could be alone for a few moments. Camau put his arm around Nisha, and they kissed just as her Uber arrived to take her back to her rented apartment in the city.

'We have all got to work tomorrow, but on Saturday we can all meet for brunch, then come back to the house and spend the day by the pool, if that works for everyone?'

'Perfect,' they all agreed.

Nisha left, and the second Uber arrived. Once in the car Anita asked Camau if he was alright.

'I am perfect. I am going to marry Nisha and spend the rest of my life with her.'

The Actress

Friday, 11th February.

After breakfast, Anita and Camau refreshed themselves about the case of The Actress.

Sophia Lazzarini was an Italian actress, who was playing in a long running Australian television soap opera, set in the outback. Although she was born in a small village, Jesolo Paese, in the province of Veneto in Italy she had emigrated to Australia when her father took a job as a chef in Sydney in the late nineteen sixties.

She had an early break in her acting career with the soap opera and had spent thirty five years playing the same character. Most of the filming was done in the studio in Sydney but twice a year, to support the local tourist board, filming took place on a set at Broken Hill in the outback so they could encourage tourists to visit. Broken Hill is a mining city, in New South Wales known as the Silver City, as it is situated on one of the world's richest deposits of silver, lead, and zinc ores. It has a community college, hospitals, shops, and hotels and is the base for a Royal Flying Doctor Service clinic. All these provided story lines for the soap opera. It has a hot desert climate and is located over seven hundred miles west of Sydney.

Sophia was the leading lady of the show and had earned a lot of money through her acting career, but also through sponsorships and advertising. Everybody in Australia felt that they knew her, and her Australian Italian accent was adored and instantly recognisable. She endorsed anything and everything from pro-biotic yoghurts to long distance truck tyres, from campaigns to save the koala bears to having her own perfume range on the main Australian shopping channel, BMN, which stood for Buy Me Now.

As she was approaching her late fifties, her personal life was increasingly troubled as her husband, Peter Lazzarini, had taken up with a younger actress, who had emigrated to Australia from Croatia. She was incensed that if they divorced, she could lose half of her assets, particularly as he was a two bit actor and hardly had any jobs on the go.

After filming for two weeks on the set in Broken Hill, Sophia was relieved to be driving back home to Sydney. She had done this journey many times and liked the solitude of driving alone, as it gave her time to relax, decompress and forget all the pressures of holding a show together. The journey was around eleven hours, and she would stop halfway for the night and to refuel.

On the trip when she died, she had left Broken Hill about ten in the morning and was cruising along comfortably when her car started to splutter and eventually came to a halt. She was literally in the middle of nowhere. She struggled to understand what had happened, as she always had her car serviced and made sure that the petrol tank was full before she left. As best she could, she checked the petrol tank several times, but it was empty. She could not see any holes in the tank, so was mystified.

There are a few petrol stations on route, but these are few and far between. The time was approaching just after one in the afternoon and the sun was fierce, as the temperature rose. It was already forty one degrees centigrade and would climb higher. There were no other vehicles passing by, but she was sure she had seen a petrol station about fifteen minutes ago, so that would be about fifteen to twenty miles away.

She decided that she would walk to the station and get help. She took her handbag, mobile phone, and the litre bottle of water that she always carried. She remembered that the road had curved gently to the right, so she reckoned that it would be much faster if she cut across the desert rather than sticking to the road, and she calculated this would save her at least thirty per cent of the journey. She worked out that she would be at the petrol station in three hours if she walked briskly.

She started to walk across the desert as she planned, as the heat intensified. After about thirty minutes, she sat down on a rock to have a drink of water, and put the bottle down next to her. She checked her mobile phone, to see if there was any reception. She waved it around as she could see one bar, but as she did so, she knocked the bottle of water over and because she had not put the top back on, the water spilt out and disappeared into the barren desert. She managed to grab the bottle and save some water but almost half had already gone.

She carried on walking and quickly ran out of the water as she constantly took small sips. The temperature rose to fifty degrees, and she became disorientated. Her body was found by an outback rancher four days later. She had died of exposure and dehydration.

Her estate sold at Mount's in twenty sixteen and raised fifty five million dollars.

Anita, Juliet and Camau had breakfast sitting on the terrace as it was a beautiful morning with clear blue skies and a gentle breeze. They ate scrambled eggs, fresh croissants, that Juliet had bought earlier from the nearby French bakery, accompanied by freshly squeezed orange juice and strong black coffee.

'So, I am going to the drama school this morning with Nisha to start planning the classes and will be back around six. Shall I ask Nisha to come back for dinner?'

Camau smiled. 'Yes please.'

'Great. And you can cook Chinese.'

Anita and Camau had an appointment this morning with the Chief Superintendent of the New South Wales Police, Jason Thompson. Sophia's death was a national tragedy and there was a period of national mourning for her. Also, the manner of her death attracted a huge amount of media attention, and the internet was rife with conspiracy theories.

Jason had been a police officer for twenty five years and had risen up the ranks. He was six feet four inches tall, well built, tanned, still with natural blond hair and enjoyed the outdoor life in Australia. He had been a state surf board champion when he was eighteen but decided to follow his career in the police and continued to surf as a hobby.

His parents had emigrated to Australia from Scotland, in the early nineteen eighties, when he was a small boy. He still retained his Scottish accent blended with his Australian one. He had always lived in, and around Sydney and was well respected by his colleagues and the public at large. He had an easy going manner and was firm, but fair.

Anita and Camau had read all the background information about Sophia's case and had a few questions for Jason. They arrived at New South Wales Police headquarters, which is on Charles Street, and were immediately shown in to Jason's office which was basic, but adequate, with a metal desk and hi-backed leather chair for Jason, and several plastic chairs for guests.

'G'day and welcome to Sydney.'

'Good morning and nice to meet you,' Anita replied as she shook Jason's hand and introduced Camau.

'Please take a seat. Some iced tea?'

'Lovely, we had coffee that was far too strong this morning.'

'We basically have two questions for you. How did Sophia run out of petrol? Why did she walk in the opposite direction to the petrol station nearby?'

'Sophia filled her car up with petrol on the morning she left. We have the details from the garage and her bank. She purchased about half a tank of petrol, so presumably the tank must have been half full when she topped it up. The car was in perfect working order and had actually been serviced whilst she was filming in Broken Hill. When we found the car, the petrol tank was empty and when we did tests the petrol gauge was working perfectly, so we are at a loss to understand what happened. We have examined the car, done forensic analyses but have found nothing. It really is a mystery.'

'Could the petrol have evaporated in the heat?'

'We thought of that, but the tank was intact with no holes, so that is not a possible cause.'

'And why did she walk away from the petrol station that was only a few miles away?'

'After you pass the petrol station we are talking about, the road makes a long gentle curve to the right. It is almost impossible to see as the road looks straight. What we think is that when Sophia got out of her car and looked back to where she had come from, her natural instincts were to go right. Most people prefer to go right when given a choice, it is just a natural phenomenon. So, she walked right which was in exactly the opposite direction to the petrol station, she ran out of water in the desert, and I am afraid the heat took its toll. When her body was discovered several days later, the dingoes had been at her, it was not a pretty sight.'

'And then her estate was sold at Mount's and her husband pocketed the fifty five million dollars.'

'Yes, it was a sensational auction because of her fame.'

'And the husband? Where was he?'

'He was out of the country in Dubrovnik, Croatia, with his new girlfriend so he could not possibly be involved.'

'Seems that once again we have another accidental death.'

'Yes, I would agree. The outback is a dangerous place.'

'But we still do not understand why a full tank of petrol would in effect disappear.'

'Yes, I agree. A total mystery,' Jason agreed with resignation in his voice.

The Wedding

Monday, 14th February.

Anita's and Juliet's wedding took place at three in the afternoon in the nearby Tree Cathedral. This was an outdoor natural church created by two rows of tall, old trees whose canopies had grown and been shaped together to form a natural roof. It was located in a pristine nature reserve. Where an altar would have been in a traditional church there was simply an open view towards the Blue Mountains.

The celebrant, Kylie, was fifty five, an Australian of Greek heritage and wore a pale blue dress. She stood facing Anita and Juliet, dressed as they had planned, with Camau and Nisha standing behind them. Camau was dressed in a stunning royal blue sherwani, embroidered with gold motifs, and Nisha wore a traditional sari in emerald green and gold. They both held hands, as did Anita and Juliet.

'My name is Kylie, and I have the privilege of performing this ceremony today. On behalf of Anita and Juliet, welcome and thank you for being here. They are thrilled that you are here today to share in their joy, during this wonderful moment in their lives.'

'By your presence, you celebrate with them the love they have discovered in each other, and you support their decision to commit themselves to one another for the rest of their lives. The greatest happiness of life is the conviction that we are loved, loved for ourselves. If there is anything better than being loved, it is loving. This afternoon we are here to celebrate love. We come together to witness and proclaim the joining together of these two people in marriage.'

'This is the union of two individuals in heart, body, mind, and spirit. Therefore, marriage is not to be entered into lightly, but reverently, honestly, and deliberately. And it is into this union that Anita and Juliet come now to be joined.'

'Anita, you have chosen Juliet to be your life partner. Will you love and respect her? Will you be honest with her always? Will you stand by her through whatever may come?'

Anita answered, 'I will.'

'Juliet, you have chosen Anita to be your life partner. Will you love and respect her? Will you be honest with her always? Will you stand by her through whatever may come?'

Juliet answered, 'I will.'

'And do you both promise to make the necessary adjustments in your personal lives, in order that you may live in a harmonious relationship together?'

They both answered, 'We do.'

'Now in the spirit of joy and affirmation, I want to ask your witnesses here present. Do you give Anita and Juliet your blessing and support this day, wishing them a wonderful life together?'

Camau and Nisha answered, 'We do.'

'Anita and Juliet, now we come to your vows. May I remind you that saying your vows are one thing, but nothing is more challenging than living them day-by-day. What you promise today must be renewed tomorrow, and each day that stretches out before you. Will you now please turn and face each other and hold hands, looking at each other.'

'Anita, please repeat after me. In the presence of our witnesses, I Anita, choose you Juliet, to be my life partner, to have and to hold from this day forward, for better, for worse, for richer, for poorer, in sickness and in health, in joy and in sorrow, to love and to cherish, and to be faithful to you alone. This is my solemn vow.'

'Now Juliet, please repeat after me. In the presence of our witnesses, I Juliet, choose you Anita, to be my life partner, to have and to hold from this day forward, for better, for worse, for richer, for poorer, in sickness and in health, in joy and in sorrow, to love and to cherish, and to be faithful to you alone. This is my solemn vow.'

Kylie asked, 'May I have the rings please?'

Camau and Nisha produced one ring each.

'Anita, I give you this ring, that you may wear it, as a symbol of the vows we have made this day. I pledge you my love, and respect, my laughter, and my tears. With all that I am, I honour you.'

'Juliet, I give you this ring, that you may wear it, as a symbol of the vows we have made this day. I pledge you my love, and respect, my laughter, and my tears. With all that I am, I honour you.'

'Now may those who wear these rings live in love all their days. Now may the love, which has brought you together, continue to grow and enrich your lives. May you continue to meet with courage any problems, which may arise to challenge you. May your relationship always be one of love and trust. May the happiness you share today be with you always. And may everything you have said and done here today become a living truth in your lives.'

'Anita and Juliet, we have heard your promise to share your lives in marriage. We recognise and respect the covenant you have made here this day before each one of us as witnesses. Therefore, in the honesty and sincerity of what you have said and done here today and by the power vested in me by the State of New South Wales, it is my honour and delight to declare you married and partners in life…for life.'

'You may seal your vows with a kiss.'

Anita and Juliet kissed, and Camau and Nisha did the same.

'It is now my personal privilege and great joy to be the first one to introduce Anita and Juliet as a newly married couple. Please greet them warmly.'

Everyone kissed and hugged each other several times, followed by thirty minutes of taking photographs amongst the stunning scenery.

During the service, two catering staff had arrived in separate cars and set up a dining table for four, a couple of hundred yards to the right of the cathedral. The celebrant left and the four of them enjoyed a glass or two of champagne and a meal of chilled oysters with vinegar, lemon juice and capers, a lobster and crab salad with mango and pineapple, followed by brandy infused strawberries dipped in dark, bitter chocolate served with vanilla ice cream topped with real gold foil. They drank Australian chardonnay and finished with a one hundred year old whisky.

By the time they had finished the meal, the sun was setting, and it was time to go home. One of the staff took Anita and Juliet back to their house and the other took Camau home with Nisha to her apartment, as they had agreed to leave Anita and Juliet alone for a couple of days.

On to Asia

Thursday, 17th February.

Anita and Juliet had spent the last two days holed up in their house enjoying some quality time together. Since arriving back from their wedding on Monday evening they had not left the house but spent the time lounging around the pool, relaxing, eating, and drinking, and of course having wonderful sensual sex. Having made their marriage vows, their love had grown and become more mysterious by the day. Both Anita and Juliet felt different, renewed, refreshed, lighter and deeply happy. They both knew they would have to get back to work today but were looking forward to their proper honeymoon in Egypt in just over three weeks' time.

Camau and Nisha had spent the last two days together as young lovers. They explored each other's bodies and made passionate love, rekindling what they both knew and felt was their ancient bond. Camau asked Nisha to marry him, and she said yes. Of course, she would have to finish her studies at drama school in London, but they agreed they would live together once back in the UK. Each had spoken to their respective parents, who were all taken aback at the speed of their romance, but they trusted their children and supported them wholeheartedly.

Anita ordered a taxi to take her and Juliet to the airport, and to pick up Camau and Nisha on the way. The flight to Shanghai from Sydney would leave at midday. At the security gates there were hugs, kisses, and tears as Anita and Camau left for the next stage of their trip. Camau would have to wait until he was back home before he would see Nisha again.

Settled in first class, the flight would be ten and a half hours, arriving in Shanghai in the early evening. They had to spend the night at the airport as the connecting flight to Beijing was at seven in the morning. They stayed in an airport hotel, located in the terminal. All these sorts of hotels are the same wherever they are in the world. Functional, but sterile, and only acceptable for a one night stay. They ate in the hotel restaurant, hardly saw any natural light, and retired early to read up on their next case.

Tea

Friday, 18th February.

The flight landed at Beijing airport at nine twenty in the morning. After getting through passport control and customs they took a taxi to the Beijing Grand Hotel, which took about ninety minutes, as the traffic was bumper to bumper. They arrived at the luxury hotel which was located in the top thirty floors of a sixty floor block, checked in and went to their rooms. The rooms were spacious and luxurious, but the views were obscured by the grey cloud of pollution that covered the city and made it look like dusk.

They agreed to meet for lunch at twelve thirty in the hotel's restaurant and had a fabulous Chinese meal with yellow tea.

'Because of the flight timings, we have a couple of days here in Beijing before our meeting on Monday with the Head of Security at The Forbidden City. We can be tourists for the weekend and see the sites.'

'Yes, I am looking forward to that. I have never been to Beijing before.'

'But you are Chinese.'

'I am actually Chinglish, half Chinese and half English, but I was born in Hong Kong, and I have never been to mainland China.'

Camau decided to make a suggestion for the weekend.

'I think we should just look around the city this afternoon, after the long journey, then tomorrow we can visit The Forbidden City, and on Sunday The Great Wall of China.'

'Great. It is cold here, so we had better wrap up well.'

'I agree. Thankfully, we have our trusted hi-tech coats and Icelandic jumpers.'

After lunch they left the hotel and walked around the city area close by. In some respects, it was just like the luxury district in any other city. There were large stores for all the major Western fashion brands, but interestingly they both noticed that there were no customers in any of the shops.

'Perhaps they just have to have a flagship store presence in Beijing to be able to do business on line in China.'

'Possibly.'

'This looks fascinating.'

'Shall we go in here?'

'Yes, I agree.'

Anita and Camau entered a traditional looking building which stood out from the modern fashion stores that looked as though it housed a market. It was decorated in classic Chinese style with lots of dragon motifs and bright colours. Once inside they saw there were several floors and many shops located on each one. Soon they realised that every shop was selling exactly the same thing, tea. All the shops were staffed and had open sacks of tea leaves and various different coloured packs of tea.

'How can this be commercially viable?'

'I have no idea, but I think we should have a quick look around and leave quietly before anyone notices us.'

They entered a shop, and that was it. They spent the next two hours and forty five minutes, tasting several different types of tea and having each one explained to them in detail. As the vendors, all three of them, discovered that Anita spoke Mandarin, the sales pitch extended to a potted history of China from two thousand and seventy BC to the present. Every time Anita indicated that she would buy some tea, another three or four varieties were brought out, solemnly brewed, and had to be tasted. As the time was approaching five in the afternoon, Anita informed the vendors that they had to go to the airport to catch a flight, so could they buy some tea, wish them health and happiness and be on their way.

The tactic worked, but Anita and Camau each left with a large selection box of fifty teas that was the size of a small suitcase and cost them each the equivalent of two hundred and sixteen pounds.

Camau was adamant. 'We are going back to the hotel and staying in. Now I know how that place is commercially viable.'

'And we will have to have these packs of tea sent back home by DHL.'

The Forbidden City

Saturday, 19th February.

After the tea experience, Anita had agreed with Camau that they would go on an organised trip to visit The Forbidden City. The hotel concierge arranged it and after parting with another fifty pounds each, they found themselves on a luxury coach with thirty other international English speaking tourists at ten thirty in the morning. The Chinese guide, Sky, was a Beijing resident born and bred, aged twenty eight, spoke perfect English and explained everything clearly and easily.

'This is much more relaxing and informative than the tea vendors,' Camau said with relief in his voice.

'I agree.'

Sky continued.

'The Forbidden City was the Chinese Imperial Palace of twenty four Emperors from the Ming to the Qing Dynasty. It was built over fourteen years in the fifteenth century and required a million workers to complete it. It is the largest, and best-preserved collection of ancient buildings in China. It covers an area of seven hundred and twenty thousand square meters, has nine hundred and eighty buildings with eight thousand, seven hundred and four rooms. It is contained within a ten meter high city wall with a fifty two meter wide moat. On each of the four sides there are huge gates.'

'The palaces are decorated mainly in yellow, symbolising respect, and red symbolising the Emperor's hope of national stability. There are many mythical animals including dragons, phoenix, lions, elephants, and turtles. Dragons represent the Emperor, and the Phoenix represents the Empress.'

'Common people were not allowed to enter the Forbidden City freely and officials were only allowed access to certain parts. Only The Emperor had free access everywhere. The Forbidden City is mainly divided into two parts: the southern Outer Court (or Front Court) which was used for ceremonial purposes such as the enthronement of the Crown Prince, the Emperor's birthday, imperial marriage ceremonies and official business. The northern Inner Court (or Back Palace) was the residence of the Emperor and or Empress and used for day-to-day affairs of state.'

'There are over one and a half million items displayed in the City's museum, including ceramics, paintings, bronze ware, timepieces, jade, and an eclectic mix of fascinating palace artifacts. There are no trees or birds in the City, and the large bronze pots that are dotted around were filled with water in case of fire.'

'The palaces known as the Cold Palaces were where concubines and princes who fell out of favour with the Emperor lived.'

Like our back bedroom when the video came to light, Anita thought to herself.

The four hour walking tour visited Tiananmen Square, The Mausoleum of Mao Zedong, The Forbidden City Palace Museum, The Hall of Union, The Hall of Great Harmony, The Hall of Preserving Harmony and The Imperial Garden of The Palace Museum.

'This was mind blowing,' Camau said to Anita as they got back on to the coach.

'Yes, it is. This is one of the greatest treasures on earth and highlights how ancient Chinese history and culture is.'

'Just like India.'

'I find it difficult to see how Ehuang Zhang died here. I did not see any wells. Did you?'

'No.'

Bits and Bobs

Sunday, 20th February.

This morning Anita and Camau had booked a trip to see The Great Wall of China at Mutianyu. The group was smaller, around seventeen people as they joined the coach for the hour's drive through the outskirts of Beijing. The weather was awful, raining, grey, drizzly, foggy, and damp.

'Looks just like London,' Camau joked.

'Yes, it does, but the traffic here is unbelievable and the pollution unbearable. I have a feeling in my throat that I just want to clear, but I cannot. Plus, when you look at many of the houses, they are really just shacks with corrugated iron rooves and satellite dishes attached.'

'All very sobering I know, but the shanty towns in Kenya and many of the villages in India are far worse.'

Anita changed the subject.

'I was thinking last night about where the well is, that Ehuang Zhang fell into and drowned. It must be somewhere in The Forbidden City that we did not see.'

'Hopefully, our meeting tomorrow will reveal the facts.'

'We are here now.'

At the entrance and ticket area to The Great Wall of China, there was a huge car and coach park that was practically deserted. There were around fifteen closed ticket offices with only one open and staffed. There was a grim looking café with a few dishevelled tourists standing outside, all wrapped in those cheap plastic, useless, disposable raincoats. They were standing under a large wooden canopy, clearly waiting for their return transport. It was raining heavily, and the cloud base had descended, so that the Great Wall was shrouded and covered in mist.

'Everybody follow me. I will get the tickets and then we can walk along the wall to the main tower over there,' the tour guide announced.

'Shall we just stand on the wall, take a photograph, and then go and get a coffee? Or perhaps they have tea?'

'Yes.'

All the other tourists in the group did the same thing. They stood on the wall, took photographs for their social media profiles, although it looked like they were actually standing on a cloud, then had a drink. The tour guide realised that the trip was not going well, so offered them a free trip to a nearby museum which would be indoors.

They all agreed enthusiastically.

When everyone was back on the coach, the guide explained that they were going to visit the tomb and museum of Tian Yi, who had served three Ming Dynasty Emperors, and that they would arrive in a few minutes.

Everybody was buzzing with excitement.

As they approached the museum Anita could see some trees in the distance with large fruits hanging from the trees' branches.

'OMG, there they are. There really are low hanging fruit. So, it is not all jargon after all.'

Camau looked at her.

'They are just jackfruits,' he said shaking his head.

What the guide failed to mention, was that Tian Yi was a eunuch, and the museum was the world's only museum dedicated to the history and life of eunuchs.

The museum contained a graphic collection of surgical instruments, and a life size sculpture of the necessary operation, with the poor boy being held down by two men, whilst the operation was performed by another. All the nine year old boy's bits and bobs were removed, and a spring onion inserted into the urethra, with the only anaesthetic used being chilli paste, according to the signs explaining what was going on. The bits and bobs were kept in a jar, and if the eunuch left imperial service, they were returned to him as severance pay.

'That puts severance pay into perspective. I think I would rather go back to the tea market.'

'Me too,' agreed Anita.

Once back in the hotel, having recovered from their rather gruesome trip, and after a late lunch, they decided to read the briefing pack about Ehuang Zhang.

Ehuang Zhang was one of the most prominent Chinese contemporary artists of her generation and was only thirty seven years old when she died. Her grandparents, on both sides, had emigrated to Madrid, just after the second world war and jointly opened and ran a successful Chinese restaurant. Her parents were both born in Madrid, and they eventually took over the restaurant from their respective parents. Ehuang was born in nineteen eighty five and it soon became apparent that she was a gifted artist, even as a child. She won many school and local art competitions and eventually went to study at The Madrid Academy of Art.

As a young woman she became increasingly interested in politics and Chinese history, and decided she wanted to become a member of the Chinese communist party. Her art career was flourishing as she combined historical Chinese art techniques with communist philosophy. In particular she created huge works of traditional calligraphy in vivid colours that promoted communist thoughts, values, and sayings.

Her work was in huge demand, and she was fêted all over the world. Her art soon started to sell on the secondary market at auction, and the prices rose inexorably. She married a film star from South Korea, Sook Zhang, who had made the transition from a wildly popular teenage pop group to be the leading actor of his generation, but whose star was fading as he aged.

Ehuang decided to take a year off and to study the history of China. Although of Chinese heritage, she had never visited the country before and started her year off by a solo trip to Beijing to see, and start to understand Chinese history.

Through her connections in the art world, she managed to secure a place on an exclusive tour of The Forbidden City, that went into the private quarters of the Emperors, that the general paying public never got to see. Only a handful of people got to see these rooms, that were deep inside the Palace. There was almost no daylight in these rooms as the Emperor lived completely cocooned, surrounded by his or her loyal servants, the most loyal being the eunuchs.

There was an inner courtyard that was highly decorated in traditional colours and patterns, with a large well in the centre. This well was the source of the water for the inner sanctum of the Palace. The well was over five hundred feet deep and about five feet across. No-one really knew how deep the water was below the surface. In the courtyard surrounding the well opening, there was a stone wall about two and a half feet tall with a ledge, large enough to sit on.

Ehuang was on the private tour with four other people and a guide. After two and a half hours the tour had reached the courtyard. Ehuang, like the rest of the group, was feeling a little tired and so they all sat on the wall surrounding the well opening. The guide continued to talk about the architecture and the Emperor's life inside the Palace when Ehuang suddenly fell backwards into the well and in five and a half seconds splashed into the dark cold water at the bottom. She drowned and her body was finally recovered a couple of days later by a diver that had to be lowered into the well.

Her estate was sold at Balfour's for one hundred and twenty five million dollars.

Spanish, Not Chinese

Monday, 21st February.

The appointment with the Head of Palace Security was scheduled for seven thirty in the morning, before the Palace opened to the general public. Anita and Camau had risen early, had breakfast, and were in a cab by seven on their way to The Forbidden City. It was still dark as the sun was just about to rise. Camau pointed out the Bird's Nest, built for the two thousand and eight Olympics.

A few minutes later they were whisked through a large wooden gate into what looked like the back of The Forbidden City, clearly an area forbidden to the general public. Two soldiers carrying live guns, halted the taxi and asked to check the papers of the occupants.

Anita explained in Mandarin that they had an appointment with the Head of Security. The guards took away Anita's and Camau's passports and went into the sentry point, picked up a phone and checked with the main office.

The soldiers returned, handed back the passports and saluted the taxi and its occupants as it moved onto the entrance. Anita and Camau got out of the taxi, paid the driver, and were escorted by two further soldiers up a long flight of stairs to a waiting area.

'Wait here,' the taller of the two soldiers ordered, then turned, and left along with the other soldier.

There were no seats, and Anita and Camau just stood looking at the place they found themselves in. It was dark, with few windows and looked just like the various palaces they had visited the previous day. The large room, about sixty feet square was heavily decorated in Imperial taste, and smelt of old dry wood, imbued with the long lost scent of incense. There were a couple of weak electric light bulbs hanging from the ceiling, but otherwise the place was dark and musty.

For some reason Camau felt he had to whisper. 'I think I prefer the precinct in New York to this.'

'Yes, I know. I feel like the ghosts of Imperial China are in this room watching us.'

They stood waiting until nearly twenty five past eight, when a door opened in the middle of a highly decorated wall with images of courtly life from the Ming Dynasty.

'Come.'

Anita and Camau went through the door, which was closed behind them by the soldier who had obviously opened it.

'This way.'

They followed the soldier down a long dark corridor, as it turned left and then right. The soldier opened another door.

'In.'

The soldier closed the door behind her as she left.

They were now standing in a much smaller room which was modern, painted in battleship grey with two fluorescent lights on the ceiling. Again, there were no seats.

After another ten minutes, the door opened and a woman, about five feet six inches tall in a dark green military trousered uniform wearing a peaked cap, entered.

'I am the Senior Commanding Officer on duty today. How may I assist you?'

'Good morning. I am Inspector Anita Wu of the London Metropolitan Police Art Squad, and this is my colleague Camau Kumar. We are investigating a series of deaths around the world that resulted in large auction sales, to see if any crimes were committed. We are here to find out more about the death of Ehuang Zhang, two years ago.'

'Yes, I know,' the officer replied.

'Ehuang Zhang sat on the wall surrounding the well, leant back and fell in. End of.'

'Were there no notices or protective guards to prevent anyone falling in?' Anita asked.

'It is the personal responsibility of everyone who is granted access to The Forbidden City to behave sensibly, and not to do anything that would jeopardise the experience for everyone else,' the officer stated.

'But what about Health and Safety?'

'What about it? The Chinese have a long history and have had no need of Health and Safety rules and regulations for the last four thousand years.'

'But what about protecting the visitors who come here?'

'This Palace is Chinese, and the Chinese people know how to behave here. It is the foreigners who are a problem.'

'But Ehuang Zhang was Chinese,' Camau added.

'No, she was Spanish, not Chinese. Her people had left the homeland years ago and this is what happens,' the officer stated categorically.

'Well thank you for your time. We should leave now.'

'Good,' the officer said abruptly as she bellowed out to the guard on the other side of the door, turned and left the room.

Anita and Camau followed the guard in silence retracing their steps they had taken earlier. The guard opened a door.

'There,' the guard pointed to the open air, as Anita and Camau walked through the door which was then slammed shut immediately.

'That was brutal,' Camau said as they adjusted their eyes to the morning daylight.

'Yes, it was. Shall we go for some tea?'

English Pub

Tuesday, 22nd February.

As they had agreed two weeks ago, Kerem and Riccardo met in Baku to discuss Kerem's new museum. Riccardo had required a visa to travel to Azerbaijan which was handled quickly and efficiently by Miriam in Kerem's private office.

Kerem had arrived on Sunday evening by his private jet, and Riccardo had flown in first class on the GB Airlines Monday evening overnight flight from London Heathrow to Baku. His flight was five and a half hours, and with the time difference of three hours ahead he landed at six thirty in the morning which was really three thirty to Riccardo's body clock. He cleared passport control and customs, then took a taxi for the twenty five minute journey straight to the Marriott Hotel, checked in, and went to bed.

Kerem's office had booked the hotel room for Riccardo which was an Ambassador King Suite. The one-bedroom suite had views of the Caspian Sea and the city, plus access to the Executive Lounge with complimentary breakfast and snacks throughout the day, soft and alcoholic beverages, and business services.

Riccardo woke at eleven thirty and ordered some brunch from room service. Whilst waiting for his food to arrive he shaved, took a long hot shower, and after drying himself put on the unbelievably soft cotton bath robe and a pair of those pointless flip flop slippers that hotels include in the room.

Thirty minutes later his brunch arrived, which consisted of:

- A selection of seasonal sliced fruits
- Goychay Pomegranate Bircher Muesli made with oatmeal, fresh cream, Guba apples, black and golden raisins, goji berries, pumpkin seeds, and pomegranate reduction

- Spiced Shakshuka, eggs poached in a tomato-based sauce with chili peppers and onions, accompanied by warm tandir bread
- Carrot juice and coffee.

One of the side effects of jet lag is the desire to eat as much as possible, as though the body wants to make sure it is fully nourished to deal with the stress of changes to its body clock.

After finishing his brunch, Riccardo dressed in black jeans, a black polo neck jumper, black Chelsea boots and put on his thick heavy black overcoat as it was just above freezing outside. He took his briefcase and a pair of black leather gloves and left his room for his two o'clock meeting with Kerem. He had already pre-ordered a taxi from reception to take him to his appointment.

The meeting took place in the nearly completed new museum building that Kerem was funding. The building was designed by a newly qualified architect from Ecuador, Jose Zubliaga. Jose had used the Fibonacci sequence and created an iconic building, that when viewed from above resembled a nautilus shell on its side, with the spirals radiating outwards and creating a series of interlinked galleries. The building was huge and dominated the skyline along with the Azerbaijani Carpet Museum and of course the three Flaming Towers. The shell like building was covered in mirrored tiles, that sparkled in the daylight, and which were illuminated from behind with twinkling lights during the night, thereby creating a mesmerising dance in midnight blue light.

Riccardo arrived at the same time as Kerem, and they were both greeted by the on-site foreman, and each handed a hard hat and Hi-Viz jacket. Riccardo was horrified at having to wear these items.

'Shall I show you around? We are now on the home stretch, and we should be finished by Friday, if everything goes according to plan,' the foreman explained.

'Yes, that would be great.'

'Come along Riccardo, you can see all the galleries where we are going to display everything.'

'Great. This building is out of this world. I love it and I am sure it will become one of the world's iconic buildings.'

'That is what I wanted to achieve.'

The building had five floors and was in effect five shells on top of one another. Several lifts connected all the floors and in the centre was an open atrium with a clear roof that let in daylight, and cleverly positioned mirrors lit the galleries by bouncing the sunlight around. The larger galleries, which were all curved, were obviously on the outer edges of the spiral floors, and each gallery became smaller as Kerem and Riccardo, guided by the foreman arrived at the central atrium. Each floor had eight galleries, so in total there were forty.

On the ground floor in the centre of the atrium would be a café, restaurant, shop, information desk, and education centre. The ticket office would be located at the outer most gallery on the ground floor. Riccardo and Kerem sat at a makeshift table on a couple of dusty plastic chairs and were joined by the foreman. All Riccardo could think about was how dusty his overcoat was going to get.

'Riccardo, I would like to see your plans for the museum after we spoke a couple of weeks ago.'

'Of course. I think each floor should have a broad theme. The ground floor will be devoted to nature and the natural environment that makes up Azerbaijan. We must only represent things that are unique to Azerbaijan, and we will have art and artefacts that truly represent the diversity and splendour of its nature. The second floor will be devoted to Black Gold, oil that has defined Azerbaijan since time immemorial. The third floor will be devoted to power, the power of groups, and the power of men, women, and children. The fourth floor will be devoted to creativity and include all sorts of things that represent the innate creativity and artistry of the Azerbaijani people. The fifth floor, the top floor will be devoted to mystery, magic, folklore, fantasy, and stories that make up the collective memory of this country. I also propose that you let the general population contribute art and artefacts, alongside others that you will buy, to create a mutual sense of ownership and pride.'

'Riccardo that is brilliant. I love it.'

'The management team and staff who will run the museum have been employed and are sourcing material.'

'Great.'

'Riccardo, I know that this is a project for you, but I want to keep your involvement because your ideas and taste are second to none. The new teams will be instructed to dress each gallery, and you will have a complete veto on everything. I would like to open the museum on May the ninth in eleven weeks' time on the President's birthday. I know it will be an evolving process, but it is best to get it open as soon as possible.'

'Perfect. My flight leaves on Thursday afternoon and I intend to spend the time writing the creative briefs for each floor, so that the teams know exactly what they are doing.'

'Great, and whilst you are here, I would like to invite you to my place for our arrangement.'

'Of course. Tonight?'

'Yes, perfect. Brad will pick you up from your hotel at seven.'

'Is Brad here?'

'Yes, he flies with me as my personal body guard wherever I go. He is dealing with something for me this afternoon but will be back to pick you up. He is such an asset to have around.'

I bet he is, Riccardo thought to himself.

Riccardo had returned to the hotel, showered, and changed into some blue jeans, white and blue sneakers, a white t-shirt, and a dark navy blue hoodie. He went down to the Executive Lounge around half past six, ate some snacks and had a glass of red wine.

Just before seven o'clock he was down in reception waiting for Brad who arrived exactly at seven.

'Mr Hofstadt, welcome to Baku, your carriage awaits.'

'Evening sexy.'

'I know you have a meeting with Kerem, but after that, do you fancy a beer after I finish work?'

'Of course, I would love to.'

'I reckon you will be about sixty minutes, so I will be waiting for you downstairs.'

'Downstairs where?'

'The main Flame Tower.'

'Kerem lives there?'

'Yes, he has the Penthouse in the tallest of the three flame towers, one hundred and eighty two metres above ground.'

'Wow, I am looking forward to seeing that.'

'Come on, we had better get going,' as Brad put his arm around Riccardo's shoulder and guided him outside to the waiting black Mercedes Maybach.

'In you get. Got to do this properly,' Brad said, again with a twinkle in his eye.

Brad drove the powerful car skilfully to the underground access to the largest of the three flame towers. The car stopped next to a lift and Brad got out of the car and opened the door for Riccardo.

'This private lift takes you directly to the Penthouse. When you have done just take it to level zero and I will be waiting for you. Okay?'

'Sure, see you later.'

Riccardo entered the lift and pressed the button marked Penthouse. In fact, apart from zero, and minus one, it was the only other button. It sped up smoothly to the Penthouse in a matter of seconds and when it arrived, the doors opened directly into Kerem's apartment.

Everything in this apartment was extremely modern, unlike the one in Paris which had a mixture of old and new. There was serious art on the walls, Rothkos, Warhols, Picassos, Lichtensteins, Richters, and a couple of large Basquiats.

'Good evening, Riccardo. Welcome to my little flat.'

'Good evening. Can I ask how many homes you have?'

'We have homes in New York, London, Paris, Baku, Monte Carlo, Hong Kong, Sydney, and Cape Town. Plus, I have several other properties that are rented out, for example to my cousin Tural, in Geneva.'

'Very nice.'

'Well, we are not here to talk about real estate, are we? Come this way into the bedroom.'

Brad was correct and Riccardo was down in reception sixty minutes later. Brad was waiting and had changed out of his chauffeur's uniform and was wearing a heavy black leather jacket, tight fitting blue jeans, a black tight t-shirt, black hoodie, and black snakeskin pointed cowboy boots with Cuban heels.

'All done.'

'Yes.'

'Come on, you deserve a beer.'

Riccardo thought to himself that perhaps Brad knew what was going on but decided not to say anything just in case he was mistaken.

They walked five minutes into the Old Town and found a bar that resembled an old English pub. Brad ordered two beers and brought them over to Riccardo who had found a table in a quiet corner.

'This place is unexpected, as is having a drink with you,' Riccardo said as Brad sat down.

'Cheers.'

'Cheers.'

'I hope you are enjoying working on the museum. It is a really big deal here and Kerem has a lot riding on it.'

'What do you mean?'

'Kerem has promised the President, and the government, that this museum will be world class and will attract hordes of tourists. It clearly needs to be a critical success as well as a commercial one. You have taken on a huge responsibility in agreeing to be an advisor.'

'To be honest I think I am more of a Creative Director, and Kerem has employed a team of people to manage and run the museum, but I get the final say, creatively.'

'Do you enjoy that power?'

'To be honest I have never really thought about it.'

'Probably the best way to be.'

'Anyway, change of subject. When we are back in the UK do you and your boyfriend want to come to dinner to my place in Chelsea?'

'Chelsea is nice.'

'Yes, I inherited some money from my parents and decided to buy a house. It is a great place to live.'

'That would be great, but we live in Zurich most of the time, but it can be arranged.'

'Good, do that,' Brad said in a firm manner.

Riccardo felt as though he had been given a military order and a refusal was out of the question. Riccardo also felt that something serious was happening here. This was not a casual invitation but one that he felt would be the start of something life changing.

They had two more beers, then Brad walked Riccardo back to his hotel.

'Take care and see you in London,' Brad said as he slapped Riccardo on the shoulder and winked at him.

Riccardo went to his room, wishing that Brad had gone with him. But in his heart of hearts, he knew that one day Brad would come back with him. Clearly this was not the time or place, and it was crystal clear to Riccardo that Brad was thoughtful, precise, and careful. He was after all, a highly trained military individual.

Pingle

Wednesday, 23rd February.

As the plane left Beijing, both Anita and Camau were relieved to see blue sky once more, when the plane climbed and passed through the grey cloud base. The flight landed in Anita's home city just after lunchtime, after a four hour flight. They quickly completed the formalities and were soon in a taxi on their way to the hotel.

'How does it feel to be back in Hong Kong?'

'To be honest, this does not feel like home anymore. I left here so long ago, and I have not been back since my parents' funeral, eighteen years ago. They loved each other so much, that when my father died, my mother died two days later, they say of a broken heart. The City has changed so much since the handover. It looks much more Chinese now than it did when the English ruled. There are, however, lots of fantastic things to do here.'

'But we do not have much time, as our flight to India leaves tomorrow evening.'

'Yes, I know.'

'But then because of the flight schedules we will have some time to relax in India over the weekend.'

The taxi arrived at the Mandarin Oriental Hotel and after checking in, Anita suggested they went for lunch to Maxim's Palace City Hall. This is the largest Dim Sum restaurant, and one of only a few left in Hong Kong, where dim sum is still served the traditional way from steaming carts, piled high with bamboo baskets, pushed around by surly uniformed waitresses.

The restaurant was like a huge warehouse with hundreds of people seated, chatting loudly, and eating all manner of dim sum. The noise was extraordinary, but the dim sum were fresh and tasty. They both had a thoroughly good lunch with green tea and felt energised and ready for their next investigation.

They walked back to their hotel through the bustling, commercial district. Virtually everybody was dressed in designer clothes and every single person walked around with their mobile phones in their hand. They had to take a couple of lifts to move between the different levels in the commercial area to get back to their hotel, and every single person looked at their screen when they entered the lift. Not one word was spoken, just the interaction between fingers and screens. The only voice was the one inside the lift, making those useless statements, that the doors are closing or opening, or that the lift is moving, as if that would be a surprise.

There were designer shops and boutiques everywhere, and the huge neon advertising boards flashing adverts for all the main fashion brands, were enough to give anyone a headache. There were simply too many brands and too many adverts, a total overload.

'This place is crazy. No one speaks to each other, and everyone looks like a mannequin with their heads bent down towards their screens. I bet their auras are in a real mess.'

'I agree.'

'Well, you have changed your views.'

'Maybe,' Anita replied coyly.

When they arrived back at their hotel there was a huge commotion, with hotel staff, police and emergency personnel running around like headless chickens. Streams of people with luggage were queuing to check into the hotel. Anita stopped an elderly English couple and asked them what was going on.

'The bomb.'

'What?'

'They are digging over by the harbour to create the new underground line and have come across an unexploded bomb from the second world war. We were staying in the hotel, right next to the construction site and along with four thousand people we have all been evacuated and we were told to come here. The bomb was made by the Americans and dropped on Japan-occupied Hong Kong during World War Two. They found an identical one last week in the same area,' the gentleman explained.

'Are you alright?'

'Yes, we are fine. Exciting really.'

'Keep calm and carry on,'

'Exactly.'

'Camau, I propose that this afternoon we should read up on Yves Gaston, who died here in Hong Kong, then we can have dinner at the Peak, and a night cap in the Peninsula hotel.'

'Sounds perfect. See you back here in reception at six?'

'That is fine.'

Yves Gaston was a French professor, academic, book collector and was fifty seven when he died. He had amassed a great collection of French Literature after inheriting a number of valuable books from his mother. His focus was on eighteenth and nineteenth century philosophy and serious novels. His collection included works by all the great male and female writers of the age, many of whom were critical of the establishment, in particular the Monarchy and the Church, and several met their untimely end at the hand of Madame Guillotine.

Yves travelled the world in search of books and manuscripts, seeking out rare volumes in the most unexpected places. There were plenty of auctions and dealers in Paris, but Yves prided himself on finding gems in former French colonies. On his final trip to Asia in twenty fifteen, he had visited Laos, Cambodia, and Vietnam before stopping off in Hong Kong for a couple of auctions that unusually included Western and French literature.

Yves travelled alone and always carried several books with him to keep him company, as he travelled around or ate by himself. He spoke French, English and Mandarin and was a kind and gentle soul. He had snow white hair, that was thinning on top, had a white neatly clipped beard and wore the sort of clothes you would expect a professor to wear. Brown corduroy suits, green and white checked shirts, and sensible brown suede lace up shoes.

His wife had left him years ago because he had no interest in the things she liked, going out drinking, theatre, fashion, and shopping. They had one daughter who had never made anything of herself and now worked as a waitress at a low quality restaurant in Lille, where she lived and was estranged from her father. Her son, Yves' grandson, Claude Gaston, left his mother when he was sixteen years old and went to live with Yves' ex-wife in the centre of Paris. Yves doted on his grandson and hoped that one day he would inherit his love of literature and ultimately inherit his collection of books.

Prior to the auctions taking place in Hong Kong, Yves was invited out to dinner by Xin Cheng, Mount's Head of the Beijing office, who was also in Hong Kong for the sales. Xin invited him to the best Japanese sushi restaurant in Hong Kong, Zema, as she knew that Sushi was one of Yves favourite cuisines.

The restaurant was located up one of the steep side streets leading away from the commercial centre. It was literally a door on the street, but once inside it was like being transported to central Tokyo. The restaurant was exquisitely decorated in classical Japanese style with bamboo, light wood, and Kyoto limestone. The staff were kimono-clad and there were white paper screens hanging between and separating each table. These were covered with white linen tablecloths, on which was the simplest of cutlery, and to finish the look a fine delicate porcelain cup for sake. Ikebana floral displays, each with three violet blue irises, were dotted around the restaurant and created a perfect sense of harmony and peace.

Xin and Yves had the finest sake, and each ordered the restaurant's signature dish, a mixed platter of the freshest sushi arranged around real coral as if it were a replica of a coral reef with brightly coloured fish darting in between the multi-coloured coral arms.

The platter consisted of eel, salmon, yellowtail tuna, sea bass, sea bream, octopus, scallop and fugu. Fugu, or Puffer Fish, is held in the highest esteem by some, and people pay a small fortune to taste it because it is said to be the most delicious of any fish. Fugu is extremely poisonous if not prepared properly by removing all the toxic organs, and one fish contains enough poison to kill thirty people.

One pinhead of poison is enough to kill a person. It is one thousand and two hundred times more powerful than cyanide. The poison in question is tetrodotoxin and it is a terrible way to die. When eaten, if the fish still contains some poison, it attacks the nervous system, switching it off, leading to paralysis whilst the diner is still fully conscious, until they die. There is no antidote.

Yves was looking forward to trying the fugu as he had never tasted it before. He picked up a piece with his chopsticks, dipped it in the small dish of soy sauce and then into the wasabi paste. He popped it into his mouth and savoured the flavour, which was mild and unique, with a hint of savoury that makes it moreish.

He felt his lips tingling, which is a recognised characteristic of eating fugu, but then the tingling moved to his tongue. In the same way that an anaesthetic injection at the dentist progresses, the paralysis travelled quickly until Yves's face was numb and then his fingers started to tingle. He struggled to breathe and when he tried to stand up, he fell over, knocking several floral displays to the ground. He tried to get up, to move but it was pointless. He laid there motionless staring at the ceiling, listening to the activity around him, but within a matter of minutes, he was dead.

His estate was sold at Mount's Paris office in twenty sixteen and raised twenty five million dollars.

Anita was waiting in reception at six as agreed, when she received a text message. It was from the French Ambassador, based in Hong Kong that they were due to meet in the morning. When Anita had contacted the police in Hong Kong when planning this trip, she was referred to the French embassy and was due to meet the ambassador at eleven o'clock tomorrow morning.

The message stated that because of a serious wasp infestation at the French embassy, he could not meet her there, but instead could meet at the British Embassy, as he had been invited to an Anglo, French, Hong Kong business reception and lunch. He apologised but asked if she and Camau could come to the British Embassy at eleven, with their passports, as he had added them to the guest list.

At that moment Camau arrived.

'Looks like we are off to the British Embassy tomorrow morning, to a business reception. The French have a serious infestation.'

'Cool. I am really excited about going to any Embassy. I have thought seriously about joining the Diplomatic Service.'

'You think it is all James Bond and exciting. Most of the time is dealt with lost passports, people dying on holiday and people complaining about everything and anything. Plus, you have to go to these tedious receptions, like the one we have been invited to, tomorrow,'

'How do you know these are tedious?'

'Because they are all show. Everyone knows that real business is done behind closed doors by the people with power and money. Receptions and the like are pretence, and make people feel that they are important. To be honest I think they are a waste of time, and I cannot abide them.'

'I see you do not hold back with your opinions.'

'Never mind. I have bought us tickets on line to go on the Peak Tram, the funicular railway that will take us up to the Peak, about four hundred metres above sea level and offers great views over the harbour and skyscrapers of Hong Kong.'

'Cool. I read it has been operating since eighteen eighty eight and takes seven minutes to get to the Peak,' Camau added.

It had been surprisingly warm today and even in the evening it was still around fifteen degrees. They walked to the station and climbed aboard the

Victorian carriage as it was hauled up the hillside by the motorised chain underneath it.

'I used to love coming up here when I was a child, as there are spectacular views, and I used to fantasise about flying away to a foreign land.'

'Well, you did.'

'But I am right back where I started as a six year old child, sitting in this train, hoping to fly away again.'

'What eats you?' Camau asked Anita.

'You are always so melodramatic, but you have a fantastic life. I do not understand what your problem is.'

'When we get to the restaurant I will tell you.'

Camau was intrigued.

When they arrived at the Peak, they went to look at the view as the sun was just setting and disappearing into the ocean.

'Wow, it is spectacular here. I know we are not, but it feels like we are on the top of the world. You can see everything from here, almost the whole island,' Camau said enthusiastically.

'Yes, it is.'

Anita's favourite restaurant was closed for refurbishment, the old traditional steak house that had been there since the railway opened. Instead, they went to the Jumbo Lumbo Prawn House.

'Guess what they serve here?'

'Ha, Ha. You are getting witty, now you are a married woman.'

They sat at a table, ordered some salt and pepper calamari, a large plate of grilled tiger prawns and a couple of Tsingtao beers.

'Cheers Camau. It is time for me to come clean and tell you why I am here.' She explained to Camau what had happened with the video, the Home Secretary, and the Mayor of London plus the consequences for her career and the initial difficulties with Juliet.

'I feel like I am carrying a lead weight around the whole time and people like you can see that.'

'People like me. What do you mean?'

'Camau, you are a wonderful person and so nice, not like me. Your cousin Jag was charming, even that Obergrupperfuhrer Monika was pleasant, and that lovely monk was divine.'

'Anita, what world do you live in? Do you know at university that everybody had videos and photographs floating around? Even at school we were circulating images of people, some naked and several of various intimate body parts. There is no such thing as privacy anymore and if you think you can be blackmailed or your career jeopardised because of a video, just search on line and you will find something to fight back with. Or better still, just let it go. If we are so frightened of employers and the like finding something on line, nobody will be able to get a job anymore. Just tell these people to get lost and mind their own business. No one has the right to dictate to you what is right and what is wrong. You are your own woman. We are living in a different and exciting age now.'

'So, I should just tell your uncle, the Home Secretary, to get lost?'

'Yes, and he will respect you for that, believe me.'

'Erm, well that is not what I expected to hear,' Anita said as she ordered two more beers.

'When we have finished here, we shall go to the top of the Peak, where you will leave all your emotional baggage and guilt up there, then we will go down and have a drink in the Peninsula Hotel. Deal?'

'Yes, deal.'

They finished their drinks, paid the bill, and left the restaurant to take the short walk to the top of the Peak.

'Now, once and for all, let go of all your emotional baggage and leave it here on that rock.'

'Okay, done.'

'Right, we are now going back to the station to take the train and then off to the best hotel in Hong Kong.'

'Okay, boss,' Anita replied realising that the roles had been reversed.

The Peninsula Hotel, Hong Kong is a colonial-style luxury hotel located in Kowloon. The hotel opened in nineteen twenty eight and is notable for its large fleet of Rolls-Royces painted a distinctive Peninsula green.

They entered the hotel and sat on two high chairs in the first floor bar. The intimate room was fitted out with deep rich mahogany woodwork, dark red velvet soft furnishings, a traditional English Axminster carpet and just enough light to be able to see what was going on, but not too much to be jarring. It felt indulgent and luxurious. The back of the bar was filled with every conceivable bottle of alcohol that existed. There were hundreds of bottles, all lined up neatly, like a row of soldiers awaiting inspection.

'I will get you a brandy.'

'That will be lovely, but are you sure?'

'Yes, I got my allowance from my parents yesterday.'

'Good evening. What can I get you?'

'Two large Remy Martin XO, please.'

The barman took two empty brandy glasses, warmed them in a brandy warmer over a lit tea light for exactly twenty seconds, then added the brandy and presented them to Anita and Camau.

'To lost luggage.'

'To lost luggage,' Anita cheered as they clicked glasses then both took a sip of the perfectly warm brandy, just warm enough to release its complex aroma.

'This trip is much more revealing than I imagined. I am still not sure whether we will discover any murderers, but I am discovering much more about myself then I ever thought possible,' Anita said as she cradled her glass. 'And this brandy is wonderful.'

'I wonder whether we are trying to find too many connections between all these cases. Perhaps there are no connections, and we should just look at each case in isolation.'

'I think perhaps you are right. In traditional multiple murder cases there are always patterns and commonalities that the investigators can pick up on and identify. Murderers, just like all people are creatures of habit and they are usually uncovered because they do the same things over and over again. Maybe it is the sort of victim, the manner of death, the locations, or some other characteristic. We have found nothing like that,' Anita said with frustration and exasperation in her voice.

'Perhaps there is more than one murderer?' suggested Camau.

'Interesting, let me think about that.'

Thursday, 24th February.

After a late breakfast, Anita and Camau checked out of the hotel leaving their luggage behind and took a taxi to the British Consulate-General, located at 1 Supreme Court Road, Admiralty. Upon arrival the taxi stopped at the entrance barrier.

'Good morning and how are you today?' the British policeman asked.

'Very good, thank you.'

'Excellent. Passports please?'

After a few minutes, the policeman returned and handed back their passports.

'Jolly good, all sorted. I am sorry you did not take up that position in London as head of the UK's Anti-Terrorism Unit Ms Wu, but I hope you have a lovely day.'

Anita had a look of shock on her face.

'OMG, they must all be talking about me. I can feel my aura waning.'

'Nonsense. Remember what Sarvajna said, that you put the past behind you and carry on, and if anybody bothers you, just tell them to naff off.'

Anita laughed.

'Yes, you are right as always, Camau.'

The taxi progressed on towards the front door, they both got out of the taxi, entered the building, and went to the reception desk where an English woman in her thirties was seated behind the desk. She looked frightfully prim and proper.

'Good morning.'

'Good morning, we are here to meet with Monsieur Renauld.'

'Ah yes, the one driven out of his embassy by a wasp, can you believe it? The French. He is in the Blue Wing, just one moment. Please take a seat over there and would you like a cup of tea?'

'Thank you, but no thanks.'

The receptionist looked at them as though they were aliens. Little did they know that she had worked for GB Airlines for ten years and was conditioned to give people a WTF face if they did not fall in line.

They waited a few minutes until Monsieur Renauld appeared and ushered them into his temporary office in the Blue Wing. The room was a large dining room with a long rosewood table that could easily seat twenty six people. The walls were lined in pale blue silk and there were several painted portraits of the previous governors of Hong Kong. The long pale blue curtains, hanging either side of the six large windows framed views of the beautiful English lawn and rose garden.

'I am so sorry about this, but it is the best we can do, given the circumstances. They found a nest, the size of a tennis ball in the rafters above my office and we all agreed to close the embassy, and have it fumigated properly. We are using Spentokil, supposedly the best company, and it will take two weeks, but at least we will be clear of them,' the ambassador explained.

'Back home in Kenya, we just spray them with a mixture of hot water and washing up liquid.'

'What? This is costing us thirty thousand Euros.'

Anita changed the subject.

'Anyway, on to Yves Gaston. Can I ask why the French Embassy is involved in a local death? Surely it is a matter for the local police here in Hong Kong.'

'I have been here as ambassador for ten years and we were monitoring Yves' activities. He was buying up some extremely important manuscripts and books, that are integral to the French state. Many of the works that he owned should have been in museums for the French people to enjoy and study. We were having conversations with him about selling his collection to the government or even better, donating it, either during his lifetime or after his death, for some honorary reward such as naming a room in a museum after him, or something similar.'

'So, what happened?'

'He refused to sell his collection at the price we wanted to pay. It eventually sold for twenty five million dollars, but can you imagine the uproar if the French government, in this day and age, spent that amount of money on some books. We offered him two million euros, over the course of ten years, but he rejected that. He wanted to leave the collection to his grandson, whom he hoped would grow and develop it. He was, as I believe you know, estranged from his daughter. The grandson did inherit the collection when Yves died ,and sold it as quickly as he could, at auction. Most of it went to American buyers who have deeper pockets. It is a travesty for the French and French culture.'

'And what about how Yves died?'

'What a truly 'orrible way to go, knowing that you are dying and unable to do anything about it. The police did a thorough investigation but were unable to prove anything. The chefs that prepare the fugu have to be specially trained and licensed. All that happened was that the restaurant fired the chef to protect their reputation. They checked all the remaining fish on both platters, and everything was as it should be. I think someone slipped a small piece of the poisonous fish onto Yves' plate, but in a restaurant teaming with staff, and no CCTV it was impossible to identify a culprit.'

'Well, thank you for explaining everything to us. It all makes much more sense now.'

'Good. Shall we go out for pre-lunch drinks on the lawn as it is such a lovely day?' Monsieur Renauld proposed.

'That would be lovely, most kind,' Anita accepted.

All three left the office and after walking down a long corridor, turned left and entered the garden. It was like an oasis in the hustle and bustle of Hong Kong.

'I have to say that I am really jealous of the English having this beautiful house and garden. My embassy is much smaller with no outside space.'

'Well, the English did pick the best spot,' Camau added.

Anita and Camau each picked up a glass of cranberry juice that was offered to them by one of the waiting staff as they mingled with the other guests. There were about twenty five guests of mixed nationalities standing around in groups of two or three.

'I now know what you mean. This reception looks awful and boring,'

A Japanese gentlemen in a dark suit and tie, and wearing spectacles approached them and bowed.

'Kon'nichiwa.'

'Kon'nichiwa,' replied Camau and bowed his head.

'Can'ichy'wah,' Anita attempted to say and bobbed her head.

'I own Pingle. You like Pingle? Pingle genuinely nice,' the Japanese gentleman continued.

'Yes very, very nice,' responded Anita.

At that moment Monsieur Renauld interrupted.

'Let me introduce you to the British Ambassador, Sir Christopher Robin.'

'Good morning, Sir,' both Anita and Camau said in unison.

'I hear you are on a murder mystery tour. That sounds most exciting,' Sir Christopher joked as he knocked back a large whisky.

'And no, Winnie-The-Poo is not with me. Everyone always asks me.'

Anita took Sir Christopher to one side.

'Can I ask, what is Pingle?'

'Ah, you mean Pringle, the Scottish knitwear company. That chap over there owns it.'

Dot to Dot

Friday, 25th February.

The Singapore Airlines flight arrived in Chennai, India, at nine fifty in the morning. As Anita and Camau had to catch a flight the previous afternoon from Hong Kong to Singapore it was the perfect excuse to escape the reception in the British Embassy, which they thought was attended by a load of crazy people. They had left Hong Kong at six in the evening, arriving in Singapore three and a half hours later and on the same time zone.

They both had a substantial meal served in the first class compartment and were relaxed and ready for bed when they checked into the airport hotel for the overnight stay.

'I am going to get all my laundry done here tonight as they do a four hour service.'

'Good thinking Camau. I will do the same.'

'Night and see you bright and early in the morning.'

As the air stewardess gave the arrival announcement, which is generally the same on every flight, thank you for flying with us and come back soon, she stated that the local time was nine fifty. Anita looked puzzled. Camau explained.

'India does time zones in half hours, not full hours. Welcome to India.'

Chennai airport is busy twenty four hours a day as there are no restrictions on night time flights. It is permanently full of people coming and going to nearly seventy international destinations. The city is one of the most important economic hubs in India and is a hi-tech centre. It has one of the highest penetrations of high-speed internet access in India and is one of a handful of cities in the country connected to submarine fibre-optic cables.

Anita and Camau were in a taxi, driving along in the middle lane of the five lane highway to their hotel.

'Gosh, this place is busy,' Anita commented as the traffic rushed by on both sides of the taxi. There were huge lorries carrying every manner of goods, small cars speeding along as fast as they could, mopeds zooming along, often with several people clinging on, and in the central reservation cows were grazing. If one stepped into the road, the traffic braked, swerved, and carried on. The traffic speed was insane, and Anita was concerned that if anything braked in front of them, they would be toast.

'Do they not realise that the laws of physics are the same in India as everywhere else? Have they never heard of braking distances?'

'It is in the hands of the Gods.'

Anita leant forward to talk to the taxi driver in a commanding voice.

'Driver, slow down and keep your distance between you and the driver in front.'

The driver did as he was requested and immediately the gap in front was filled by several cars, lorries, and mopeds, so they were back to where they started.

'Anita, just close your eyes until we get to the hotel. You will love it there.'

'If I ever get there alive.'

They did get to the hotel after nearly a fifty minute drive.

'I will never complain about the traffic in London ever again,' Anita vowed.

The Taj Fisherman's Cove Resort and Spa is situated in a beautiful location, south of the city on the Bay of Bengal. Camau had booked two individual cottages for them, and they rode on the hotel's golf buggy from the reception area down to the complex of cottages through the perfectly manicured tropical gardens. Side by side, their cottages were detached, mini-colonial style bungalows with a sumptuous bathroom, luxurious lounge, double bedroom, and a large terrace which opened onto a lawned area which then gave way to the beach, fringed with swaying palm trees, and then the Indian Ocean.

Anita breathed in deeply.

'Camau, this place is beautiful and almost worth that journey.'

'Yes, I agree. Shall we unpack, get refreshed then have some lunch? I would suggest the Bay View restaurant.'

'Perfect.'

They met in the restaurant an hour later and sat under a thatched gazebo with a view of the ocean. The temperature was thirty one degrees with a gentle breeze.

'Camau, this place is out of this world. I think it is the best place we have visited.'

'I thought we were on a business trip, not a pleasure trip.'

'Well, we have to enjoy life as well as working. Nobody on their death bed ever said they wished they had worked more.'

Camau was stunned at Anita's change of attitude.

'I would like to suggest that we have the daily mixed seafood board, which will have a mixture of the freshest fish caught this morning.'

'Sounds perfect Camau. Then this afternoon I want us to go down to the beach, discuss a few things about work whilst we are sunbathing, then go to the spa for some treatments, on me.'

'Fine by me.'

They ate the most wonderful fish, accompanied by a fresh ginger mocktail, and finished with a coffee.

After lunch they went down to the beach, found a couple of loungers and immediately a beach boy brought them towels. They settled down and Anita noticed that the beach was protected by armed guards. Clearly this beautiful, privileged place was for the few.

'Firstly, Camau I want to review our budget. We seem to have been away for ages and I am concerned about how much this is all costing.'

'Of course, I have been tracking all our expenses and here is the summary sheet.'

Camau passed his iPad to Anita.

'Can you print this out?'

'No, Dyllis I will not. I will e-mail it to you.'

'Let me explain it to you.'

Budget: Suspicious Deaths - World Tour							
	Number of Nights	Number of People	Hotel Nights	Cost/Night	Total Cost Hotel	Expenses Per Night @ $100 per person	Flight Tickets
Iceland	2	2	4	$250	$1,000	$400	
New York	3	2	6	$175	$1,050	$600	
Miami	4	2	8	$135	$1,080	$800	
Jackson Hole	2	2	4	$250	$1,000	$400	
San Diego	5	2	10	$125	$1,250	$1,000	
Sydney	8	0	0	$0	$0	$0	
Shanghai	1	2	2	$135	$270	$200	
Beijing	5	2	10	$95	$950	$1,000	
Hong Kong	1	2	2	$145	$290	$200	
Singapore	1	2	2	$195	$390	$200	
Chennai	4	2	8	$95	$760	$800	
Mumbai	2	2	4	$145	$580	$400	
Dubai	7	2	14	$145	$2,030	$1,400	
Cruise	7	0	0	$0	$0	$0	
London	0	2	0	$0	$0	$0	
Total	52		74	$144	$10,650	$7,400	$16,000
Grand Total $							$34,050
Grand Total £							£28,140

'The title sounds like the world tour of a rock band, I like it.'

'By the time we get back to London we will have been away for fifty two nights, from January twenty forth, to the eighteenth of March. In Sydney we stayed with Juliet, so that was free, you will be on your honeymoon in Egypt, so you will have to cover that and when we get back to London, we cannot claim expenses. In total we will have stayed seventy four nights in hotels at an average of one hundred and forty four dollars per night, therefore a total of ten thousand six hundred and fifty dollars.'

Anita interrupted.

'Those rates seem cheap for the hotels we have stayed in.'

'My father got us trade rates. All I have to do is to post positive reviews on some websites.'

'Cool,' Anita replied and smiled. Camau as resourceful as ever, she thought to herself.

Camau continued the explanation.

'We have been spending on average about one hundred dollars per day each on taxis, incidentals, and food, so a total of seven thousand four hundred dollars.'

'Does that include the snorkel trip?'

'Yes, all included. Some days we have not spent much at all,' he explained.

'I booked the round the world flight tickets, with fifteen stops, through my father's travel agent in Nairobi, and we got first class tickets for the economy price, otherwise he threatened to move his account. Our flights cost us sixteen thousand dollars in total. For the record, our flight itinerary is as follows.'

Flight	From	To	via
1	London	Reykjavik	
2	Reykjavik	New York	
3	New York	Miami	
4	Miami	Jackson Hole	Houston
5	Jackson Hole	San Diego	Los Angeles
6	San Diego	Sydney	Honolulu
7	Sydney	Shanghai	
8	Shanghai	Beijing	
9	Beijing	Hong Kong	
10	Hong Kong	Singapore	
11	Singapore	Chennai	
12	Chennai	Mumbai	
13	Mumbai	Dubai	
14	Dubai	Cairo	
15	Cairo	London	

'So, all in all we have spent, or will spend, thirty four thousand and fifty dollars, which at today's exchange rate is twenty eight thousand, one hundred and forty pounds.'

'That is amazing Camau, given all the places we have been to. My only concern is that we do not come across anything and I get in more trouble for having wasted this money.'

'Remember that I got your budget increased so you will still have around twenty thousand left, less of course the expenses for Penny and Stephen and their safari.'

'Yes, I regret agreeing to that now.'

'Anita, can I ask if anyone is on your case from back home?'

'I have not heard a word from anybody. It is as if I do not exist.'

'Can I say something that might upset you?'

'Of course.'

'My uncle asked me to spy on you and report back, but only in person which obviously I have not been able to do.'

'I am not surprised. I would have done the same thing.'

'Really, I thought you would be angry.'

'Not at all. We have been together for several weeks now, and I have nothing to hide. I have learnt my lesson and I am trying to do the right thing, and as your monk friend said, to put everything behind you and move on as a better person. Just out of interest what would you say to your uncle?'

'Honestly, I would say that you are hardworking, diligent, thorough, frugal and a bit too hard on yourself. Plus, you are a really nice person who has spent too much time focused on your job and career, and not enough on you, and your life.'

'Thank you, that is kind of you.'

'Camau, the other thing I want to discuss with you are these cases we have been investigating.'

'Yes, I have been putting all the information we have been collecting into their respective files in the cloud. We will have a lot of analyses to do when we get back to London.'

'You know when you are a kid, and you do dot to dot pictures. You start off not knowing what you are going to create, and you keep plodding on until suddenly everything makes sense and the drawing in front of you is as clear as a bell. I think that is where we are Camau.'

'One thing that is bugging me is that in nearly all the cases the person, or people, who have benefited from the death of the person in question and inherited millions of dollars, were generally nowhere near the scene of death. Do you think they were employing a hired murderer or assassin?'

'That is an interesting idea, Camau.'

'On that note, I want to go for a swim in the sea, which true to my frugal nature is free.'

After they had enjoyed a refreshing swim, they continued their discussions.

'I have been keeping a summary of all the deaths so far, sorted by year, which I thought might prove useful. Do you want to see it?'

'Yes please Camau.'
'It is on my iPad, of course.'
'Ha, ha.'

Who	Occupation	Location	Cause of Death	Beneficiary	Estate Value	Year	Auction House
Eleanor Dupre	Cosmetic Queen	New York	Sat in her chair	Granddaughter	$352	2016	Mount's
Darian Amani	Film director	Jackson Hole	Balloon fall	Wife	$735	2016	Balfour's
Sophia Lazarini	Soap Actress	Australia	Exposure	Husband	$85	2016	Mount's
Yves Gaston	Book Collector	Hong Kong	Fugu sushi	Grandson	$342	2016	Mount's
Johannes Blomfeld	TV Journalist	New York	In front of a train	Foundation	$68	2018	Balfour's
Myra Sharma	Jeweller	San Diego	Bitten by Spider	Sister	$38	2019	Balfour's
Patrick Van Roots	Philanthropist	Puducherry	Snakebite	Sister	$145	2019	Seton's
Melvin Easton	Retailer	Iceland	Hypothermia	Son	$290	2020	Mount's
Ehuang Zhang	Artist	Beijing	Fell into a well	Husband	$135	2020	Balfour's
James Settle	Cartoonist	Everglades	Eaten by 'gator	Wife	$18	2021	Seton's

'This is interesting. I think you should keep updating this as we carry on our trip and something might pop out to us, like a dot to dot drawing.'

'Yes, boss.'

Bedroom Window

Monday, 28th February.

Over the weekend, Anita and Camau had enjoyed the beach, swam twice daily in the ocean, ate wonderful local food, and had a range of spa treatments in the hotel.

On Saturday, they had visited the San Thome Church, officially known as St Thomas Cathedral Basilica and National Shrine of Saint Thomas. This is where the tomb of St Thomas the apostle, the original doubting Thomas, is located. It was a surprise to both of them to find the tomb of one of the twelve disciples in Southern India, and although its authenticity is in question, many faithful Christians visit it each year. They spotted two nuns dressed in grey, knee length habits, walking on their knees towards the tomb, kissing it and praying when they reached it, then walking away, again on their knees.

'That is dedication,' Camau commented to Anita as they walked passed the tomb and touched it.

'Yes, I admire those nuns and people like them. They seem content in their faith and to have everything sorted. I wish sometimes I could be like that.'

'You want to become a nun?'

'No way. That looks like far too much work for my liking.'

'Good. Shall we go to the shopping district?'

'Yes.'

Anita bought several high quality loose gemstones, as a wedding present for Juliet, which cost a fraction of the price she would have to pay in the UK. When she got back home, she decided that she would have them set into two brooches, one for her and one for Juliet.

Camau bought Nisha a heart shaped gold locket on a gold chain. This was his first gift for Nisha.

On Sunday, they visited the Dakshin Chitra museum, which is a living museum of art, architecture, lifestyles, crafts, and the performing arts of South

India. The museum has a collection of eighteen authentic historical houses with contextual exhibitions in each house. All the original houses were bought and reconstructed to represent the regions where they came from.

It was on Sunday afternoon that Camau plucked up the courage to tell Anita that tomorrow's journey to Puducherry was a two hour drive away. He had arranged for a driver to take them there, in a large Mercedes people carrier and the driver had been given special instructions to drive carefully. Anita was not happy at all about the thought of a total of four hours on India's roads.

They left the hotel at eight thirty for the drive south to Puducherry.

Puducherry, a former French colony is known as The French Riviera of the East. The streets of the French Quarter, also known as White Town, are dotted with charming mustard-yellow colonial structures with bougainvillaea laden walls. These are interspersed with cosy cafes and chic boutiques that offer French cuisine and beverages.

The drive was not as bad as Anita had anticipated, but it was still hair raising. She eventually decided not to look out of the window but to put on her sunglasses and close her eyes. Whilst they were travelling, Camau read to her the details of the case of Patrick van Roots.

Patrick was only thirty six years old when he died. His parents had divorced when he was only two years old and three years later his father inherited a fortune from his father who had been a major shareholder in a Dutch car company that had been sold to General Motors a few years ago. Patrick's mother was furious that her ex-husband had inherited six hundred million euros after her divorce settlement. Patrick was therefore the sole heir to his father's millions.

A few weeks after inheriting the money, Patrick's father was in the Dutch countryside on a wild duck shoot. He was with four other hunters as they were having a successful day shooting around eighty ducks. As they were on the final few minutes of their shoot, his hunting rifle failed to go off. He lifted the gun off his shoulder and stood the butt on his left boot, holding the barrel in his left hand. He looked down the barrel to see if there were any blockages, when the cartridge shot out of the barrel blowing his head apart. At the age of five, Patrick inherited six hundred million euros that was in a trust until he was twenty one. His mother could not touch a penny.

His mother started to date a new French man, Gilles, and she quickly became pregnant. As soon as Gilles realised that she did not have any access to the inheritance, he left her and went back to live in France. Patrick's half-sister was born a few months later and they all lived a rather frugal existence in a flat in Rotterdam where his mother worked as a security guard at the Port of Rotterdam. Patrick never liked his half-sister as he viewed her with suspicion based on her father's motives.

When Patrick finally inherited his money, he invested some of it in several Dutch Old Master Paintings and the rest he decided he would use to fund philanthropic initiatives. He wanted to avoid the trap of charitable donations, which merely offer temporary support for a particular problem, and instead to ensure that his philanthropy would make a real, lasting change.

He set up a foundation, called Roots, which aimed to provide a good quality education for children from the age of four to eighteen. The majority of his money was permanently transferred over to the foundation and the proceeds from the investment income was used to fund his initiatives.

Roots Schools were based in rural communities in Africa and India. There were twenty seven schools educating around twelve thousand children for free. Patrick's full time job was the Chairman of the Foundation, and he would travel around visiting each school with his girlfriend, Beth, who was an art advisor. The Foundation was supported by several illustrious board members who provided guidance, advice, and sometimes political assistance.

Four years ago, the Roots Foundation was opening its latest school thirty miles outside of Puducherry to support children in rural communities who were unable to afford to travel to the city for their education. The school was housed in a converted clothing factory that had closed a few years earlier. The building had been gutted and refurbished to include fourteen classrooms, an assembly hall that could be used as a gymnasium, kitchen, offices, laboratories, and several workshops for practical skills. There would be about thirty pupils in each class and the response from the area was enthusiastic and the school was soon oversubscribed.

Patrick was visiting alone as his girlfriend was attending the Art Fair in Basle, Switzerland, one of the world's major Art Fairs and an absolute essential stop on the global merry go-round of auctions and fairs. He had hired a car and driven from Chennai airport to the small village of Kaymakam, where the school was located. There were no hotels in the village, so Patrick was the guest of one of the teachers at the new school, Mrs Nadar.

Mrs Nadar lived with her husband, their three children, both her mother and mother in law, her two sisters, and her brother in one of the larger houses in the village. The complex was surrounded by a breeze block wall with a secure steel gate to gain entry in to the central courtyard. The house was u-shaped with the doors to each bedroom, six in total, off the main courtyard and there was a semi-open plan area under a veranda made of corrugated iron. The family, cooked, ate, and lounged in this semi-open area. The weather was always warm and at this time of the year was particularly hot and unpleasant. It was generally in the high thirties during the day and only falling to the late twenties at night, which made sleeping difficult.

Mrs Nadar, a teacher, was the main breadwinner as she had benefited from an education from a French missionary school when she was growing up, but unfortunately the school had closed due to lack of funds a few years ago. She was delighted to have the opportunity to work in the new school near her home, rather than travelling thirty miles each way, every day there and back, on her moped to her old teaching job in Puducherry.

Patrick arrived around six o'clock in the evening, parked his car and was welcomed by Mrs Nadar and her family. He was treated as a guest of honour and was given the best bedroom in the house, usually used by Mrs Nadar's mother, who was moved to sleep with her grandchildren, much to her annoyance.

Patrick put his things in his room and because it was stifling hot, he opened the small single window that was high up and looked towards the wasteland at the back of the house. He went to sit with the family on their low seating outside and chatted about the school opening ceremony that was going to take place in the morning.

As the sun set just after half past six the temperature started to cool a little. The family had all prepared a special meal in Patrick's honour which was laid out in the outdoor area on fresh banana leaves on the ground in the traditional manner. The meal consisted of chapatis, three sorts of chutneys, several vegetable curries, lemon rice, tamarind rice, sambal, and flatbreads. Only Mrs Nadar spoke English, so she translated their conversations with Patrick.

They had a wonderful evening and expressed their gratitude to Patrick and his foundation for funding the school and providing a much needed boost to the village, since the only employer, the clothing factory had closed down five years ago due to global economic forces.

Around ten o'clock it was time for bed as the whole family would be up at six in the morning with sunrise to get on with their daily lives. They bade each other good night and Patrick went off to his room carrying a kerosene lamp.

Whilst all Indian villages are connected to the National Grid, only about ten percent of houses in rural villages have access to electricity. He undressed and climbed onto the cot bed. He checked his e-mails on his mobile phone, which worked remarkably well and connected it to the battery pack he had brought with him. He turned off the lamp and despite the heat, he was relaxed after the meal and the company, and fell asleep in a matter of minutes.

At six in the morning the whole household was up, getting dressed, cleaning up and the children playing with a football in the courtyard. Mr Nadar made traditional filter coffee to which milk and sugar are added and is then poured from dish to dish several times to create a frothy coffee. In effect it is an Indian cappuccino.

Patrick was nowhere to be seen and Mrs Nadar's seven year old son took a cup of coffee to Patrick's room to wake him up. When he entered Patrick's bedroom, he dropped the coffee on the floor, screamed and ran to his father.

A large cobra was curled up in the corner of the room and Patrick was dead.

The whole family came to the bedroom to see what had happened. Mr Nadar quickly got an old sack and a hook stick to capture the snake, put it in the sack and take it away. Mrs Nadar's mother was wailing as she told her daughter that she had checked the bedroom just before they ate and closed the window which was open.

The police were called on Mrs Nadar's mobile phone and they arrived three hours later. They took Patrick's body away to the mortuary in Puducherry.

Patrick's collection of Dutch Old Master paintings was sold at Seton's in twenty nineteen for fifteen million dollars.

Anita and Camau arrived in Puducherry around ten twenty. It was a glorious day, the sea was calm, and the beach deserted. It was strange to think that several years ago this whole coastline was overwhelmed by the boxing day Tsunami nearly eighteen years ago, but the city itself was mainly protected by a three centuries old sea wall. Clearly tsunamis had happened before.

They had an appointment with the Assistant Director General of the Police, Subham Rajan.

'Driver, can we stop here, and we will be here in two hours for you to take us back?'

'Yes of course, whatever you want.'

Anita and Camau got out of the car and went to a nearby beach front café where they sat at a table outside under an umbrella and ordered a coffee. The waiter brought two dishes and two cups and proceeded to pour the coffee from one dish to the other, extending the distance between the dishes each time. After five transfers the frothy coffee was poured into the waiting cups and served.

'We are meeting Mr Rajan here. He thought it would be more pleasant for us and I do agree.'

'Yes, it is beautiful, but we are here to work Anita.'

'Yes, I know.'

Mr Rajan arrived in a police car and parked directly outside the café where there was clearly a sign painted on the road that said no parking.

'Good morning lady, and gentleman. Welcome to Puducherry. What do you think of our little piece of paradise here?'

He pulled up a chair, sat down and clicked his fingers to the waiter and ordered a coffee.

'It is beautiful here, just like our hotel in Fisherman's Cove.'

'Yes, this part of India is the best. So how can I help you with your case? I read all the notes but if you sleep in the rural part of India with your window open, you are almost certain to get visitors. Did you know that there are around fifty thousand deaths a year in India from snakebites?'

'OMG, I had no idea.'

'I would have thought that you would have known that young man, You are Indian, are you not?'

'Yes, sir, I am Indian, but from Nairobi.'

'Okay, that counts for it then. You are probably more used to deaths from mosquitoes and hippos.'

'Do you think there was any foul play as there was a lot of money involved?'

'It is hard to say. I believe that his half-sister inherited the proceeds from his auction because his mother had committed suicide twelve months ago, the girlfriend was not entitled to any inheritance, and she was his only living relative.'

'Do you know where she was when Patrick died?'

'She was in the Netherlands. We have checked with the authorities there and it turns out she was arrested for being drunk and disorderly on the night that Mr Roots died.'

'That is convenient.'

'So, I am afraid Lady and Gentlemen that Mr Roots was just one of the fifty thousand snake deaths per annum. Remember, not to leave your bedroom window open at night. They can smell their prey miles away.'

'Understood and thank you for talking to us. Most illuminating.'

Mr Rajan waved at the waiter. Your bill is sorted, nothing for you to pay.'

'Are you sure?' asked Anita.

'Of course. I never pay for anything here. Where are you off to next?'

'We are flying via Mumbai to Dubai to investigate another death there and to visit the Dubai Art Fair.'

'Well, good luck with your investigations.'

Mr Kumar got up, nodded, and returned to his car and drove off.

'That is why he wanted to meet us in this cafe. He obviously does not pay for anything here. Well, Camau, that is another mystery to add to our list, plus we have to drive for another two hours. Let us get it over with and hopefully we can go for a swim when we get back to the hotel.'

'Great.'

The Gateway to India

Monday, 28th February.

The drive back to Chennai was longer than planned as they were stuck behind several large lorries that were driving in convoy, but in all the lanes. No one could pass and the traffic was slowed down to a crawl. Later they learnt that it was a protest about road deaths, not humans but cows. Anita sighed deeply when she heard this, and once they were finally back at the hotel she went to her room to change and go for a swim.

They had dinner in the hotel sitting on the terrace overlooking the Indian Ocean and discussed their plans for the following few days. Camau explained the itinerary for the next few days.

'Because of the round the world ticket that we bought, we can only travel on certain airlines. Our flight tomorrow to Mumbai is at one in the afternoon and arrives one and a half hours later. We will stay in the Taj Mahal Palace Hotel for two nights then we will fly to Dubai on Thursday morning.'

'That was the hotel that was attacked in two thousand and eight. I remember studying the details on a training course about how to deal with terrorist incidents.'

'Yes, that is the one, but it is safe now and my father got a good deal for us as his cousin is the General Manager.'

'Do you have cousins in every hotel?'

'I suppose so. Anyway, it is a wonderful hotel, steeped in history and I am sure you will enjoy it.'

'I hope so. After the cow protest, I am not sure if I can cope with anything stressful,'

'But we will have to drive sixty minutes from the airport to the hotel, but there is a motorway.'

'That gives me no confidence at all. Just means everybody will drive even faster,'

'Do you want something to relax you?'

'What do you mean? Drugs?'

'No, some herbal tablets that we can buy here at the hotel to take with us. They will help to soothe your nerves when we are travelling.'

'Okay. We will get some.'

Tuesday, 1st March.

They duly arrived in Mumbai on time and took a cab to the hotel. The relaxing tablets, whatever they were, worked a treat and Anita was smiling and waving at the cars as they drove along the Rajiv Gandhi Sea Link, which is the express highway connecting the North of Mumbai to the South of the city. Mopeds are not allowed on this road and Anita felt positively enthusiastic about the journey as they sped along the modern road that cuts across the Mahim Bay.

When they arrived in the hotel, they first passed through airport style security, which Anita thoroughly approved of, and they entered a different world. Opened in nineteen hundred and three, the Taj Mahal Hotel was the first in India to have electricity, American fans, German elevators, Turkish baths, and English butlers. Later, it also had the city's first licensed bar, India's first all-day restaurant, and India's first discotheque, Blow Up. All the rooms had en-suite bathrooms and it was the height of luxury, as it still is today.

They were greeted by a team of people dressed in traditional Indian dress. The young women in scarlet saris and the men in classic light gold sherwanis. Their luggage was taken away from them, as if by magic, and they were each presented with a garland of fresh marigolds that was placed around their necks. Red dots were placed on their forehead between the eyebrows, and they were offered a drink of sweet tea.

'This is over my sixth chakra,' Anita announced proudly as she pointed to the red vermillion dot on her forehead.

'Exactly. You have learnt a lot.'

They were escorted to their rooms, and both showered and relaxed for a couple of hours before meeting again downstairs for an early drink, and then dinner.

'We must have the signature Taj Harbour Cocktail,' Camau insisted.

'Of course.' What is in it?

'Gin, flambé green chartreuse, peach liqueur, pineapple juice, cranberry juice and topped with fresh apple and pomegranate.'

'Wow, that sounds fantastic.'

They went to the Harbour Bar and ordered two cocktails.

'Will you meet your father's cousin whilst you are here?'

'No, he is in Doha as they are opening a new hotel there and he is helping to recruit the General Manager.'

'Okay.'

As they were drinking their cocktails Anita announced that she wanted to go to a local restaurant in the city, and to walk. Camau was slightly taken aback at her suggestion but agreed. Anita was clearly becoming more relaxed and adventurous or perhaps the herbal tablets had not yet worn off.

After they had finished their drinks, they left the hotel and walked the streets of Mumbai. The sun had just set, the traffic was busy with the sound of car, bike, and moped horns a constant backdrop. As always, cows wandered wherever they wanted and did their necessary excretions wherever they happened to be.

'I think we should go here.'

'But this is a Jain restaurant.'

'So, what is that?' Anita asked.

'The Jain diet is a strict form of a vegan diet. Jains are the followers of Mahaveer Jain, and they believe in an extreme form of non-violence. Not only do they reject any animal products, but they also reject eating any product, which can potentially hurt a living being. A strict Jain diet would exclude common vegetables like potatoes, onions, and carrots because these are root vegetables and have to be dug out of the ground.'

'Great, well when in Rome.'

They ate cucumber and lettuce soup, flatbreads with dal and various chutneys, followed by some date, chocolate, and coconut balls. They drank plain boiled water.

'That was a lovely meal, but I am done with being a vegetarian,' Anita said to Camau as they left the restaurant and walked back to the hotel.

Wednesday, 2nd March.

Anita and Camau had the whole day ahead of them to explore Mumbai. After a good night's sleep, they had breakfast in the hotel restaurant which was extremely busy and looked like a meeting of the United Nations. Serving staff were everywhere and when anyone ordered a coffee the pouring ritual happened every time, for every cup.

'Camau, how can it be cost effective to have a server do that for every cup of coffee?'

'It is a tradition and costs are much cheaper than in the UK.'

'Okay, what shall we do today?'

'I thought we could hire a rickshaw driver this morning to take us around the city at a leisurely pace to see the sights.'

'Great, I like that idea.'

'And then this afternoon we can lounge around the pool in the hotel and discuss our trip to Dubai. I arranged the dates so that they would coincide with the Dubai Art Fair, which opens on Saturday. You will be able to see the art world in its full glory.'

'Perfect. I am looking forward to that. It is time we got to grips with all these suspicious deaths. They all look too convenient but as I said, when you join all the dots together something will appear.'

After breakfast they walked over from the hotel to the Gateway of India, the huge triumphal arch built in nineteen eleven for the visit of the King-Emperor George V and Queen-Empress Mary, the first British monarch to visit India. They wandered around the causeway, looked out at the Arabian Sea, and took the obligatory photographs.

Next, they hailed a rickshaw driver from the street and asked him to take them around the city. As ever the traffic was insane but after a while Anita, in particular, started to go with the flow. Somehow all the cars, lorries, mopeds, bicycles, rickshaws, people, and cows all seem to move along without bumping into each other.

They spent about seventy minutes careering around the city and drove passed the former Victoria Station, now the Chhatrapati Shivaji Terminus, the huge, monumental train station which is like a meringue of Victorian, Hindu, and Islamic styles all whipped into an imposing Daliesque structure of buttresses, domes, turrets, spires, and stained glass.

They then decided to spend the rest of the morning in the Chhatrapati Shivaji Maharaj Vastu Sangamaya museum, previously the Prince of Wales Museum, which houses a vast collection of Indian art and artefacts.

'I feel like I am overwhelmed with too much art,' Anita announced as they left the museum after two hours.

'Wait until you get to Dubai. There will be lots more to see there,' Camau said as he hailed the rickshaw driver over, who had been waiting for them whilst they were in the museum.

Once back in the hotel they got their things and went down to the pool bar. Anita ordered a club sandwich and a full fat coke, whilst Camau ordered a cheese burger, fries, and a diet coke.

After lunch they lay by the pool and Anita started to talk.

'As you know we have deaths from various causes in different locations over a number of years and interestingly all since Kerem Akbarov inherited Mounts, but we cannot link him directly to any of the deaths. All the deceased had different occupations and were of various ages and nationalities. There are a wide range of beneficiaries, the values of the estates vary enormously, and the sales are spread across all three auction houses, but predominantly Mount's. Some of the people died alone, others with one or two people, others in a large group. What I do think is a pattern is that auction house staff, from all three auction houses, are generally around the areas where these deaths occurred, not in all cases, but most. See I have put this chart down on paper.'

Who	Location	Event
Eleanor Dupre	New York	Birthday party with art people invited
Darian Amani	Jackson Hole	Gala event for Mount's Emeritus Chairman and he knew all the people in the balloon from the art world.
Sophia Lazarini	Australia	No art people involved
Yves Gaston	Hong Kong	Mount's Beijing representative at dinner
Johannes Blomfeld	New York	Had attended his own exhibition with lots of art people
Myra Sharma	San Diego	Her sister was a gallerist
Patrick Van Roots	Puducherry	No art people involved
Melvin Easton	Iceland	He was part of the group exploring Viking heritage
Ehuang Zhang	Beijing	Was an artist and with some art interested people on the tour
James Settle	Everglades	No art people involved

'I like this thinking. So, it is looking as though auction staff from all three houses may be involved. I will add your thoughts to my database on my iPad so we can add to it in the future.'

'Perfect. Right, more sunbathing then we will change, have some dinner in the hotel and bed, ready for the trip to Dubai tomorrow.'

The Aquarium

Thursday, 3rd March.

Anita was extremely happy when she arrived in Dubai. The weather was perfect, sunny, a gentle breeze and twenty five degrees centigrade. She was also glad to be back on full hour time zones. Although the flight was three hours, the time difference was one and a half hours behind but now aligned with time zones across the rest of the world. Her body clock felt restored to equilibrium, and it was nearly lunchtime.

Additionally, as they travelled in a taxi from the airport to the hotel, Anita was pleased that the roads were of a high standard, the traffic was orderly and a sense of calm prevailed.

Dubai is clean, tidy, well maintained and pleasing to the eye. Dubai is one of those places, like Monaco, where weeds do not grow in the flower beds, they simply dare not. The journey to the main commercial district, where they were staying, was uneventful and twenty five minutes later they were checking into the five Star Dubai Four Seasons Hotel.

The hotel was brand new and only recently opened. Everything sparkled, including the impossibly smooth, shiny marble floor and the over one hundred especially commissioned huge crystal Murano chandeliers that were hanging in the reception area. The lifts to the rooms were the fastest and quietest that either of them had ever been in. They agreed to meet for lunch in forty five minutes downstairs in the International restaurant.

Once seated in the restaurant, the server handed each of them a menu that was the size and weight of an encyclopaedia.

'My room is enormous, almost as big as that condo we had in San Diego,' Anita whispered to Camau.

'Yes mine is the same and we only have standard rooms.'

'The wealth here is unlike anything I have ever seen before. In London and other cities, people hide themselves and their wealth. Here it is on full display,'

Anita said and gasped as a six foot tall blond woman in her thirties wafted by leaving her trail of perfume.

'That woman is dripping in diamonds. I am surprised she can walk, and nobody is batting an eyelid.'

'Yes, this is Dubai. I am used to it as we always come here for holidays from Nairobi. It is only five hours away.'

'Lucky you.'

They flipped through the encyclopaedic menu, astounded at the range of food on offer, and finally chose goat luwombo stew from Uganda, served in banana leaves. To drink they selected San Pellegrino.

'Camau, what is our schedule here in Dubai?'

'We can mooch around this afternoon and get acquainted with the area. Tomorrow is Friday, obviously the weekend here, so we can review the case of Aoki Fujiki who died here. On Saturday evening there is the opening event for the Art Fair itself which opens to the general public on Sunday afternoon. We can mingle with the art cognoscenti at the fair on Monday and see who we meet. This really is the best place to see all the major players and key influencers in the art world, they will all be here. We have our meeting with the Investigating Officers on Tuesday, then we leave on Thursday to Cairo.'

'Good. I am looking forward to the next few days. I have a feeling in my water that we are going to uncover something important here.'

'Feeling in your water?'

'Yes a sense, a woman's intuition.'

'And you thought chakras were mumbo jumbo.'

After lunch they had a stroll outside. The commercial centre was like a combination of Canary Wharf in London and a large shopping mall, but without a roof. There were several different levels all connected by escalators and lifts. There was a range of art galleries, shops, commercial offices, three other hotels and innumerable cafes and restaurants, all with outside seating areas. Most of the people walking around were dressed in smart, fashionable Western clothes but there were a few men and women dressed in traditional Arab dress.

'This place is cool,' Anita commented as they were walking around.

'This is nothing as it is the business district. Wait until we see some of the other parts of the city.'

'Shall we take a taxi from the hotel and ask the driver to give us a tour of Dubai and then to drop us off at the largest shopping centre in the world where we can check out the aquarium?' Anita suggested.

'Yes, great idea.'

The driver of the midnight blue E-Class Mercedes taxi took them first to the beach area, where the Palm Island is located, the largest man-made island in the world. They drove passed the Burj Al Arab, the famous sail like seven star hotel. Wherever they went they could always see the Burj Khalifa, the tallest building in the world at over half a mile high. They passed by several construction sites where more apartments, villas and hotels were being constructed.

'Who are all those people in the orange dungarees?' Anita asked the taxi driver.

'They are the workers that come here to build everything. It is a tough life for them. They work for a fixed period on a contract then they will be allowed to leave.'

'Allowed to leave?' Anita said with surprise in her voice.

'Yes, that is the way it is. Everybody, whoever they are, apart from the Dubai nationals, has to work, and if you have no job you have to leave. There is no unemployment and no benefits system. It is a unique model that has enabled it to become so wealthy over the last fifty years or so.'

'I see.'

'Here we are on the edge of the desert where you can experience the life of the Bedouins.'

'No thanks. It is beautiful but I know what happens in deserts, just like the Australian outback. Can we go to the shopping centre now please?'

'Yes, of course.'

The taxi pulled up outside the Dubai Mall, the world's largest shopping mall and Camau paid the driver and thanked him for the tour. The Dubai Mall receives more than one hundred million visitors a year. It has twelve hundred shops, two hundred restaurants, an amusement park, a twenty two screen cinema, a kids' zone, an underwater zoo, and the largest indoor aquarium in the world.

Anita and Camau wanted to see the aquarium as this was where Aoki Fujiki had died in two thousand and eighteen. The aquarium located in the middle of the shopping mall is fifty metres long by twenty metres wide and eleven metres deep. It holds over ten million litres of water and contains over thirty three thousand aquatic animals. You can walk underneath it via a tunnel and get close to all the creatures including a large collection of sand tiger sharks, stingrays and over one hundred and forty other species.

'Wow, this place is extraordinary, out of this world,' Anita said as she entered the mall.

'I have never seen so many jewellery shops and there are no customers, just like the shops in Beijing. We are not going into any of them. I know what will happen if we do.'

'Well, you do not have to go into a shop to get some gold. Here look. You can just use this ATM,' Camau said proudly.

'What?'

'This ATM here will give you twenty four karat gold in different forms, from gold bars and coins to wearable jewellery, in varying weights. You just tap the screen to make your selection, pay with cash or with credit card, and out pops your purchase.'

Anita was practically hyper ventilating.

'This is like money laundering heaven; I think I need to lie down.'

'It is no wonder all those art people like to come here. I told you I would uncover something.'

'I think we should go for a coffee, and you can recover.'

'Yes, and a brandy.'

'Remember where you are.'

'Ah yes, coffee then.'

They had coffee and agreed to return to the hotel. Anita went to her room for a rest, but Camau jumped in to another taxi and went back to the mall and the ATM. He showed his passport to the guards who allowed him to enter the foyer where the ATM was located.

He put his credit card in the machine and selected a twenty four karat, twenty two inch heavy gold chain and a link bracelet, both of which cost him just over three thousand US dollars. His parents had credited his card with that amount for him to specifically buy some gold in Dubai, which they always did when they were on holiday there.

For Indians, gold is a status symbol, a sign of purity, and an indicator of family well-being. He was building up his own collection of gold for Nisha. He could wear the items when travelling and breeze through airport security easily, but decided it was best not to say anything to Anita.

In the evening they went down to Al Seef, the old quarter of Dubai on the creek, which is a world away from the modern sky scrapers and twenty first century life. The light was fading, and strings of lanterns flickered and created a magical feel as traditional dhow boats sailed passed. It was like stepping back in time, especially as they wandered through the old souk where there were more jewellery shops, stalls selling every known spice, and exquisite, small boutiques selling perfumes.

'I love it here,' Anita gushed as they wandered through the souk with the heavenly and heady aroma of spices and perfumes.

'Yes it is wonderful here. It feels timeless.'

'Right, in here.'

They entered one of the small perfume stores and were greeted by a wonderful local man in his twenties, dressed in the purest white cotton trousers and Nehru shirt that either of them had ever seen.

'As-salaam "alaykum".'

'wa "Alaykum as-salaam",' Camau replied.

'I would like to buy four perfumes. One for me, one for him and two more for women,' Anita asked.

'Of course,' the owner of the shop replied.

Anita told Camau that she was going to buy a gift for him, Nisha, Juliet, and herself.

'But we cannot take them through security,' Camau added.

'No problem, sir. We can have these sent anywhere you like by courier, all free of charge.'

They selected a musk perfume for Camau, a jasmine one for Nisha, an amber one for Anita and an oud one for Juliet.

'What is oud?' asked Camau.

The shop owner explained.

'Oud comes from the wood of the tropical Agar tree. When the wood of this tree gets infected with a parasitic mould called Phialophora parasitica, it reacts by producing a precious, dark, and fragrant resin. This is the perfume ingredient oud.'

Anita paid for the perfumes and the shop owner arranged to have them sent to the UK. They ate a splendid meal sitting in a local restaurant overlooking the creek then wandered slowly back to their hotel.

TikTok

Friday, 4th March.

After breakfast, Anita and Camau sat down in the hotel's quiet business lounge to refresh themselves about the case of Aoki Fujiki who was Japanese.

Aoki was sixty seven when he died in Dubai in two thousand and eighteen, He was a successful industrialist who owned a company that produced components for the burgeoning electric vehicle industry. His company had made the transition from producing traditional car components and was now the leader of such products in Asia. Like many Japanese art enthusiasts, he had bought several Impressionist paintings in the early nineteen nineties, before their value started to rocket. The paintings were stored in a bank vault in Yokohama, the second largest city in Japan.

Aoki was unmarried and devoted all his spare time to marine conservation. He had established a well-known foundation in Japan, to support research into the preservation of marine life. He had decided that he wanted to expand the reach of his foundation to the wider world and had been engaged in setting up a number of exhibitions around the world to promote the cause.

Through this work he had become good friends with Dr Abdul, who headed the Oceanographic Institute in Dubai. They had collaborated on many projects around the region, to raise awareness of the fragility of the ocean ecosystem, and the impact that its slow destruction would have on the human race.

With support from the Royal family, Dr Abdul and Aoki had put together an amazing exhibition of photography and videos that showed the beauty of the ocean environment alongside images of the devastation that was happening everywhere.

The exhibition had toured several countries in Asia, and in early two thousand and eighteen it was on show at the Aquarium in the Dubai Mall. Accessed by a lift, the general public were encouraged to go to the top of the aquarium where a whole floor surrounding it, allowed the public to stand at the

257

water's edge, and in some areas to touch the Manta Rays and other fish, who had become accustomed to human contact.

The public could take boat trips on the surface of the aquarium accessed from this floor and there was always a queue of people wanting to have the experience of sailing on top of the world's largest indoor aquarium.

On the day that Aoki died, the floor was closed to the public at six in the evening for a charity event to support Aoki's foundation, which would be attended by many of the people who were in Dubai for the Art Fair. It seemed appropriate to have the exhibition next to living sea creatures to add an extra dimension to the messaging that Aoki and Dr Abdul wanted to get across.

Aoki was five feet four, slim with a completely shaved head. He always wore black cotton pyjama style trousers and a loose fitting black shirt, fastened at the neck and with long sleeves. His only extravagance was Christian Louboutin black ankle sneakers.

At the charity reception, there were perhaps two hundred and fifty people, most of whom would only be making a brief appearance. They would spend the minimum amount of time to show their face and would then move onto another two or three events that evening. Individual's status on the art circuit was determined by how many events one attended and even better if they could choose which ones to attend and which ones to miss. The worst horror of all, was only having one event to attend.

The exhibition was well received as the guests chatted and drank tea, fruit juice or water. Naturally, a group of people huddled around the edge of the aquarium where the fish gathered to be pampered. Aoki was standing with them, explaining how sand tiger sharks hover around the water's surface, having taken air into their stomachs to achieve buoyancy. He was surrounded by perhaps thirty people, when his grip on the rail he was holding loosened and he slipped into the water. Sharks, rays, and a myriad of fish splashed around as Aoki's lifeless body started to sink.

It gradually fell deeper and deeper and soon the shoppers in the middle of the mall gathered to look at the spectacle before them. Everyone, without exception, took out their mobile phones and started to film what was going on.

'What a great way to promote Christian Louboutin,' a young Italian teenager said to his friends.

'Yeah, I am filming this live for TikTok. It will increase my number of followers. Fantastic, awesome, sick,' said one of his friends.

Aoki was not attacked by any of the fish as they were all well fed, and sand sharks are not interested in humans. He died from drowning and his body was removed from the tank with a combination of two robotic submarines with arms and a lasso. Despite the real tragedy that had occurred, the shops and cafes did not close and by the time the distraction was over, all the guests at the reception had dwindled away onto their next evening event.

Aoki's collection of Impressionist paintings sold at Mount's in two thousand and eighteen for five hundred and seventeen million dollars.

The Opening Event

Saturday, 5th March.

The Dubai Art Fair had become a major meeting point for the art set since it was founded in two thousand and seven. The fair, held over six days, had firmly established itself on the art circuit and all the major dealers, artists, clients, and auction houses now attended. There was a whole host of exhibitions, auctions, breakfasts, lunches, drinks, and dinners to keep everyone entertained as well as the fair itself which had over two hundred exhibitors this year, showcasing and selling art from across the globe, and in every category. Following its absence during the pandemic the fair this year was even larger and more spectacular.

As usual all the main players from the auction houses were there, including Kerem and his wife Rosemary, Adrianna Fraganese from Balfour's, and Hased Soydon from Seton's. The team from Mount's consisted of around twenty staff who along with Kerem and his wife were staying in the five star opulent Hotel Tarif in the centre of the commercial area of Dubai, where the fair was being held.

Each staff member was staying in a standard double room, whilst Kerem and his wife had the Presidential Suite on the thirty fifth floor. As usual, when Ursula and Riccardo arrived from Zurich and checked in, Ursula gave her second room key to Riccardo.

The opening event was on Saturday evening starting at six o'clock. As part of Kerem's plan to create a world class museum in Baku, he had persuaded, or rather his team had, a large number of museums, institutions, and individuals to loan several items for the opening exhibition supported by the Royal family. The exhibition was titled "Ten" and showcased ten works of art from the ten most famous artists in the world: Michelangelo, Leonardo Da Vinci, Raphael, Van Gogh, Rembrandt, Monet, Picasso, Renoir, Cezanne, and Vermeer. In addition, there were ten cars used in the James Bond films and fabulous jewellery pieces, ten of each created with diamonds, emeralds, rubies, sapphires, and pearls. To complete the exhibition there were the ten rarest carpets in the world. All these objects were displayed in a series of ten galleries that were pitch black inside with the exception of the illumination on the objects themselves which all looked as though they were suspended in space. The walkway through the galleries was lit by the faintest of floor level lighting that provided a guide for the visitors but did not detract from the overall effect.

Kerem was delighted with the exhibition as it achieved exactly what he set out to do. He wanted to demonstrate that Mount's was the superior art institution in the world and could put on an exhibition that left all the others behind. He wanted to support the Dubai Royal family in their aim to make Dubai the rich capital in the world, which they were well on their way to achieving, if not already succeeded. He also wanted to show all the visitors, and in particular the wealthy ones, that Mount's had access to the best things in the world. The fact that almost all the items on display were not for sale merely heightened rich people's desires.

The whole evening started with a drinks reception, serving non-alcoholic drinks, for the two thousand guests in the grounds of the Royal Palace, adjacent to the exhibition. Following a speech by the Emir at seven o'clock, the exhibition was opened to the invited guests who trailed through the ten galleries and marvelled at the priceless items on display. Everyone was impressed by the beauty and majesty of the exhibition and those that could heaped praise on Kerem and his team for creating such an outstanding exhibition. The Emir was ecstatic.

Anita and Camau were not on the guest list for the opening event, so spent the day in the gym, swimming pool and spa, then during the evening having dinner in the hotel and an early night.

The Private View

Sunday, 6th March.

The main fair opened to the general public at two o'clock in the afternoon. Prior to that there was a private view so that the VIPs, by invitation only, would not have to mingle with the general public. The private view opened at eleven so they would have three hours to wander around the fair at their leisure, and importantly to show interest in, or buy any of the items on display that they fancied. It would encourage the general public to open their wallets once they knew that the best items had already been sold, or had serious interest, by having a red sticker attached to them.

Kerem and his wife were amongst the VIP group, but not the team from Mount's. They would all have to wait until the main fair opened later that day. Whilst wandering around the fair Rosemary spotted Adrianna Fraganese and moved to greet her. They air kissed, not wishing to disturb their makeup and were soon joined by Kerem.

'The opening exhibition last night was amazing Kerem.'

'Thank you. My team did a great job, and everyone is happy. It was a lot of hard work but worthwhile and I am extremely supportive of the Emir's ambitions. Dubai is a wonderful place, everything works beautifully here, and it is full of beautiful people, just like you, Adrianna.'

Rosemary shot Kerem a glance, but in her heart of hearts knew that he was simply working Adrianna. At this point, Hased from Seton's arrived and joined the small group.

'Congratulations Kerem. A fantastic exhibition, really world class. I have never seen anything so stunning in all my life,' Hased said as he managed to shake hands with all three.

'We have finally created our new lines of Gocce D'Amore chocolates, that we mentioned at the dinner in Paris,' announced Adrianna. 'I will have my assistant send over a package to each of you containing all twenty one lines. We will be launching them at Rome Fashion week in June, which we are sponsoring.'

'Thank you, well done and I wish you all the success in the world,' Rosemary added.

'Well, we must get on and see everything. Have a good fair and I hope to see you both soon,' Kerem said as he moved on with Rosemary.

At two o'clock the fair opened to the general paying public who each had to pay the equivalent of sixty five dollars to attend. The fair was thronged with people, almost like a football match. Everybody, without exception, was dressed immaculately and both Anita and Camau felt a bit under dressed in their blue jeans and white shirts.

The exhibition hall was enormous with several walkways allowing access to the stands on each side. Some stands were large, others small, but they were all showcasing their wares as best they could.

'It is just like a big market,' Anita commented.

'Exactly, that is what it is. As was explained to you by Stephen, the dealers move around the globe from fair to fair and the clients follow, like groupies,' Camau added.

'Yes now I see. So, where are all the VIPs?' Anita asked Camau.

'Oh, they have gone. Some will have already left Dubai on their private planes, others will be in their hotel suites and will request artworks to be brought up to them to review and maybe purchase,' Camau explained.

'How do you know all this? Does your cousin work here?'

'Ha, ha. I have been here a couple of times with my parents who collect abstract paintings.'

'I see.'

'There will be lots of people here from the auction houses and we might see some of them,' Camau added.

'Will we be able to meet the owners? Do you think they are here?'

'I am certain they are here, but we are unlikely to meet them. We are not in their league, and they stay away from the general public at all costs. Have you never thought that you rarely see really wealthy people? They live in a parallel universe that the vast majority of people have no chance of accessing.'

'I am now starting to understand how these people think they can get away with things. They do not think that the laws that apply to everyone else, apply to them. I can see it now.'

They spent the rest of the afternoon wandering around the fair looking at all the different stands and marvelling at the exquisite artworks on sale. Anita was gobsmacked by the jewellery that was on offer.

'This whole place makes me feel so poor. I have worked all my life, have a reasonable house to show for it, still with a large mortgage, and felt lucky to buy a few loose gemstones in India and some perfume at the souk. Maybe I am missing out.'

Camau responded instantly. 'No, stop being silly. You have the best thing in the world, love. You love and are loved. That is priceless and worth more than all the art and jewellery in here.'

'Thank you Camau, I know. But I do like that sapphire ring over there.'

The Chocolates

Monday, 7th March.

Overnight Adrianna had arranged for twenty one packages of her new chocolates to be flown over from her Italian factory. Each package contained twenty one hexagonal boxes in three stacks of seven, one box for each of the new lines. All the stacks were wrapped together in water soluble cellophane finished with an organic ribbon, dyed naturally of course. The packages were delivered by nine in the morning, to Kerem Akbarov in the Presidential Suite, Hasad Soydon in his suite, one to herself in her own suite and the rest to the VIP lounge that was used by guests visiting the fair. All in all, four hundred and forty one boxes of chocolates were delivered.

Before the fair opened again at two in the afternoon, the Mount's team, all fourteen of them, had agreed to meet for lunch in the hotel. They had spent the morning enjoying the spa facilities in the hotel and met at twelve thirty for lunch in the hotel's outside terrace restaurant. They sat at a long table, six on either side and one at each end. The choice of food in Dubai is unlike anywhere else in the world. One can simply have whatever one wants from any cuisine around the world at any time. Xin from Beijing proposed Chinese and suggested that they order several dishes rather than having to make a choice individually, and everyone agreed.

She spoke to the waitress in Mandarin and in due course sixteen different dishes arrived served with exquisite jasmine tea. The team chatted excitedly about the fair, about how awesome the exhibition had been, and about how proud they were to work for Mount's. At one fifteen Ursula finished eating, pushed her chair back and announced that she had a meeting, would have to leave and she would see everyone else later at the fair. Nobody thought anything of it as it was standard form for people to come and go at staff events.

Ursula as always was dressed immaculately, today in a fuchsia two piece suit with matching shoes, accompanied by her trusty handbag. She left the restaurant, went to the lift, entered it as the doors opened and pressed the button for the floor number she was visiting.

During the afternoon, the whole team walked around the fair, meeting and greeting clients. There was always an intense rivalry between the dealers who were exhibiting at the fair, aiming to sell their works of art, and the auction house staff who were keen to strengthen their relationships with clients. Everybody of course was extremely polite but if the dealers could have their way, they would have auction house staff banned from art fairs. That was about as likely as the sun failing to shine in Dubai.

Kerem had asked Riccardo to escort Rosemary to one of the stands in the fair to look at something, as Kerem was busy having a meeting.

Anita wanted to go back to the fair as she was mulling over buying herself the sapphire ring she had seen the day before. She had some money in her savings account that she had inherited from her parents which she was keeping for a rainy day. Perhaps it would rain today in Dubai.

As Anita and Camau were wandering around the stands, Camau heard his name being called.

'Camau, hey is that you? Remember me, we met a few weeks ago at breakfast in the Bridge Hotel. Riccardo.'

'Ah yes, good to see you.' How are you?

'Exhausted, talking to all the clients and listening to their woes,' Riccardo replied. 'Apologies. May I introduce Rosemary Akbarov, Kerem's wife?'

Camau shook Rosemary's hand and introduced Anita as The Head of the Art Squad, Metropolitan Police.

'How nice to meet you?' Rosemary said as she shook hands.

'How are you getting on with your investigations?' Riccardo asked Anita and Camau.

'What investigations?' Rosemary asked.

'They are investigating the rise in single owner collection sales at the auction houses. They seem to think there is something afoot,' Riccardo explained to her.

'Oh, how intriguing. You are like Agatha Christie and Hercules Poirot,' Rosemary said as she winked at them both.

'Anyway, Riccardo come along. I want you to give me your advice on that sapphire ring over there. Kerem said I can have it for my birthday if you think it is a good stone. Nice meeting you both and happy hunting.'

'Who is that Riccardo?' Anita asked Camau.

'He works for Mount's in Zurich, and I met him and his boyfriend in London a few weeks ago as we shared a breakfast table as the restaurant in the Bridge Hotel was packed.'

'What were you doing in the Bridge Hotel?' Anita asked.

'When I was packing for our trip, I realised I had left my chargers in the office, so decided to pop in to pick them up and treated myself to a breakfast. All Stephen's fault as I fancied a full English breakfast.'

'Okay. Without your chargers you would cease to function,' Anita said, hoping to wind him up a bit.

'Very funny.'

'You do realise that Rosemary has just bought your ring?' Camau said as he gestured over to the jewellery stand where Rosemary was leaving wearing the ring with Riccardo.

'What? Now I feel like nothing. These VIPs can do what they want and ignore the rest of us.'

'There are plenty of sapphire rings here and in the rest of Dubai.'

'That is not the point. I wanted that one.'

'Well, the lesson you need to learn is to take every opportunity that comes your way when you can, and not let it slip away. Understand?' Camau said firmly.

'Yes, I understand. And that Rosemary woman thinks we look like Agatha Christie and Hercules Poirot, who are both ancient.'

The Hard Rock Cafe

Tuesday, 8th March.

Anita's and Camau's meeting with the investigating officer from the Dubai police was arranged for ten o'clock on the terrace of The Hard Rock Café, near their hotel. It was a glorious morning and there were a few people walking around, but generally it was a bit too early in the day for most people.

'The climate here is great,' Anita said to Camau as they sat at a table and ordered cappuccinos.

'Have you been in the summer?' he asked.

'No,' she replied.

'Well, you know all the hysteria in the UK about the heat in the summer these days, you should spare a thought for the people that live here and in other similar places. The temperature here gets up into the high forties. It is unbearable and people just stay inside all day. It is lovely at certain times of the year, like now, but when it is so hot, those that can, decamp to Europe and especially around our office in Knightsbridge.'

'Two cappuccinos,' the waiter announced as he placed two large frothy cups of coffee on the table.

'Thank you.'

The investigating officer arrived at the café and after a brief conversation with the waiter, came over to Anita and Camau. He was five feet ten inches tall, wearing a stone coloured police uniform and wearing a peaked cap. He had jet black hair and a thick moustache. Anita thought to herself that he was an extremely attractive man.

'Good morning. I am Inspector Muhammad Aziz. How lovely to meet you?' as he shook their hands.

'Good morning. I am Anita Wu, and this is Camau Kumar. Please take a seat.'

Another cappuccino arrived for the Inspector.

'I thought we were meeting two of you?' Anita asked.

'My colleague has been transferred to Royal security, so he is unable to meet I am afraid.'

'Okay. Can we discuss the death of Aoki Fujiki?' Anita asked.

'Of course. He is the only death we have had in the aquarium, apart from fish of course. We are so careful with all the people that take boat trips and stand by the water's edge. The glass panel where you can touch the fish is forty five centimetres tall so that children can experience the magic of connecting with them. We have lots of closed circuit television and although we have studied it time and time again we cannot see anything that would cause poor Mr Fujiki to fall in the tank. It is as though he just fell in and that was that. I will tell you something that was not in the official paperwork. When we did the toxicology reports, we discovered that he had a lot of vodka in his system. When we checked his hotel room we found several bottles of vodka. That was kept out of the report, because it was a Royal sponsored event and things like that do not happen here.'

'So, he was drunk?' Camau asked.

'Seems so,' the Inspector replied. 'That is why he just sank to the bottom of the tank. Because it was filmed by so many people on their mobile phones we went along with the notion that it was a clever promotion by Christian Louboutin and actually paid them to agree to the cover up. We simply cannot afford to put off one hundred million visitors to the mall for the sake of one drunk person. Sorry, but that is the truth.'

'Well, thank you Inspector for being honest with us and explaining that he was drunk. We could not see that from the case notes. I understand the religious sensitivities and commercial realities,' Anita said as the Inspector got up to leave.

'The coffees are on me,' he added.

'Camau, I want you to update your charts with this final case as we have now seen everyone we are going to see on this trip. We will just wait to hear from Stephen and Penny when they get back to London then we can all meet up. I have to say that every case is opaque. There always seems to be some reason that explains each death, yet there are also unanswered questions in all these cases. Perhaps there are multiple murderers, with different motives, using a range of methods to kill their victims,' Anita said wearily.

'Or perhaps, there is nothing in it, as you say, and we are on a wild goose chase set up by Penelope so she could have a free holiday,' Camau added.

'I am not sure. My instincts tell me they are here in Dubai.'

'Well, we have until Thursday before we leave for Cairo,' Camau said trying to give Anita some encouragement.

The Discovery

Wednesday, 9th March.

The Mount's team had agreed to have a meeting at nine o'clock in the morning to discuss how things were going at the fair. They wanted to compare notes on who they had met, and what information and gossip they had picked up during the fair. Hakam Noor, from the Dubai office, had arranged the meeting so that he could collate all the data. The intelligence gathering exercise was like a spy network, picking up snippets of information here and there, and importantly feeding them into the Client System so that SPOT could analyse them in due course.

Many of the team had risen early and gone to the gym or swimming pool for some early morning exercise, after which they went for breakfast. As it was nearing eight thirty, Riccardo thought to himself that he had not seen Ursula this morning. He sent her a text message and put his phone down on the table and continued chatting with Barbara from New York.

Five minutes later he checked his phone again and saw that he had not had a reply.

'Excuse me, I am just going to check on Ursula,' he explained to Barbara as he stood up and left the restaurant, forgetting his mobile phone on the table. Her room was two doors away from his on the fourteenth floor. He knocked twice and got no answer so went to his room and picked up Ursula's second key. He put the electronic key into the slot, opened the door and entered.

He immediately gasped as he saw Ursula lying face down on the floor next to the sofa with the contents of her handbag strewn around her, including her insulin pens, along with a box of Gocce D'Amore chocolates that looked as though it had fallen off the coffee table. He touched the back of her neck which was stone cold. She was clearly dead. He noticed a small black notebook that was on the floor and instinctively he picked it up and put it into his jacket pocket. Realising that he had left his mobile phone on the breakfast table, he thought about using the room telephone to call for help, but stopped himself as he wondered whether, if there had been foul play, it might have fingerprints on it. He went to leave the room to get help and as he opened the door, he bumped into Rosemary who had just left the beauty salon also located on the fourteenth floor.

'My God, what is it?' she asked Riccardo. 'You look awful.'

'It is Ursula. She is dead.'

'Oh my God.'

'I am going down to reception to get help. You stay here and do not touch anything.'

'Okay.'

Riccardo called the lift and went down to reception.

In a matter of moments two members of the hotel staff accompanied Riccardo to Ursula's room. They all entered and saw Rosemary weeping uncontrollably. The staff checked Ursula and used their walkie talkie to call a doctor.

'It looks as though she went into a coma after eating these chocolates and did not have time to use her insulin pen,' one of the staff members surmised.

'Yes, it looks like that,' Riccardo agreed.

Riccardo noticed another black note book on the floor near the box of chocolates. He had not noticed it before but thought nothing more of it as his mind was all over the place with the shock of finding Ursula who he had genuinely liked.

'Can I ask you both to leave and we will be in touch later?' requested the second member of staff.

'We have called the doctor and the police.'

'The police?' screamed Rosemary.

'It is standard practice in Dubai when a guest passes away in a hotel,' explained the first staff member.

Riccardo guided Rosemary out of the room with his arm around her waist and they walked towards the lift.

'This is awful. Ursula is, was, such a lovely person and so dedicated to Mount's,' Rosemary blubbered as she continued to sob.

Once inside the lift, Riccardo asked Rosemary for her exclusive pass to access the Presidential Suite. When they arrived the lift door opened directly into the suite's reception area which they passed through to enter the lounge. Kerem was laid on the long white sofa, wearing a white bathing robe which was open between his legs. It was obvious what he had been doing, pleasuring himself.

'Kerem, it is a tragedy. Ursula is dead,' screamed Rosemary as Kerem stood up and Rosemary fell into his arms.

'What?' Kerem exclaimed.

'I went to check on Ursula as she had not come down to breakfast. I always have her second key, in case of situations like this. When I entered the room, I found her lying on the floor, stone cold, with a box of chocolates and her handbag contents all around her. It looks as though she went into a diabetic coma before she was able to administer her insulin pen. As I left the room to get help, I bumped into Rosemary who was coming out of the beauty parlour,' Riccardo explained.

'Oh my God, I am so sorry,' Kerem said to both of them.

'Darling, come and lie down in the bedroom,' Kerem said as he guided Rosemary out of the lounge.

'Riccardo, let yourself out and I will come and find you later.'

'Yes, I will go and tell the others who are downstairs having breakfast and I propose we cancel the meeting that Hakam had arranged to review how we are doing at the fair.'

'Yes, yes of course.'

Riccardo went to the restaurant, but everyone had left and moved to the meeting room where the meeting was just about to start. Riccardo entered and immediately everyone could tell that something was seriously wrong.

'What is it?' asked Barbara.

'It is Ursula. I am afraid she is dead.'

'Oh my God,' Cecelia shouted as she stood up to comfort Riccardo along with Hakam who was standing at the front of the room.

'What happened?' Barbara asked.

'Let him sit down first,' insisted Lady Cecelia.

'Would you like a brandy, dear boy?' asked Gresham.

'Yes please,' Riccardo replied.

'I will go and get one,' Gresham said as he left the room.

'In God's name what happened?' Barbara asked again.

'As you know I went to check on Ursula as she was late for breakfast. She always gives someone her second key when she is staying in a hotel. I knocked and got no reply, so entered and found her lying on the floor, dead as a dodo with chocolates and her handbag contents all around her. It looks as though she ate the chocolates and started to go into a diabetic coma but did not have time to administer her insulin.'

'Why on earth was she eating chocolates? She is always so careful,' asked Sadi.

'There are boxes of those new Gocce D'Amore chocolates everywhere. They are all over the VIP lounge,' stated Barbara.

'Yes, and they have those different variations. I heard there are twenty one different options, including sugar free,' Hakam added.

'Maybe Ursula picked up the wrong box or somehow they got mixed up,' suggested Sadi.

'Well, the police and the doctor should be there by now so they will no doubt work out what happened,' Riccardo stated.

'The police?' questioned Sadi.

'Yes, it is standard procedure when someone passes away in a hotel in Dubai.'

At this point Kerem entered the room.

'Everybody, this is so awful. I do not know what to say. The doctor is taking Ursula's body to the hospital for an autopsy, and we will then fly her home. I have just spoken to her husband; the poor man is broken. I suggest that you all pack up your bags and head home to be with your loved ones.'

The whole room agreed.

The doctor arranged for an ambulance to take Ursula's body to the local morgue where a post mortem would be carried out to determine the cause of death. The police packed up all Ursula's belongings and took them for safe keeping to the police station until her body was released and could be flown back to Zurich for her funeral.

Anita and Camau were sitting in the indoor café in the hotel's reception area having a hi-vitamin smoothie. The temperature was climbing outside so they had agreed to follow local custom and stay inside.

'What is all that noise going on over there? There are police and an ambulance,' Anita observed.

'I will go and find out.'

Camau bumped into Riccardo who explained to him what had happened.

'Seems that a member of Mount's staff has died in her room. Apparently she was a diabetic and it looks like she had been eating chocolates.'

'That is sad. What a shame. I would like you to come with me to the shopping mall to find a sapphire ring.'

'You mean like Rosemary and Riccardo?'

'Well better Rosemary and Riccardo, then Agatha and Hercules.'

Tears

Thursday, 10th March.

After buying a sapphire ring for five thousand pounds, Anita was in turmoil. Should she declare it as she was passing through customs, or should she do as Camau had suggested and just wear it? She finally decided to wear the ring, but the waves of guilt were causing her serious hot sweats. She imagined being locked up in a women's only prison in Dubai or Cairo, and quickly decided that this was not a fantasy she wanted in her head. She sat on the plane from Dubai to Cairo, glad she had escaped one potential prison, but now might be headed into another. She resolved never to buy anything like this again.

She could not decide what was worse, being an unsuspecting porn movie star or a jewel smuggler. Perhaps she should not have become a police officer, perhaps she really was a criminal deep down. Should she get counselling or therapy, or both when she got home? Her mind was racing with all the questions, doubt, and guilt.

'What is the matter with you? I can see that something is not right.'

'My chakras are in meltdown; all my fuse boxes are blown.'

'What on earth are you talking about?'

Anita pointed to her ring.

'Is that all? Look,' as Camau undid the top button on his shirt and pulled up his left cuff.

'Oh my God, so you are a criminal as well,' she said under her breath.

'Here, take some of your herbal tablets.'

'Okay. I will, as I am losing my mind.'

Anita took two of her tablets that she had asked Camau to carry as she did not want to be a drug smuggler as well. Soon she was admiring the ring on her hand, and the gold chain and bracelet on Camau.

They landed into organised chaos. Despite being in first class, all the passengers from about ten flights were queuing together to go through passport control. There was no orderly queuing system that they could fathom and Camau thought it was a good job Anita was a little high, otherwise she might have a breakdown.

'Stay here a moment. I have to go and buy two visas for us and as I have US dollars they will process me first.'

Camau duly returned and they eventually located and joined a fast moving queue that got them through passport control and customs.

'Thank God we have hand luggage,' Anita said as they left the airport and exited into the dusty Egyptian air outside the airport.

Suddenly, a black people carrier with dark tinted windows arrived in front of them, and the driver greeted them. They got in the back of the air conditioned vehicle, the doors closed automatically and soon they were leaving the airport to travel to the centre of Cairo.

'Camau, that was amazing. Thank you for arranging that. If I were on my own, I would still be waiting at passport control and probably be arrested. Anyway, there is something I want to tell you. Juliet invested some money in the play that she was appearing in, and because it was a great success in Australia she has received a huge dividend. So huge in fact, that she has bought you a ticket for you to come with us on our honeymoon down the Nile.'

'No, I cannot do that. I was planning, as you know, to backpack around Egypt until we fly back to London. No, there is no way I can go on your honeymoon. No.'

'Will you wait a minute, there is something else.'

'What?'

'Juliet has also bought a ticket for Nisha to join you as well. They have become close friends on the tour and Juliet, and I have been discussing inviting you both along for a couple of weeks now.'

'Are you sure?'

'Yes of course.'

Camau started to cry tears of joy. 'Thank you. How can I ever repay you?' he sobbed.

'There is no need for that. It is a gift. You have given me so much on this trip and opened my eyes to a whole new world. Now stop crying. You do not want Nisha to see you like this, do you?'

'You mean she is here already?'

'Yes. Both Juliet and Nisha arrived yesterday and are waiting for us in the hotel.'

Camau hugged Anita and held her tight. He cried again, then regained his composure, opened the window to get some fresh air and took several deep breaths.

When they arrived at the hotel, Juliet and Nisha were waiting for them in reception. There were hugs and tears all around as all their emotions overflowed.

'We have a few hours here in Cairo before we leave on the cruise tomorrow morning, so I have put together a plan,' Juliet informed them.

Camau was holding Nisha's hand as if his life depended on it.

'Great, and both Nisha and I want to thank you both from the bottom of our hearts.'

'Good. Unpack, lunch, then the pyramids and the museum this afternoon,'

Stephen and Penny had taken the overnight GB Airlines direct flight from Heathrow to Cape Town, which landed around nine in the morning. They had travelled in business class, as Anita had refused to pay for first class fares. The minute Penny got on the plane and turned left, not right, she made the crew's life hell.

'I am not sitting there, next to the lavatory,' she shouted loudly and collared a steward as he walked passed.

'Young man. I am not sitting there. We have paid a fortune for this flight, and I want another seat.'

'Madam, let…'

'Lady, young man.'

'Yes, milady. Let me check and I will come back to you in a jiffy.'

He duly returned and offered them two seats right at the front of the cabin. Penny gave her hand luggage to Stephen to carry as she went to inspect the seats.

'Yes, I suppose these will do,' she said as if she had been asked to go down a coal mine and sleep on a bed of nails.

'You can have the aisle seat as I want to look out of the window and see the animals.'

'But it will be dark all night.'

The business class seats, that transform into a flatbed, were side by side with one facing forwards and the other backwards. Penny settled into her seat and the steward asked her if she would like some champagne.

'What sort of champagne is it?'

'I do not want any old rubbish.'

'Moët et Chandon Brut Impérial,' the steward replied.

'Alright then. And none for you, Stephen, otherwise you will be going to the loo every two minutes.'

'Yes, Pen.'

As she was waiting for the champagne she looked around her seat and then pressed the call button. The steward arrived.

'Yes, milady?'

'It is dusty down there, look in the corner on the floor.'

'I will get someone to clean it up for you.'

'Good, and where is my champagne?'

The steward realised that his WTF face would not work on her ladyship. He would have to employ some other techniques in due course.

'Milady, your champagne.'

'Thank you.'

A cleaner was brought on board to remove the offending dust and soon the whole cabin was ready for the departure.

It had been a number of years since Penny had flown in business class and there were so many new gadgets and buttons to press. She started adjusting her seat up and down and it was almost flat when the steward told her to return it to its original position for take-off.

'Madam, we…'

'Lady.'

'Milady. We cannot take off if your seat is not in the correct position,' as he adjusted it.

'Socialist,' she muttered into her glass of champagne.

She then found the button that raised the dividing panel between her and Stephen and duly raised it. The steward returned.

'Madam. Sorry milady, the panel must be down for the safety briefing.'

'Why? Is it sound proof?' she asked.

'No, it is so that you can see how to fasten your seatbelt, put on the life jacket and see where the emergency exits are when we demonstrate them.'

'I have been flying since before you were even thought of young man, and the demonstration is the same on every plane world-wide. Do you think I am stupid?'

'No, I do not think that you are stupid. We are just following the rules?'

'Just like the Nazis,' as she was about to raise her right arm.

'Penny, shut up for God's sake. These guys are just doing their job,' Stephen snapped.

She then decided to raise the personal video screen from its docking station and pulled the remote control out of its pocket which was attached with a spring loaded cable. She pressed every button she could think of, but the screen was blank.

She pressed the call button again.

'Yes, milady, what is it now?' the steward asked.

'There is nothing on the telly.'

'Not until we are airborne, and the captain has switched off the seat belt signs. Please return it to its docking position.'

Penny huffed and as she let go of the remote control it shot back into its holder and at the same time knocked over her glass of champagne onto the floor.

The pilot announced, 'Cabin crew, please take your seats for take-off.'

Once the cabin crew were released after take-off, the steward went to the location where all the video equipment was located. He opened a panel and made a couple of adjustments.

The call button went again.

'Yes, milady,' the steward asked.

'What are they over there?'

'What do you mean?'

'Those people in that row over there.'

'They are children, milady.'

'What are they doing in business class? They should be at the back in children class with all the others. This cabin is for business people, like me, on important business.'

'I am sorry milady, but they have paid to sit in business class, just like you.'

'Ridiculous,' as she pressed the button to raise the dividing panel between her and Stephen, released her personal video screen again and put on the headphones. She pressed the call button again.

'Yes, milady. What is it now?'

'There is no sound on the telly.'

'There is a snag with your seat. The audio system is not working apart from the channel for the Norwegian language,' the steward explained.

'Well, where is the channel? I studied Norwegian at University in Hull so that will not be a problem.'

The steward found the right channel and Penny relaxed watching the new Top Gun movie dubbed in Norwegian.

The steward walked back to the galley area and spoke to his colleague. 'I am going to lynch that woman in seat 1D, she is a nightmare.'

'Leave it to me. Give me your iPad.'

His colleague walked up the gangway to where Penny and Stephen were sitting. She pressed the button to lower the privacy screen, as Penny removed her headphones in protest.'

'Lady Greyshot, my name is Violetta, and I am the Cabin Services Director on this flight today. The captain has personally asked me to introduce myself and I must say it is a pleasure, and honour, to have you, and Mr Smith, on board this evening. I understand you asked about the children sitting over there. They are the Prince and Princess of the Royal House of Sweden. They are flying down to meet their parents, the King, and Queen of Sweden. I hope you do not mind sharing the cabin with them.'

'How delightful, Violet, and of course I do not mind sharing the cabin with royalty. We aristocrats have to stick together you know.'

'My name is Violetta.'

'Well, yes, but I will call you Violet.'

'The captain allows me to offer a half bottle of champagne to selected guests. Would you care for one, milady?'

'Thank you Violet, yes, I will, and I will have his as well,' she replied, pointing to Stephen.

Violetta returned to the galley to get the two bottles of champagne.

'She is a right old cow, that one,' she commented to the steward.

'See, I told you. I tried to scupper her audio channel, but would you believe it, she speaks Norwegian.'

Penny drank the first bottle of champagne and quickly fell asleep. As soon as she was snoring, Stephen lowered the privacy panel and took the second bottle of champagne, drank it, then also fell asleep.

When they arrived in Cape Town they went straight to their hotel to relax and prepare for their meeting tomorrow.

After lunch, Juliet had arranged for a horse and carriage to take them the short distance to the Giza Plateau on the outskirts of the city to see the pyramids of Khufu, Khafre and Menkaure, and the Great Sphinx. This was their first taste of the ancient country of Egypt and what is probably the most fascinating country on earth.

As they were riding along amongst the traffic Camau asked them, 'Did you know that the three pyramids are aligned with Orion's belt in the heavens, and that the Great Pyramid is aligned perfectly with the cardinal points, north, south, east and west?'

'No, that is news to me,' replied Juliet.

'And the Great Pyramid is a scale model of the earth and incorporates important mathematical relationships, for example Pi,' he continued. 'Plus, it is located at the exact point where the lines of latitude and longitude each cover the maximum amount of land on the earth's surface. Inside it is always twenty degrees centigrade, no matter what the temperature is outside.'

'How do you know all of this?' Nisha asked.

'We studied this at Cambridge when I was doing my mathematics degree. I do not believe that the pyramids were built by the Egyptians, and they were never intended to be tombs. There are mysterious chambers inside them with angular shafts that connect to the pyramid surface and point directly to certain stars. They are something else.'

Anita was fascinated as Camau continued.

'And if you look at the Sphinx, it has marks on it consistent with water erosion, and it has not rained here for thousands of years. It is much older than we are led to believe.'

'Perhaps it is just an old rock that the Egyptians carved?' Juliet suggested.

When they arrived at the pyramids they got out of the carriage and walked around the bases of the huge monoliths.

'They used to be covered in white limestone, so they must have looked out of this world when they were built,' Camau explained.

Everyone was stunned into silence as they attempted to process the mysteries around them. When they arrived at the Great Sphinx they could see the rivulet channels running from top to bottom.

'Wind erosion is horizontal, water is vertical,' Camau added.

'Awesome,' they all exclaimed in unison.

After taking all the obligatory photographs they got back into the carriage and drove to The Egyptian Museum in which there are over one hundred thousand artefacts, far too many to see in a couple of hours.

Juliet went first to the museum shop and bought everyone a book about the history and culture of ancient Egypt. She handed them out and explained.

'We can all read these on the cruise as there is simply too much to take in. Over thousands of years there have been different kingdoms, lots of wars and the construction of monumental buildings on a colossal scale. The Egyptians were sophisticated people with complex religious beliefs, belief in the afterlife, which is where of course, mummies come from, and had developed lots of practical things that we still use today. I think you will find it interesting.'

They all thanked Juliet and agreed that they would just visit the Tutankhamun section of the museum. They wandered around the exhibits and marvelled at the range of objects on view, including of course the iconic and world famous funerary mask in solid gold.

'Hey, Camau, look at these.'

Nisha pointed to a small display cabinet that contained a small wooden box and some elongated linen pieces of fabric, like the fingers of a glove that have been detached.

'These are Tutankhamun's original condoms.'

Anita tutted and shook her head.

'I do not believe you two. You are in one of the world's greatest museums, surrounded by centuries of history and stunning objects, and what do you focus on? Condoms.'

Camau replied. 'Just goes to show there is nothing new.'

'Come along children, let us go and get a drink,' Juliet proposed.

'Good idea,' Anita agreed.

They went to the café and picked up some bottled water.

'Make sure the cap is sealed,' Nisha urged everyone. 'You have to be careful here. We are not immune to most of the local viruses and bacteria which can make you extremely ill indeed. Be careful about eating salads, and do not have ice cubes in your drinks. Plus be careful touching the money, and always clean your hands afterwards before you start touching your face and mouth.'

'Will we be okay on the cruise?' asked Anita.

'We should be okay, but better to be safe than sorry,' Nisha replied.

Phones 4 U N Us

Friday, 11th March.

Stephen and Penny were refreshed and ready for their meeting with Cape Town's Chief of Police. Penny was dressed up to the nines, wearing a blood red, body hugging, sleeveless dress, red tights, red flat shoes, and a huge silk scarf wrapped around her neck in daffodil yellow. Her hair was in her trade mark pigtails, and she finished the look with a pair of huge black sunglasses. Stephen wore khaki shorts, a khaki shirt, with the cuffs turned up, and a pair of brown ankle boots with thick knee length, woolly socks. They were going to discuss the death of Gavin Johnston who had passed away in twenty seventeen.

Mr and Mrs Johnston came from Yorkshire. In the mid nineteen nighties, before she was married, Clare had started a business selling mobile phones in her hometown of Halifax. She was a no nonsense, down to earth, northern woman. She had cropped, naturally blond hair, was five feet six inches tall and for business always wore a grey two piece suit with a soft pink blouse.

Her unique approach was to target and sell mobile phones to women. She sold the same phones as everyone else, but her staff were all female who could therefore relate to her customers' needs, unlike staff in most mobile outlets who were all young men, technically obsessed and frequently introverted.

The approach she developed focused on the same technical aspects of the various phones she sold but tailored the sales techniques to each customer. A local business woman may have different needs to a stay at home mother or a female student who was out and about late at night and concerned about safety and security. The business was a roaring success and over several years had expanded into a chain of fifty outlets, located all over the north of England.

At a mobile phone conference in Harrogate, she decided she wanted a coffee break after a gruelling day talking to suppliers and looking at new technological developments. The coffee bar was full, but she finally managed to find a small empty table with two seats and sat down after buying her cappuccino in the obligatory paper cup with a plastic lid. Whatever happened to good old reusable cups and saucers, she thought?

She closed her eyes for a moment to let the day wash over her, and to seek a moment of peace and tranquillity. When she opened them, she saw standing in front of her a vision of a man. He was tall, beautiful, tanned, chiselled face with shoulder length immaculate black hair. He was wearing a perfect black suit, black polo neck jumper and black lace up shoes.

Where the hell has he been she thought to herself, and she instantly glanced at his left hand to see if he was wearing a wedding ring. He was not.

'Mind if I sit here for a moment? It is packed here today.'

'Of course, be my guest.'

'May I introduce myself? I am Gavin Johnston.'

'I am Clare. Pleased to meet you.'

'Likewise.'

'So, what brings you here?' he asked.

'I have been meeting with my suppliers. I have a few shops in this field.'

'How interesting, me too. It is the first time I have been here as I have been really busy over the last couple of years building my business. Here is my card.'

She took the card and read it. He was the Managing Director of Screens R Us.

'Interesting,' she replied as she handed over her business card.

He read it and his mouth dropped open.

'Wow, so you own Phones 4 U. I have obviously seen your shops around. I am based in Carlisle and have just opened my fifth shop in Kendal.'

'Excellent.'

'I have a couple of more meetings this afternoon, then do you fancy dinner this evening?' Gavin asked.

'Yes, that would be lovely. I am staying in the Harrogate Hydro. You?'

'I am in the same hotel. Shall we say seven thirty in the bar and there is a lovely looking Italian restaurant just across the road. I will call and reserve a table for eight.'

'Perfect see you later, handsome.'

They met in the bar, had one drink, dinner at eight, and by ten fifteen they were in Gavin's hotel room ripping each other's clothes off. They had a night of passionate sex and agreed to meet again at the weekend in Leeds.

Not only did their businesses complement each other, one selling phones, the other repairing them, their relationship flourished, and they soon married in Hebden Bridge eighteen months later. As the mobile phone phenomenon continued to explode, their respective businesses expanded and were soon operating in joint sites under the new brand name, Phones 4 U' n Us, selling new phones, refurbished second hand phones and the repair business.

The business expanded rapidly and was soon a national brand with outlets in most UK towns and cities. In two thousand and eleven they sold the business to one of the largest Dutch mobile phone operators and found themselves with just over two billion pounds in cash. They bought Scaitliffe House in Todmorden, an old fifteenth century manor hall that had seen better days. Bringing the hall up to modern standards of living took an enormous amount of money, and then Gavin started buying art to line the walls and spent considerably more. Clare was not amused as she thought art was frivolous, ridiculously expensive and did not sit well with her Yorkshire sense of value for money.

They bought a two hundred and sixty foot yacht and spent the British winters somewhere warm and sunny, and the summers in their historic home.

Gavin liked spending money and would buy more and more art, most of which was not necessary, but then art is not a necessity, it is a nice to have. Clare thought that when they met, her business was ten times the size of Gavin's, but through marriage he had become an equal partner in the business and the subsequent sale proceeds. She seriously regretted not having a prenup agreement as her solicitor advised her against it, saying it was better for husband and wives to be equal. He was spending her hard earned money and she started to resent him. Paintings were delivered almost daily from dealers and the auction houses.

In the winter of twenty seventeen, the crew had sailed the yacht down to Cape Town for Clare and Gavin to join it, and sail around the coast of South Africa for Christmas and the New Year. The yacht was moored in the Victoria and Albert Marina, sideways on to allow for ease of access. Two days after they arrived they held an evening reception on board their yacht, sponsored by one of the main art dealers in Cape Town. One hundred people were invited to view the Johnston's art collection on board, as well as an exhibition of thirty works that the dealer was offering for sale.

The guests were dressed in their evening finery and on the top deck of the yacht there was a well-stocked bar and several food stations where the guests could take some food and sit at the open air dining tables dotted around. The rear of the top deck overhung the lower deck by several feet with the sea water directly beneath it. At this point there was a salad bar where the guests could order a made to order salad from the range of ingredients on offer and have a dressing prepared to their choosing.

Gavin agreed to buy five of the dealer's pictures, without consulting Clare. When she found out, she was livid.

When the guests had all left, around eleven forty, Gavin went to their cabin to change into some shorts, a tee-shirt, and some flip flops. He came back to the top deck and he and Clare had a major argument about his latest purchase. She eventually left him and went back to their cabin, locking the door behind her after she had closed it. She resolved she was going to pack up in the morning and get the first flight back to London and her beloved Yorkshire.

Gavin was standing around the various food stations, that were going to be removed in the morning, and walked to the back of the boat near the salad bar. He picked up a couple of radishes and bit into them. He followed with a swig of vodka from a glass he had just filled up at the bar.

At midnight, the Queen Charlotte monstrous cruise ship left the harbour, and as she passed the yacht marina, created a huge backwash that caused all the tethered yachts to move up and down in the water by several feet. Gavin could see the backwash coming, a bit like a tsunami, and held onto the railings at the back of the vessel. The yacht went up about seven feet, then down about fourteen feet. Gavin slipped off the edge of the deck and straight into the midnight, inky black ocean.

His body was washed up on the main tourist beach about ten thirty the following morning. Clare sold his collection of paintings at Mount's in two thousand and eighteen for four hundred and seventy eight million dollars.

Penny and Stephen arrived at police headquarters just before eleven o'clock. Penny had completely taken over the investigation from Stephen and had a large file with all her notes and paperwork. She had studied this case forensically and had a myriad of questions for the Chief of Police.

Why did the yacht have an overhanging deck?

Who designed it?

Where were the crew when Gavin fell?

Where was the CCTV footage?

Why were the food stations not removed that evening?

Where was Clare Johnston?

Did she push him?

Why are large cruise ships allowed in the port and allowed to create huge backwash?

Was the Queen Charlotte scheduled to leave at midnight?

Why did Gavin's body end up on the beach?

The Police Chief was bamboozled by all her questions. He responded. 'Lots of yachts have overhanging decks, and it is easy to look up the designer on line. The crew were all in bed, or in their cabins and the CCTV footage showed the argument between Clare and Gavin and then him standing at the rear of the deck drinking vodka. Catering staff only work so many hours a day and had planned to remove everything the following day. Clare Johnston was in her cabin as the CCTV footage showed and her mobile phone locator proved, so she did not push him overboard. The big cruise ships always leave at night to minimise disruption. They all steer by radar so the dark is not a problem. The tides and backwash dragged Gavin's body to the beach which was washed up by the morning tide.'

'So that is that then?' Penny asked.

'Yes I am afraid so,' the Chief replied.

'Well, I never. It looks like we have been sent on a wild goose chase by Anita for some guy that just fell off a boat, stupid idiot. Come on Stephen, time to get back and get on with our safari.'

'Yes, Pen.'

Biblical Scenes

March 11–18th.

Juliet and Anita had booked their Nile cruise just after Christmas and were lucky enough to be able to get a second cabin for Nisha and Camau. The coach journey from Cairo to Luxor took a few hours, and then they boarded the five star luxury MS Royal Karnak, a Nile cruise ship with four cabin levels, housing one hundred and twenty cabins in total. The ship, like all the Nile cruise vessels, had a short draft, was relatively slow, and narrow enough to access the various locks on the river cataracts.

Inside, the ship was the height of luxury with fantastic public areas, bars, restaurants, two swimming pools and a spa complex. Unlike the cheaper cabins, theirs were on the top deck, away from the noise of the engines, with balconies so they could watch the mesmerising scenery glide by. The ship was about half full, so it felt calm and peaceful. It had outstanding hygiene awards so there was no need to worry about salads or ice. They could all relax and enjoy their week whilst being transported back to ancient times.

Nisha and Camau gave Juliet and Anita as much time alone as they could, partly because they did not want to interrupt their honeymoon, but also so they themselves could spend time together. They were besotted with each other and would sit on their balcony when the evening sun was setting, arm in arm, watching the biblical scenes before them. The Nile is magical and the scenes on its riverbank as old as time. Blossoming beds of lotus flowers, irrigated fields of crops, houses built of mud, and local Egyptians dressed as though they were straight out of a biblical movie, only this was real life. The setting sun, the gentle hum and motion of the boat, and the odd fish coming to the surface to see what was going on, completed the scenery.

'Camau, this is magical. We are so lucky,' Nisha whispered in Camau's ear.

'Yes we are. We should drink in every moment, every image and hold them dear. There is no-one else I would rather be with, to see this, than you.'

Nisha kissed Camau.

The packed itinerary for the week included excursions to the valleys of the Kings and Queens, the Karnak Temple complex, the Temple of Hatshepsut, the Medina Habu Temple, the Temples of Khum, Edfu and Kom Ombo, the Aswan dam, the unfinished obelisk, the Temple of Isis at Philae Temple, and Abu Simnel.

When they had the chance to take a trip on a felucca to visit Elephantine Island, Anita flatly refused.

'There are crocodiles in this river and just like alligators they are happy to have a human or two for lunch,' she insisted remembering what had happened to James Settle in the Everglades.

Likewise, when an early morning balloon ride was on offer, over the Temple of Karnak and the valleys of the Kings and Queens, she declined remembering the fate of Darian Amani in Jackson Hole.

At Aswan, they had to change ships so they could travel to Abu Simnel on Lake Nasser, which as a large man made reservoir is nearly three hundred miles long. The Abu Simnel temple complex was moved in nineteen sixty eight to avoid it being flooded by the creation of Lake Nasser after the Aswan Dam was built. It is now located on higher ground about one hundred and forty miles from Aswan.

As they cruised along the Lake to Abu Simnel, their mobile phone reception disappeared, and apart from the movement of the boat there was silence. The sort of silence that is rare these days as there were no signs of civilisation, no aircraft and only a few birds who were silent anyway.

'This silence is amazing,' Anita said to Juliet as they were standing hand in hand on their balcony.

'Yes it is. It is as profound as my love for you,' Juliet replied.

Anita smiled. 'Are you enjoying our honeymoon?'

'Yes, this is the best time of my life, and I know it will only get better as the days and years follow.'

'Good. I am glad that we got married and happy that we came to Egypt,' Anita said as she kissed Juliet.

When the boat docked all the passengers disembarked and went for a tour of the temple. In the evening there was an amazing Son et Lumiere show with fantastic laser lighting, images projected on the stone facades and powerful, eerie classical music. It sent shivers down everyone's spine.

As they were all having breakfast on their final day sailing back to Aswan, Juliet asked everyone what their abiding memory of Egypt and the cruise was.

'I was fascinated by the depiction of medical instruments carved in stone in the temple of Kon Ombo that are still used today,' Camau answered.

'I was blown away by the image of the annunciation by an angel to Hatshepsut's mother on her temple built in one thousand four hundred and seventy nine years before Christ. It proves to me that the Christian tradition is rooted in ancient Egypt,' Anita answered.

'I was amazed at how all the inscriptions and paintings were created in the tombs without natural light. If they had used candles or oil lamps there would be lots of soot marks. I think that the rumours that they had some sort of electric lamps or batteries are true,' Nisha answered.

'I felt a powerful force in the temple of Karnak as if I had been there before,' Juliet added.

'Perhaps you were Nefertiti or Cleopatra in a past life,' Anita joked.

'Ha, ha. Now onto the coach for the journey back to Cairo to get the flight home,' Juliet ordered.

It Rains

11–18th March.

Stephen and Penny arrived at Nairobi airport for the transfer to their fifty minute flight to the Masai Mara. Penny had to crouch to get on the plane as she was seated in the rear seat and had been handed a small plastic tray with a ham sandwich, a sealed glass of water and a small apple. There were no staff that she could complain to, as there was only the captain and co-pilot on board, along with seven other passengers.

The plane took off with the propellers whizzing round at full speed, causing the whole aircraft to vibrate. Once in the air it soared over the shanty towns on the outskirts of Nairobi, which is a shocking and sobering sight. It rather subdued Penny, and she realised that she was lucky to have her sandwich, apple, and water.

Soon the aircraft was flying over the savannah, and like all the passengers, Penny and Stephen could see herds of animals below them.

'Stephen, this is wonderful. I feel like Meryl Streep in "Out of Africa".'

In a Danish accent she continued, 'I 'ad a farm in Africa, at the foot of the Ngong hills.'

'You mean Karen Blixen darling?' Stephen asked.

'Yes, I think I will channel her for our trip. I have been reading her book which is exquisite and a beautiful passionate love story. It brought tears to my eyes.'

'Are you alright Pen?' Stephen asked her as she hardly ever expressed any emotion.

'Yes I am fine, I feel alive, and connected to nature and mother earth.'

Stephen thought she had been drinking.

The plane landed and a guide driver took them in a Suzuki people carrier to their base camp for the next few days. Penelope had not realised they would be camping and got agitated when they passed through the welcome entrance gate with, "Mara's Adventure Camp" painted in wobbly letters on the overhead wooden sign.

'Stephen, you never told me we were camping. I thought we were going on a luxury safari. Has that Anita Wu person booked us on a down market holiday?'

'Pen, just be patient.'

'How can I be patient?' she shouted at the top of her voice.

Two bellboys took their luggage and guided them to their tent through beautiful tropical gardens that were being watered by the gentle rainfall that was falling. The birds of paradise plants were almost as tall as Penelope.

When they arrived at their tent, Penelope exclaimed, 'Oh my God, this is beautiful.'

They had a stunning, huge, canvas tented set of rooms with two en-suite bathrooms, built with proper brick walls and a regular roof. There were luxurious sofas, two huge king size beds with mosquito nets, seemingly layers of Persian carpets and electric lamps everywhere.

Penelope busied herself unpacking her suitcase when she heard Stephen calling her.

'Come, Penny. There is a herd of elephants over there.'

Penelope picked up the courtesy umbrella in the room, opened it, and went to join Stephen to look at the elephants that were in the distance. Thankfully, there was a fence between them and the herd of elephants. She lowered the umbrella to get a better view and was then shaking from head to toe as she laid the metal tip of the umbrella on the electric fence and got an electric shock.

'Oh, help me. I am shaking all over,' she screamed.

The elephants trumpeted back.

'I think we should have a gin and tonic, then have dinner and we can think about tomorrow's safari,' Stephen suggested to distract her attention.

At dinner, their driver guide explained to them that they would be leaving at six in the morning to see the animals feeding.

'No. I am not getting up a five o'clock. We shall leave at nine. The animals will still be there, eating or not,' Penelope countermanded the driver.

He simply dare not question her.

Over the next three days, Penelope and Stephen had a private safari with the driver guide, who drove them around the Masai Mara showing them all the animals. They saw lions, cheetahs, leopards, rhinoceros, more gazelles than they care to count, herds of bison, zebra, and majestic giraffes.

'This is just like "The Lion King",' Penny exclaimed and insisted on singing the "Circle of Life" whenever she saw a lion.

On the Monday evening, after the sun had set, they attended a camp barbecue down by the local lake, where Penelope regaled her guests with her new found role as a sleuth. They ate a whole selection of meats including ostrich, gazelle, antelope, giraffe, and crocodile which tasted just like chicken. As they were eating, hippopotamuses came out of the water onto land to feed in the nearby grassy areas, and everyone could see how dangerous these animals are. They kill around five hundred people a year, twice as many as lions.

'Stephen, what are those things moving over there? They are the size of tea cups,' Penny asked.

'I am not sure. Excuse me, what are those things moving over there on the ground?' Stephen asked a fellow guest sitting at their table.

'Those are dung beetles. They collect dung and roll it around into a ball, to store it for later.'

'How positively disgusting,' Penny shrieked.

'Well, you are in Africa. What do you expect?' the guest replied.

On the following morning, as they were having breakfast, a troop of monkeys descended from the nearby trees through the semi-open ceiling and attacked the breakfast tables. They were skilled, and as one of them distracted the camp staff and guests, a couple of monkeys would steal croissants, bananas, and pieces of bacon. When the waiting staff chased them, they simply waited for a minute or two and then re-attacked. Eventually the guests gave up and left the room as the waiting staff cleared up, dodging as best they could their attackers.

'Now I know where the phrase, cheeky monkey, comes from,' Penny muttered as she left the dining room.

Today they had a different itinerary. They were going to drive to visit a Masai village to see how they lived. This would be followed by a ride on an elephant, then a flight to Lake Nakuru to see the splendid flocks of flamingos.

Once again this morning it was raining, When they arrived at the Masai village, or boma, which was a group of about fifteen round homes in a large circle in a clearing in the savannah, there was no one about. Each low house, or kraal is made of mud, sticks, grass, and cow poo, and are about two to three metres in size.

'Where is everybody?' Penny asked.

'I will go and check,' the guide replied.

He came back and told her that the village people were not getting up as it was raining.

'What? How rude. I have come all the way from England, where it rains constantly, and they want to spend the day in bed. It is beyond.'

'Never mind, Pen, We can go for our elephant ride now,' Stephen suggested to calm her down.

'Well not if the elephants do not feel like getting up because it is raining.'

They drove a couple of miles and came to the elephant riding centre. There were four other people in the party, and they all proceeded to the area where the elephants were kneeling down ready to be mounted.

The guide took Penelope to the sweetest looking elephant with long curly eyelashes that fluttered her eyes when she saw Penelope.

'Penelope, this is your elephant. She is called Juniper.'

'Good morning, Juniper.'

Penelope climbed onto Juniper and sat on a plaid woollen rug, across her wide neck, holding onto a rope harness. Juniper leant forward and then stood up. Penelope felt on top of the world as she was so high up. All six elephants, with their mounts on board, walked one by one onto the path and into the savannah. They passed a few luscious looking trees and Juniper decided it was time for breakfast. She veered off the path, leaving the other elephants and made off for the trees. Penelope pulled and tugged on the harness, but that just made Juniper go even faster, rampaging through what had become a large clump of trees, and snapping off juicy leaves whenever she could.

'Did no one give this elephant breakfast?' Penelope shouted out to the guides who were walking with the other elephants and were powerless to halt Juniper.

Juniper caught sight of her fellow elephants and did an about turn and charged as fast as she could to join them. Penelope held on for dear life until they were all finally back at the centre.

'Get me off this stupid animal now,' Penny screeched to Stephen, who was secretly giggling at the whole episode.

Once back in the people carrier they were going to drive to the nearby airport to take the flight to Lake Nakuru. It would have taken them six hours to drive there, but by flying it would be less than an hour each way.

They flew to the banks of Lake Nakuru, one of the highly alkaline, soda lakes in the Great Rift Valley. It is famed for its huge flocks of vibrant pink flamingos. Penny, Stephen, the pilot, and a couple of other tourists on the trip had a lakeside lunch of freshly caught fish prepared by local people. After lunch, the pilot took them on a low flying flight across the lake swooping over the flocks of flamingos that seemed to stretch as far as the eye could see.

'Stephen, this is so much better than lazy villagers and stupid elephants,' Penelope said as they made their third return flight over the lake. The other two guests on the plane recoiled in horror at this extremely rude English woman.

The following day their next trip was a flight to see Mount Kilimanjaro, from Kenya, although it is located in Tanzania, as Stephen and Penny did not have the right visas to enter the country. The two other guests from the previous day had cancelled their trip as they did not wish to spend the day with, as they said, the rude, arrogant, and ignorant English woman. Penny and Stephen flew down to a nearby airport and took an open topped land rover with a driver.

Kilimanjaro is the tallest mountain in Africa and the highest single free standing mountain in the world. It is a snow-capped volcano and on the day they visited, after the rains had stopped, the sky was electric blue, the snow was gleaming white, and vegetation had sprung to life with green shoots everywhere following the rains.

They stopped to take a photograph just as a single giraffe walked by. It stood there majestically and turned its head towards Stephen as he took the perfect shot.

'That will make a perfect Christmas card this year,' Penny informed Stephen.

Their final trip, before they returned to Nairobi, was to Mount Kenya and to straddle the equator.

'Did you know Stephen, that the Europeans in the nineteenth century, carved up Africa between them, with a pencil and a ruler? That is why so many of the borders are straight lines. Queen Victoria got Mount Kenya, and her grandson, the Kaiser, got Mount Kilimanjaro, so they had a mountain each. It was disgraceful carving up this ancient land.'

'Yes I know. History is the best teacher and the more history you know, understand, and appreciate, the better informed you are to deal with today's challenges,' he replied.

'That was profound for a Thursday morning.'

'Well, it is true.'

They flew passed Mount Kenya and took as many photos as possible. Once on the ground they had a great lunch in a restaurant with picture postcard views of the mountain. After lunch they wanted to straddle the equator and get a certificate to say that they had stood in both hemispheres at once. They did so as they watched two buckets of water with holes in them being held up, demonstrating how water goes down a plug hole clockwise in the north, and anti-clockwise in the south.

As this was their last activity on their safari, Penelope took Stephen to the side, away from the other tourists.

'Stephen. I have really enjoyed this holiday and I have loved being with you. I know I am an old dragon and can be a real bitch, but most of the time it is all bravado. I have had four marriages and I like being married. Although we live together I miss that feeling of being completely enveloped in a marriage. Will you marry me?'

Stephen was gobsmacked and felt like his mind was affected by the equator with one half going clockwise and the other anti-clockwise.

'Wait a minute.'

He moved north of the equator, holding Penelope's hand as she crossed it to be in the same hemisphere as him.

'Yes I will, there is no doubt about it. I have loved you for years, and as you play the dragon, I play the fool, but we are well suited to each other.'

They kissed, first in the Northern Hemisphere and then in the Southern.

'Never say that I do not take you anywhere,' Stephen joked. 'Shall we go home to Burford?'

'Yes.'

Part Three

Return to London

Friday, 18th March.

Landing back at Heathrow was a rude awakening for Anita, Juliet, Camau and Nisha. As is often the case, it is a total surprise when a plane lands at Heathrow and it has to wait, along with all the entombed passengers, until a gate is available, in this case forty five minutes.

Once released from the aircraft, they then had to navigate passport control, where there was a work to rule by the Border Force staff, resulting in it taking over one hour to pass through the passport control. Next, it was baggage reclaim because Juliet and Nisha had travelled with large suitcases. Due to staff shortages the wait was two hours until their bags finally appeared. To cap it all there was a tube and train strike, so Juliet had ordered a taxi to take them all back to Putney for the night. The taxi driver who had arrived on time, left, did another job, and returned but still had to wait thirty minutes for his passengers to come through arrivals.

'We have been round the world with lots of different airlines and in many airports and it was nothing like this. This country is collapsing,' Anita said as they got into the taxi.

'Yes and just wait until you see the prices. Everything is going through the roof,' the taxi driver added. 'Nearly two quid for a litre of petrol and the price of food, gas and electricity are insane. My missus is giving me a hard time, telling me that I have got to work more, but after driving a black cab for forty one years, I think it is time to hang up my keys.'

'What a great welcome home,' Anita responded with resignation in her voice.

The taxi driver did his best to get back to Putney with the congested traffic and roadworks everywhere.

'That took us five and a half hours since we landed to get home and it only took us five hours and twenty five minutes to fly back from Cairo,' Juliet calculated.

She paid the taxi driver eighty five pounds for a journey that used to cost thirty five to forty.

'Jesus, we are going to have to budget big time,' Juliet informed Anita.

Anita had other thoughts as this trip had opened her eyes, but she decided to leave this topic alone for now and would come back to it another day.

They were greeted by their dog, Mabel, and the next door neighbour who had been looking after her whilst they were all away.

'What a lovely dog,' Nisha said lovingly. 'When we get married we will have a dog, or two,' she simply informed Camau.

It was early evening, cold and dark outside. Anita decided to order a Chinese take away for everyone which duly arrived thirty minutes later and after eating, they watched a thriller on Netflix, then an early night for everyone as the events of the last few weeks seem to have caught up with them.

Saturday, 19th March.

Penny and Stephen's direct flight from Nairobi landed at six thirty in the morning. The airport was quiet, they glided through passport control, picked up their luggage and Deidre, Penelope's sister was waiting for them to drive them to Burford. Deidre had been staying in their house so she could look after the chickens and sheep. They were home an hour and forty minutes after landing.

Back in the Office

Monday, 21st March.

Nisha and Camau left Anita's and Juliet's house on Saturday morning, and after popping into Camau's flat, in Parson's Green, to pick up some things they went to Nisha's family home in Wandsworth to meet her parents. Everyone got on like a house on fire and Camau was invited to give up his flat and move into Nisha's large family home, so they could start saving. Everything seemed to be moving at lightning speed, but no-one had any reservations at all.

Juliet was going to be in a new play in London, so she had rehearsals to attend before the opening in the West End on April sixth. Nisha was going to work backstage over the summer until she went to drama school in September.

Anita and Camau arrived in their office which of course was untouched. Nobody in the Metropolitan Police seemed to care about either of them, or the Art Squad. They re-opened the office, sorted through the piles of junk mail, and generally got the office back up to speed.

'We need to create a facts, figures, and clues board for each case including all the additional information we have picked up on our trip,' Anita explained to Camau. 'Then when we meet up with Penny and Stephen we can review them and see if we can join the dots. I suggest you get some large white board so we can see them all together and move them around if need be.'

'Just like in that thriller the other night,' Camau joked.

The phone rang and Anita answered.

'Hello Anita, Stephen here. We got back on Saturday morning. Did you have a good trip?'

'Yes thanks, it was most interesting, but we have not cracked the cases yet, so it will be useful to review all the information together. Camau is pulling together boards with all the data.'

'That is fantastic. Penny and I will go to Surrey on Wednesday to follow up on the Zena Sparks case. We will meet with my old colleague, who was a junior sergeant when I left the force. Penny has just invited you to come to Burford for the weekend. She is standing next to me gesticulating and mouthing that you can come on Friday evening, just like before and leave on Sunday.'

'That would be wonderful Stephen, thank you. May I bring my wife, and can Camau bring his new girlfriend?'

'Of course, the more the merrier. See you same time on Friday, bye.'

Anita was furious. Not only had Stephen and Penny not yet been to Surrey, but another weekend in the country was also almost unbearable. She decided she was going to dispense with both Penny and Stephen after this weekend and he could start his formal retirement, and Penny would be out of her hair forever.

'I will make the boards so they can fold up and we can take them with us,' Camau explained in an attempt to calm her down.

'That bloody Penny woman dictates everything and controls Stephen like a puppet. Who does she think she is? I would not be surprised if she was the murdering type. She has had four husbands after all,' Anita ranted.

'Want a tablet?'

'Yes, please.'

The Coroner's Report

Thursday, 24th March.

The authorities in Dubai had tendered to hold the twenty thirty six Olympic Games. They planned to build a completely covered Olympic town that would hold all the events and house all the Olympians, officials, and visitors. Dubai had just been announced as the winner. Whilst the final decision making process was underway there was a complete moratorium on the issue of any documents or information that could over shadow the proceedings.

The coroner's report into Ursula's death, which had been produced the following day on March the ninth, was consequently held back. When it was released the whole world was shocked.

Ursula Baumann had died after going into a diabetic coma after eating some Gocce D'Amore chocolates, which were not diabetic, even though the chocolate box lid said they were. She had eaten the chocolates after returning to her room and was unable to administer her insulin in time, so died during the night. She was discovered dead, by Riccardo Hofstadt the following morning.

The thing that was really shocking was the little black book that was discovered next to her specially designed handbag. It contained the details of the six people that she had murdered, that had all resulted in large and successful sales at auction.

The press went insane, and it was global news that a respectable Swiss lady of a certain age, sixty two, had been travelling the world murdering people in order to win business for the auction houses. It was interesting to note that five of these sales went to Mount's auction house and one to Balfour's.

The entire art world was stunned, and the news channels were having orgasms reporting on this story, which dragged on for days.

The reaction of the art market and Ursula's colleagues was one of profound shock.

Sadi Leclere was completely traumatised that her best friend had been travelling around the world bumping off clients. As all the key players in the art world travel on their never ending circuit, it was inconceivable to Sadi that Ursula had murdered clients in the UK, USA, China, South Africa, and Dubai.

Adrianna and Michaela Fraganese were furious that the reputation of their Gocce D'Amore chocolates had been tarnished by being responsible for such a high profile death. They were not sure if their chocolate business could survive such a blow.

Altan, Hasad and Neval, the owners of Seton's were relieved that none of the collections they had sold had been implicated. They ran a clean ship, and they recalled asking Kerem when they were all at the dinner in Paris, how Mount's was winning business. Now they knew.

Kerem was irritated that his plans and strategies had been blown apart by the evidence that Ursula had been murdering clients. How could anyone ever trust the Mount's brand and business again?

Rosemary took the death of Ursula badly. She began to convince herself that there were more killers at large as she remembered meeting the police at the Dubai Art Fair. She had not really paid much attention to the Asian policewoman who said she was investigating murders. But now, Rosemary could see killers in every shadow and Kerem was worried for the state of her mental health.

Penny and Stephen were relieved that they had got back from their paid safari before this news came to light. Any earlier and their adventure might have been cancelled.

Anita was intrigued. How had she missed this in all the investigations that she and Camau had undertaken in the last few weeks? Apparently, Ursula was responsible for the deaths of Darian Amani in Jackson Hole, Eleanor Dupre in New York, Aoki Fujiki in Dubai, Gavin Johnston in Cape Town, Ehuang Zhuang in Beijing, and Zena Sparks in Surrey. She asked Camau to check the attendees at all the events where the above people died. In every case Ursula Baumann was there.

Riccardo was devastated. He had no idea at all what Ursula had been up to. He knew that she was successful and a great business getter, but he was truly stunned that murdering people was her modus operandi. He had just arrived in Gran Canaria for a two week beach holiday as he had not had a break since Christmas. He was exhausted from doing his own job, as well as keeping up to speed with the demands of advising on the new museum. On top of all that, there was the pressure of Kerem, who was demanding and clearly had Riccardo at his beck and call, wherever he was in the world.

When the news about Ursula came out, Riccardo remembered that he had picked up a little black book when he discovered Ursula and put it in his jacket pocket. Before flying back home that day he had changed out of that summer suit and into warm clothes for his arrival in Zurich. The suit was unpacked and hung in the wardrobe. In all the commotion that day, Riccardo had completely forgotten about the book, until now. He resolved that he would see what was in it when he got back from his holiday.

Ursula's husband was bereft.

Soon the story about Ursula was eclipsed on the news channels by a blue whale that had become stranded off the coast of Newfoundland. Deluded campaigners set up a crowd funding website to save it, which was a complete and utter waste of time and money, as once beached that is it, the whale's organs are crushed without the support of the water and death follows.

Regroup in the Country

Friday, 25th March.

Anna, Penny's bi-weekly help, had been preparing Burford House on Penny's instructions for the weekend guests. There would be seven people in total; Anita and Juliet, Nisha and Camau, Deidre, Penny's sister, and of course Stephen and Penny. It had been a long time since so many people had stayed for the weekend and the house was in full swing. There were fresh flowers in all the rooms, clean bedding on all the beds, and Deidre, an excellent cook, had been delegated to cook for the weekend.

The party of four, travelling from London, took the same train that Anita and Camau had taken previously. They were collected by Stephen and driven to Burford House. The guests were welcomed, shown to their rooms, and invited down to the drawing room for cocktails.

'Anita, this place is beautiful. I wish we had a house like this. I cannot wait to see it in the daylight,' Juliet said as she unpacked her things.

'Yes, it is beautiful, but you will have to get used to Penny. She is an acquired taste and not what you expect at all.'

'Well, she looks lovely in her vibrant African print dress and headgear.'

'Oh God, you are not telling me that you fancy her, are you?'

'Mmmm, Well maybe,' Juliet said playfully.

'Drinks now, wife.'

They arrived in the drawing room and joined all the other guests.

'Let me introduce you to my sister, Deidre. She is the one that does deaths at Mount's.'

'Does deaths?' Nisha said with alarm in her voice.

'I collate all the death notices and put them on file, then inform whoever is the best person at Mount's who can deal with the client's family to win the business,' Deidre explained.

'Were you aware of the people that were murdered?' Juliet asked.

'Yes of course. All those people were on our radar as they all owned substantial collections.'

'Do you believe that Ursula, now dubbed the auction killer, had killed all those people?' Anita asked Deidre.

'I would not be surprised. When you have read as many death notices as I have over forty five years, nothing shocks me. People die in the most unexpected and unusual circumstances. I could write a book.'

Penny changed the subject.

'It is a wonder that I am here at all, after the traumas on the safari.'

'What do you mean?' asked Camau.

'I was almost killed. I think Stephen was trying to get rid of me for my money, just like that murdering woman Ursula who worked for Balfour's.'

'She actually worked for Mount's,' Anita corrected Penny.

'Well, it does not matter. All the auction houses are the same anyway.'

'So, what happened?' Juliet asked.

'Well, on the first day I was electrocuted?'

'Oh my God, you poor thing,' Juliet said in her best compassionate acting voice.

'Why would the camp give you a metal umbrella and surround you with an electric fence? Honestly. When I lowered the umbrella to get a better view of the elephants I got a thousand volt shock.'

Stephen rolled his eyes.

'Next, I was attacked by monkeys who stole all my breakfast and the hotel staff just stood there and watched.'

Stephen rolled his eyes again.

'Then a rogue elephant who had not had any breakfast tried to kill me by storming off into the jungle,' Penny continued.

'Penny, Juniper was lovely. She had lovely long eyelashes,' Stephen added.

'Totally stupid elephant. I thought it would be like Dumbo.'

'Dumbo is a cartoon,' Anita said thinking she was being constructive.

'Then to cap it all we went to a Masai village, and they were in bed.'

Stephen changed the subject.

'Nisha tells me that you two got married in Sydney and that she and Camau are going to be married. Well, we have some news. We are getting married as well.'

'I thought you were not going to get married again,' Anita asked Penny.

'Yes, I know I said that, but the truth is that I like being married and Stephen is such a sweetheart.'

'Where did you propose Stephen?' Camau asked.

'Well actually it was Penny who proposed to me, but of course I had been thinking about it. We were standing on the equator and we both got a bit light headed.'

'That is so romantic,' Nisha gushed to Camau.

Champagne glasses were filled, and everyone cheered each other, took a drink then kissed each other.

'I know that we have the Coroner's report from Dubai, but I insist that tomorrow we review all the information on all thirteen suspicious deaths and murders, just to make sure that we have covered everything,' Anita explained.

'Perhaps it is fourteen,' Camau suggested.

'What do you mean?' Anita asked.

'Ursula. Perhaps she was murdered.'

'I am not so sure about that. There is no motive. She just ate those stupid Gocce D'Amore chocolates,' Anita said closing down the discussion.

'Right, we are having a celebratory dinner this evening with lots of wine,' Deidre explained. 'We are having smoked salmon, from the Smokery, served with my Scandinavian, home baked nut, and seed bread, followed by roast chicken with all the trimmings. Actually, Pen it is Felicity we are having, she was plump and ready for the table.'

'No problem, of course, I am sure she will be delicious.'

'For pudding we are having coffee crème brulé, accompanied by a shot of rum, and chocolate coated coffee beans.'

Everybody agreed that it all sounded absolutely wonderful. They finished another bottle of champagne, then went to sit in the formal dining room that Deidre had prepared.

The dining room was half panelled in mahogany and the remainder of the walls lined with soft green raw silk. On the walls were several oil portraits of men and women dressed in Georgian finery.

'Who are all these people?' asked Nisha.

'They are our ancestors. The Harringtons of Burford who built this house. That is the Count and Countess, and that is Lord and Lady Harrington. The family subsequently lost all their money, and Deidre and I grew up always knowing that we came from landed gentry that had fallen on hard times. It is pure serendipity that when I met my forth husband he already lived here. It felt like coming home when Deidre and I first came here,' Penny explained.

'That is an amazing story,' Juliet gasped. 'That would make a wonderful film.'

'And would you play me?' Penny asked Juliet.

'Shall we sit?' Anita said forcefully, deliberately moving the subject on from what she could see was becoming a lovefest between Juliet and Penny. She thought to herself that we have not been married long, and she remembered Juliet looking at the waitress in the restaurant in Sydney, then of course the girl in Edinburgh and now this. She was going to have to keep a close eye on her wife.

In the stone fireplace, at the end of the room, a log fire was roaring. There was more silverware on the table than the four guests had ever seen. The whole room was lit with candlelight from five huge candelabras on the table, and another four, standing two each on the two mahogany sideboards. The mahogany table, that could seat ten comfortably, had no tablecloth, silver cutlery, crystal glassware and crisp white linen napkins. Each diner had their own solid silver salt and pepper pot. Sitting on the table, in a precise pattern were nine silver beakers all planted with snowdrops, that hung their flowers as if in respect to all the diners.

'Deidre, this is wonderful,' Penny exclaimed as she kissed her sister. 'Thank you.'

The dinner was a huge success, the conversation lively and the wine flowed. Deidre's food was exquisite and by midnight everyone was sated, a little drunk and ready for bed.

Saturday, 26th March.

Penny was up bright and early and went off to feed her chickens and three sheep, who lived in the field next door to her house. Stephen prepared the breakfast after clearing away the dining room and kitchen from last night's dinner. By eight thirty everyone was down for their hearty breakfast in the kitchen.

'Good morning everyone. I slept so soundly last night, must be the air,' Juliet said as she came into the kitchen.

'Or perhaps the red wine,' Deidre added.

'It must have been your cooking and glorious food,' Camau suggested.

'You are such a darling, Camau,' Deidre replied. 'Nisha, he is a keeper.'

'Yes, I know,' as Nisha pecked him on the cheek.

By nine fifteen, Anita, Camau, Stephen and Penny were in the dining room to review all the materials. Camau had brought all his prepared boards and either laid them on the table or propped them up on the sideboards between the candelabras. He handed everyone a one page summary. Anita explained that they were going to look at all the details and see if there were any connections that they had not seen before.

'I honestly do not know why we are doing this,' Stephen stated. 'There is practically a full confession from the auction killer, Ursula, as she was keeping all the details in her notebook.'

Who	Occupation	Location	Cause of Death	Beneficiary	Estate Value	Year	Auction House	Event
Eleanor Dupre	Cosmetic Queen	New York	Sat in her chair	Granddaughter	$352	2016	Mount's	Birthday party with art people invited
Darian Amani	Film director	Jackson Hole	Balloon fall	Wife	$735	2016	Balfour's	Gala event for Mount's Emeritus Chairman and he knew all the people in the balloon from the art world.
Sophia Lazarini	Soap Actress	Australia	Exposure	Husband	$85	2016	Mount's	No art people involved
Yves Gaston	Book Collector	Hong Kong	Fugu sushi	Grandson	$342	2016	Mount's	Mount's Beijing representative at dinner
Johannes Blomfeld	TV Journalist	New York	In front of a train	Foundation	$68	2018	Balfour's	Had attended his own exhibition with lots of art people
Gavin Johnston	Retailer	Cape Town	Fell overboard	Wife	$478	2018	Mount's	Had attended art event on his yacht
Aoki Fujiki	Industrialist	Dubai	Fell into aquarium	Cousin	$517	2018	Mount's	Marine exhibition during Art Dubai
Myra Sharma	Jeweller	San Diego	Bitten by Spider	Sister	$38	2019	Balfour's	Her sister was a gallerist
Patrick Van Roots	Philanthropist	Puducherry	Snakebite	Sister	$145	2019	Seton's	No art people involved
Melvin Easton	Retailer	Iceland	Hypothermia	Son	$290	2020	Mount's	He was part of the group exploring Viking heritage
Ehuang Zhang	Artist	Beijing	Fell into a well	Husband	$135	2020	Balfour's	Was an artist and with some art interested people on the tour
James Settle	Cartoonist	Everglades	Eaten by gator	Wife	$18	2021	Seton's	No art people involved
Zena Sparks	Popstar	Surrey	Fell down steps	Daughter	$1,213	2021	Mount's	70th birthday party

'Yes, but that only covers six of the cases. What about the others?' Anita asked.

'Just as Deidre said last night, people die in all sorts of ways. In all my time in the police I can assure you that once you have a confession there is no need to spend any more time looking for another answer,' Stephen stated confidently. 'I think we should have a cup of coffee, a bracing walk then we can all go down to the pub for an early lunch.'

'Yes I agree,' said Penny. 'It all looks cut and dried to me. As far as we are concerned the guy in Cape Town simply fell off his boat. It happens to the best of people, remember Robert Maxwell?'

Anita was despairing. She realised she had made a big mistake, and spent a lot of money, asking Penny and Stephen to do anything. They had simply made up their minds.

'I will go and get some coffee,' Stephen said as he stood up and left the room.

This was just like the first time she met Stephen. She decided once she left Burford House, that was the end of the involvement of Stephen and Penny. They were done.

Stephen soon returned with Deidre carrying a tray of coffee mugs and Nisha a cafetiere. They were followed by Juliet.

'So, I hear you are all done,' Juliet said as she sat down at the table.

'No. I want us to look at each case in turn and see if there are any connections,' Anita insisted again.

'Everybody get a coffee; take a seat and I will take you through each case in turn.'

Camau outlined the details of each case with information on the location, manner of death, beneficiaries, value of the estate and which auction house sold it. He had photographs stuck on each board. As Camau was going through the case of Sophia Lazzarini in the outback in Australia, Deidre put her hand up, as if she were at school.

'One thing that is bothering me is how could Ursula, who was relatively tiny, kill all those people without being noticed. Can we look at her details?'

'Sure of course,' as Camau picked up her board and held it at the front of the room.

'This is the photograph of where she was found, the Gocce D'Amore chocolates, the contents of her handbag strewn around her and her insulin pens,' Anita explained.

Nisha stood up and approached the boards that Camau was holding up.

'You say these are insulin pens?' she asked.

'Yes, apparently she carried them around with her all the time,' Anita explained.

'My grandmother has diabetes and I know what they look like. The cap on that one looks different unlike any pens that I have ever seen before,' Nisha explained as she pointed to one of the pens in the photograph.

'Are you sure?' Anita asked.

'Yes, positive,' Nisha replied.

'Were these tested in Dubai?' Deidre asked.

'Not as far as we know,' Camau replied.

'Just go over the manner of deaths again split between the ones Ursula killed and the others,' Deidre requested.

Camau explained how each person died as requested.

'What I deduce is that all the ones Ursula was involved in, all fell. Out of a balloon, out of a chair, off a boat, into an aquarium, down some steps or down a well. All the others died as result of heat exposure, eaten by an alligator, eating sushi, hypothermia, pushed in front of a train, bitten by a spider or snake,' Deidre explained.

'Of course. Why did we not see that? We could not see the wood for the trees,' Anita commented.

'If I were you, I would see if you can have access to those pens and have them tested,' Penny suggested.

'Thank you, that is what we will do,' Anita agreed.

'And if there is something not right with the insulin pens then perhaps Ursula was murdered,' Stephen added.

'Exactly and thank you Nisha and Deidre,' Anita said gratefully.

Camau added.

'I believe all Ursula's belongings were returned to her husband when her body was flown back to Zurich. I will find his details and we can call him.'

'Right. Off for a walk and then down to the pub for lunch. I will book a table for twelve thirty,' Stephen offered.

Camau found the contact details for Ursula's husband and Anita called him. He was pleased to receive a call from the Metropolitan Police and more than happy to help. He did have the pens and her handbag, and they agreed that Anita and Camau would fly to Zurich on Wednesday morning to meet. Somehow Anita felt that this was a breakthrough at last. All they had to do now was to endure the rest of the weekend. The evening was going to be a slide show prepared by Stephen and Penny, not only of their safari, but also their Caribbean cruise.

Visit to Zurich

Wednesday, 30th March.

Prof. Baumann welcomed Anita and Camau into his home. Ursula's funeral had taken place in Zurich a few days after her death, once her body was repatriated, and the shock of the coroner's report was evident on his face.

'Good morning and thank you for coming over from London. I am eternally grateful. Would you like some coffee?'

'Guten Tag, and yes some coffee would be lovely,' Anita accepted on their behalf.

The house was a Bauhaus style nineteen thirties detached property, that was immaculately decorated and furnished. There were many contemporary works of art adorning the walls, and the furniture was a mixture of eighteenth, nineteenth and twentieth century pieces. The house was filled with light from the huge windows which looked out over a garden and with mountains in the background. Prof. Baumann brought the coffee into the lounge where Anita and Camau were seated.

'May I just say that we are profoundly sorry for your loss, Prof. Baumann.'

'Thank you, but please call me Tomas,' he replied. 'I cannot believe that my darling Ursula was involved in all those murders. She absolutely loved her job and devoted her life to Mount's. I am completely shocked by the coroner's report, and I have hardly slept since. I feel like the world is watching me as the story is on all the news channels and there are some nasty things being written on social media. My colleagues are also at a loss to understand how this could have happened.'

'Yes, I am sure, it is a nightmare. As I mentioned on the phone, one of my team spotted that Ursula's insulin pens look a bit off. Can we possibly see them?' Anita asked.

'Yes of course. They are with all her things that came back from Dubai. Come with me.'

They all went into Tomas's office and saw her suitcase and handbag. Anita put on a pair of rubber gloves and Camau produced an evidence bag. She opened the handbag and took the three insulin pens and put them into it.

'We are going to have them analysed to check what is in them,' Anita said as she sealed the bag.

'Thank you and if you need to see anything else just let me know.'

'Should we also take the chocolates and her handbag?' Camau suggested.

'Yes good thinking. Put them in the other bags. I know the chocolates were tested in Dubai, but it will be good to confirm the first results,' Anita agreed.

Anita took the evidence bags and added them to her overnight flight bag that she had brought with her. They thanked Tomas once again and left in an Uber, that Camau had ordered on his mobile phone.

The taxi took them to the train station so they could catch the direct train to Geneva. As Anita's department was so insignificant in the Metropolitan Police Force, she had decided to use a private laboratory in Switzerland to do the analyses in order to get a quick result. They were travelling to the Institut de Medicine.

A couple of hours later they arrived in Geneva and took a taxi to the Institut which was located about fifteen kilometres outside the city. The Institut was a pure white two storey building with no windows. As they entered the reception area, it was like walking into a sterile clinic. The whole place was white with not a speck of dust anywhere. Even the receptionist look immaculately clean as he asked them who they wanted to see and issued them with visitor's badges.

They waited perhaps five minutes in the reception area when they were approached by a woman with long blond hair, wearing a white lab coat.

'Good afternoon Ms Wu, and Mr Kumar. My name is Helga and bienvenue to the Institut de Medicine.'

'Bonjour and thank you,' both Anita and Camau replied.

'Please follow me and we can discuss your requirements.'

They followed Helga down a corridor and up a flight of stairs into an office which had one side made of glass overlooking the laboratory below, which looked pristine.

'I understand that you are from the Metropolitan Police and would like us to do some analyses.'

'Yes, we are from a small department, and I would like to get these results quickly. If we go back to London it could take several days as we will be at the back of the queue,' Anita explained.

'I understand. So, these are the items you wish us to analyse?' Helga asked.

'Yes, these are from the woman you have probably heard about who allegedly killed several clients. Three insulin pens, a box of chocolates and her handbag. We would like to know if the pens are insulin, the chocolates are diabetic or not, and if there are any unusual fingerprints on the handbag.'

'Do you have any fingerprints of the deceased?'

'Unfortunately, not. She was cremated, but I will ask the authorities in Dubai if they took any,' Anita confirmed.

'Okay, understood. We will have your results by ten o'clock in the morning if you would like to come back then.'

'Great. See you then.'

Anita and Camau left the Institut, took a taxi, and went to check into their hotel for the night.

Thursday, 31st March.

At ten o'clock Helga greeted Anita and Camau and showed them into the same room.

'Would you like some coffee?' Helga asked.

'No thanks. We would prefer to get on with business,' Anita replied.

'Excellent. Firstly, the chocolates are regular chocolates, not sugar free or suitable for diabetics, despite what the packaging says. The handbag only has fingerprints from the same person, so we assume that it is the deceased. The issue is the insulin pens, or to be honest, one of them. Two of them are standard insulin pens, but one of them looks similar apart from the cap, and it does not contain insulin. We have tried all our standard chemical and toxicology tests, but nothing has shown up. We are at a loss as to what it contains. We are currently running the contents through our latest equipment which can deformulate what a compound is. We should have the results in about forty minutes if you care to wait.'

'Of course,' replied Anita, 'And perhaps we can take those coffees whilst we wait?'

'No problem,' Helga said as she left the room and sent in the coffees.

As they drank their coffee Anita and Camau discussed that they had just heard.

'There are clearly two issues to consider here. Firstly, why would someone who was a severe diabetic have regular chocolates, and secondly why have an insulin pen that does not contain insulin?' Anita summarised.

'There were apparently four hundred and forty one boxes of those chocolates circulating around the Dubai Art Fair, many of them open in the VIP lounges. Do you think the Fraganese sisters are involved?' asked Camau.

'I honestly do not know. Anyone could have switched the lids around but why would Ursula have a box of chocolates that could harm her?' Anita mulled.

'Perhaps someone gave them to her that she trusted?' Camau suggested.

'Difficult to say.'

Helga knocked on the door, came into the room, closed the door behind her, and sat down.

'It seems that we have a completely new compound which has not been picked up by any of our tests. The compound looks to be a variant of Botulinum, but one that we have never seen before, and it is in an extremely concentrated form.'

'Botulinum. What is that?' asked Anita.

'It is commonly known as Botox, which is always highly diluted for cosmetic purposes, but we think that in the concentration level in the pen it would only require the smallest amount, and I mean a microscopic amount to cause complete paralysis in a matter of moments,' Helga explained.

'Oh my God. Kerem Akbarov has a plastic surgery practice that specialises in Botox treatments. Perhaps he was the one that directed Ursula to murder clients as he and Mount's benefited most of all. Maybe Ursula really did murder all those people by giving each one a jab with her pen that paralysed them and explains why they all fell without any problem,' Anita exclaimed.

'But why did she not use her insulin pen when she realised she might be ill in her hotel room? It does not make sense,' Camau added.

'I agree. We are going straight back to London to interview Kerem Akbarov.'

'Yes, boss.'

Police Interview

Wednesday, 6th April.

When Anita got back to London she contacted Kerem's office but was told that he was out of the country in Azerbaijan. She insisted on making an appointment to meet him and was finally allocated ten minutes at five twenty in the afternoon the following Wednesday when Kerem would be back in London.

She arrived at Mount's at five to five and was escorted up to Kerem's office and introduced to his secretary.

'Good afternoon Ms Wu, please take a seat. Would you like a cup of tea?'

'Yes, that would be lovely,' she replied as she remembered the look on the receptionist's face in the British Embassy in Hong Kong.

At precisely five twenty the phone rang on the receptionist's desk, and she indicated to Anita to enter Kerem's office.

'Good afternoon Ms Wu.'

'Good afternoon Mr Akbarov.'

'Please take a seat. What can I do for you Ms Wu?'

'I head the Art Squad which is part of the Metropolitan Police Force, and we investigate crimes in the art world,' Anita answered.

'Never heard of it. Should I?'

'That is irrelevant. We are looking into the death of Ursula Baumann as part of our investigation into the rise in single owner sales at auction over the last few years. In fact, almost since you inherited Mount's.'

'Yes Ursula's death was a real tragedy. She was a great business getter, but I was horrified that she had been murdering clients in order to win business. That is not what we do. We employ the best people, have the best systems and I reward people well, so they are motivated.'

'We have discovered that one of the insulin pens discovered in her hotel room in Dubai was filled with a highly toxic concentrated form of Botox.'

'What? What do you mean?'

'Concentrated Botox, that if injected into a person would cause almost instant paralysis. It looks like it was the method Ursula used to first paralyse her victims then when they fell, or were pushed, there was no resistance,' Anita explained.

'What has this got to do with me?' Kerem asked.

'I understand that you own a plastic surgery practice that specialises in Botox treatment.'

'Yes, that is true,' he replied.

'So where did Ursula get the Botox she used?'

'I remember now, there was a theft from the clinic a while back. Ursula was a long standing patient and so must have stolen some when she was having a consultation.'

'If something was stolen, why did you not report it?' Anita asked.

'Officer, I have never heard of your little squad and what is the point of reporting anything to the police as nothing is ever done about it?'

'Mr Akbarov. That is unfair,' she continued.

'Well, the statistics speak for themselves. And I will tell you what is unfair, is you coming into my office and practically accusing me of aiding and abetting that murderous woman, Ursula Baumann. I think you had better leave,' Kerem said angrily as he gestured to the door with a flick of his raised hand.

Anita was shocked at his high handedness, dismissive attitude towards the police and laissez faire attitude to the theft of Botox from his clinic. He was either up to his neck in this or innocent. She could not work out which. The one thing that kept coming back to her was if Ursula was the killer, why did she mistake the Botox pen for insulin? Was she confused, disorientated, was it suicide? The possibilities were endless, and she was going round and round in circles.

Perhaps it was just easier to accept that Ursula Baumann stole the concentrated Botox when she was having a consultation, selected certain clients to murder on her business travels and reaped the financial rewards as she clearly lived in a beautiful and well-furnished home. Maybe the other deaths that they looked into were just accidents or natural deaths and there was nothing further to consider. After all, several police forces around the world had looked into all these cases and were not able to pinpoint anything.

She thought that she should just go into the office tomorrow, write the last few weeks off to experience and settle down into the hum drum existence of dealing with minor crimes in the art world. She had found no people or drug smuggling, no money laundering and no serious crimes that would interest her. She would be forty eight next birthday and would only have nine more years to go before she could retire on whatever meagre pension she would now have. She was thoroughly depressed as she waited for the bus outside Mount's to take her home.

The Little Black Book

Friday, 8th April.

Riccardo had enjoyed his two week holiday in Gran Canaria with Stephan and was relaxed and tanned when he arrived back mid-afternoon to his apartment in Zurich. The first thing he did, was to go into the bedroom and look in the wardrobe for the suit that he had been wearing when he discovered Ursula. He slipped his hand into the inside pocket and retrieved the little black book he had picked up when he first saw her.

He closed the bedroom door and sat on the edge of the bed. He opened the book, but it was upside down, quickly righting it. He read the pages, then re-read them.

He was absolutely devastated by what he read.

He was shocked to his core.

The Reckoning

Monday, 9th May.

Today was the opening of Kerem's new museum in Baku. The President and his wife along with a whole host of politicians and dignitaries were invited to the ceremony that would take place at eight o'clock in the evening. Kerem had been in the city for a few days finalising everything with his management team, and Riccardo had been in and out of Baku as his job allowed. He was due to arrive in Baku at two this afternoon on the GB Airlines direct flight from Heathrow.

He landed at just before two and after clearing all the formalities arrived at Kerem's apartment just before two forty five.

'Hi, good to see you,' Kerem said as he welcomed Riccardo.

'Likewise. Is everything going okay for this evening?'

'Yes, everything is in order. Rosemary arrives around seven o'clock this evening direct from Paris and the museum looks great. Obviously, there are still a lot of exhibits to put on show, but the barebones are there. The President was keen to get it open ready for the summer tourist season.'

'Great. I am looking forward to this evening. It should be a seismic event. As we have a couple of hours before we have to get going would you like to pop into the bedroom for some fun?' Riccardo asked.

'What a great idea. Give me five minutes to send these e-mails to my lawyers then I will be with you. Go on through.'

Riccardo waited in the bedroom until Kerem came in and closed the door.

'I thought we would have a bit of extra fun this afternoon. Get onto the bed,' Riccardo ordered.

Kerem laid on the bed and almost instantly Riccardo climbed on top of him and straddled him. In a flash, Riccardo produced a pair of handcuffs and attached one end to Kerem's right wrist and the other to the bedstead. He then produced a second pair and secured his left arm.

'Well, this is different,' Kerem said with excitement and anticipation.

Riccardo went to the wardrobe and took two Hermes ties and secured both of Kerem's ankles to the foot of the bed after removing his shoes. Kerem was spreadeagled securely to the bed and attempted to struggle, but it was fruitless. Riccardo moved over to his briefcase and took out some silver gaffer tape. He tore a strip off the roll and fastened it securely over Kerem's mouth. Kerem continued to struggle. Riccardo closed all the curtains and left the bedroom to go into the lounge. He made a phone call and in a few minutes there was a knock at the door.

'Come with me, he is in there, nice and secure,' as Riccardo led the way into the bedroom.

Kerem continued to struggle and attempted to speak but the tape held tightly across his mouth prevented him. He saw the figure that came into the room with Riccardo. The man was dressed in black military tactical gear with black lace up army boots, body armour, thick black gloves and completely masked with only the smallest aperture for his eyes. He stood in the corner of the room with his legs astride and his arms folded, watching Riccardo and Kerem intensively.

Kerem tried again to get free and made lots of muffled sounds.

'Shut up,' Riccardo shouted at Kerem. 'You are going to listen to what I have to say. When I discovered Ursula I found a little black book that was on the floor, which for some unknown reason, I picked up and put in my pocket. I left it in my suit pocket when I changed to fly home and only remembered to look at it when I heard about the coroner's report and after I got back from holiday. The book contains the details of thirteen murders, who committed them, who else was involved and how each one was arranged. The mastermind behind all these murders was you.'

Kerem tried as hard as he could to speak and break free of his bonds, but neither were possible.

'You, Akbarov are mentioned on every page. I am going to give you a choice. My father has helped me to draw up a Deed of Sale, for the sale of Mount's to me for the sum of one Swiss franc. If you do not sign the document, my friend here who works for the Azerbaijani secret police, and is being paid by my father, will arrest you for male prostitution as well as for masterminding the murders. You will spend the rest of your life in an Azerbaijani prison and will be known as the gay murderer. You will not have a fun time in prison.

If you sign the document, witnessed by my friend here, I will leave Azerbaijan on my father's private plane, which is waiting at the airport and once

I am out of Azerbaijani airspace I will message him to release you, just before Rosemary arrives. You will then be able to attend the opening reception, and nobody will know anything about our little transaction. The only difference will be that I will own Mount's, not you. And just in case you get any ideas, the original little black book is in a vault in my father's private bank, and if anything happens to me it will be released, and you will be arrested wherever you are. So, the price of your freedom is Mount's. I am going into the other room for a cup of coffee whilst you think about your options.'

Riccardo left the room leaving the masked military guard watching over Kerem who was tugging at his bonds and attempting to speak once again. Thirty minutes later Riccardo returned to the bedroom with the Deed of Sale and a pen.

'Are you going to sign?' Riccardo asked Kerem.

'I said, are you going to sign? Otherwise, I am going to leave you here in the hands of my friend.'

Kerem nodded as best he could. Riccardo beckoned the masked man over to the bed and gave him the key to undo Kerem's right wrist.

'Now sign there. I will also sign, and my friend will witness.'

After Kerem signed the Deed, Riccardo slapped the handcuffs back on him and attached his wrist once again to the bed.

'Thank you, and here is one Swiss franc which he placed on Kerem's mouth. Now that you are relieved of Mount's you can concentrate all your energies on your new museum which I truly hope will be a great success. I am going to the airport now, and when we are airborne I will call him to release you. That should be about six forty five, fifteen minutes before Rosemary arrives. I wonder how you are going to explain to Rosemary that you no longer own Mount's. Anyway, that is not my concern. Auf wiedersehen.'

Riccardo left the apartment and got into a waiting taxi to take him to the airport. He boarded the Gulfstream V private jet and was quickly airborne. As soon as the plane left Azerbaijan airspace the pilot sent a message to the guard asking him to free Kerem.

The guard released Kerem and threatened him to stay calm or else. He took away the handcuffs and put the Hermes ties back in the wardrobe. He straighten the bed and left the apartment.

Kerem was all over the place. His wife was arriving soon, and they had the reception to attend with the President. He was shaking all over and could not think straight. He quickly decided that he would tell Rosemary that the death of

Ursula had upset him so much that he did not want to be involved with Mount's anymore. He had sold the business to Riccardo Hofstadt for an undisclosed sum, so that a new generation could run the business.

When Rosemary arrived just after seven o'clock, Kerem explained to her what had happened.

'I think that is a great idea, darling. Mount's is a nasty business, and you are better off without it. All those murders and deaths, who wants to be in a business like that? Now shall I wear the red Gucci or the blue Chanel?'

You All Work for Me Now

Tuesday, 10th May.

When Riccardo's plane landed in Zurich he was greeted by his father and whisked to the family home in the chauffeur driven Mercedes.

'Congratulations Riccardo. You have done well, and I am really proud of you. It is great that you now own Mount's. You will be a new broom that sweeps away all that controversy and you can run the business properly. Whoever heard of a business that murdered its clients to win business.'

'Thank you father for supporting me. I really appreciate it.'

'Son, your mother, and I love you dearly, and will do anything to make your life happy. You and I will keep the details of this transaction just between us, the fewer people that know the better. Secrecy is the way of the world here in Switzerland.'

'Yes, father.'

Wednesday, 11th May.

After spending the night in Zug, Riccardo flew to London to take up his new role as owner of Mount's. Riccardo's father's office had coordinated the press release with Kerem's private family office. It was released to the Press Association late Tuesday evening.

'Mr Kerem Akbarov has agreed to sell Mount's Auction House to Mr Richard Hofstadt of Zurich, for an undisclosed sum. Following the tragic death of Ursula Baumann and the discovery that she had acted alone in murdering clients, after apparently stealing concentrated Botox from Mr Akbarov's private clinic, it was felt it was best for the business, clients, and staff, that a new owner takes up the reins. Mr Akbarov wishes Mr Hofstadt all the best for the future.'

Once again the art world was in turmoil.

How could such a young man take over Mount's?

Where did he get the money?

Why were no other suitors involved?

The social media platforms were in meltdown and Mount's staff were buzzing with excitement and anticipation. The staff liked Riccardo and appreciated his investment in the company, or rather his father's. Mount's was now the largest and most successful auction house in the world. The staff had received record bonuses for the second year in a row, all driven by the profitability of the business, even though they now knew that it had all been achieved by murdering clients.

Riccardo landed at Heathrow on the first flight out of Zurich and took the VIP passport control option. Brad was waiting for him at the terminal and greeted him warmly.

'Well good morning and welcome back to London, Mr Hofstadt,' Brad said as he smiled at him.

'Hey, call me Riccardo, even though you now work for me,' Riccardo said teasingly.

'Yes, boss,' as they both laughed.

They drove out of the airport and along the M4 and A4 towards central London.

'Well, this is a surprise you taking over Mount's, but a nice one,' Brad said as he was driving along.

'Yes I never expected this, but Kerem felt that a change was in order, and he has enough money anyway,' Riccardo explained.

'I would love to know how this all came about. Shall we do that dinner on Friday evening as we planned, then you can tell me all about it?' Brad asked.

'Yes, that would be great, but it will only be me. Stephan is away at a crypto conference in San Francisco.'

'All the better. Just you and me, so we can have a good chat,' Brad confirmed.

'Here we are boss,' Brad announced as the car drew up at the front door of Mount's.

An all staff meeting had been arranged in the largest gallery for eleven o'clock and would be streamed to all the offices and staff who were travelling.

Riccardo took centre stage, standing on the rostrum and surveyed all the staff looking at him. His first words were.

'You all work for me now.'

Everyone in the room laughed, clapped, and cheered loudly. This is going to be fun, he thought to himself.

Dinner in Chelsea

Friday, 13th May.

Riccardo was wearing a black polo shirt, casual black trousers, a black leather hoodie and sneakers, all Giorgio Armani of course. He arrived by black bus for dinner at Brad's house just after eight o'clock. He knocked on the door and Brad opened it. He was wearing a tight black t-shirt, which emphasised his muscles, blue jeans, and his trademark black snakeskin cowboy boots.

'Hi, come in.'

'Thanks. This is a lovely house and so hidden away.'

'Yes, it was a great find. It was built in eighteen fifty four as part of this group of forty eight workers' cottages,' Brad explained.

'Yeah really, workers' cottages, here in Chelsea. This house must have cost you millions,' Riccardo said.

'Well, that would be telling, but it is fantastic to have a three bed, three bathroom house with a south facing garden in Chelsea, and in a private gated complex. Come downstairs.'

The main bedroom and ensuite bathroom were on the first floor, the two other bedrooms and bathrooms were on the ground floor along with a terrace, and the dining kitchen, utility room, guest loo and lounge were on the lower ground floor with direct access to the garden.

'I have some champagne on ice to celebrate your new role in life. Let me get it. Take a seat on the patio, as it is still pleasant outside.'

Riccardo went outside to the patio and sat at the oak outdoor table. In a couple of moments Brad arrived with two crystal champagne glasses, an ice bucket with the bottle snug in the ice, and a dish of peeled quails eggs nestled around an open salt cellar holding Hawaiian Pa'Akai Alaea Sea Salt, the best salt in the world. Brad placed the items on the table, sat, then opened the champagne filling the two glasses.

'Riccardo, to you, boss, and congratulations.'

'Thank you, but less of the boss, please.'

'I am glad that you came for dinner. You know I have been longing to meet you properly since we first met in Paris in January, and whilst we had a drink in Baku it was not the right place to get to know each other better,' Brad explained.

'Thank you, and yes I know. I feel completely overwhelmed when I am near you,' Riccardo replied.

'Well, that is good to know that we are both on the same page,' as Brad smiled and topped up the glasses.

'Brad, can I ask you something?'

'Of course.'

'Given that I have taken over Mount's, are you happy to remain as Mount's world-wide Head of Security, my personal body guard and chauffeur?' Riccardo asked.

'Riccardo, I am, and I will be there for you for whatever you want, whenever you want. It is my destiny.'

'Brad, that is the nicest thing anyone has ever said to me.'

Riccardo stared into Brad's eyes as the electricity flowed between them. He leant forward and kissed Brad.

'Brad, can I talk to you?'

'Of course. I promise to keep whatever you say to myself.'

'When I found Ursula Baumann in her bedroom in Dubai, remember she always gave someone her second hotel key, I saw a little black book. For some unknown reason I picked it up and put it in my pocket. Then I forgot about it until the Coroner's report came out, when I was on holiday. When I got back, I read it and it was truly revealing. In her own handwriting it listed all the details of thirteen deaths. The manner of death, who was involved, who benefited and by how much. It was all planned and arranged by Akbarov. It is a well-known secret that his wife, Rosemary, is not too hot in the bedroom, but Kerem's sex drive is excessive. He has a number of men and women, all employees at Mount's, that he has been using for sex. I think you know that he also almost blackmailed me into doing the same, otherwise my career would be over. When I discovered what he was up to, I discussed it with my father, and we agreed to use the situation to my advantage. I gave Kerem a choice. He could either sell Mount's to me for one Swiss franc, as I had him spreadeagled to the bed.'

'What, spreadeagled?' Brad interrupted.

'Yes, I gave him a taste of what he does to other people. He either sold to me or he would have been arrested, for male prostitution and murder, by a member of the secret police in Azerbaijan, that my father had organised and who was with me in the room. Kerem would spend the rest of his life in prison. He signed and when I left Azerbaijani airspace on my father's plane we messaged the secret police guy to release him. And just in case he gets any ideas, the little black book is in a vault in my father's bank and will be released and published if anything happens to me.'

'Nothing will happen to you, I can assure you of that,' Brad swore.

'Thank you.'

'Riccardo, I have to say that I am impressed with your ingenuity and getting even with Kerem. He was always pleasant to me, but I know of all his little arrangements with certain people and the one with you. I wanted to stop him seeing you but that was not possible. That is why I arranged to have a drink with you in Baku.'

'Again, thank you Brad. I am glad I could talk to you about all of this. There is only my father apart from me that knows about this, and now you.'

'And that is where it stops,' Brad said confidently as he topped up the glasses with the rest of the champagne.

'I think we should go inside as it is getting a little chilly now,' Brad suggested.

'Yeah.'

'Dinner can wait a bit. Come with me upstairs,' Brad insisted.

'I thought you would never ask,' Riccardo agreed without any hesitation.

They went upstairs to the main bedroom on the first floor.

Around ten o'clock they came downstairs, had dinner accompanied by a couple of bottles of red wine and without even discussing it, Riccardo spent the night with Brad.

The Informant

Wednesday, 18th May.

Following the interview with Kerem six weeks ago, Anita had settled into a daily routine of going into the office, arriving at nine, working all day, with an hour for lunch and leaving by five. She had actually become used to a more regular working day and between her and Camau they dealt with the myriad of minor crimes that were either reported directly to the Art Squad or were handed to them by their colleagues in the Metropolitan Police.

She had accepted that Ursula was the killer of the six clients listed in her little black book, having stolen Botox to render her victims helpless. She was clearly a greedy money grabbing woman who caused untold heartache for her own personal gain. It was impossible to exhume the bodies of the victims, as they had all been cremated, so too late to do any forensic tests. All the other cases that they had investigated had just been unfortunate deaths, as Deidre had pointed out.

Her current case load included some thefts from dealers on Church Street in Kensington, a couple of cases of buyers using fake identities at Balfour's and a number of burglaries in the Boltons in Chelsea where jewellery and watches were stolen. Serious as these crimes were, Anita felt underutilised and frustrated.

Camau continued to be a valuable asset to her team and was enthusiastic and hard working. She realised she had been extremely unfair when she first met him and misjudged him. He was a remarkable young man with a bright future ahead of him and a beautiful girlfriend. She was lucky to know him, and they became close friends as well as working colleagues.

Through a combination of circumstances Camau had been unable to meet with his uncle, The Home Secretary who had been travelling extensively across the United Kingdom and to a couple of international meetings on security, one in New York and the other in Seoul.

As Camau was working at his desk, the phone rang, and he answered it. The caller asked to speak to Anita Wu who was out of the office visiting Balfour's. Camau asked what the caller wanted and if they would like to leave a message.

'Yes, please. I have some important information about the deaths of auction house clients, but I will only speak to Ms Wu if I and two others are guaranteed anonymity and immunity from any potential prosecutions. That is the deal, take it or leave it.'

'Thank you. I will pass your message onto Ms Wu. May I ask who is calling?'

The line went dead.

When Anita returned to the office around four in the afternoon Camau relayed the message.

'That is not going to happen. Whoever it is can provide me with the information first, then we can think about any immunity and anonymity. Plus, it is the Home Secretary who approves these,' Anita responded.

'Okay.'

Thursday, 19th May.

The caller rang again at ten in the morning, but Anita was out of the office having emergency dental work as a tooth filling had fallen out and needed to be replaced. The caller refused to leave any contact details but repeated the request for guaranteed immunity from any potential prosecutions for three people and anonymity.

Friday, 20th May.

The caller rang again at lunchtime, but Anita was out having lunch with Juliet, and again refused to leave any contact details but repeated the request for guaranteed immunity and anonymity.

Sunday, 22nd May.

Camau's mother had flown into London from Nairobi to attend a magazine editors' three day conference the following week, that was being held at the Mayfair Hotel. She arrived on the early morning flight and had invited Camau, her brother, the Home Secretary, his wife, and children for lunch to meet Nisha. Whilst she had taken part in several Zoom calls with Nisha she wanted to meet her in person.

Lunch was arranged for one o'clock at Amazonica in Berkeley Square, the Brazilian restaurant that was her favourite in Dubai. The party of seven arrived and had drinks before lunch. Camau's mother was enchanted by Nisha and thoroughly approved of the match between her son and her soon to be daughter-in-law.

Camau chatted with his uncle, the first time they had met face to face since before going on the world-wide trip.

'You look great, Camau. You are clearly enjoying the police and the Art Squad.'

'Thanks. Yes it is fascinating and I have learnt a lot.'

'It seems that your round the world trip was a bit of a waste of time. Good for you, but not a good use of taxpayers' money. How did you find the Wu woman? She did not uncover anything.'

'She is really nice, and I thoroughly enjoyed my time with her. She is a bit tough on herself but when she relaxed, she blossomed.'

'So, nothing for me to know about?'

'No, not really. It seems that Ursula Baumann was responsible for the murders and the rest of the cases we investigated were all accidents. We have had someone ringing up three times this week offering to be an informant but wants immunity and anonymity for three people. Anita dismissed the request as she said that you need to approve it.'

'Yes that is true. What does this person want to say?'

'Apparently something about the cases, we investigated.'

'So, you and Wu have been round the world, discovered nothing, have been blindsided by the revelations about Baumann and you have an informer offering to tell you something?'

'Yes.'

'I approve the anonymities and immunities for whoever they are. They probably want letting off some parking tickets. If this caller has something juicy to say, it might be the end of Wu, who is a liability and even when given a new role has delivered nothing.'

'You mean the porn movie?'

'How did you know about that?' the Home Secretary asked Camau.

'She told me.'

'Interesting. Anyway, tell her on Monday that I have approved the anonymities and immunities and we shall see what happens?'

The waiter invited the party to take their drinks to their waiting table.

Monday, 23rd May.

When Camau arrived in the office he made two cups of coffee just in time for when Anita arrived. He greeted her and they chatted about their respective weekends. He then broached the subject of his uncle and the anonymities and immunities he had granted.

'He approved them just like that?' Anita asked.

'Yes, he thinks it will be about some parking tickets, or something similar, so he is not concerned. He thinks that the Ursula Bauman case was just a lucky discovery. If she had not died, no one would be any the wiser, so if there is an informant offering some more information it is worth it,' Camau replied.

'Do you have the phone number of the caller?' she asked.

'No, it was withheld every time. I checked the phone records on the computer, but nothing. We will just have to wait and see if they call again.'

'Okay. There was another burglary at the weekend of several Rolex watches from a house in Chiswick. I will pop over later this morning. Want to join me?' she asked.

'Sure, but what if the caller calls back?'

'We can route the phone to my mobile, so no problem,' Anita explained.

'Okay, great.'

Wednesday, 25th May.

The caller had not yet called back, and Anita was confident that the whole situation was a hoax, to distract her attention, probably from the people doing the latest spate of burglaries. At ten fifteen the office phone rang and Camau answered.

He waved frantically in the air and whispered, 'It is the caller?'

'Good morning, this is Inspector Anita Wu. I can confirm that the Home Secretary has granted your anonymities and immunities. You will need to come into the office and provide me with the details of the persons in question.'

'No problem. I am on my way.'

Anita had asked Camau to leave the office and go home so she could meet with the informant privately. Forty minutes later there was a knock at the door and the informant was welcomed into Anita's office. She produced the relevant papers which were completed and signed by both of them, including a Non-disclosure Agreement. Then Anita closed the door and listened.

Two hours later, Anita emerged white as a sheet and went to Camau's office and closed the door. She called the Home Secretary. The informant left and ten minutes later she was in a squad car, under a Section Two notice on her way to Whitehall.

Anita met with the Home Secretary and explained what she had just been told by the informer. He called the Foreign Secretary, and they all agreed to go and see the Prime Minister in Number Ten Downing Street. The Home Secretary's assistant, James, called Number Ten and was informed that the Prime Minister was in a meeting with the President of…. The Home Secretary exploded and said he did not care which President of Diddly Nowhere the Prime Minister was with, they were coming to see him now.

Anita, the Home Secretary, and the Foreign Secretary met with the Prime Minister in the cabinet room. You could have heard a pin drop when Anita had finished outlining what she knew.

'How did you discover this?' the Prime Minister asked.

'I appointed Anita as the head of the Art Squad last year and she has done an outstanding job with her team uncovering all this evidence,' the Home Secretary replied.

'Excellent. I am impressed Anita. This will no doubt lead to a promotion for you,' the Prime Minister said.

'Thank you, Prime Minister. That is generous of you,' she acknowledged, not wishing to contradict anything that had been said, even though she knew it was stretching the truth a lot.

'You can all work together to coordinate an international plan to arrest all these people and let me know when it has all been done. I will speak to my counterparts in China, Croatia, The United Arab Emirates, The United States, India, Italy, France, Japan, Netherlands, Spain, and Australia. This is such a mess and an embarrassment for our country. Anita, once again I am grateful for your efforts in uncovering all of this,' the Prime Minister stated.

The Arrests

Monday, 30th May.

Twenty six people were arrested in twenty one locations, in twelve countries around the world, in a highly coordinated police effort. It had been assumed that the drug addict in New York had died, although without any concrete evidence the person was still on the list. The media went into overdrive trying to understand what was going on, but the party line in all locations was that those who had been arrested were simply assisting the police with their enquiries.

The people arrested were:

First Name	Last Name	Country	City
Drugged	Addict	USA	New York
Joy	Amani	USA	Jackson Hole
Xin	Cheng	China	Beijing
Gunter Kurt	Denhart	UK	London
Andrea Maria	Denhart	UK	London
Suzanne	Dupre	USA	New York
Gary	Easton	China	Macau
Eric	Felps	UK	London
Haru	Fujiki	Japan	Yokohama
Claude	Gaston	France	Paris
Lala	Greggs	USA	Los Angeles
Clare	Johnston	UK	Todmorden
Ernesta	Lavender	USA	San Diego
Peter	Lazzarini	Croatia	Dubrovnik
Janete	Litz	UK	London
Kalvin	March	USA	New York
Mr	Nadar	India	Kaymakam
Hakam	Noor	UAE	Dubai
Cristoff	Russo	Italy	Rome
Flora	Settle	USA	Florida
Paavni	Sharma	USA	San Diego

Javinda	Singh	India	Mumbai
Jane	Sparks	UK	Surrey
Freida	Van Roots	Netherlands	Rotterdam
Nancee	Wilson	Australia	Sydney
Fang	Wong	China	Hong Kong
Sook	Zhang	Spain	Madrid

Over the next few days, depending upon the legal processes in each country, all the arrestees were charged. It was agreed between all the respective police forces and politicians that the first trial would be in London at the Old Bailey.

The Old Bailey

Monday, 5th September.

During the last three months the main case was prepared and at ten o'clock the courtroom was filled with legal staff and there was not a single free seat in the public gallery.

'All rise,' the clerk of the court ordered.

The judge, His Honour Joshua James QC, entered in his full scarlet red robe and wig and took his seat. Everyone else sat down as well.

'Would the defendant please rise?'

The defendant stood up in the dock.

'Please state your full name.'

'Rosemary Dawn Akbarov.'

'And your permanent address?'

'Which one? We have eight houses?' Rosemary replied with a smile across her face.

There was laughter in the courtroom.

'Ms Akbarov. May I remind you that you are in a Court of Law and these proceedings are of the upmost seriousness. Please provide your main residential address in the UK,' the judge said sternly.

'Well, okay. Apartment three, twenty one Mount Street, London, W1A 6QH.'

'Thank you,' the judge said.

The clerk of the court continued. 'You are charged with fourteen counts of conspiracy to murder. How do you plead?'

'Not guilty, your majesty.'

The room burst into laughter again.

The judge banged his gavel down hard.

'One more inappropriate comment from you Ms Akbarov, and you will be charged with contempt of court. Do you understand?'

'Yes.'

'Yes, your honour,' the judge said firmly.

'Yes, your honour.'

'Please be seated. Ms Salehem for the prosecution, please proceed.'

'Thank you, milord.'

Ms Salehem stood and started her case for the prosecution.

'Rosemary Dawn Akbarov. That is not your real name, is it?'

Rosemary failed to answer.

The judge addressed Rosemary.

'Ms Akbarov, you must answer the question truthfully. Ms Salehem, please continue.'

'Rosemary Dawn Akbarov. That is not your real name, is it?'

'No.'

'Please state your real name?'

'Andrea Maria Denhart.'

'And why did you assume the identity of Rosemary Dawn?'

'So, my husband would not find out about my history,' Andrea replied.

'Andrea Maria Denhart. You are a fraud, who along with your twin brother, who is not Charles, but Gunter Kurt Denhart, have been living a lie.'

'You were born in Germany in nineteen seventy seven, along with your brother at the Wurttemberg Hospital for unmarried mothers in Freiberg. You were the illegitimate offspring of Count Freedenberg and a maid that worked in his castle. You were given up for adoption and grew up in Munich with your adoptive parents. They were humble, good decent honest people who strived to give you and your brother the best in life. They were always honest with you that you were adopted and who your father was.'

'You, and your brother, both longed for the social status and lifestyle that you believed you were both due. Your biological father died when you were a child and you had no recourse against him, his family or estate. You briefly studied History of Art, without completing the course, or gaining any qualifications, whilst your brother, who was obsessed with computers worked for Google in Berlin. In your early twenties you and your brother were both petty criminals, stealing money from your respective employers, and you committed three burglaries during which you stole jewellery and watches. When the authorities in Germany were hot on your trail you arranged for new identities and moved to the UK.'

'You assumed the identity of Rosemary Dawn Wilson and your brother, that of Charles David Wilson. You conned your way into getting a job at Mount's, in the Impressionist and Modern Department, by convincing them that you were an expert on German Expressionism. Your brother set up a technology company and created a website that was full of lies, with false case studies and client endorsements.'

'You, deliberately and specifically targeted Kerem Akbarov just after he inherited Mount's Auction House. You decided that the easiest way to a rich lifestyle, and the social status that you craved, would be to marry Mr Akbarov. You also knew that profits in an auction house are difficult to come by, because of the triopoly of the three houses, in which it is almost impossible to gain a sustainable competitive advantage.'

'You married Kerem and introduced your brother when there was the opportunity to develop new computer systems. He created the systems and gave you unrestricted access to SPOT. You used SPOT, and the information it provided, to target the clients that you intended to arrange to be murdered in order to generate more business for Mount's.'

'You withheld your sexual favours for your husband, pushing him into the arms of others, all of whom you arranged. Once they were caught in your trap, you blackmailed each one of them into doing your bidding, murdering clients. You, or rather SPOT, selected clients that had a grievance and would benefit from a sizeable inheritance. The beneficiaries, who were all accomplices, were instructed to award most single owner sales to Mount's, but certain others directed towards Balfour's or Seton's to deflect the trail. You thought that by targeting clients around the world, that there would be no pattern or connection.'

'As you may know, milord, winning business is the key to the survival of auction houses. It is a brutal and competitive battle fought on a daily basis.'

'Thank you, Ms Salehem,' the judge replied. 'Please continue.'

'Ms Denhart, you intended to crush the competition, Seton's, and Balfour's. When Mount's had become the dominant world-wide auction house, you were going to murder your husband, Mr Akbarov, making it look like an accident and you would inherit Mount's.'

'Your husband, Mr Akbarov, genuinely believed that everything he was doing at Mount's was delivering the results. He employed the best people, rewarded them well, implemented great state of the art systems, changed the travel policy to send a message to the industry that his staff were focused on clients, encouraged management meetings, and brought in consultants to create an air of professionalism. He held the private dinner in Paris to convince the other auction house owners that his strategy of good staff and client service was the winning strategy. He even used his powerful Botox to hook in clients. Mr Akbarov believed that he was uniquely successful when no other auction house owners had ever broken free of the triopoly.'

'I will outline briefly for the court, milord, how each person was murdered and by whom. In due course we will go into each case in considerable detail with witnesses that I will call, and there will also be several additional court cases around the world, following this one. I will go through the cases year by year, starting with the earliest milord.'

The judge interrupted.

'Thank you Ms Salehem. In addition to the charges listed, Ms Akbarov, or Ms Denhart will also be charged with perjury for lying to this courtroom and assuming a false identity. Clerk, please ensure that these are added to the charges.'

'Yes, milord,' the clerk confirmed.

'Please continue Ms Salehem.'

Ms Salehem addressed Andrea.

'The case of Sophia Lazzarini who died in twenty sixteen in Australia. You conspired with her husband, who benefited from her death, and Nancee Wilson from Mount's Australian office who was the murderer. She tampered with Ms Lazzarini's petrol tank by inserting and inflating a balloon in the tank, the day before Ms Lazzarini travelled. When the tank was topped up, the petrol gauge showed full when it was not. Wilson followed Ms Lazzarini in the outback and on discovering the empty car, she simply retrieved the balloon from the tank, leaving no evidence behind and everyone puzzled as to how Ms Lazzarini ran out of fuel. Ms Wilson had sex with Kerem Akbarov, which you encouraged, then blackmailed her threatening that she would be sacked. Sophia's collection was sold at Mount's.'

'The case of Yves Gaston who died in twenty sixteen in Hong Kong. You conspired with his grandson who benefited from his death, a kitchen hand, Fang Wong in the restaurant, and Xin Cheng, the Head of Mount's Beijing office who were both the murderers. The kitchen hand added a piece of poisonous fugu fish to his plate, just before it left the kitchen. Ms Cheng had sex with Kerem Akbarov which you encouraged, then blackmailed her, threatening that she would be sacked. Yves' collection was sold at Mount's.'

'The case of Darian Amani who died in twenty sixteen in Jackson Hole. You conspired with his wife, who wanted all his money so she could marry her lover in Jackson Hole, without having to divorce and accept a financial settlement, and Eric Felps, the Head of Mount's Old Masters Department in London who was the murderer. He was on the balloon trip and using gloved hands he slid the lock open so that when Darian leant on it he fell to his death. Ursula Baumann was also on the balloon trip but was not involved. Mr Felps had sex with Kerem Akbarov on occasions, which you encouraged, then blackmailed him threatening that he would be sacked. Darian's collection was sold at Balfour's which you engineered with his wife to deflect attention.'

'The case of Eleanor Dupre who died in twenty sixteen in New York. You conspired with her granddaughter, who wanted full control of the Dupre company, and Kalvin March from Mount's New York Office who was planned to be the murderer. He intended to administer a shot of concentrated Botox from an insulin pen, which would have paralysed and killed Ms Dupre. However, Ms Dupre died of natural causes at her birthday party before this wicked plan could be executed. Ursula Baumann was at the party but was not involved. Mr March had sex with Kerem Akbarov on occasions, which you encouraged, then blackmailed him threatening that he would be sacked. Eleanor's collection was sold at Mount's. You actually thought that Mr March had administered the Botox and falsely accused Ms Baumann of murder.'

'The case of Johannes Blomfeld who died in twenty eighteen in New York. You conspired with Lala Greggs from Mount's office in Los Angeles and Janette Litz from Mount's African and Oceanic department in London. Ms Greggs' lover is Janette Litz who conspired with you as well because she wanted to own the Benin face mask, which she stole on the night of his death, telling everyone that it was a gift. You arranged for Ms Greggs to pay a drug addict to push Mr Blomfeld in front of a train. Ms Greggs is bi-sexual and had sex with Kerem Akbarov on occasions which you encouraged, then blackmailed her threatening that she would be sacked. Johannes' collection was sold at Balfour's, again to deflect attention which Ms Litz arranged as she was a trustee of Mr Blomfeld's foundation.'

'The case of Gavin Johnston who died in twenty eighteen in Cape Town. You conspired with his wife who wanted to avoid a divorce and losing half her money, and Hakam Noor from Mount's Dubai office who was the murderer. He attended the party on the boat and instead of leaving with the other guests he hid on the top deck near the food station. When Mr Johnstone was stood nearby Mr Noor administered a shot of Botox in his calf, just at the right moment as the cruise ship passed by creating the swell causing Mr Johnston to fall into the water and drown as he was already paralysed. Mr Noor jumped into the water immediately after Mr Johnston, unseen by the CCTV and swam ashore. Ursula Baumann was at the reception on the boat but was not involved. Mr Noor who is bi-sexual had sex with Kerem Akbarov on occasions which you encouraged, then blackmailed him threatening that he would be sacked. Gavin's collection was sold at Mount's.'

'The case of Aoki Fujiki who died in twenty eighteen in Dubai. You conspired with his cousin, Haru Fujiki, and Hakam Noor from Mount's office in Dubai who was the murderer. The cousin wanted Mr Fujiki's money to buy more paintings and resented Mr Fujiki's wealth being spent on marine conservation. Mr Noor plied Mr Fujiki with high strength vodka then discretely administered a shot of Botox as they were standing by the edge of the aquarium. Ursula Baumann was at the event in Dubai but was not involved. As I already mentioned Mr Noor is bi-sexual and had sex with Kerem Akbarov on occasions which you encouraged, then blackmailed him threatening that he would be sacked. Aoki's collection was sold at Mount's.'

'The case of Patrick Van Roots who died in twenty nineteen in India. You conspired with his sister, Freida Van Roots, Javinda Singh, the head of Mount's Office in Mumbai and Mr Nadar who were both murderers. His sister wanted her brother's money and Mr Singh and Mr Nadar worked together. Mr Nadar ensured that the bedroom window was open, even though Mrs Nadar's mother closed it, enabling Mr Singh during the night to introduce the cobra from outside. You paid Mr Nadar a healthy amount of money as he was frustrated at not having a job and therefore being supported by his wife. Mr Singh had sex with Kerem Akbarov on occasions which you encouraged, then blackmailed him threatening that he would be sacked. Mr Roots' collection sold at Seton's, again to deflect attention.'

'The case of Myra Sharma who died in twenty nineteen in San Diego. You conspired with her sister, Pavani Sharma, the afore mentioned Lala Greggs from Mount's office in Los Angeles and Ernesta Lavender, the insect expert who were both murderers. Ms Sharma's sister would have lost out on her sister's estate if she married her new lover from Oman. Ms Lavender was easily persuaded to assist by introducing the Sydney Web Funnel spider into the ones she prepared for Ms Sharma to study. Ms Lavender was well aware that there were no stocks of the anti-dote and in return she accepted a sizeable grant for her department. Ms Greggs is bi-sexual and had sex with Kerem Akbarov on occasions which you encouraged, then blackmailed her threatening that she would be sacked. Ms Sharma's collection was sold at Balfour's, again to deflect attention.'

'The case of Melvin Easton who died in twenty-twenty in Iceland. You conspired with his son and Cristoff Russo, the head of Mount's office in Rome who was the murderer. Mr Easton's son wanted money from his father to feed his gambling addiction. Mr Russo was on the dive with Mr Easton and as they were swimming along, he held Mr Easton back, managed to give him a shot of Botox in the small area of skin that was exposed next to his face mask, and pushed him into the side channel where he got stuck and died of hypothermia and paralysis. Mr Russo had sex with Kerem Akbarov on occasions which you encouraged, then blackmailed him threatening that he would be sacked. Mr Easton's collection was sold at Mount's.'

'The case of Ehuang Zhang who died in twenty-twenty in Beijing. You conspired with her husband and the afore mentioned Xin Cheng, the head of Mount's office in Beijing, who was the murderer. Ms Zhang had become a fervent communist and admirer of the Chinese state. She planned to give all her art, money, and future royalties to the Chinese government. Her husband had other ideas. Ursula Baumann was on the tour of the hidden parts of the Forbidden City, but it was Xin Cheng who was leading the group and administered a shot of Botox as Ms Zhang sat on the well. Within seconds she leant back and fell in. Ursula Baumann was not involved. As I have already mentioned Ms Cheng had sex with Kerem Akbarov which you encouraged, then blackmailed her, threatening that she would be sacked. Ehuang's collection was sold at Balfour's, again to deflect attention.'

'The case of James Settle who died in twenty twenty-one in the Everglades. You conspired with his wife and the afore mentioned Eric Felps, the head of Mount's Old Masters Department in London who was the murderer. His wife was furious that Mr Settle would not give their daughter a significant amount of money to start her newly married life, after having had such a torrid time with her first husband. Eric Felps was on the boat trip and dropped a few drops of his own blood into the water as the boat was positioned next to the nursery, attracting the watching alligator mother who snatched James. As I have already mentioned Mr Felps had sex with Kerem Akbarov which you encouraged, then blackmailed him, threatening that he would be sacked. James' collection was sold at Seton's, again to deflect attention.'

'The case of Zena Sparks who died in twenty twenty-one in Surrey at her birthday party. You conspired with her daughter, and the afore mentioned Cristoff Russo who was the murderer. Jane Sparks was livid that her mother spoke openly about donating all her money, whilst she and her daughter struggled after her husband's death. Cristoff was at Zena's birthday party and was stood right at the end of the semi-circle as Zena was singing. As she approached the end of the line and stretched out to shake hands, Cristoff gave her a shot of Botox from the insulin pen that was held in his hand. With the combination of the Botox, her high stiletto shoes and being close to the edge of the steps the stage was set for her finale. Ursula Baumann was also at the party but was not involved.'

The judge interrupted. 'Ms Salehem, who is looking after Zena Spark's granddaughter?'

'Fortunately, milord, the daughter, Amy, has been adopted by Jane's closest friend, Jenneke and now lives in the North of England.'

'Good, please continue, Ms Salehem.'

'As I already mentioned Mr Russo had sex with Kerem Akbarov which you encouraged, then blackmailed him, threatening that he would be sacked. Ms Spark's collection sold at Mount's.'

'Now I come to the final charge. Ursula Baumann knew that you were not who you said you were. Ms Denhart, you have a birthmark on your left shoulder that is in the image of a butterfly that you have embellished to make it more attractive. Is that correct?'

'Yes, your highness,' Andrea answered.

The courtroom burst into laughter again.

The judge banged his gavel down so hard on the bench that the vibrations could be felt around the room.

'Silence in court,' he bellowed. 'Ms Denhart, I have warned you already. You will now be charged with contempt of court. Clerk, please note that.'

'Yes, your honour.'

'And if there is one more sound from anybody else in my courtroom you will also be charged and receive a custodial sentence.'

There was silence.

'Ms Salehem, I apologise, please do continue.'

'Yes, milord.'

'Ms Baumann gave birth to a child at the same time, and in the same hospital, where you and your brother were born. Ms Baumann was sixteen years old when she became pregnant, and her strict parents sent her to Germany from Zurich to have the baby which would then be adopted. There was no discussion.'

'Ms Baumann remembered you because of the unique birthmark and that you were a twin. When you married Kerem Akbarov she soon suspected who you were, as you often wore off the shoulder dresses at social occasions and even more so, when your brother started to work for Mount's. She stayed quiet for fear of upsetting the apple cart.'

'Four years ago, Ms Baumann was contacted by her son who had been adopted. She was overjoyed at meeting him and loved him instantly, as only a mother can. She did not mention him to anyone, including her husband, as she was still deeply ashamed about having a child out of wedlock.'

'She met him frequently over the last few years to get to know each other and at the Bridge Hotel about eighteen months ago she told him about her suspicions about you. He told her not to say anything to anyone and he would do some digging for her. They continued to meet, and he confirmed what she already suspected, but that the situation was far more serious. He discovered what you were up to, but wanted time to collate all the evidence he could.'

'He gave Ursula, his mother, as much detail as he could, and she noted it down in a little black book that she always carried around with her in her handbag as insurance in case you found out that she knew who you really were.'

'About a month before her death, Ursula came to see in your apartment in London where you were alone, and she confronted you about your identity. She told you that she was keeping notes on you in a little black book. You dismissed her as a crazy person and threw her out. In Dubai, at the Art Fair, you were unnerved when you met the police woman from the Art Squad. You felt the walls closing in on your plans. When the Gocce D'Amore chocolates were in circulation, you used that opportunity to get rid of Ms Baumann by making it look like a tragic accident.'

'You asked Lala Greggs to give Ursula a box of chocolates which she did, after switching the lid to one that showed sugar free. You then asked Xin Cheng to follow Ms Baumann into the ladies, and when Ursula went into a cubicle she left her handbag on the counter top next to the sinks. Xin deftly replaced all her three insulin pens with lookalikes but filled with the deadly concentrated Botox. Ms Baumann subsequently ate the chocolates in her room, felt unwell and administered her insulin pen. She paralysed herself and died.'

'When Ursula Baumann's body was discovered by Mr Hofstadt, you had been waiting in the beauty salon for Mr Hofstadt to enter her room. When Mr Hofstadt asked you to stay whilst he went to get help, you planned to switch the little black book that you knew Ursula kept in the hidden compartment in her handbag. You tried frantically to find it but as you could not, all you could do was to leave the book that you had created, copying her handwriting exactly in order to frame her for six of the murders that I have just outlined to the courtroom. You did not know that Mr Hofstadt had picked up Ms Baumann's book and put it in his jacket. You also intended to replace the Botox filled pens with the original ones, but you only managed to replace two before the hotel staff arrived with Mr Hofstadt. When the police was mentioned you went wild and screamed.'

'So, to summarise milord. Rosemary Dawn Akbarov is not who she says she is. We know convincingly that she is Andrea Maria Denhart, a German national and petty criminal. She is driven by greed, status, and money. She coveted designer clothes and the finest jewellery. She wanted to be the most famous woman in the world, eclipsing the likes of Jackie Kennedy and Princess Diana, but without doing any of the hard work. She selected the art world, and the auction world in particular, because it is always at the centre of things and is not affected by fashion or celebrity.'

'She thought she had created the fool proof plot by arranging the murders all over the world, ensuring there were no patterns and she herself was never at the scene of any of the murders. Her accomplices did it all for her.'

'When she went to have Botox injections at Mr Akbarov's clinic she stole a vial of concentrated Botox and got the idea for using insulin pens after seeing how easily Ms Baumann travelled all over the world with hers in her handbag.'

'When Ms Baumann confronted her, she knew she had no choice other than to get rid of her, otherwise her whole world would come tumbling down. What she did not count on was Ms Baumann's son collating a dossier of evidence that police forces around the world had failed to do. Andrea is an extremely clever and devious woman who thought that she had covered all her tracks carefully.'

The judge stopped Ms Salehem. 'Do we know the name of Ms Baumann's son?' he asked.

'Sorry, milord. That is sealed by the Home Secretary who granted anonymity and a guarantee of immunity to prosecution for three people.'

'Three people?'

'Yes milord. We do not know the names of these people, we only have the dossier,' she replied.

'Not ideal, but there is nothing we can do about it. The Law is the Law.'

The court case lasted just over another thirteen weeks until on December the seventh, Andrea Maria Denhart was found guilty on all fourteen counts of conspiracy to murder, one count of perjury, one count of false identity, and one count of contempt of court. She was sentenced to a whole life sentence, without the chance of any parole.

Life Goes On

Thursday, 8th December.

It was exactly one year since the final lot had been sold, in Mount's auction room, at the single owner sale of Zena Sparks. Riccardo sat in his office in Knightsbridge, the one that Kerem used to use, but was now his. The oak panelling and tasteless furniture had been replaced, and it was now a contemporary office with a black swivel leather chair, a smoked glass desk and high quality contemporary art on the white walls. What a year it had been. From operating out of the Zurich office, he was now the owner of the oldest and most successful international auction house, and he was looking forward to the years ahead.

The death of Ursula had been a horrible shock, compounded when the news about her murdering clients had come to light. He had discovered however that she was totally innocent, and the truth was in her little black book, Akbarov was behind everything. The lucky mistake that Riccardo made was assuming that Akbarov referred to Kerem, thereby he was able to blackmail him in to handing over Mount's for one Swiss franc. Maybe he should have gone to the police, but if he had, he would still be working in Zurich and he would not be where he was today.

He was doubly shocked that Rosemary Akbarov, or Andrea Denhart, was really behind all the murders and was now safely behind bars for the rest of her life. He did wonder to himself why Kerem had not been in touch given the news about his wife. Surely he would want Mount's back.

Riccardo decided to go to Knight's bar for a drink after he left work. He was still staying in the Bridge Hotel when in London, as he had not had the time to sort out a permanent place to live. As soon as he walked into the bar he bumped into Camau, who asked him to join him. They sat at the bar, ordered a couple of gin and tonics, and started to chat.

'I have not seen you since Dubai,' Riccardo started.

'Yes, we went onto Egypt after that and now back doing the day job. The last few months have been a revelation with the death of that woman in Dubai, the Coroner's report, and then the world-wide arrest and trials of all those people. Who would have thought one woman Rosemary or Andrea, could have masterminded all those deaths?'

'It was terrible, and we are having to work hard to restore the reputation of the business.'

'Ah, yes. You now own the auction house. Lucky you. How did you manage to do that?' Camau asked.

'Kerem Akbarov was devastated by the murders and wanted nothing more to do with the business, so he was happy to sell it.'

'I bet he was,' Camau added. 'Do you see him?'

'No, I have not seen him at all. It is as if he has disappeared. I think he does not want to show his face after his wife was imprisoned. I hear he is divorcing her,' Riccardo continued.

'So, Camau, what are you doing now?'

'I am working in the UK's Anti-Terrorism unit as an intern, only in the back office at the moment. I am going to Police College in January and when I qualify I have been offered a place, if my grades are good enough, to join the fast track stream in the department. Anita Wu, who was the Head of the Art Squad was promoted as a result of uncovering the auction murders and offered the original position as the head of the unit that she was going to take up last December. The person they had appointed in her place turned out to be a complete disaster and the Home Secretary fired him,' Camau answered.

'I remember, your uncle is the Home Secretary. He is never out of the news these days, even I have noticed that.'

'Yes, he is now the Deputy Prime Minister, as well as Home Secretary and the betting is that he will get the top job sometime next year. He is lining up the Mayor of London to be elevated to the House of Lords and to replace him as Home Secretary. She has proved to be the most effective operator within the Home Office and has been making all sorts of changes.'

'Good for her,' Riccardo said.

'They got off to a terrible start when the whole Anita thing blew up.'

'What do you mean?' Riccardo asked.

'Anita was caught in a porn movie set up by the Chinese and The Home Secretary demoted her.'

'What for a porn movie? How ridiculous?' Riccardo scoffed.

'Shall we have another drink?'

'Sure.'

'So, how is your love life?' Riccardo asked Camau.

'Perfect. When I was in Sydney I met my soul mate, the love of my life, Nisha, who was in a play with Anita's wife, well girlfriend then, as we were witnesses at their wedding. We are living together now whilst she is at drama school here in London and when we have finished studying we will be married.'

'Congratulations and cheers,' as Riccardo tapped Camau's glass. 'Who is Anita's wife?'

'Juliet Brioche, the actress.'

'I saw that play last week; it was fantastic. What a small world we live in,' Riccardo said as he smiled.

'We are invited to another wedding in the Cotswolds,' Camau continued.

'Whose is that?'

'Stephen and Penny, the other members of the Art Squad.'

'I thought there was only you and Anita?' Riccardo asked.

'Well, officially yes, but Stephen was the old head of the department, Penny is his girlfriend and then there is Deidre, Penny's sister, who works at Mount's.'

'You mean Deidre Harrington?'

'Yes.'

'She works for me in our Deaths Department. I have a regular meeting with her every week to review the latest obituaries. She has transformed since the court case and has now embraced technology. She loves SPOT, our main system and checks every obituary notice with him or her. She treats SPOT like a person.'

'It was actually Deidre who identified that the people Ursula supposedly murdered had all fallen, and Nisha who spotted the fake insulin pen from the evidence we had,' Camau continued.

'We had an informant, but we have no idea who it was. They got anonymity and immunity from prosecution for three people in return for providing the evidence,' Camau replied.

'Three people, interesting. Let me get this straight. The Head of the Art Squad, a senior policewoman, and you, travelled around the world meeting up with the police in all those countries and none of you were able to identify the killer. It took Deidre, who is seventy two, your girlfriend, an aspiring actress, and a secret informant to produce all the evidence?'

'Yes, that is right?' Camau confirmed.

'Astounding, and that Anita woman gets promoted.'

'Yes, that is correct.'

'Well, I do not feel so bad then,' Riccardo said, with relief in his voice.

'What do you mean?' Camau asked.

'Nothing,' Riccardo replied.

'How is your business?' Camau asked changing the topic.

'We are doing really well considering everything that has happened. The business is remarkably resilient, no matter what happens. The competition though are having a really tough time.'

'Balfour's overall strategy has turned out to be a disaster. Their chocolate business has gone down the plughole, as Gocce D'Amore are now nicknamed Gocce D'Morte, Death Drops instead of Love Drops, and sales have collapsed. Their fashion business has been a disaster as people do not want to buy recycled clothes and they have not been focusing on the auction business. All their best people are coming to us, and we have a number of vacancies as several of my ex-staff are now in prison.'

Riccardo continued. 'Seton's has struggled as the price of sneakers and second hand handbags has plummeted, once people cottoned on to the fact that they were just buying old, second hand goods. Tulipmania, all over again.'

'Yes, I studied that at University,' Camau added. 'Looks like you have a promising future ahead of you.'

'Yes, it does. I am lucky and have the best team around me,' Riccardo added. 'Anyway, great talking to you and I wish you all the best for Christmas and the New Year. I know it is a bit early, but hey ho.'

'Cheers, and the same to you,' Camau said as he shook Riccardo's hand.

It Was Me

Friday, 9th December.

After work, Brad drove Riccardo back to Chelsea for dinner and a night in. Stephan had gone to see his parents and would be coming to London the following week to start his new job. He had quit the cryptocurrency job in Zurich and was going to head up the new NFT department at Mount's, focusing on the new frontier of digital art.

Stephan had met and knew all about Brad. He was relaxed that Riccardo was spending time, including nights with him. It meant that there were no issues when Stephan wanted to have sex with other men and would spend the night away. The arrangements suited them both and did not affect, in any way, the fact that they loved each other.

As they were driving back to Chelsea, in the Friday night rush hour traffic, Riccardo told Brad that he had just fired Woody Smith, the ex-Human Resources Director.

'He thought he was something and expected special treatment. He started to threaten me in my office this afternoon, so I just fired him. He was stunned.'

'Well done, that is the only way to be, ruthless,' Brad said as he smiled at Riccardo and put his left hand on Riccardo's knee as he continued to drive.

When they arrived at Brad's house, he parked the car and opened the door, disarming the alarm as he did so.

'I thought we would have a take away this evening as I want to talk to you,' Brad said with a seriousness in his voice that Riccardo had never heard before. Riccardo thought to himself that perhaps Brad was bored with him, resented the fact that he owned Mount's and was now his boss. Maybe Brad was going to resign and leave Mount's, or worse still he was going to stop seeing him. His mind was dancing all over with negative thoughts.

'Let me get some wine whilst you take a seat in the lounge,' Brad said as he went into the kitchen.

He returned with an open bottle of Barolo, offered a small amount for Riccardo to taste, who approved of the luscious wine, then Brad poured two glasses.

'To us,' Brad said as he clinked Riccardo's glass, savoured the wine, then took a drink.

'Thank you. I thought you wanted to stop seeing me,' Riccardo said with a tremble in his voice.

'Hey, nothing could be further from the truth. I want to talk to you about the court case this week now that the verdict is secure.'

Riccardo breathed a sigh of relief.

'You remember when we first met in the car in Paris?'

'I certainly do,' Riccardo answered as he smiled broadly.

'I told you that I was American.'

'Sure, so what?'

'Well, it is only partly true. When my father died just over four years ago, two years after my mother, I was going through all their things when I came across some paperwork. It turns out that I was adopted as a baby. I was born in Germany and my mother was Ursula Baumann, or Ursula Vogel, as she then was. I had absolutely no idea and obviously it was a shock.'

'Brad, I am really sorry to hear that,' Riccardo said as he took hold of Brad's hand and held it.

'I eventually tracked my birth mother down, after working with several agencies both in the USA and Germany. I contacted Ursula and she agreed to meet.'

'I obviously knew about Ursula's baby from the court case, but I never imagined in a million years that it was you,' Riccardo said as he tightened his grip on Brad's hand.

'We met first of all in Paris, and as I was looking for a job, after leaving the Navy, she proposed to Kerem that I would make a great Head of Security. I met Kerem and the rest is history. As I had a German mother I applied for and got a German passport to enable me to work in Europe, then after Brexit I applied to have settled status and will apply for a British passport, now that I am based here. As I travelled around with the Akbarovs I would meet Ursula in various locations depending upon where she was.'

'That all makes sense now. Ursula was always popping out for mysterious meetings. I was completely convinced that she was having an affair. I remember

357

she came back from lunch one day with the back of her head as flat as a pancake. Obviously, lunch on her back.'

'Yes, she told me about that. Her husband had flown into London to surprise her on her fortieth, ruby wedding anniversary. They had lunch, then a quick visit to her hotel bedroom. She did not realise what had happened to her hair until she visited the ladies. She thought it was highly amusing,' Brad explained.

'Just over eighteen months ago now, Ursula told me about her suspicions concerning Rosemary Akbarov, simply that she was an impostor. I told her to say nothing to anyone and I would see what I could find out. As I was driving Rosemary around, she always made phone calls and because of her attitude, she assumed I was nobody and was not listening. I quickly latched on to what she was doing, but building up the evidence took a considerable amount of time. I had to record her calls, study her phone logs, access her computer, observe her behaviour and mannerisms, and in effect create a dossier of evidence.'

'So, you are the informant, that was mentioned in court?'

'Yes, I am, Ricardo. It was me.'

'As I realised how dangerous that bitch Andrea was, I kept my mother informed, and she wrote down the basic details in a little black book so she would have a record to be used as an insurance policy, if ever Andrea confronted her,' Brad explained.

'My mother made the fatal mistake, against my advice, of confronting Andrea at her flat in London. That sealed her fate, as we now all know what happened in Dubai.'

'Brad. I am so sorry. Ursula was a fantastic person and did not deserve any of this,' Riccardo sympathised.

'Yes, I know. I was determined to nail Andrea for everything that she had done, including murdering my mother. It took me a bit longer to complete the dossier of evidence. But in the meantime, before I could hand it over to the police, you told me when we met here in May that you had found Ursula's little black book, and because Akbarov was mentioned on every page, you assumed Kerem was the killer. You did what you did, and as a consequence he handed over Mount's to you.'

'Oh my God, did I mess things up for you?' Riccardo asked.

'My first instinct was to protect you, Riccardo. That is why when I took the dossier to the police I insisted on anonymity and immunity from prosecution for you, your father and me.'

'Brad, I do not know what to say?'

'We are legally protected; you own Mount's, and you deserve it. That bitch was grooming you to be her next murderer. As always she encouraged Kerem to find sexual partners, then she would pounce threatening to destroy your life unless you did as you were told.'

'I remember the first meeting that Kerem and I had in Paris, she must have set up the encounter at the Louvre event, and she knew I was meeting with Kerem in his apartment, when she returned from the jewellers, and you took me to the station. Wow, I have been played. I thought I was smarter than that.'

'Yes, I know Riccardo. When we met in Baku I wanted to kill Kerem for meeting with you, but instead we went for a beer. I am sorry that I let that happen to you, but I needed to get all the evidence to ensure a water tight case.'

'Brad, it is fine, honestly,' as Riccardo hugged him and held him as tight as he could.

'I love you, Brad.'

'And I love you, Riccardo.'

'One thing that bothers me is why Kerem has not come back and threatened me as I was wrong about him?'

'Kerem knew what his wife was doing, but never let on to anyone, including her. He had always recorded her phone calls and monitored her e-mails. It suited him to have her do his dirty work and he reaped all the benefits as the profits at Mount's soared. He did not know that I knew, as I once caught him running a spreadsheet on his computer as I was standing in front of him with my mobile phone, and I could see his screen obliquely. He must have thought that I could not read round corners. He had a running list of single owner collections, including the ones that had not yet occurred, when I saw it. He quickly closed the file down and I drove him to the airport in Paris. He asked me if I had seen what was on his screen and I acted dumb as I told him I was checking the traffic levels on the Périphérique on my phone.'

'Once I knew what he was doing, I used my contacts to get the secret police in Azerbaijan to hack into the museum's computer network, so they could see everything. They found that file, in Kerem's encrypted private folders, and after a visit from the Head of the Secret Police, they put the fear of God into Kerem. One whiff of a scandal that could impact the President's re-election campaign and something horrible would happen to him. He might be dissolved in acid and poured into the Caspian Sea, or something similar. By opening that museum in

Baku, he had tied himself inextricably to the President's success. If Kerem says a word about you, he will be liquidated.'

So, nothing will happen to you, you are as free as a bird.'

Riccardo kissed Brad.

'We are going to have fun running Mount's. Stephan will develop the new NFT business, Cezary Bukowski is joining us in the Marketing department, and you and I will have the best time ever. I am really looking forward to the New Year,' Riccardo concluded.

'Yes,' Brad simply replied.

'Shall we have another drink?' Riccardo proposed.

'Yes.'

'And Riccardo, when you go to the office on Monday, log on as Kerem. I have his password here. You will be surprised what his screensaver is.'

'Okay, will do.'

'Now after all that, I am starving. Shall we order?' Brad asked.

'Yes, then I want to cuddle up with you and watch that new movie "Bullet Train".'

'Perfect.'

The Password

Monday, 12th December.

After a great weekend together, Riccardo and Brad arrived at Mount's around eight thirty and went straight up to Riccardo's office. Riccardo logged onto the system using Kerem's password and saw that the screensaver was a video of Liza Minnelli and Joel Grey singing, "Money makes the world go round."

Riccardo turned to Brad.

'Murder make$ the world go round.'

To be continued…